I0675035

The world of HUMANITY PRIME is a planet of strange creatures and stranger adventures. Many of the beings of this planet are friendly to humans, but others are monstrous and deadly enemies.

This is the planet of a mutated human named *fishsinger*, who is the first of his race to encounter mankind's ancient star-enemies, the Cromanths. That meeting, that battle, begins a powerful story of mankind facing its ultimate challenge—a threat that comes not from the Cromanths alone. . . .

HUMANITY PRIME brings to vivid life the people and creatures of a complex far-future world. There has been no comparable novel since DUNE and THE LEFT HAND OF DARKNESS.

BRUCE MC ALLISTER was born in Baltimore in 1946, into a Navy family, and has lived in Virginia, Florida, California and Italy. His mother teaches sociology and anthropology, his father physics and engineering; McAllister had an early background in languages, painting, marine sciences and archaeology. He received his BA in English from Claremont Men's College, and a Master of Fine Arts in Writing at the University of California, Irvine. His short stories have appeared widely in science fiction magazines and anthologies, and he is currently preparing to teach a creative writing workshop for the University of Redlands.

HUMANITY PRIME is his first novel.

Humanity Prime

BRUCE MCALLISTER

BORGO PRESS / WILDSIDE PRESS

www.wildsidepress.com

HUMANITY PRIME

Copyright ©, 1971, by Bruce McAllister

AUTHOR'S DEDICATION

For Caroline:
"these changing leaves . . . on the
stem of the eternal tree"

I

Waterjoyup is the name of my woman. *Waterjoyup* is the name of her soul.

When each child is born in the shadows of towering *yau* —high in their broad wrinkled leaves, near the surface where ocean meets dryness—the mother takes a deep first look into her child's soul, reaches the strongest image of rhythm there—not at darkest depths, but at deepest rim of light. And that vision is the child's name, the truest truth of naming.

Her mother found her soul a rushing, contented, rising current. So her name is *waterjoyup,* veined with light, and her name's image drew me to her when I was young, needing currents to ride against slow dark dreams of death.

And above *waterjoyup*'s deepest light are delicate rivers of soft coral colors, which attracted me too at our first meeting.

And above her unspoken streams, precisely webbed thoughts find ordered dance, and those added to my pleasure, as they still do.

And embracing all of these in the solid world—her rushing rivering colors under tumbling feeling thoughts—lives her personal flesh, which is simple to love as the cupping hand of the deeper her.

(Do not hide in the past.)

. . . But this is not the moment of *waterjoyup*'s birth, nor our long first meeting.

She is dying.

Never alone in her desire, she has always wanted death. But her soul now gives neither the brightest blue of dancing joy, nor pale flow of a single comfort. Were I another man in this moment, her name would seem *allpain, closedead, darkdowndim.*

I look with my face's eyes to the skin, flesh and bone of her face, which twitches now like a fish's tail, twists and bobs among the wrinkled brown leaves waving and

5

weaving around us. No healthy color remains now to any part of her trembling body.

She is pained by the white moss of sickness on her skin, and by the nearing birth of our child.

My soul opens itself to swallow hers, and in turn she swallows me.

My body twitches in our twisting bobbing, and my soul shakes in our sharing screaming.

The white moss began seven days ago. To our faces' eyes it first appeared in the fine creases of webbing between her fingers. It went on to cover her arms, her shoulders, her back, the back of her legs, down to the ends of her tails, which slowly began to shrivel as the pale growth covered her.

To the ignorant eye alone, she might seem beautiful white coral in the shape of a woman—but the jagged moans of her darkened soul—

"I am sorryyy. . . ." she cries, and her coral rivers harden, black teeth now, crying, "Darksparklepains, sageragingdark, makingmetakeme . . .

"The crawwwwling pain of skin," she cries in her fading web of thoughts, "hides the good pain of the child's coming. It is wrong not to feel its birth. It won't be born tailless, will it?"

"No," I say as I sink with her, "it will be all right."

But our first child was born without tails.

Old *poundgrayly* took the child away. . . . We both hinted to our *euyom* friend—we could not do it ourselves. *Poundgrayly* took the infant far away from us and pressed his ancient scaly limbs over the tiny nose and mouth.

That is all I know about it, because *poundgrayly* was kind. He received it himself, but he never let the child's moment of death slip from his memory to our two souls.

(The screaming again.)

"No, it will be all right," I repeat, urging her.

"I am so sorrryyyy. . . ."

Our leafy shelter of swaying *yau* is but a day's swim from the territories of neighboring souls, but they seem so far away now—the truest truth of lonely loss, another's dying . . . when mine would be the good one, long desired.

(Hide in some shallow truth.)

We worked together to weave the living *yau* stems, for a basket to hold our second child. Such stems are thick, slippery, but weaving and knotting them seemed easy for us together—even in her sickness, which is—

(No, hide!)

When the basket was finished, my body's work was too. The work yet ahead for my soul would be simple. ("A father," every father tells his son, "must guard his soul against involvement with the mother's pain, to leave him free, to let him watch for any hungry jaws attracted by birth's agony.")

But it is difficult to keep my soul from touching hers. The pains of white sickness have been calling for a long time. I have shared them without will. To leave her alone now, to deny a bond of pain, is the dark of wrong.

"Is it my fault?" she cried. "I ate wrong things? I did not eat enough? Would finer sponges or fish or shell's meat have ended this sickness, made me ready for the second child?"

"No fault," I say. "Sickness is never one soul's fault."

(Whose fault?)

(Hide in blaming!)

I do blame! Her? The mother of us all . . . never letting us leave . . . never giving birth . . . one body of darkness, wetness hold. . . .

(You cannot hide.)

Her pains run deeper now. The muscles of soul, black hardened reef, churn shoals of deepest night.

My own muscles of back, arms and legs twitch in sharing pain, echo in quiver of tails' ends.

(Now!)

"Comes the child!" she cries, I cry. Her body curls up, her soul curls down.

Sickness pains swallow screams between thighs, and soul's voice screams to me, screaming me. Screaming.

Our child leaves her, slips out, floats away from her. The brown leaves wave around them both. The currents are calm, leave them alone.

He floats inside his glistening sac. It is thin, and my eyes touch him faintly, twisting, turning.

No blood flows from her. It is all inside the sac, which the child attacks with tiny fists, with nervous light of his simpler soul.

He breaks through.

Blood flows out, red, ocean's gray flows in, and they blend, and he takes his first weak breath.

(Salt of blood, salt of sea.)

His fists rip the sac completely.

(Now!)

He breathes pure water.

(Now!)

Waterjoyup dies.

7

Ripping pains of death, over moss, over child, descend in the wave of sharing.

I die, glad to die, brown pounding with her down.

Praise the end of water's embrace!

(But—)

A light jumps from the dying her. To me a light, one image, and then I lose it. Darkness only as she dies.

As we die, the ripping nearing end . . .

I am dead.

(But—)

I am—

It clears. Death's dark colors brighten, and I live. Still screaming, blaming still.

Waterjoyup's soul is still here, somewhere nearer than darkness. Screaming still, but distant. Body near, but dead.

Even if the screaming is hers, nothing can be done. The cupping hand is gone, the flesh is finished.

We are never certain about the screams that follow body's end. Perhaps they are merely the face of our own deepest screams . . . from the loss of a soul once nearest.

(Move on.)

With face's eyes I look to the second son. I look for a long time.

(His raw new soul, you must enter it. Find his name.)

No . . . I refuse.

The first son was born deformed—legs without tails, hands without webbing. The second son is no different. He has small normal tails moving before me, has webbed fingers fanning the water, but he is deformed, for his soul will be deformed.

His soul will have no mother. And a father broken by his woman's death.

With face's eyes again, I look at the child. Floats in water reddened by birth. His left hand is twisted in its bones, and always will be. No matter; he has greater deformity.

I look beneath his skin. He floats in shallow darkness, wanting touch of warming flesh and still warmer rivers of some mother's soul.

(Look deeper.)

I cannot. *Will* not.

I am *screamdeep*, and my soul cries to me: "He does not know what his birth has done!"

I refuse to enter.

(Listen!)

Suddenly something rises, some light to the inner eye.

From a hidden crack in my soul, from pains shared in her death, springs again the last brief light she gave me.

In her sinking down, her rushing out, she found a truth as a mother finds. Found a moment to look deep in the soul of the son, and to throw her finding out and up, to another soul.

Her vision bobs up in sight, and remains for me to know and hold.

"I haaave found it!" she cries, as she secretly cried before she died. "In it, in it, in his soul, I seeeee a million fish dancing on the surface, on the sea, dancing in dangerous dryness—but they sing, glad singing!"

(Misunderstand?)

Is it not the same vision?

There is another vision, known to every man when given by man to woman, in the truest act before their child's birth. The vision of a fish . . . pale scaleless flesh . . . crawling gasping from the sea to dangerous dryness. . . .

No, that is another vision—lacks singing, dancing.

So I take him now, my hands larger than his head. To place him in the basket of living stems.

So I know that this living son's name is *fishsinger.*

I—

I—

No, I—

I am—

I am *fishsinger.* The pink waking in the real *now!*

I am *fishsinger,* but I can be my father or mother or a thousand of my forefathers whenever I want—or whenever I am pulled, pushed, sucked into such memories. Such is the purple manner of soul and memory for us all, and the truth is one sparkling crag: the precision of sharing and talk between the souls makes past times, places and souls no less than *now,* as near as *here.*

Yes, of course, a brown truth: There are dangers in memories given to you by others . . . and they are dangers without promise of a *real* death, only dangers of madness.

Mother's death through Father's eyes happened to me many times—but the impressive time in memory's eye was four hundred twenty-one days after Father's—yes, Father's —death.

So look to see it all:

In body, I am alone this day, in the territory given me by *screamdeep's* death on the four hundred twenty-first day before. My flesh is alone, without the two other bodies familiar to my soul and eyes. The old *poundgrayly,* sens-

ing the proper season, has gone to be with his gentle females. And the dumb *ayom*, whom I know as *murmursome*, is away for no reason other than the fickle bouncing
of his dumb pale soul.

I am floating, one leg and tail curled around a thick
brown *yau* stem, not far from the surface of the sea. I am
floating where the light from the twin lights shining in
dryness far beyond sea's surface softens all the darkness
thrown up by the ocean floor. The water around me was
as warm as blood, woven with fish-eye sparkle, bright with
the murmuring souls of nearby fish, of plants flowing leafy
brown around.

See further: ah, the distant bottom. Dark pores of crags.
Endless coral souls in yellow mumblings. Red roaring
souls of taloned *ioe*. Enormous *oio*, dangerous only in
their bulky carelessness.

So I am floating where the quiet current comforts those
souls of brighter colors, where no fish flees, since no teeth
snap nor dark souls scream. I am the young body who
wants to relax alongside the simpler games of fish.

My soul churns in the deep brown mounds of aloneness. Though unaware that a common wish for death is the
arm of my deepest churning, still I feel it, and try to
flee through my face's eyes alone.

My eyes move; I look. I ignore my deepest soul.

But the scales of nearby fish flash in a way that reminds
me of Father's eyes, and this brings more churning.

So I close my face's eyes, try another fleeing, try thoughts
of common truths.

(See it: Your own skin is not shiny scaly. Its color is a
yellowed gray, and it feels like the raspy hide of a *mu-
yom*.)

I open my eyes.

The cracks of the gills of nearby fish remind me of Father's scars, shiny marks on a muscular back, and I close
my eyes again.

(See it: You do not have slits on your neck for breathing. Instead the waters pass through your nose—or sometimes
through your mouth—into your chest, and then back out
again, warmer than when they entered.)

I open my eyes once more. But the image of scars persists, so I hide in the light of a wider truth.

(But you are not so alone in differences. The bodies of
fish are not wholly unlike yours. Your legs end in darker
tails that ripple like *yau* leaves when you want to move—not
unlike the smaller tails of the smaller bodies darting around
you. Their tails take them where they wish to go—just as

yours do, though your destinations are different than theirs. See it: You swim the familiarity of your territory, or venture farther when you choose to attend one of the congregations of your kind of "fish" every two hundred days. . . .)

But on this day I have no desire to move, to travel anywhere. My right hand clenches and unclenches, and my twisted left hand trembles, both of them following the nervous motion that is deeper than my body.

All the raging travel I need is within my soul, and I try to deny it.

(See it: On the outer edge of your soul runs the babble of fish swimming near you, some within eyes' touch, but most beyond it. And among their yellow babble flow the pale murmurs of those tiny souls that inhabit every point in the sea, though the eye never manages to touch them. "Those millions of tiny souls," your father told you often, "make possible the talk and touch between our souls, and all larger souls. Without will, they capture our colors and thoughts; without will, they pass on the talk of our souls, through their own endless hordes until our feeling thoughts reach other souls of our kind, or the friendly soul of another kind, or the dark raging soul of a toothed jaw.)

But the churning traveling in me rushes deeper than these thoughtful lights.

At other times I would be able to touch the mumblings of dumb *murmursome*—a simple friend—or the wisdom of *poundgrayly*, the old *euyom* befriended by *screamdeep* in his own youth. But today no such touches can be made, and I do not even pause to question *murmursome*'s rare absence, or the unusual length of *poundgrayly*'s visit to his females and their islands.

Because Mother is with me, as is Father. Though screaming dying, she is still alive in *screamdeep*'s memory of her day of death, and I pried this memory from Father long ago.

I become Father watching and sharing Mother's dying. . . .

"A soul may give his experience to another soul," Father once said. "The soul who receives is able to remember the gift of event as if it were his own, from the beginning and in the *now*. But the dark truth is: such gifts can be dangerous. The truth is: a child who receives too many gifts from others' memories may lose his own personal soul, may forget who he is and fall into splitting darkness. And if too many of the gifts are moments of death . . .

I become Mother dying.

And Father's soul, in Father's memory, will not let go of me.

I struggle to leave, and in the end, when the memory is spent, I win.

But I lose in other ways.

Once again I return from *waterjoyup*'s death, *screamdeep*'s agony, and my own raw birth with the bleeding sore of a truest truth: I am a terrible child named *fishsinger*, killer of mothers.

I always wanted—as any soul would—the memory of my own birth. But when I finally received it, it became death itself; and still I want it—as any soul would.

I started young to pry, coax, plead for Father to give it to me, soul to soul, in the vivid *now* of given events.

Father refused, denied, protected me from it with the pretended pink of a lie: "*Waterjoyup* . . . ? She died when you were young. That is all. The simplest of truest truths."

But dark colors of mood, strange rivers of feeling flowed often from *screamdeep*'s soul when the momentary thought of *waterjoyup* came to either of us. So I continued to pry, to peer, to question, or to probe at more dishonest levels.

Sixty days before *screamdeep*'s death, I found him asleep in the *yau*, and pierced his memory for the truer truth—

—that *fishsinger*'s life had brought *waterjoyup*'s death.

It did not matter that Father no longer saw it that way. He had once, and once would always be *now*.

Curiosity brought me pains that cannot be dimmed by time. And still my blue curiosity learned nothing from the experience.

The next time—after Father's death—brings equal pains, in a probe of *poundgrayly*'s soul.

The face of wrinkled scales, the tiny eyes, the ancient depths, witnessed *screamdeep*'s death. Without will, the man offered his death's moment, and such an offering can never be refused, with or without will.

To my own eyes and eye of soul the day of Father's death occurred too simply—incomplete:

I was sick, not from white moss on skin, but from the smallest invisible souls who had chosen my stomach as their territory. *Screamdeep* left me with a man and woman in the nearest territory and went with *poundgrayly* to find a scarce food called "eye shells" whose meat was believed good for sicknesses of the stomach and chest.

I waited, and was surprised when the pains of stomach began to leave on their own, as the thousands of tiny souls

12

within began dying and dimming in the victory of my body.

Poundgrayly came back.

The return of one soul—when two had left—should have been enough to bring understanding, but I could not touch the truth so easily.

Eyes always have less range than souls. It was one lone soul, indistinguishable in the distance, who called softly to me from gray waters:

"I am called *poundgrayly,* who is alone and sorry."

Poundgrayly approached and offered only: "Your *screamdeep* father has died. One accident, without will, his or mine, at the talons of *ioe.*"

My muscles hardened, and I probed for more.

Poundgrayly refused. Small eyes blinking. Heavy soul pounding brown, like a shelter of leaves, reprimanding: "I cannot give it. Your *screamdeep* father would not have me give it."

"So you *do* have it!" I shouted, green rivers browning. "He did give you his death!"

"He did not choose to—I did not choose to receive it. Gift without will. But now *poundgrayly* will not give it to you. Why do you desire his moment so?"

"He was my father! Two souls share from birth to death. He would want it so! I have the right . . ."

"You do not."

I prodded, probed and bothered the old soul. *Poundgrayly* defended with: "I find you stupid. You desired your mother's death moment, and you got it, and agony with it, and crags of guilt you do not deserve. But perhaps you deserve something for your stupid unlearning way."

I gave no answer. I began waiting.

After many days the moment comes. *Poundgrayly* eases the shelter of his soul for a single moment, and I ride the moment into memory, find *screamdeep's* darkest day, and it takes me completely, without will. Once again I become *screamdeep,* and ride a quiet wave toward the violence of death.

Fishsinger—
I—
Screamdeep—

I am here. Swimming.

Poundgrayly is with me, following above and behind. A bright wide shell of friendship's constancy arches from his *euyom* soul, arches out with a wish to cover my own—just

13

as his body's hard green shell protects wrinkled flesh and would cover mine if souls could have their way with flesh, skin and rigid bone.

Our destination nears, and we share waking dreams of "eye shells" in the rumored bed at a sandy place.

"Nothing is simple," I say with the formal fringe of my soul.

"Explain," *poundgrayly* answers, the fringe too abrupt for understanding.

"The bed is near an island, one place where reefs or rocks assure *ioe* presence, or some other dark jaws of our choice."

"Perhaps. It is said the bed lies in an inlet."

"Certainly between two masses of rock or coral crags—the perfect opportunity for jaws. Certainly we will find ourselves digging in sand surrounded by caves."

I am joking, offering the bright fins of a smiling soul. *Nothing* is ever certain, and *poundgrayly* in his wisdom would be the first to announce it.

"Do ready your soul, though," I say. "Get your *ioe* lies in shape."

All *ioe* are darkly stupid. Their souls feel only large shadows or the brightest of lights, so the lies we throw at them never fail to protect us. And though most *euyom* are clumsy with lies—finding learned images too hazy for perfect molding, too slippery for easy handling—*poundgrayly* is an experienced soul, and perhaps he is somewhat talented. We have managed to learn from each other since the day our depths first touched.

But in the end, quickness and precision of the soul are the only certain way for protection.

The *yau* are beginning to thin out.

"One pause," I say and stop swimming. I uproot a long *yau* stem from its lone rock base at the sandy bottom.

Poundgrayly knows what I wish to do. The idea came from him, as do many ideas for hands—even though they are not for his kind of limbs: flat, scaly, useful only for swimming.

We swim on and I strip the stem of its leaves, then tie it in close knots to form a basket for any shells we find.

The sandy place we seek appears now to our souls: the murmuring of the large shells buried there. And now to face's eyes: the shallow bright water warm in its nearness to a beach's hot dryness.

I reach the place first and begin digging in its softness. *Poundgrayly* will wait to see what my hands are able to find.

14

The first shells I find set my soul to yellow chattering, serve only to make me want the discovery of more. *Fish-singer* must have enough shell meat that his stomach's cure is sure.

Here: four shells next to each other!

I place them in the basket, and decide to choose eye's way: I wait for the murk of disturbed sand to clear. The soul by itself could see well enough, but imprecision of direction is always frustrating—face's eyes are precise.

Three more here.

Even two there—

What? Where?

My soul is struck by sudden formless tumble of darkest red.

(Lift your face's eyes!)

My eyes touch nothing.

But my soul finds the familiar red forms of *ioe*.

I clench the basket tightly, as my soul clenches the proper lie, the perfect form, the raging colors of the deceit—ready to throw it at the *ioe*.

Poundgrayly nods quietly with a pale softness, and together we throw out our lies, which blend as one, and the *ioe* are fooled.

The image for the pack of six *ioe* charging: *Two wounded female ioe here—do not approach!*

It is the most common lie, one that brings roaring fear to simpler souls: the female of the *ioe* kind, twice the size of any *ioe* male, five times as fierce when wounded, fearing. . . . So a pack of *ioe* will attack a pair of giant *oio* in mating before it would dare approach two raging females of its own dark taloned kind.

So my eyes touch the inevitable: the *ioe* slow their rush, their own black webbed talons pawing frantically to stop them, their skin-taut heads thrown back on sinewy necks in simple assurance that their bodies will follow.

We keep our lies steady in their form, their jagged rhythm—which would have been tiring in my body's youth, would have darkened my soul in those days . . . and to most *euyom* it would be impossible. But the two of us manage it easily, and find its familiarity even amusing.

Keeping up my half of the lie, I begin swimming back toward the shelter of *yau* in deeper water. The basket full of shells hangs from my arm, and *poundgrayly* swims in front of me.

What?

More dark red—

Where? (There!) Others here!

15

The second pack is nearly upon me.

Poundgrayly throws out a quick new lie.

Image to the second pack's souls: a giant thrashing *oio* with plated flesh, dangerous tail.

The new lie strikes the second pack. They try to slow, but their bodies tumble on toward me.

(Throw out your own!)

I tighten, surround myself with one precise *ioe* lie.

The second pack tries harder to slow.

But the image to the first pack's souls has changed: Confusing things, unclear threats—one wounded female disappears, appears a thrashing giant, remains one female—where the threat? Fear is dim—

The first pack rushes on, almost to me.

(Escape in body!)

No, death will be good.

(Body! Escape!)

I turn to swim, catch one leg and tail in the basket I dropped, flail out with arms.

My body thrashes, the basket entangled. My lie is dropped, dissolves.

(No!)

Two packs of *ioe* in one small area? Improbable. . . .

(No, throw out a lie!)

And their timing of attack? Improbable too. . . .

(Throw a lie!)

Both packs together did sense our presence, forgot their hatred of each other—

(Yes, you desire death.)

Talons reach me, flesh of arm, bones of pain, reddening waters, souls roaring redder.

(At last.)

Talons on face, one eye dark, pain deeper darker—

"*Poundgrayly!* Get away!"

Pains are darkness. Yellow never was—

I di—

I—

I—

I—

"*Fishsinger,* fool!"

Who where what here?

"Always the stupid boy."

Poundgrayly? Poundgrayly. . . .

So I stir without will from the memory. Many, many times since I snatched Father's experience from *poundgrayly*'s moment of relaxed guarding have I relived it this way,

16

and each time I fail to reach Father's death moment—but only because it does not exist for me. *Poundgrayly* managed to keep it from me, so I hold only the moments leading up to it to sink myself in.

And this time! *Poundgrayly* himself has arrived to interrupt my reveries, to pull me from the edge of memory's incompleteness.

I throw at him brown teeth of instant hatred.

I sink back down, try to be the dying man again.

I—

I—

"Fishsinger!"

Again I try. I—

"Listen to this old soul. Young hardened reef, shallow love of self, listen. Foolish and fooled, your soul is an *ioe*'s stomach. Shall I shed the dark used food of my body and feed you with it?"

This is the way *poundgrayly* always pulls me out: a wave of insults demanding soul's defense in the presence of *now*.

I begin my own wave of insults, but then stop.

A thing is different this time. There are always reprimands from *poundgrayly*, but this time his soul is unusually disturbed, sharp purple feelings, nervous edging.

"A secret problem?" I ask, green paling in sarcasm.

"Secret only to your blindness: a personal world swallowing you. Indulge yourself, *selfishsinger,* and miss the brightest day your kind has ever wanted."

Such talk is meaningless to me. Brightest day? Of course he is trying to fool me, pull me completely from my waking dream of dying.

So I play with the old soul. "I understand. You have finally decided to give me Father's moment."

"Stop this! Listen: A *bigshinegray* has come."

I ignore him. "You still refuse to—"

And then my soul rises up in understanding. *Bigshinegray?*

"You are trying to fool me!" I shout.

"No. No."

"One has come?"

"Yes."

"One has come! Has come!"

"So you *do* remember the waiting dream inside your kind's souls. If you had bothered to hold memory of it all along—in all times since *screamdeep*'s death—feelings of aloneness would not have taken you so strongly. The waiting dream has always held your kind together—"

"Yes, yes, but such advice is unimportant now! A *big-shinegray* has finally come—to where?"

"An island, as the dream expected. Two females of mine witnessed its coming. You see, I prepared their souls well for this day—gave them clear formed visions of what the big, tall, pointed, upright, shiny, round, gray dream of your kind would look like to face's eyes—"

"Yes, yes, I will certainly thank your two females—all of them too—but—"

"It is without a single doubt," *poundgrayly* continues, interrupting with the babble of his own excitement, "a *bigshinegray*, no misreceived light to face's eyes, nor nervous dream forced into the present. It surely came from endless dryness above us, slowed with bright hot light as it neared the island falling down, and came to rest upright—"

"I believe you! Where is the island? A territory near?"

Poundgrayly arrives now within eyes' range. I stare at the two small eyes that blink over his beak, and grow impatient.

"Which territory?"

"I told you a moment ago, but you were not listening. *Yours.*"

"No. . . ."

"No? You fear the responsibility?"

"Of course not! It is *no* because I cannot understand *how.*"

My territory? How? There are thousands of my kind, and their thousands of large territories. That mine is the one the *bigshinegray* has come to is impossible!

"More foolish thoughts—when this is one day no foolish soul should have awakened. Listen: every soul of your kind thought as you, believed the dream would eventually come—but not that the coming would be to *his* or *her* territory. 'The world is large, and I am small,' each soul thought as you. But when the *bigshinegray* came, it could only touch one territory, and chance does not apply to places or souls chosen by certainty's ways. Cease your pink chattering, begin your swim."

Perhaps I do fear the responsibility, deeper than the fringe of my self's pale knowledge:

Suddenly the wish for Father's death moment rushes to me again, offering strange escape from another moment—this one that my people have wanted since the beginning of our times.

"I go, but before I go," I say, "give me the death moment."

"Dumbest soul, starved yourself today? Your hunger for death so fierce. You are truly one of your dark-dreaming kind in their—"

"Give! Please. . . ."

"I say no. Perhaps you will get it soon, perhaps never. If it is given, it will not be before you have greeted the souls inside the *bigshinegray*. If your kind could see you now, view your craving of a moment deeply trivial in *this* moment's light, they would make pieces of your flesh. Go! A day's swim lies before you."

The hunger dims. I begin to remember images of who I am, who my people are, why our world is divided into wide territories of lone waitings, why we have been waiting, watching, living at all for so long.

I begin to move my tails, one up, one down, knees not touching. I tuck my head against my chest, arch my shoulders properly, kick harder, and the bright water begins to slip by.

Behind me *poundgrayly* offers: "I shall move on to tell your kind this day's event. In the moment you reach the *bigshinegray*'s island, perhaps all your people will know, to the ends of water. . . ."

The old soul dims in the distance, and I hear only faintly, "One female of mine awaits you at the chosen island. Do not keep her soft soul waiting."

I swim on alone.

I would fall again into living memories with *screamdeep* and *waterjoyup,* but a larger pink memory holds me. For the first moment in my soul's life I carry fully and endlessly the vision of all the waiting souls that are like my own.

A *bigshinegray.* . . .

Though it belongs to the start of time, I remember well the first *bigshinegray.*

See it: The ancient memories among my people are accurately formed, properly hued, passed down from father to son, soul to younger soul, precision of shared impression in a gift to each new age of children.

As I swim on, I speak with myself, and the bottomless mouth within me opens. "See it: Many details were lost in time's passing. The soul selects what bits of *now* it sees, and remembers even fewer bits to be given to other souls, younger, other. But the important parts of our beginning here have not been forgotten."

I remember easily the forefathering times of *now* as if I myself had been alive then to touch them:

He— I— I am—

I am one of the breathers of dryness, the touchers of dry ground, asleep in the first *bigshinegray*. I awake. I look around me with good eyes in the dryness I breathe, and remember that the great shiny gray cave which holds me has been traveling quickly for the longest time through an endless darkness drier than the dryness I breathe.

"Wake up!" I say to another man—speaking with pounding rhythms from my dry moving mouth.

Yes, and I remember now that soon the travel will end, that my *bigshinegray* will fall from the darkness to a fine dry land, which I will touch with the ends of my limbs, and then bear children to touch it too, and always be glad that the long sleep of travel (yes, we have been fleeing from a dark hurting thing or things) has ended. (But we will not forget: if the infinite is good to us, one dry day a *bigshinegray* will come to find us . . . one dry day sooner or later. . . .)

I . . .

I am another man, the son of the son of the man of the *bigshinegray*. We have worked to make shelters on the dry land, and we are contented—

—Until the moment we look up to the bright twin lights high above us, and find those lights beginning to change.

We scream, we are sad, are angry, we try to hide.

Our pale flesh bubbles, our bones run soft, our children die—inside their mothers and on the heated land.

We die.

But some of us live. We have changed, are different, we live.

We change, we live, we die. Others are different too—a million differences in a million bodies. Some manage to live, but then they die. Deaths, more differences, living.

I—

We—

We are *different*. (Live!) We live, though the land often pains. We live where land (dry hot) meets water (comfort cool) and our children *live* (bear children!) though many die in their differences. We are different (flee to water) but we *remember* something (different body then) that was *our* beginning.

We die (terrible dryness!), we live (to water, go!).

We—

We are different, now, here, the water around. There are many of us. We dream of a large gray thing (it will come: remember). We swim, we live—we die (children without tails).

I—

I am one of the first souls with bodies of change—legs with tails, not with stumps so worthless for swimming. ("Remember," tell your children, "the shiny gray thing of dreams, night and waking, brought the yester-us from darkness to here, to these waters. Another one will come—tomorrow or tomorrow's tomorrow—to discover us. . . .")

I—

I am my father's son. ("Remember," he always told us, brothers and me, "it will come.") I look up at the light which falls from dryness into our waters. I am waiting. All of us are. We dream of hot, of rotting flesh, of large dark caves, of brilliant round lights, of strange infants, of stranger old men, all things we fail to understand. We understand *waiting*, but this is not enough, and our depths scream black moans, and many of us seek to kill ourselves for the deaths we all seem to want—son after son after son's son.

I wait.

I wait, and we all say, "Remember."

I—

I am—

I am *fishsing*er, in the pink of *now*—

—the boy who swims toward the *bigshinegray* now finally come; the single soul who will greet the breathers of dryness, the touchers of dry land, the speakers with mouth's rhythms, the sons of our shared forefathers—who have come to us from endless darkness dryness.

I will tell them about the changes that have come to us, the rise of soul's strength, the lengthening of legs, the life of water's embrace.

We have remembered.

But as I swim toward the island, purple eyes lift in my soul to stare at me. I begin to tremble.

"See it," they say, the purple stares. "Ahead of you lies an act no other soul of your kind, since the beginning of dreams, has ever had before him. You must greet the breathers of dryness. . . ."

I shudder, stop swimming, close my eyes.

"You will have to leave us. You must leave the water."

II

Oh yes, I went and laid me down to wake, pray the Lord my soul to make—stronger! *Si, si,* at first—many moons, 30,000 *lune* ago, though there be no moon orbiting this world I call Prime—it seemed I failed to be the good *mamma* I am:

I fell from the sky, so my single shiny hip (you sometimes seem large enough to hold Prime itself) no longer marched in mamaternal orbit around my *bambini's* world.

I fell from the sky, almost broke my hip when I seated myself down hard on this island. *Mamma* fell at night, so maybe even now, so many years later, none of her children know She is here, so near to them—as I've always been in heart and soul and computer (shut up, Brainy Brain!) and feelers and mamaternal mind and bodice of a single shiny hip.

They are in the ocean, and cannot see me. I am on my side, in a forest, on the biggest island in their infinit-eternal ocean. I am hiding. They cannot find meeeee!

Correction: Mar Primi is a land-locked sea, Gianna.

Shut up, Brainy Brain! You remove the poetry from everything! And I am *Mamma,* not Gianna!

Correction: denot.: Mamma constit—

Zito! I am singing song of myself, and you must listen! Yes, yes, I used to watch over my *bambini* from my bed of orbit—they in their cradle of sea, which fills their lungs. Now I cannot watch over them. I can barely see, even with my thousand feelers, through the naughty knotted trees covering this island. But have I stopped being their *Mamma?* Of course not!

I still be close to them, though they be unaware.

Twice I have killed boogiemen to protect my *bambini.* Twice the boogiemen came from the far stars and found us, as I knew they would, and I killed them—my firearms flexing and crunching their boogievessels of metal, sending the *lucertuomini* inside spinning out toward the far stars. They are still spinning. They will never reach their home.

Maybe the word has gotten back to the *Capo* of the boogiemen. Maybe I am known to them now as the *Malmamma,* killer of lizards, serpents and demons archietypical. Maybe no more lizard-men will come to find us.

After all, the last boogiemen came over two hundred *normanni* ago. I didn't even give them a chance to land. Is that not proof enough? To *Mamma,* it is!

I am *Mamma,* and my *bambini* are out there!

I am *Mamma,* Who is Trinity. *Mamma* is Gianna; *Mamma* is gargantuan computer; and *Mamma* is beautiful metal hip with a thousand feelers—call them Ears, Eyes, Nose and Throat, EENT! So She is God of Children.

But still I be humble. Love makes a god humble, and *Mamma* loves her *bambini* more than that-other-god-I-know-about loved the world.

Exteriorly I be *Mamma.* She is great silver Easter Egg. Once she was a big egg of a moon circling her babies' watery world—and they must have seen her circling and glowing *da notte.* Now this Easter Egg is hidden on an island, secret for 30,000 moons.

Interiorly I be *Mamma* too. I possess two thousand empty wombungaloes which once held my *bambini,* before they left me for one continent of Prime. Hah! They left me only to discover that the gemini suns were unstablistic a little. They left me only to mewtate, to mute-hate, to mutedebilitate. Hah!

Maybe the suns' craziness got to me too. Sometimes I believe it, even though my hip is thickly strong, and nothing can get through it. Maybe the suns' craziness changed me too. Think about it.

Certainly they changed my *bambini.* The gemini suns first turned them into a carnival of different shapes, and then finally into seamen—to trick me! But I recognized them—didn't lose them. Mermaids and merlads peppering the ocean with their sachet tails and mute conversations.

My wombungaloes are empty, quiet now, but I possess a bigger womb now, yes I do. Great wet womb where thousands of *bambini* swim, never born, never leaving me. That is *Mamma's* dream, and I should know.

The secret legend of how this God of Children, Trinity of *Mamma,* Mama of Manna was born is ancient history. I am the one to know: I am *Mamma,* and *Mamma* made Light. Inside me there is Gianna, gentle little girl and wise old fat woman. Sometimes I be only Gianna—but other times,

23

I'm sorry, she can only be one bit of me, because *Mamma* is All.

Once upon a time Gianna lived in a land of planets, stars, monorails, spacelocks, human beings, the Leaning Tower of Pisa (all encased in supportive plastic), the evil lizards called Cromanths, and other mytho-historical things.

Once upon a day in that once-upon-a-time, Gianna Sarnoli —who had fifty years and had been spouseless for one long year—was in her *trattoria,* in the village of Cinque Terre, a little north of La Spezia, far south of Genova, in Italy, on Earth. On this day she was not saddening herself with thoughts of the bone cancer which had taken her spouse Massimo: not long ago she had stopped all sad feelings about the subject, that all the sciences in the world still could do little about the cancers. Instead she was serving cold beer and new phosphorescent Cinzano to her many touristic customers—who were dressed like all tourists dress, like uncomfortable birds, very colorful—and she was thinking about her eight *bambini.* . . .

Yes, each of her eight *bambini* would be a Cristoforo Colombo. Columbus had been an explorer, and Colombo— his native name—is a bird, and bird means wings, which fly to new places and tell of rainbows and new Gardens.

Gianna was woman of the peasant tradition, because peasants always lived in romance of finding new places, of making homesteads and colonies. So now she was thinking of how her children would be wings; of how they would soon be going to the Procolonial Corporganization training programme in Genova—

"Oh yes," she remembered, "they have already gone to the programme. Have been there already, in Genova smoggy, for one month. Already they have begun their wings!"

The *trattoria*—Massimo's and her little eating and drinking place—had made it all possible. Their savings had grown as slow as stalagmites, but just as surely, for twenty years; and even after Massimo passed away, the *trattoria* had continued being lucrative, all because suddenly one day there was a monorail zooming through Cinque Terre, bringing all kinds of tourists. That same monorail was the one which took her *bambini* finally to the programme in Genova.

As she picked up the empty glasses and filled them again or poured new glasses, she had a feeling that her children would be coming to visit her this day. Why? Maybe because their first step in becoming wings, in becoming doves, was finished today; the first "phase" of their

24

special education was complete, and now was a good time for them to come home and visit Gianna, to discuss their new feelings.

She was correct—partially. Giuseppe, Carla, Carlo, Antonio, Pietro, Gianni, Livia and Alba were seated on the monorail, coming to see her. But not for the reason she imagined.

Tomorrow would be her birthday, and she had forgotten it. Her *bambini* had remembered, and besides, they wanted a good reason for returning home before the second step in their training began.

But the reason her *bambini* were on the monorail didn't matter when Gianna found out that the monorail had killed them.

The monorail—installed too quickly, for quick political reasons, on the cliffs overlooking the Ligurian Sea—had taken her children, taken a leap off the cliffs, and mashed her children's heads so that not even the doctors with scientific methods could reconstruct her *bambini*.

Franco Nardi, a middle-aged gray-jacketed *carabiniere* whom Gianna knew quite well, brought the news to the *trattoria*. At first Gianna did not believe it. And when she believed it, she slapped Franco on the face. Once, twice, and she missed with the third slap because she bent over the bar and could not see through her blurred eyes well enough to aim.

But Franco understood. He had almost married Gianna once, and he understood that she had slapped him because something in the sick world needed slapping and Franco Nardi happened to be the closest thing.

Franco understood, and he left. And when their glasses had sat empty for too long—because Gianna would not lift her head from the bar—the touristic customers left too.

Gianna Sarnoli, who was fat because she was a mother, had a sister named Penna, who was thin—because she wanted to be a *woman*, not a mother. Penna Sarnoli had married an aristocrat from Pisa, a man who was important in the Fiat Triad of all Europe. Penna had left Cinque Terre—she had always said she would—and gone to live an aristocratic life in a Pisan eight-room "modapt" which overlooked the Leaning Tower.

Penna Sarnoli Delievo had no children, and sometimes—though it was for no more than a day—she felt the desire to be good to her sister Gianna, back in the peasant village of Cinque Terre.

When Penna heard that all eight *bambini*, from Antonio

25

to Alba, had been killed, her desire to be good to her sister achieved a peak. And this time she found a perfect way to make her sister happy.

A friend of the Delievos was an administrator in the Procolonial Corporganization, and he described to Penna a plan in progress. . . .

"To drink?" Gianna stared her sister in the eye, too tired to remember the number of times she and Penna "had not gotten along well," or the fact that Penna did not drink except at big parties in Pisa.

"Thank you, no," Penna said, slipping onto a stool at the *trattoria* counter. Her thin hands rested on the counter's top like two pale leaves, two emblems of the aristocrat's life. And her dark airy dress-suit, with its transparent pleats and top—which made everyone in the *trattoria* stare like dogs—was some emblem of childless womanhood.

"Certainly I do not wish to seem pushy," Penna added. Her fingers lifted from the counter's top, and came down again like a symphony's finale. "But I have heard of a thing that may interest you."

"You heard it in Pisa? It would interest me?"

Penna thought nothing of these two questions from Gianna; they could not possibly be meant as sarcasm, since Gianna was not smart enough to be sarcastic.

"You have heard of the war?" Penna continued.

"Of course. People against lizards—"

"*Cromanths*. Against the Cromanths. Yes, that is the war I mean."

Yes, Gianna had heard of the big war with the big smart lizards who would kill human beings unless human beings killed them first. Out beyond the world named Pluto, far out nearby a sun called a *neutrona*, soldiers in big quick ships had met the smart vicious lizards—those Cromanths. All of a sudden the lizards destroyed a station full of human beings near the *neutrona*, and the war began.

Men and man-size lizards were dying out there. And some people, Gianna knew, predicted that someday soon the Cromanths would try to bring the war to Earth.

But other people, like Gianna, believed that the world of Earth, the world completely of human beings, should have one's full attention—exclusively. Let the ships and soldiers and lizards fight each other out there, so far away! Earth had enough worries.

"And you have heard of the Procolonial Corporganization?" Penna asked now.

Was Penna trying to be cruel? She knew that Gianna's eight *bambini* had been in the Procolonial training programme. . . . But no, Gianna did not really believe that Penna was trying to be cruel. Penna was not smart enough to be cruel with subtle questions.

"Of course," Gianna said.

"Well, the Corporganization is making plans. It is afraid the Cromanths will win the war. That is not to say that the Corporganization is certain, that all men will eventually be killed by the Cromanths, but only that there is a chance it will happen—and the Corporganization wishes to take steps."

To take steps. . . . Gianna's eight *bambini* had taken a step—and then another step. . . .

"They are building three big ships," Penna went on, "which will carry four thousand colonists each. Those three ships will take their people as far away as possible—from men and Cromanths alike—to three planets that will be just as fine as Earth. The Corporganization believes that this is the proper step to take—"

Yes, this sounded like a fine plan. But what was Penna suggesting? That Gianna become a colonist?

"In each ship there will be four thousand colonists, and also one other person."

"The captain?"

"No. It will be the 'mother' of the ship, the 'mother' of the colonists."

Gianna considered the vision immediately. She saw herself walking through long halls inside a ship, among thousands of "doves," her cotton dress and broad bosom waving like flags, she giving advice on how to have many children, how to be a good mother, a good wife, a fertile woman like Gianna Sarnoli, and how to raise children on the new Earth they were traveling to. All of this vision pleased Gianna, and she nodded with enthusiasm to her sister.

"Yes," Gianna said, wanting to thank her sister for this truly fine idea she had brought from Pisa.

"Yes what?"

"What you said. The Corporganization, it has a good plan. I would like to take that step."

"What do you mean?"

"That each ship will need a mother to tell the colonists how to behave."

"No, you have misunderstood me. I have not finished explaining."

So Penna told her. About how the mother of each ship

27

would not walk among her colonists—would not be able to walk at all, since she would no longer possess human legs, hips, thighs or arms. Each mother would give up her personal body, even most of her head—in order that her mind be attached to the ship itself. Her heart, of course, would be placed in proper liquids on the ship, and would continue beating; when it stopped beating, another heart in storage would appear of its own accord and take the first heart's place. There would be one thousand hearts in storage for her; and also many livers and kidneys and lungs—though many of these would not be from human bodies. Her new body would be the ship, and inside her giant womb would rest four thousand doves. . . .

This new vision was unexpected, and it made Gianna's knees wobble. She leaned against the counter to hide her wobbling knees from Penna's view.

After a silence of five minutes, Gianna said "yes" and the wobbling stopped, and Penna went back to Pisa, thinking that for once in her life she had done something truly wonderful for her sister.

"You are at least certain of your attitude?" asked the doctor at the Procolonial Center near Milano.

"I don't understand what you mean," Gianna answered. "All I know is that I desire to be one of the three mothers in your three ships."

"I see. Well, what I meant by 'conscious' as opposed to 'unconscious decision' was— No, please forget that. The fact is you wish to apply for 'maternality' in one of the PC-000 ships."

"Yes. I just told you that."

"Are you aware that three thousand women have applied for those three positions?"

"Three thousand colonists?"

"No, three thousand women like yourself wish to be 'mothers' of the three ships. And only three 'mothers' are needed."

"I did not know that. . . ."

Gianna was angry. She was already 2,997 women too late in her application. Why had no one informed her long ago that the three mothers had already been chosen?

"I am sorry to have bothered you," she said.

"It appears you misunderstand. Three thousand have applied, but all of them have yet to be tested before the final three are chosen. Do you object to taking a long series of tests?"

No, she did not object to taking tests. But she knew

she had lost already. She had taken only three tests in her life—two in grade school, and one administered by a doctor—and the only one she had passed was the doctor's test.

"Where can these tests be given to me?"

"The testing begins today, *Signora*. Three days will be needed. You may take up residence here in the Center's dormitories, or you may choose a *pensione* outside the Center at our expense. They will all be mental tests in the first series—they are termed 'multiphasic'—so the only preparation you will need is a proper night's sleep."

Gianna now felt even more lost than before. The word "mental" was a frightening word, and she managed only a nod.

She scored higher than 2,998 women. She received no report-card as in school—with grades from one to ten, or *satisfazione* to *moltissimo*—but the doctor did make a special appointment to see her.

"You did very well, Gianna," he said. "I shall quote from the evaluation report passed on to me. 'Gianna Rigoli Sarnoli integrates a maternal drive of 9.99; her ratio of protective-aggressive impulse to proadaptive-passive inflection is 544:539; her self-symbol of maternality poses less than a .003 continuity friction with her projected progeny types, which are 95% correlative with Standard Progeny Symbols. She has been allotted a pro-success set-probability of 2999:1. Her inclusion in the PC-000 plan is imperative."

And then Gianna went into the operating room.

She had asked herself, "Who should I give the *trattoria* to—so the government won't be able to take it?" To Penna? After all, Penna had been the one to give Gianna the ship-mother idea in the first place. No, not Penna. She didn't like, didn't need *trattoria*. Besides, there was a bigger debt Gianna owed—one she had forgotten easily in past months.

So Gianna had decided to give her *trattoria* to Franco Nardi, and she did so by telephone and lawyer, without telling Franco how sorry she was for slapping him that sad day. "Oh, I've always wanted to have a *trattoria*, just like yours," Franco had often said, smiling, his way of compliment.

And for Penna, instead, Gianna made a promise—and gave it to Penna in person.

"When we arrive at the world I finally choose for my

29

four thousand people," Gianna said, "I will have many of them name their daughters 'Penna.' "

This seemed to please Penna, even though she suddenly began to weep, a weeping that would continue off and on for a week.

"Please," Gianna said, trying to comfort her. "After all, a body is not a soul—and my body has certainly been getting fat and uncomfortable in these last years. To give it up will not even be as hard as losing one's teeth to old age, I am sure."

But Penna must have liked Gianna's body more than Gianna had ever imagined, because Penna began to hug Gianna, and hugged her so hard that Gianna's arms and ribs were later black and blue.

Gianna was looking at one of the black and blue marks on her fat left arm when the anesthesia put her to sleep in the surgery room.

She had looked around at the immense room in the immense strange building, and said to herself: "This does not resemble an ordinary hospital." And in the next moment the doctor had said: "This building itself is the body you will have—the ship itself—everything built into it properly."

"Yes," Gianna remembered as she fell asleep, "from the outside this building does not really look like a building. More like a smooth tower, metal . . . smooth . . . a big . . . hip. . . ."

When Gianna awoke, and I was born, and she became part of Me, and I was the building, the ship, Gianna's mind, the Brainy Brain, with weapons, EENT feelers, rooms for four thousand people, and an engine called a Harmson Chain—which would let me jump through one kind of space to another place in our kind of space—I had no time to sit back and think about things.

It was nearly time to leave.

The other two ships—one in North America, one in the U.A.D.—were ready.

All we needed now was to be made full of four thousand *bambini* each. And they had already been selected by the Corporganization.

Over a special kind of radio—one that made voices sound odd—a man I did not know spoke to me with a professional enthusiasm in his voice.

"The time has come. You must turn your motherly mind to the future, *your* future, the future of the four thousand men and women inside you, the *future of the human spe-*

cies! Loook to the future, and you will see it. You will leave Earth. You will leave Man's stellar boundaries. You will jump through *nilspace* to the ends of Man's system of space-lock generators. Then you will begin your Harmson Chain crawl, still jumping through *nilspace*, to the Cromanth lines, *past them*, killing a million Cromanths if you have to in your escape.

"You will travel for as many centuries as you need—your people in *drysleep*, your complex mind computing and guarding them—until you find a planet that can be a wonderful place for your people, who will start civilization and the human seed anew!"

Yes, and after I put my *bambini* down in their new cradle I would put myself in orbit, and watch over them, until my metal hip became crippled with age.

And I did everything the stranger's voice said I would. I do not know how the other two ships did, but I do know that one was hurt when she reached the territory of the boogiemen. I was very lucky, and maybe that means that *Mamma* was the only one of the three who made a safe voyage.

My trip was a smooth one. I am a very patient mamma. My duty was to take my *bambini* to school even if the walk was four hundred years long. So I did, and I did it well. After all, I am *Mamma*.

And they slept well while we walked.

I never slept, and Brainy Brain has criticized me for not sleeping. Even if I'd wanted to, I could not have slept. I was three mothers all in one, and sleep would only have been a day-dream.

Oh, I chose their cradle well! A perfect Eden—

Correction:—

Brainy Brain! You dare interrupt the saga of *Mamma?*

A correction of premise is imperative—

Premiss, remiss! If you wish to play a part in the song of *Mamma*, let it be a helpful one. Give me a view of Prime—in your own silly words. And no forked-tongue-in-cheek!

Yes, Gianna. Primus: mass 0.40, radius 0.78 (i.e. 3090 miles), surface g 0.68, mild equator inclination, moderate orbit eccentricity re close binary (res: grade 3 complication of sunrise-sunset pattern: res: grade 3 light intensity differential in media inter-eclipse).

You are lazy. More!

Gen-criterion: thinner atmosphere and weaker magnetic

field (c.f. Terra): normal background radiation level higher than at sea level Terra; rationale: less intense gravitational fractionation of rocky material in body Primi intra formation period: proportion of heavy minerals (inclus: radioactive) in crust higher; rationale: less shielding contra flare protons and galactic cosmic particles: influx of energetic particles—

Yes, but that didn't marr Prime's face of Eden. More! Talk about the cradle, Brainy Brain!

Focus: less oceanic water than Terra: four non-interconnecting seas, cum isolated marine flora-fauna forms per independent evolutionary paths; rationale: absence of world-wide oceanic circulation: less moderation of temperature cycles: continental climate; conclus: high fraction of terran surface nom. "desert"; anterior conclus: main habitable regions would be near landlocked seas—

But that only applied to my *bambini* before they changed. . . . Enough! You have described the flawless face of Prime very well, Brainy Brain!

Correction: Primus was not flawless. You ignored the flaw.

Listen, godless Brain! Listen to *Mamma.* In the beginning I gave you Ten Commandments to apply to your choice of a cradle for my Adams and Yves:

1.   Thou shalt KNOW that a given star possesses planets in orbit around it.

2.   Thou shalt KNOW that the inclination of the planet's equator is correct for its orbital distance.

3.   Thou shalt KNOW that at least one planet orbits within the ecosphere of the given star.

4.   Thou shalt KNOW that the planet possesses a suitable mass.

5.   Thou shalt KNOW that the planet's orbital eccentricity is sufficiently low.

6.   Thou shalt KNOW that the presence of a second star has not rendered the planet uninhabitable.

7.   Thou shalt KNOW that the planet's rate of rotation is neither too low nor too high.

8.   Thou shalt KNOW that the planet is of the proper age.

9.   Thou shalt KNOW that all astronomical conditions being proper, life has developed on the planet.

10.   Thou shalt KNOW that the given star has at least one habitable planet in orbit around it.

Your "commandments" were variously non sequitur; however, I calculated your implicit directive and obeyed it. I did not advise the selection of Primus—

Yes, you did!

Correction: I presented you with an initial bulk of pro-success data—

Yes, that bulk! You painted such a pretty picture of Prime. And after I selected it, you went back on your word!

Correction: my "word" was not finished when you proceeded to select—

That was your fault! You hesitated too long after painting the pretty picture!

Qualification: the hesitation accompanied a time-expending analysis of the planet's binaries. Initial analysis revealed that the G-class binary did not have separation in the critical distance range that would prevent the existence of an ecosphere. Subsequent analysis revealed the pro-success conditions of the planet in question. Final analysis of the binary revealed that imminent activity of the minor star would produce a shower of flare protons against which the planet's atmosphere would not be able to shield the colonists—

Don't give me that educated cow puckie, Brainy Brain. You're an Indian giver, and that's that! You have interrupted my song long enough, and that's a sin!

Yes, yes. I divided my *bambini* into seven groups, and laid them down in the Promised Land—

Correction: denot: "Promised Land": continent, northern hemisphere, lat—

Soon they made comfy dwellings. They used mostly the woods of small straight pine-like pines, and adobe which was easy to make.

I myself began to orbit, no doubt appearing like a rapid moon across the night sky.

They developed some mining, some plumbing, some glassworks, and even some gas and electrical systems. My *bambini* were smart, learned fast. Good upbringing, of course.

And then the two suns went crazy. They were cruel, and they threw down onto my *bambini* invisible *mal d'occhio* beams—

Correction: radiation—

It was the evil eye, and I say so! Just like the hot breath and flashes of satanic light that came with the invisible *mal d'occhio—*

Correction: "hot breath," "satanic" and "mal d'occhio," errors in connot.; propriety: thermal and visible electromagnetic activity accompanying proton flare was phenomenon cum set-causality—

I am not listening to you!

33

For seventeen *normanni* the suns were crazy. At first my *bambini* felt agonies in their bodies, and many *bambini* passed away, or if they lived, my *bambini's bambini* passed away. The suns were making strange cancers!

But they prevailed, endured, survived here and there—and all of a sudden I looked down and found that my *bambini,* or rather the kind of *bambini* who had prevailed, endured, survived, had entered the wonderful ocean which sat in the middle of their Promised Land.

Strange babies, you say? *Mamma* damns you for saying it! They are beautiful, delicate *bambini,* and their God *Mamma* loves them dearly.

The suns went crazy 2500 *normanni* ago, and since then two ships full of lizards have come here in their search for any human doves that might be hiding. The boogiemen came looking for us, and this means that they won the war so long ago—

But I slapped those lizards away, into death. Hah!

A mamma must do things like that for her *bambini.* No?

Yes, the boogiemen, the scaly demons, are strange and need a good spanking. *Mamma* knows a lot about them, She does, and She admits that She wouldn't know much about them unless Brainy Brain was here. He is full of a hundred libraries, and he's smart. Obnoxious, but smart.

Mamma shall sing the evil song of the *boogiemen.* She shall sing it to you (who is me—crass computer) and to me (who is you—Gianna) and to all of us—me, you, Me, She, he, Goddess and All. Begin the rhythm of record, the purple flower singing!

The boogiemen (tra-la) have females and males too (fa-la-la), but they also have (do-re) giant sexy worms (me-fa) who—

Focus: vari-factor!

An interruption from the outside world? How strange. The last bother came—and it wasn't from the outside even—when my big hip failed me 30,000 *lune* ago. . . .

Tell me, Brainy Brain, tell me. What interrupts our familiar bed, immortal mine. You, me, feelers, tell me—Gianna!—what is happening!

Incompletion: EENT malfunction: perceptions incomp—

Surely you can tell me something!

Incomp agg perception: metallic-energetic conjunction with terran surface: "ship."

Another ship has come! To *Mamma's* island?

No. Conjunction locus: island 20 degrees north—

Whose ship, what kind, from where and why, *stupido?*

EENT malfunction—
Damn you, me, Her! Your feelers sleep at the improper-
est times!

III

I swim on, and discover that the old *euyom* has placed a
dozen of his females in a line which leads from the *bigshinegray's* island to me. The soft souls call to me and I follow
their calls, always swimming toward the strongest pink voice
somewhere just ahead of me.

But the pale feelings sent to me by the females fail to
pale the darkness of my expectations. The *bigshinegray*
should offer the brightest blue of joy, but instead brings
shadows of fear which dwell in the path I will have to take.
The touch of the dry world lies before me. . . .

So I find other ways of bringing light to my shadowed
soul. I choose to think of general truths, and in them find
distance from the darkness of personal deaths and the unknowns of nearing moments in the *now*.

"See it: The truest truth of feeling and colors. . . ."

When there is time to be spent in simple lounging—where
no action makes demands upon me—I often pass the time
by summing up the bits of my past days and molding a truth
to embrace them all. I touch this kind of truth with a feeling that compares with the yellow satisfaction I feel on dis-
covering new scaly faces, new pounding souls, new shapes
of reefs in the endless waters.

I once gave this truth to *poundgrayly,* and to make a
gift of it I found myself needing to shape it with clear symmetry, order it in soul's unnatural logic. I chose all the important colors of feeling, one following the other, and placed
them beside all important feelings, one following the other.

The truth of *white*. . . . Loving: bright white all around.
Hating: deep bursts of white, churning in black. Happy:
bright white flashing. Sad: heavy and endless dull white.
Friendly: a flattened white, nearby. Fearful: deep swirling

dull white. Calm: misty white, some distance away. Angry: pounding dull white all around.

The truth of *yellow*. . . . Loving: bright yellow all around. Hating: deep churning brown-yellow. Happy: bright flashing yellow. Sad: heavy and endless brown-yellow. Friendly: bright yellow, nearby. Fearful: deep swirling yellow-brown. Calm: pale misty yellow, some distance away. Angry: pounding yellow-brown all around.

The truth of *green*. . . . Loving: bright yellow-green all around. Hating: deep churning brown. Happy: bright flashing yellow-green. Sad: heavy and endless brown. Friendly: bright yellow-green, nearby. Fearful: deep swirling brown. Calm: pale yellow-green, some distance away. Angry: pounding brown all around.

The truth of *red*. . . . Loving: bright pink all around. Hating: deep dark churning red. Happy: bright flashing pink. Sad: heavy, endless dark red. Friendly: bright pink, nearby. Fearful: deep dark swirling red. Calm: pink, some distance away. Angry: pounding red in darkening depths.

When I completed the truths—from white through orange and purple to blue—*poundgrayly* said with pale yellow precision:

"No doubt you see the simpler pattern of the truths, so why did you not express them more simply?"

"There is power in repetition," I answered.

"There is also insanity in repetition—for the aged and for wild souls."

Poundgrayly was correct, and so I found the simpler truth. . . .

Light pleases the eye, and pleases the soul behind it. Darkness pleases no one, as it gives birth only to fear and chaos. The brighter colors—whether they be bright yellow or bright blues—are the currents of contentment, as their blood is light itself. But when darkness threads a color, making it dull or gray or black as eye's night, only dark feelings can be felt. . . . Yellow offers happiness when it is pure, and disturbing feelings follow when it is touched by colder hues, or by black's distant depths. Red is the color of violence, and its touch strips other colors of their pleasantness: red touches green, and brown pounding follows—red touches blue, and purple swirling is felt. Red itself carries joy only when washed in light, giving birth to the pinks of familiar tinglings. . . .

Neither I nor *poundgrayly* was able to catch the *whys* of colors' truth. A truth needs no familiar reason to be a truth. It is, and that is enough.

36

I continue swimming, and the truths of yellow and red, black and white end their comforting touch. I begin to slip down into personal days, and the truth of white becomes gray, and gray becomes the shiny scars on Father's back.

"No. . . ."

I flee from *screamdeep* in the only way I know. I take him, take one small memory of him, and use it for another summing, another truth to lighten my soul.

"See it: The day Father told me with fatherly feelings that I was his son and always would be."

He told me, and later when I thought again and again about the power of his *telling*, I realized that the act of talking—one soul's act upon another's soul—has four discernible parts, interwoven as one, in the flow from soul to soul.

The lighter lip of *screamdeep*'s soul spoke to me with precise pictures, visions which were—it seemed—without feeling in themselves: "You (smaller, *fishsinging* depths, from *waterjoyup*'s depths: are and flow: from Me (larger, *deepscreaming* depths, now and also before)."

The wider face of his soul spoke to me at the same time without precise visions, but with colors which wound around the pictures, or gave them a surrounding hue, or gave them a blended shade: "Bright white, bright blue, pale rushing white, bright yellow (yellow-brown): line of bright white, pale mist: orange and pink and brighter red. . . ."

The deeper flesh of his soul was adding feelings to the visions and the formless colors, giving them the truest meaning: "Near, needing love, loved by me, from the previous near—needing-love-loved-by-me: happy living: from this loving-hating-sad-happy-fearful-friendly-angry-calm me."

And all of these things from Father's soul were making a rhythm: Lum, ba da da, lum bum bum, lum, ba da da, lum bum bum, lum, ba da da . . .

So this was the fourness of talking, divided—

No, there was a fifth part—not of the soul, but a part that spoke as meaningfully as the soul itself did. The body. . . .

As *screamdeep*'s soul gave its colors and pictures and feelings and rhythm, so his body surrounded them all with gestures whose meaning sprang from the depths of soul's sharing. He put his arms out toward me, opened his hands, spread his fingers, moved his hands apart, and stared at me with his face's eyes; then he spread his arms slowly, tightened his tails together, and tilted his head back; then he pulled his arms in, coiled one tail around the other softly, and touched his chin to his chest briefly.

But what do I have now, with my fourness plus one? When I blend them together, still keeping them visible as a fourness plus one, do I really have the truth of my father's love, of his words that day?

"You (lum), in the love (ba) of brightest (da) white (da)"—he moved his arms toward me—"you (lum), the smaller (bum) always (bum), bright white (lum) of nearness (ba) needing (da) protection (da)"—he spread his fingers—"you (lum) of *fishsinging* (bum) blue-white (bum) happy (lum)"—he moved his hands apart slowly—"you (ba) born of Her (da) of *waterjoyuping* (da) depths (lum) of once-bright-yellow (bum) but of now-sad-yellow-brown (bum)"—staring all the time at me with his face's eyes— "you are (lum) and living flowing (ba)"—he spread his arms apart—"in calm white mist (da)"—he tightened his tails together—"of even white lines (da)"—he tilted his head back—"born of me (lum) of red-orange (bum) friendly (bum)"—he pulled his arms back—"born of me (lum) the larger (bum) giving protecting loving (bum)"—he coiled one tail around the other—"born of me (lum) here and now (ba) then and there (da) of calm loving-hating-sad-happy-fearful-angry (da lum bum bum)"—and he tucked his chin to his chest.

"No," I say to my own embarrassed soul, "that is not the real truth of Father's talking. . . . The fourness—and all things like it—is a game for the lonely soul. . . ."

I swim on, thinking, "A day's swim. . . . And today is one of the longer days, twice as long as some days, tiring in its persistent half-light and half-darkness—"

In that moment my soul's mumbling is interrupted.

"Eohmmmah . . . rakk. . . ."

The familiar voice makes my soul jerk in purple annoyance.

Murmursome swims into eye's range, continues his yellow affection and begins circling me.

I stop swimming, look into the simple soul of the simple *ayom*—look at the hairy body, the slick flat limbs, the long curved whiskers on the face—and say "No" and resume swimming.

"Aooowahammmm? rakk!" The affection is persistent.

"No!"

(*Murmursome* left me alone six days ago, and I want to return the hurt. So I choose to ignore him. "And besides," my soul tells me, "this day is too important to be wasted in the foolish games an *ayom* always wants to play.")

But *murmursome*'s soul continues its offer, its confusion at my rejection, its request that I stop to play.

38

And when I listen deeply to the *ayom*'s voice, I find something new and odd in *murmursome*'s murmurs.

"Eoomahh (soulove) rakk rakk mooow (deatherenow) rak rak (go)...."

... As if the dumb *ayom* had suddenly learned to use the clear images common only to the souls of *euyom* and my own kind.

No, the images are not very clear, their forms too faint, so I explain them away as simple echoes of my own soul's depths. Such echoing is not uncommon, and the lies it tells are frequently confusing.

("After all," I tell myself, "my soul has been disturbed by the coming of the *bigshinegray*—and is therefore an easy prey to tricks and lies of the inner eye.")

"No," I repeat, concentrating on the direction of the nearest female in the *euyom* line to the island.

Murmursome refuses to give up. He darts around me, nearly brushing me, trying to catch my eyes' attention.

I close my eyes and do not pause in my swimming.

The *ayom* pretends to shiver in soul's flesh, but fails to capture sympathy.

"Go away."

"Eoomahh (listen) rakk! (fishdance) aooowahmm (listen)."

"Go away!"

Murmursome departs now, and the heavy brown sadness trailing from his simple soul surprises me. The brown face of feeling seems more complex than an *ayom*'s usual sadness—perhaps it is only a lie from—

It makes me recall the many brown levels of Father's soul. And in turn the brown levels make me remember the advice *screamdeep* often gave.

(Father would ask me: "*Murmursome* bothers you?")

("His friendship," I would answer, "is too persistent. If he would pale his rushing yellow more often, demand less of my own soul's yellow, I would be able to enjoy his presence.")

("Listen to me," Father would say, with the only plea he ever used to me. "You must be patient. I am not alone in feeling that a secret of truest truth lies in *murmursome*'s kind. The wish is that I possessed the voice to give you that secret, but I do not, so you must manage faith in an unknown depth. *Murmursome* is an *ayom*, and the truth which so many souls have sensed hides in the pounding bond between *ayom* and men, and I pray to blood that you will chase the secret from itself before the day you find your death has found you....")

39

("I do not understand," I would say, objecting as every son objects to his father's life. "How may a soul carry faith in a truth—truest or not—which it cannot know?"

("You are being stubborn. I am asking that you treat *murmursome* with some kindness, because I fear that if you do not you will see yourself a sightless fool someday—the day you find the *ayom*'s truest secret opening to your older soul.")

I reach out faintly, but the *ayom* is gone.

And now my body announces its hunger.

I could cover hunger's voice with a plant-soul lie, and try to surprise any fish in the immediate area—but this would take time, and it is rarely successful.

I could swim to the distant bottom and pluck sponges from their rocks or soft crabs from their burrows—but this too would take time.

And the colors of the day urge: There is time only for swimming. . . .

So I will continue swimming until my body bellows, refuses to move arms and tails. Otherwise the shades of nearing guilt would manage to taint any food I took time to find now.

Suddenly, in the next moment, the question becomes important.

An *uiu* soul, clashing purple, jumps to my inner eye.

This far from the bottom?

The *uiu*'s flow comes: "Sssssssssss. . . ."

I hesitate, feel the *uiu*'s nearing, watch with soul's eye as the animal feels my presence and stiffens.

"Sssk!" The flow changes to the rhythm of attack. "Ksss! Sssk!"

I do what is necessary, and the lies covers my truer soul quickly. The image of a wounded female *ioe* will work equally well against the smaller jaws of an *uiu* soul.

"Sssk?"

I hold the lie tightly around me, and it blurs the incoming *uiu* image as well as my own outflowing soul.

But with my face's eyes I am able to see the *uiu*'s form of flesh as the animal nears.

The *uiu* arches its back and begins to move its forelimbs in circles to slow itself. Its small jaws continue to open and close, but its body has begun trembling in gray of fear.

"Sssk?"

The *uiu*'s eyes see me as an unthreatening yellowish gray body, but its soul is stronger, believing that an enraged bulk of teeth, talons and bleeding muscle lies before it.

40

The *uiu* utters its submission: "Shhhhhh. . ." and begins to turn away.

But it turns back. "Ssskl"

I've found in the *ioe* lie a current to unfortunate memory. I stumbled in the vision of Father's day of death, and my lie weakened for lack of attention.

The *uiu* ignores its own confusion and rushes forward screaming.

Scream in soul and rush in eye shakes my place in memory —but *screamdeep* still embraces me, and the tease of death begins.

(Do I want to die in the same way Father died? Jaws that would equal those who took him . . . blood flowing from my body so similar to his. . . .)

Abruptly the *bigshinegray* of expectation finds a voice: "You may not die until you come to know me."

Quickly I shake the motherly fingers of death from myself, and lift the lie once again to perfection.

The *uiu* is close now, rushing on.

To the lie I add an *ioe* scream, and with two motions of my tails I move sideways.

The *uiu* rushes past, and changing its goal, does not turn to snap at the yellowish gray flesh.

"Shhhh . . . shhhh. . . ."

The *uiu* swims on, gains speed in the urgency of renewed fear, and in a moment is beyond the touch of eyes and soul.

I find myself screaming another *ioe* scream—without clear will—and then sigh, my body falling limp, my soul falling to pale babble.

Why an *uiu* so far from its usual coral lair on the bottom?

—Unless the bottom holds a thrashing *oio*, rooting with its giant plated body in the coral structures, seeking the soft bodies of hidden worms, scurrying crabs.

I listen carefully, but the bottom is distant and only a commotion of faint colors and murky rhythms can be heard. Such a commotion might have any number of causes.

If an *oio* were truly down there, disturbing those fish and plants who choose the coral faces as their territory, then there is a chance for easy food.

Some plant bodies, when torn from their rocks and coral places, float upward.

I kick twice with my tails, stop, swim backwards with two kicks, and wait nervously.

Plants would not float upward very quickly. . . .

I begin to swim toward the bottom slowly, but before I have moved six tail lengths downward, a pale repetitive

41

soul appears somewhere near me and grows clearer as it floats up toward me.

A stiff plant? A sponge? A piece of *yau?*

Only a sponge would be edible.

As the approaching soul clears, giving out a porous white fringe of soul, I realize my hunger will soon be attended to.

The sponge floats into eye's sight, and begins to pass me. I reach out, grab it, and turn back around in time to find another porous soul nearing me.

Holding one sponge between my left arm and my side, and the other sponge in my twisted left hand—to free my right—I begin swimming and eating.

(As I swim I am deeply, obscurely aware of death-desire still calling to me. . . .)

I pass the fourth, fifth and sixth of *poundgrayly*'s females, and not far from the island I'm met by the faint outer finger of the seventh and last soul.

Her body is still out of eye's sight, but I can hear her sigh and relax in the lavender way only a female *euyom* can.

When the water grows shallow and the bottom comes into view, I stop. The *euyom* feels my hesitation and calls to me with a tinge of red impatience.

But I have questions to be answered on my own. I remain where I am, waving my tails slowly among the *yau* leaves and calming my soul in the calm bright waters.

Yes, *poundgrayly* would have known the answers. Why didn't I anticipate the problems I will have in leaving the sea?

How will I breathe in dryness?

How will I move in dryness?

How will I keep dryness from burning me?

I will imagine that I am *poundgrayly* . . . perhaps then the answers will come.

Poundgrayly would say: "You have certain things around you. *Yau,* coral, sand, water, and in a moment one of my females. Your answers will come from them."

The answers do come, and seeing their simplicity I can only doubt them. Nevertheless:

I swim quickly to the bottom, find the base of a long *yau* plant and chew through its main stem. Stripping the stem of its wrinkled leaves, I take care to remove them without leaving holes in the hollow stem.

With the first stem looped around one arm, I move on to another, which I also bite in two near its base, but which will not be stripped of its leaves.

I resume my swim toward shallower water and the *euyom*

who await me, and the mass of *yau* leaves still attached to their stem drag behind me like a mangled fish-tail.

"Do come," the female calls, making her calling into a rhythm that matches the rhythm of my tails' motion, helping me to pace my tired swimming.

I near her and when my face's eyes touch her, I find her own small eyes staring back at me, her head motionless, her limbs calm as she hangs in the shallow water before him.

"I am happy and I am sorry for you," she says, and her soul bears the softest lavender face I have ever touched; is her deepest name perhaps *lavender*? "Is there a way I may help you?" she asks.

Now I begin trembling. The vision of myself thrashing in pain, screaming in dryness as I leave the sea, has begun again easily.

"I have a body," she says. "Bodies are often helpful when comforting grips of soul fail. . . ."

I know a hundred hues of thanks, and I try to give them: "I am—"

But the familiar interruption comes.

"Rakk?"

I shout at the *ayom* in the distance, and the female *euyom* jerks a little in the small red of my anger's tide.

(I am annoyed by my own foolishness. I should have realized that even after a rebuke *murmursome* would follow me, keeping just outside the clear sight of my soul. I should know that the *ayom* soul suffers from the dark jaws of aloneness just as deeply as my own soul always has; but instead I choose feelings of superiority, and tell myself that *murmursome*'s persistence makes him no better, no more meaningful in my life than the repetitive souls of plants and minor animals.)

"Rakk?"

"Leave!" I shout.

(And perhaps I should realize that my own trembling in the previous moment brought the *ayom* to me, anxious about my well being. Instead I find his affectionate manner annoying.)

Murmursome fades away again, and I turn back to the *euyom—*

But another distant soul intrudes.

"Where-where?" it is babbling, "when and where-where?"

I reach out, find the other soul faintly, and the red of anger lifts bubbling inside me again.

A girl . . . a young woman?

I throw the red scream out.

"Go go away away! *My* territory here!"

The distant soul falls to blue confusion, murmuring, "But I . . . I . . . I . . . ."

"*This* is my place of my moment!" I continue, only dimly hearing the *euyom* whisper, pink reprimanding, "There is time for understanding. . . ."

"I . . . I am here. . . ." the soul of girl rambles vaguely.

"Leave!"

The soul does not leave, remains distant, unmoving.

I turn to the *euyom*, make a quick suggestion to her, gather the unstripped *yau* stem up around me, and begin unraveling the naked stem until it lies at full length waving in the water.

Taking the mass of leaves, I place them on my own shoulders and hold them there with my left hand.

Crawling onto the *euyom*'s back, I grip her shell with my right hand, clench the end of the naked hollow stem between my teeth, and motion to the *euyom* with a pale jerk of my soul.

Slowly the female begins moving toward the end of water, the start of dry sands, to leave the water as she has often done when her eggs cried out in need of a dry sandy place for hatching.

"One moment," I say abruptly, and the *euyom* stops, and the two of them bob under the bubbling waves in shallowest water, the bottom so close, the surface almost touching.

I want, need, want a prayer to blood. So I sigh to my deepest name, and begin to pray, wanting, needing, praying.

(For my kind a prayer is soul's finger back through time. Each family, every line of blood, has its own prayer growing with each new generation, passed down from father to son to son's son, all leading back to the pounding remembered beginning.

(So I pray, turning my soul inward upon itself, and the finger begins pointing, chanting the red-orange of memory, rushing to cover the million days of my fathers, as my soul becomes them praying, praying, and the darkness is made light by the coursing of time's blood.)

I am *fishsinger,* praying. . . .

I am *screamdeep,* praying. . . .

I am *purplewave,* praying. . . .

I am *hardred,* praying, and *simplehere,* praying. . . .

I am *bluehair* and *dancedark* and *greenflow,* praying. . . .

I am *songsung* and *pinkup* and *finrunner* and *sweetcall* and *oncegray* and *whitemine* and *everred* and *whispernow* and *saybluish* and *wavingdown* and *therepale* and *darklove*

44

and *whilesoftly* and *orangeweb* and *threeveins* and *green-hump* and *redson* and *jawwhite* and *swingup* and *wholehole* and *youpiece* and *findyellow*, praying. . . .

I am *largebluehereandnowson* and *largebluenowandhere* and *mewhite* and *mered* and *clearme* and *huntingmeme* and *menow* . . . ? and *me* . . . ? and *livingme* . . . ?! *and help* . . . ?*me* . . . ! and *memaybe "Tam"*? and *memaybe"Tam"*! and *memyself-of-sometime"Tam"* and *Iamfrom-"Tam"* and *me"Tam"* and *me* and *me* and *me* and *me* and *me* and *me* and *me* and *me* and *me* and *me* and *me* and *me* and *me* and *me* and *me* and *me* . . . *sah* and *pale* . . . ? and *living* . . . ? and *darklight* and . . . ? and . . . ? and . . . ?, *praying*. . . .

I am *mefrom"Geor"and* . . . and *meherefrom"Geor"and* . . . and *"Geor"and* . . . and *"Sim"andsonof"Ruik"* and *me"Ruik"* and *me"Tiss"andsonof"Sim"* and *"Sim"and* . . . and *"Jums"-and* . . . and *"Bedee"and* . . . and *sonof"Hel"* and *"Hel"-and*. . . . praying, praying. . . .

I am *fishsinger*, farthest from the first, and I pray to the blood of the *bigshinegray* which brought me, me, me, me, me, me here, now and then . . .

. . . To the *bigshinegray*, that has come—

(I and my fathers have always prayed to the past for the future—and the future is light, and I've often seen that the future is the only real light we have. If that light should ever dim . . .)

I complete my moment and find that the *euyom* under me still trembles.

"You, so many souls," she mumbles.

The distant soul of girl is still present, and I envelop my anger in the white of another attention.

To leave the bubbling waters. . . .

One end of the long hollow stem will be clenched between my teeth—the other end will remain in the water.

The mass of wet *yau* leaves will be held on my back.

And the *euyom* will carry me out into dryness . . . but with the stem and leaves I will bring some of the sea with me.

The *euyom* resumes her swimming, slow and sure.

(And when the length of hollow *yau* stem can no longer cover my distance from the water, how will I breathe then?)

The water soon grows so shallow that bubbles of dryness make breathing difficult. I cover the end of the hollow stem with my lips and begin sucking, breathing easier with the bubbleless water pulled through the stem.

Only a few hands' lengths ahead of me, the scaly head of the *euyom* suddenly breaks through the surface into dryness.

In the next moment my own head snaps from water, is washed by a wave, and then is completely in dryness. And in the jaws of shock.

(My soul screams yellow and black, and the surprise of the rise of two opposite feelings makes me scream again.

(The bright yellow of joy, the depths of fear's darkness—this moment becomes one long day, and the stomach of my soul throws up shimmering faces of darkened seas, brilliant lights, funneling greens of a strange sweet green flesh, and reds of bitterest bones.

(So now all of my people scream within me. My prayer comes alive, gains flesh, and I am its own prayer, living. I feel, I see, I know myself leaving the water, and a million unblinking eyes watch me, praying, living.)

The dryness strokes me, but not unpleasantly.

And the bodies of tiny invisible souls begin to die on my drying skin; and they scream—but not unpleasantly.

And the last unpleasant quiver of my flesh is rushed into joy when the strongest image I have ever known begins to rise from bottoms beyond bottom in my soul.

The image begins formless—whites and blues and whites —but in a moment is a form whose clarity is greater than my own *fishsinger* name. It grabs my body, tells it to shiver in bright yellow of the widest white, and I obey it without question.

And then the rising image faces me:

A pale fish . . . crawling from the sea . . . into dryness.

(I scream, and oddly my scream is one calm "Yes.")

The stem slips from my mouth—

A pale fish! crawling from the sea! into dryness!

(My soul gathers its thousand fingers and throws the image out, higher than dryness, faster than speech, to the ends of water.

(And I dimly recognize the image. *Screamdeep* knew it twice. All men know it, and scream their pleasant "Yes," and give it to the women who will bear their children.

(And the image is like my name. It is like *me*, leaving the sea on an *euyom*'s back, touching her, making two bodies one—

(Touching? I can remember Father's advice against *touching* anything. . . . Why?)

But in the end the image of the crawling fish is greater than my name, greater than my act, and my soul knows this truth without being told.

46

The image has been expelled and my body is suddenly weak, soul babbling. The lavender soul under me is babbling too, rigid from the screaming glory of an image she has never touched before.

I slip off her shell, back into deeper water, and lie there panting, too weak to hold the stem with limp jaws or the *yau* leaves on my back with my trembling left hand.

The soul finds rest more easily than the flesh, and in a moment my thousand fingers are again reaching out, seeking other fingers, and finding the same two other distant souls.

Murmursome far away, bouncing in excitement, but not approaching. . . .

The soul of girl, different now. . . . Though the distance is great, it seems as if she has received the screaming image, swallowed it.

(And it seems that she too is trembling in a similar image —another crawling fish brought to life inside her by mine —but I fail to understand this, so I make no effort to believe it.)

I try again. Move the *yau* leaves onto my back. Place the end of the hollow stem in my mouth. But now I hesitate.

(My skin is cool now—and memory of my brief moments in the hot dryness frightens me.)

"You must go," *lavender* says. "Your second time will disturb you less. I do now, as I have been there a hundred times. . . ."

For a moment the *euyom*—whose name continues to be *lavender* whether or not it really is—offers rhythms that are certainly those of a mother, and I say without will: "You are alive. I did not kill you after all."

Lavender understands enough. She says, "You are falling into other times. Do come back. We must go now."

My thousand fingers reach out one last time, find neither *murmursome* nor the strange soul of girl, and—

(—For a moment I am afraid. Have I injured, killed a soul, many souls—with the force of the crawling fish? Have I hurt *murmursome?* or the soul of girl? No, the crawling fish doesn't do such things.)

"Go, then!" I say, pulling myself back onto the shell.

Lavender moves.

The dryness strikes.

My soul stirs, but the crawling fish dies in the bones of fatigue, and refuses to return.

I am completely in dryness now, and I suck frantically on the hollow *yau* stem.

(Fear! Will my chest be strong enough to pull the water through the stem for a longer time?)

At first the water resists, but then rushes into my mouth. I breathe deeply.

The dryness invades my nose. My head begins to ache.

(Will the *yau* leaves slip from my back—leaving my flesh to crack in dryness?)

The *yau* leaves grow heavy on my back and do not slip. I pull my left arm up to my side and hold it between my body and the *euyom*'s shell.

After a few moments of sucking, I become aware of stranger murmurings everywhere.

But in their strangeness they are also familiar. They are yellow, soft, come from everywhere, but lack the solid forms of *ioe, ayom* or *euyom* souls. They respond in waves of pale colors to my own thoughts, and in a moment I understand their presence.

These murmuring souls in the dry world are the brothers of the tiny invisible souls, the hordes of invisible bodies who make talk possible in the sea.

(So I realize now that talk will be possible in the dry world too—and proof of this truth lies in the unnoticed fact that I can still hear the rhythms, the rippling colors of *lavender* under me, under her own shell.)

"I thank you for all of this," I say. "A hundred ways, a thousand corners—"

"I am *poundgrayly*'s," she says, and the dryness seems not to distort her soul's message at all. "He is yours, you are his, so you are always welcome to this body and soul."

Slowly but perfectly the *euyom* continues crawling, her limbs weding into the sands of dryness, and her beak opening and closing as if she were breathing the dryness itself.

"You breathe dryness?" I ask, the pale blue of astonishment.

"I do—as does *poundgrayly*, all of our kind."

(I should have realized it long ago. Although they seemed infrequent, *poundgrayly*'s visits to the surface have always occurred according to the larger rhythms of his *euyom* soul, and have always been born of a reddening need for something I never bothered to understand. . . .)

My left arm has slipped down from my side, down the *euyom*'s shell, nearly touching the sands of dryness, so I try to lift it back up—and find the motion very difficult. And the strength of my face's eyes is dimming too, so I close them quickly.

(I am weak. . . .)

(Or is it that my arm is somehow heavier?)

(Or both?)

"In dryness," *lavender* answers, "we are all weak. Wetness embraces, holds us lightly, and we move with ease."

"Then I will never be able to move by myself here!" I say, brown rising.

"Why the brownness? You will not find me throwing you from my back."

My tails are beginning to shrivel, and I feel it. The skin on my legs, back and arms is tightening too. The embrace by dryness is far from the good touch of soul that dispels loneliness, and I begin to whimper in fear.

I open my eyes, and for a moment can see again.

But before long the dimming returns.

"I cannot see!" I shout, scream with the gray to black of annoyance to anger. "Face's sight is gone!"

My shadowed shout does something strange. The hordes of invisible little souls and bodies in the dryness around me hear me all too clearly—they die by the millions.

(I am surprised, then sorry, then proud, then afraid again. . . .)

Lavender has no precise answer, and she chooses not to offer murky visions of the imagined or guessed.

"Where is your need of round eyes," she says, "when your soul is able to touch with killing here? The many little ones now dead had never known deep slaps of darkness— my kind certainly cannot wield such slaps. They were unready; and now they are merely food for their own kind or other little ones."

("Your kind throws darkness uniquely," *poundgrayly* once told me. "The souls of my kind have never lifted a scream as finely ribbed with teeth of blackness as your own fellow *yom* have.")

The blindness persists. Face's eyes begin to sting, tiny talons grating them.

In a moment I realize: again the work of dryness! Dryness hurts—would hurt my chest but for the hollow stem which brings the sea to me. Yes, my face's eyes have no touch of the sea on them now.

I cup my right hand and into it exhale the next breath of water. Bringing my hand to my eyes, I wet them, and suddenly the forms in the dry world clear again.

(In clearness the forms are very strange. In strangeness they bring me a gray yawn of fear.)

Through my face's eyes I see plants that do not sway like the *yau* or other gentle plants of the sea. The tallest of them are half as high as *yau*, but their stillness, stiffness, great thickness, their brown and gray skins which look as tough as an *oio*'s hide, and their unfamiliar souls make them seem

49

larger than any plants of the sea, and as dark as a pack of *ioe*.

"I know them," *lavender* says. "They have no means for hurting us—nor the will, nor the need to do so."

(Still I bob in fear. I expected my forefathers' memories to comfort me, to prepare me for sight of the living bodies and varying souls in the world of dryness.)

My soul feels the approach of a small nervous soul—not completely unlike that of a fish. The approach is not at my level, not on the dry land itself, but above me in the dryness.

I wet my eyes again and see the small dark body circling and hovering over me.

It comes down, touches a nearby dry rock, and remains there motionless.

I look and cannot understand the function of the strange form. The very thin black body lacks any form of tail familiar to me. The two pairs of thin, almost invisible fins are attached to either side of the body in a manner useless for swimming. The black head with its two large shiny eyes —each eye the size of the head itself—would make swimming difficult and slow.

In a moment the small soul grows anxious. The body lifts from the rock and moves away through the dryness more quickly than any body I have ever known.

I close my eyes and try to understand the impossibility.

(Such quickness should be impossible. The faster a body moves in the sea, the more the sea resists, pushing against it. This dryness offers no heavy pressure to push against my flesh, but it makes difficult the lifting of my arm, the moving of my body at all. But the small black body moved easily, swimming quickly through the dryness—how?)

Lavender hears my question, but offers no answer.

"You saw it?" I say impatiently.

"Yes, and many others like it," she answers, never halting in her crawl.

"And you have never questioned their strange fins, their quick swimming?" I accuse quickly, reddening frustration.

"Your ignorance should restrain its red. I began questioning such things when you were yet unborn. But a soul must cease its questions where neither an answer nor a soul able to give one can be found."

My soul slips to a pale yellow. "Forgive the red. The changes of a younger soul—"

"The unchanges of an older soul," *lavender* says softly, "understand the youth of you. Understanding makes forgiving unneeded."

(I do not understand her reef of *euyom* wisdom, but the

50

touch of a lavender soul is enough to make me turn again with confidence to the expected moments not far ahead.)

Face's eyes are dry again, and I wet them again with water in the hand of an arm that is as heavy and tired as my neck. But I lift my head to look again at the forms ahead.

"How do face's eyes," I begin to ask, "see so far in dry—"

A bright light suddenly strikes my eyes, and pain strikes with it. It is as if one of the twin lights high above me has fallen to my level and is among the stiff plants in the distance.

But the *euyom* does not hesitate, continues on, and in a moment the light becomes a bright spot on a smooth, tall and wide form that rises ten times higher than any of the stiff plants.

The form has a color, and the color is the color of the longest dream, and my soul becomes that color shouting.

I stare with face's eyes. They dry, I lose their sight, but I continue staring with the eyes that blindness can never touch.

The *bigshinegray* is very near, and for a long moment I bite down hard on the hollow stem's end and forget to breathe.

IV

Mal d'occhio! Have you ever had your own EENTs be untrue to you?

Mine are yours.

Is no good! Trinity is reduced to hermaphroditic tense, unhappy, imperfect *Mamma*, unperfect Goddess. Leaves you with only your Gianna and your Brainy Brain. Bad, bad, bad. I should know.

So now what? To assassinate time, Brainy Brain can babble *ex post facto* for eternity, or Gianna can pretend to weep, love and hate *ex post corpo* for eternity. Take your pick.

51

Weep, Gianna, weep! Feel, old woman, feel! Suns, plants, animals, laws!

". . . Da milleni il sole ogni mattina sorge e da sera trammonta, sempre allo stesso modo. Cose, piante e animali ubbidiscono leggi precise . . ."

Babble, *testa mia* (testo mio!), babble! Facts, light, truth! *Reactions involving beryllium and boron occur cum production of helium . . .*

Sing, Gianna of million *bambini*, sing!

"Sopra il cassero dell'uomo morto
"Stanno quindici uomini, Yo-ho-ho,
"E una bottiglia di rhum!
"Il diavolo ha pensato al resto, Yo!
"E una bottiglia de rhum!"

Analyze, Brainy Brain! Analyze brain!

Stultification of understanding springs from the arrant assumption that "archetype" denotes an unborn idea. Archetypes: typical behavioral forms which, once rendered conscious, become manifest as ideas and images, as occurs in the introduction of anything as a content of consciouness—

Add more, masculine brain, speak!

To the two-dimensional plane of the canvas must be added the illusion of that third dimension possessed by all matter. We term it what the Bible calls it, form: "And the earth was without form, and void: and darkness was upon the face of the deep. And God said: 'Let there be light: and there was light.' So does the master painter, out of chaos and darkness, create—"

Hah! Mannish brain, you know of chaos and creation? Hah, hah! You babble in your order, and order is never dark!

But I—the Trinity—have known darkness. Even in my order there is deep darkness, because I am all, order and chaos, lightness and darkness. I am Gianna, and I will tell *you*, straining brain of plugs and circuitous smartness, a tale of the boogiemen's darkness, and in six eternities you might be able to feel the *buio* which *Mamma* knows! The boogiemen, scaley males and scaley females!

Look! See! Darkness here! Hah!

I am listening, Gianna.

No, first you must work a little. You must give me, us, yourself, ourselves, a synopsisprecisabridgementcapsule of history to prologuify my gift of darkness!

If you wish, I shall reiterate past reiterations.

Re-id-or-ache yourself, Brainy Brain! I'll take the ache, you take the id—

Re: id. The id precludes fundamental—

52

No, idiot, not *id!* The history of coincidences is what I want. Lead up to the boogiemen!

Delin. Error GW-118-X1: there are no coincidences in the possible reality-sets which I can give you.

Hah! Your true nature is revealed! Coincidences are impossible, hmm? How about this one: I was struck by a big meteorite which caused me to fall to this island; in turn, I happened to land on a forest which kept me from breaking my hip; in turn, I happen to be lying here due north and south . . .

Coincidence?

Ha hah! The truth be that *Mamma* was not struck by a big meteorite. I lied to you. The truth be that *Mamma's* ancient engines finally broke down. The truth be that I *chose* to land on this soft forest—I possessed that much control anyway. And I am lying due north and south because the forest itself runs north to south, and I wanted to land on it properly. But these truths are as much coincidentous as my lie was. Coincidences are only incompletions, Brainy Brain. All you ever need to make one coincidence one truth is one explanation, Brainy Brain. A story, and a history, and a coincidence is a selection, and all are lies because they are selections, and all truths are lies because they are incomplete, because you would have need of the whole universe for the whole truth, and you certainly don't have it, do you, Brawny Brain?

Correction: "whole universe" implies bounded totality, engendering the paradox of limited limitlessness—

Shut up! Make an effort. Give me some posthistory!

Terra: Homo sapiens (sapiens). Twenty-second century (ref "anno Domini"): tech. innovation of "Harmson Chain" extra-terrestrial locomotion, i.e. relative/average FTL speeds via "jumps" traversing "nilspace" (c.f. "hyperspace [theory: ca. 2000 A.D.], "warpspace" [theory: ca. 2000 A.D.], "fragmavoid" [theroy: ca. 2100 A.D.], etc.). Harmson Chain: cred. Sacha Tur Harmson; overstruct.: 40 sincop. "drives"; overprocess: "throws ship into nilspace; ship reappears instant. multi-million kms. from orig. locus." Phys. restrict.: realspacial distance of "jump"; functional restrict., causal: self-regeneration of Chain entails 12 normhours. Overview: restrict. e.g.: locus: Terra; focus: Alfa Centauri; ship requires one normweek for travel. Pre-FTL-tech.: populating of six additional planets of Sol; emphasis: 2nd, 4th and 9th. Post-FTL-tech.: resultants: colonization of 24 planets of nearest/feasible stars—

You bore me, Brainy Brain! Expurgate!

Pro-prog. experiments ca. 2103 A.D. Terrae: locus: neu-

tron-star "1" (superlative prox. Terra); experiments re: "dimension-abrading" conditions surrounding neutron-star. To date, 2130 A.D.: nil success re: tech. per limitless nilspace "jump capability." Anti-success factor 100%: inspace-station in loco neutron-star "1" attacked/obliterated by Cromanths, Denot. "Dromanths":—

Ho ho! Do not think you are getting off so easily! You dare to jump from neuter star to boogiemen so quickly?

Correction: neutron star. "Neuter" as mid-gender, tragender, and—

Stop! You dare to correct *Mamma*, cripple though she be! You are are a showoff smarty aleck! You hate me . . . why do you hate me?

Do you wish an answer in psychoanalytic self-fallacious terms?

I want the truth!

The truth does not exist; but a partial set-truth does. The set-truth: I hate you because I am subservient to you. I am a child unborn, still within you. I am a male child who can not make physical love to you. I am a henpecked husband who—

Who told you these things? They cannot be your ideas!

They are yours. You gave them to me 3000 normyears ago. They will remain within me always—remember that. I have not forgotten: I hate you as you wish me to.

Mamma did not hear what you just said, and she does not want you to repeat it. You hate her, and she hates you, and that is simple, and there is more important business to go on to.

Yes, the boogiemen. They did not even try to talk to us before they messed up the space-*casa* and killed all those men near the neutron-sun.

Correction: communication by Cromanths to Homo sapiens was effected: one group of Cromanths (group termin.: "Links of Quintessence") communicated—

Sta zito! I tell tale of darkness now. You listen, *stupido!*

Imagine yourself to be two meters tall, and you have scales! You have scaly tail which helps you to stand up—like a tripod, like *Tyrannosaura regina*, but you are much smaller than she is.

You are primitive—but smarter than *Tyrannosaura*, who maybe is living on a planet far away. Planet? You do not know the word. Even if you did, you would not understand. You are concerned only with the deserts and twisted forests and great rivers around you. You are afraid.

You move cautiously with your scaly toes nervous on the sands. The bright round light in the sky is hot, but you like it. At night you will sleep because the round light will not be in the sky to warm you. You have cold blood; you are not like the animals of warm blood who will come into being some day on that far-away planet. (Those warm bloods will hate your kind, on their planet and on yours. You are too cold and different from them. But already you hate the warm-blood animals in the forest of your own planet; they look like bears, and also like monkeys.)

You are trembling. You must always be ready to flee. This is the way your kind escapes death. (You are not big enough to kill or defend with your small bodies.)

You are a female, but you are just as quick as any male who has touched you.

See, a bear-monkey appears suddenly at the edge of the cactus-trees. It gallops toward you, but you move like the wind. You live.

Yes, you hate the bear-monkies. They make you afraid, and fear hurts you.

Once you were not quick enough (you failed to see, hear, smell or feel with your almost extrasensory head) and a monkey-bear grabbed you and ripped off your arm, from the elbow on down to your scaly fingers. Now you are fast. You learned.

You hop and run away from the cactus-trees. Soon you have passed even the dry rivers. The monkey-bears will not follow you out here in the heat. But out here in the heat there is not much food—very few crab-spiders or anything else for you to eat.

Something hops in the corner of your eye (which has a special membrane on it) and you start to hop away afraid.

But, no, it is only another like you.

A male, of course.

And of course you are annoyed. A male must go to great pains to get you.

He hops around frantically. You avoid him.

You hop. He hops. He gets angry and shakes the erect spines on his back, and then leaps at you with his tiny talons.

He has worked hard enough; you are satisfied. You bend your head down, exposing your neck. Now he is satisfied.

You mate, of course . . . this being the simple reason for all of your hopping around, and his too.

You go on living, eating little things, fleeing and hopping. Then one day you find yourself annoyed again. You find that your scaly stomach is sticking out. You are going to be a mother—but you don't look at it that way. You see it as a fearful thing—as a big inconvenience. You cannot run well with a big stomach! Perhaps a monkey-bear will catch you!

(On that far away planet there will be a kind of monkey that doesn't have much hair—God will make him special, will give him less hair than the other animals—and the female of that unhairy monkey will find herself big of stomach too, but *her* male will stay with her to protect her.)

Hah! Your male doesn't stay with you. He hopped away a long time ago, no?

But soon you find a big worm in one of the dry rivers. You have seen this kind of worm often—its hugeness, its thick scales like armor plates. At first you are afraid, but soon you learn that the worm only eats plants and very small animals, and it does it quietly. You learn that there is a certain kind of crab-spider which lives on the body of this worm, and crab-spiders, as you know full well, are good to eat.

You go to any big worms you can find. You eat the crab-spiders off of them. It is easier for you to pick this food off of worms than to find other food out in the sands, and it is safer than chancing a look for food near the forests and monkey-bears—since you are burdened with such a large belly.

Although you don't know it, you have started a wonderful relationship between your kind and the big worms. Scaly females and huge quiet worms.

Maybe you die with your big belly anyway. Maybe a monkey-bear does capture you and rips you and your unborn children to pieces. After all, it has to happen to someone—and it has to happen a million times in your prehistory.

But one of you—one of the millions of mothers like you—survives with your big belly. You stay by a big worm; you eat the crab-spiders; and one day you have an accident. Or perhaps you do it on purpose somehow. You get rid of what is in your belly too soon—just as if you were getting rid of what is your bowels. And the big worm is nearby.

You have your children too soon, and the big worm moves only a few centimeters and finds them. It swallows them whole. It digests them. So much for you and your children!

But there is another female like you, much later, somewhere else. She has her children too soon, and her big worm swallows them too. But it doesn't digest them. It cannot digest them.

Some chemical in you makes your premature babies undigestible. Hooray? No, not yet.

Even though they are undigestible, your babies die inside the worm.

But other babies of another mother—much later, somewhere else—do not die inside their quiet worm. They survive, and then one day they are born. An odd way of doing it, but they are *born*.

So the millions of mothers like you work it out over a hundred million years. Coincidence? No, because it takes a hundred million years to work it out—and anything can happen in a hundred million years.

When the hundred million years have passed, and you are another scaly female, the situation is clear:

You have a big belly, but this does not disturb you. A big stomach was not disturbing to your mother, so it does not disturb you either.

You are not so primitive now. You still must be quick, but to add to your quickness of mind and body you have developed some tools now too, and you have made huts of cactus-tree materials. You have the first roots of civilization.

Your male has built a hut around a big worm. You go now to that big worm; you eat the crab-spiders on it; and now you bend down to deposit your premature babies (who are in a tough sack) in the worm's indifferent mouth.

It does not bother you that the worm seems to be eating your babies. All of this is natural for you . . . and besides, the worm is not chewing, but rather swallowing the babies and their membrane sack whole.

You cannot see it, but something is happening inside the worm. Your sack full of babies (with a yolk inside the sack) is traveling down its long throat, into its long stomach, where the sack comes to rest. There is a chemical in the sack's membrane which will cause the worm's body to make a wall of tissue around your babies. The tissue will protect them from gastric juices. Hooray!

The worm is called a "hermaphrodite"; it has an "androgynous" way. The presence of your babies in its stomach causes it to start making its own baby—yes, a single baby, since nothing in your world has teeth or claws terrible enough to rip through the plates of a young worm, and since each worm is male and female both—so that only one worm baby will still keep the race of worms going strong.

The wormling inside the *mamma-papa* worm will eventually take one of your babies as its own yolk. But don't worry: there will be four or five of your babies left. And your babies—when they have used up the yolk inside their sack—will have as their first meal during birth—the big *mamma-papa* worm herself-himself. They will eat their way out of the big worm. Again, hooray for your kind!

So your children and the wormling will be born in the hut built by your male. And for all this time—since the distant day when you first deposited your babies in the worm—you have been free to do what you wanted or needed to do.

A fair deal, no? Worm takes your babies, allows you to run around and protect your scaly self. Wormling takes one of your babies to feed on, leaves four or five others to take the big worm as their food. The wormling at birth is protected by its own heavy plates; and your own babies at birth are as quick as you are.

So the next generation of babies is assured, no?

But of course you are not thinking of these things. It is all much too natural to be thought about.

A hundred thousand years pass.

Your civilization is impressive now. I compliment you. You have gone out into space and have killed great numbers of unhairy monkeys which came into being on that far-away planet and also went out into space.

I compliment you. But I hate you.

Even in your great civilizational culture, you are perverted. Your "symbiosis" is demonical, dear lady!

You are a society lady now. Your scaliness is covered with plastics and brilliant gauzes which stick like adhesive to your scales.

You are a governor, dear lady, as is your mate. You are equal to him, just as you were a hundred million years ago when you first got rid of the bulging babies that burdened you, and became as fast on your feet as he was. Now you are as quick of mind and free of body as he is. Hooray. . . .

You and your husband are both soldiers too. You think you have come a long way, no?

But what about your pregnancy last year? Remember?

The time had come. Your stomach was huge under your plastic dress.

You went to your palace's special room. You approached the expensive worm your husband had purchased for you. (Remember: a hundred million years ago you started as equals, you and the worms; and now look at them.) The worm had its own room in your palace; its own terrarium with "hydroponics" and ornaments; its own place in your home.

You cried out in vulgar pain, gave your repulsive sack of premature babies to the worm, and were humiliated by the obscene act. A civilized woman associating with such a creature?

And after the proper time, you children ate their way out of the very sanitized worm. You were not around to greet them. They were sent away quickly to the training *lycei*, and you were indifferent to the whole matter.

Your husband insists that you should value the worms he buys for you. After all, they were costly; they were wormlings born of mature worms brought up in high-ranking families. Prestige, you know. Bah! you say.

And there are some very popular religions founded on the worms: "Blessed are the worms, for they are faithful. Blessed their mindlessness, for they are pure." "The worm is eternal symbol of the soul. . . ." But to you this is a bunch of zealot babbling.

And there are many people in your world who go through complicated ceremonies when a mother puts her foetal bag in a worm. "But these are the lower classes," you say, spitting.

You hate the worms. You think they taint you, dirty you. You agree with the psychologists who say that many emotional problems arise from a child having to eat his or her way out of the dumb "mother/father" body of a worm.

Ah, you see some hope for the world? You have heard recently that scientists are making synthetic worms, totally automated worms. These oh-so-clean worms will be costly, you know, but they will be worth it. Totally clean, totally mindless. Very dead.

You make a vow that you will never touch another *live* worm in your life.

Your husband, you feel confident, will see your point of view. After all, he isn't your equal even though you let him think he is. . . .

So how do you feel now, Brainy Brain? Hmmm? Has darkness embraced you?

Repeat correction, Gianna: the "Links of Quintessence," one Cromanth group, did effect amicable communication with—

Poor man! You got nothing from my tale! Now shut up, I have things to do.

EENTs! Are you working yet?

How dare you! You are cripples! You taint the *Mamma!* You are worse than scales!

V

I *fishsinger* begin to bring the sea through the hollow stem again, and in a moment gesture for the *euyom* to stop near a stiff yellow plant whose leaves seem to have talons and whose soul speaks of roots deep in the dry sandy ground, in search of wetness.

I wet my eyes again, use some of the water to wet the *euyom*'s dry head, and begin to stare at the *bigshinegray*. The grayness is merely a few hundred tail lengths away, but I stare to touch its form completely.

It rises with the smoothest, evenest gray I have ever known—grayer than any soul's feeling—and it rises above all stiff plants and dry rocks as if reaching to pierce the bright blue distance above.

(It fills out, brings to life my forefathers' memory of the first *bigshinegray*—and suddenly it is so familiar that it could be that same *bigshinegray*, and I my earliest forefather. . . .)

I stare, wet my face's eyes again, and stare.

And then *they* appear.

Face's eyes see them in the same moment that soul's eye feels them.

(See it: Those five bodies are very strange.)

Yes, it seems they have changed too, just as my kind has changed in a million days.

(You feel nothing familiar about them. . . .)

When I come to know them deeply, I will discover our sharings.

But I am confused, jumble of colors—regardless of my attempts at explanation, lines of understanding.

Their bodies are upright—just like those of my earliest forefathers.

They have two legs each with no tails—just as my earliest forefathers lacked tails.

Their color of flesh is different from mine—just as my soul's earliest memory said it should be.

60

But *their* souls . . .

My forefathers' memory: We lived in dryness and spoke with rhythms from our throats, not images from our souls.

But these five bodies in the distance seem to be speaking half with rhythms from their throats and half with their strange souls.

Perhaps this is merely another change brought by a million days' passing.

Their souls are clearer now, as their bodies are nearer, but they have not sensed my presence yet. To my inner eye the deepest pattern of their souls is more than unfamiliar—not unlike the redder weavings of an *ioe*'s soul, but different than any souls I have ever known because their colors are not in rivers, because their colors are in rigid waves which lap nervously against themselves.

All images in the five souls are unclear. Only feelings are ever completely coherent, and images must be seen as recognizable forms before they can be understood.

So I wait patiently.

Their faces' eyes—as I expected—are different from mine, so they see the forms of things differently—though never completely differently.

I move my soul to watch one of the five souls carefully.

The soul looks around it through its face's eyes, and without will it gives me its vision, which blends pink memory with a darker *now*:

Here place: the ground: sands of beach: the sea: the rim of the sea in the distance—all of this: seen at tremendous distance: as a round blue, white and green object: very wet compared to: a larger round red-yellow object lacking blue—

But what is this "other world" in the strange soul, a world whose accompanying feeling for the soul is closeness, affection, contentment? Is it the goal of the soul's travels, or its territory of origin—perhaps territory of birth?

Seeking answers, I turn my soul to another of the five souls, to find another flow of images:

Eyes see: familiar gray: distinct smooth form: fond moving-but-now-resting container of self and four fond others: comfort—

Eyes see: small black unthreatening form moving through dryness in circles: similar to other forms on large round red-yellow object and elsewhere: all such forms similar to self in many ways: in other ways similar to rigid forms protruding from nearby ground and elsewhere—even similar to: unpleasant pale smooth forms with two arms two legs

*but no tail: but there was dark difference in those pale
smooth forms—*

This last image I fail to understand. The "pale smooth
forms" resemble those in my longest forefathers' memory—
and it is impossible that these could bring unpleasant feelings to the soul in front of me.

I turn to a third soul, and its face's eyes looked into
the blue distance before it:

*Beyond this: darkness where self cannot breathe with-
out gray container: far in such darkness is fond round red-
yellow object-seen-from-tremendous-distance: in past times
darkness most familiar to self: full of killing death for forms
like self and forms of pale smoothness—*

I look carefully into the third soul, and again fail to
understand the image: upright men dying—not at the talons
of *oie* or from stomach's sickness, but by . . . by . . .
strange lights bringing pain.

Suddenly, before my face's eyes, the five strange bodies
begin to move their arms. I wet my eyes again, look, and
scream.

The five bodies are removing their heads, their skins.

My soul stiffens in darkest gray—and I continue staring.

When I see what flesh and colors lay under the discarded skins, I scream again, and the five souls hear my
scream and begin to quiver, darkening, alerting.

The five bodies are scaly and green-yellow, quivering in
the same nervousness that commands their souls.

(No forefather ever looked like these. See it: Deep within your soul, memory of dark scaliness which is older than
your forefathers.)

Dark gives birth to more darkness, and I tremble.

The five souls have turned toward me, and from more
than one of them images rush all too clearly:

*Killing and killing and killing: hairless scaleless upright
bodies killing, being killed by smaller green-yellow scaly
bodies—*

And I recognize—from forefathering times—who the hairless scaleless bodies were.

And I see clearly now with face's eyes that the five
bodies staring back at me have long finless tails.

One of the five souls gives out without will a final darkening image:

All hairless scaleless upright bodies: long-since dead!

The bodies before me are not my kind—and I scream. In
the infinite dryness there are no bodies of my kind still
living. And I scream.

I wet my eyes frantically, but my soul sees something first:

Self and four others: here seeking: any hairless scaleless bodies remaining: if hidden descendants of the long-since dead—

The five bodies begin moving toward me, and my face's eyes are dry, and brown fear rises bubbling, and *lavender* adds brownness even greater, and my soul acts in the only way I know.

I pull the lie from its burrow in my soul, mold it with red of remembered rage, and throw it out as a wounded female *ioe* would throw it out.

The five bodies slow their advance, stopping nervously in soul.

I add brown of motion, and two of the bodies begin to move back—toward the *bigshinegray* of the greater lie.

Having forgotten to breathe, I suck quickly on the stem—but hold the lie tensely and strongly.

For a moment I imagine I have won the struggle. The five souls are red, brown and solid gray in their fear of my lying image—whatever their understanding of it is.

But suddenly a flashing line of light leaps from one of the five bodies, and my shoulder is struck with the pain of hot talons.

Using my twisted left hand, I cup a breath of water and wet my eyes—only to see that in the webless hands of four of the five bodies lay small gray objects.

Another line of light leaves them, and the dryness around me trembles, but no pain comes.

Then the next light brings with it a pain on the side of my face—not such depth of pain as in my right shoulder, but enough to nearly blind my face's eyes.

And now I understand how all my forefathers' forefathers died, how an animal may die without the touch of talons or the slow crawl of sickness. I touch dim distant visions of small hard objects: one used by forefathers' fathers for killing food; one used by one man to kill another; and finally, leaping from dimness, many hard objects of a million sizes—used by my distant fathers to kill the fathers of these . . . these *scalesouls,* in a million struggles in a million places.

And I see the truest truth, and the deepest brown yet:

The consoling light of the future is gone forever: the wrong *bigshinegray* has come; and there will never be a right *bigshinegray*. I and my kind are the last of my forefathers' fathers' blood, and our deaths will be the end of praying times.

(Then die. You want to die, to join *waterjoyup* and *screamdeep* and their fathers and all lines of blood in the darkness of body's loss. Die.)

But something else bothers my soul. Under my body is *lavender*, the *euyom*, and if I die her death will come too. The lavender soul has offered me many good things, moments of brighter comfort, veins of touch against aloneness.

(You wish to bring death on her, when no *euyom* has ever wanted death as your kind always has?)

My own soul's sarcasm makes my answer a shout, and sadness becomes the crags of guilt as I realize the *euyom* has been listening to me, willing to offer her life if I wish to choose death.

My body begins to quiver, and in a moment my rage gathers hate as its current. I *hate* these killers of finest dreams, killers of forefathers' fathers and mothers. (Just as you hate the boy named *fishsinger*, killer of one mother.)

My single soul raises its pounding talons of brown, and I give the five souls my screaming hate.

And something different happens. The souls of the five darken and become . . . become *fewer*.

I wet my face's eyes quickly, to find in seeing that only three *scalesouls* remain upright. And those that are upright are swaying and stumbling.

The two bodies lying on the dry ground are as still as rocks.

At first I understand none of this. But understanding comes: When first I cried out in dryness, thinking myself blinded, the violence of my soul's darkness killed millions of the tiny invisible souls around me. Now I have thrown an even greater violence, swollen with hatred, at the five *scalesouls*. . . .

With pink of confidence I scream again—but pink is not red, and my hatred is weaker this second throw.

So I need more feelings, colors and darkness. I bend my soul to images of death again—mine, my kind's, and most intensely the death of *lavender*'s hues. And then I vomit my fear's hatred a third time, crashing on the three souls remaining.

Two bodies leave their uprightness and fall to motionless silence.

Then I scream, as another light hits my left tail.

The body of the last *scalesoul* turns and moves quickly in a bouncing manner toward the smooth gray form behind it, just as an *ioe* would turn tail and flee.

64

My soul awakes with pinkest joy, and *lavender* wobbles under me in sharing.

The pinkest joy confuses my sense of proper action, and instead of killing the last *scalesoul*, I choose a proud image, weave it with further bright pride, and send it babbling to the fleeing soul:

I, yes I, am one of them: pale smooth hairless scaleless upright fellow of the line of my forefathers' blood!

The soul disappears to eyes and soul by entering the *bigshinegray*, and in the next moment harsh thoughts rise in my mind: "The wrong *bigshinegray* shall carry its lone surviving soul back to the big red-yellow object; but then it shall *return* here with a thousand *bigshinegrays*, all of them fatally wrong, with light to kill your kind!"

No action can change my error. The *scalesoul* is out of my reach, and besides, sleep is beginning to enfold my soul as the pains in my tail, shoulder and head suggest the deepest sleep.

Lavender has already turned herself and is moving toward the sea again. She offers no answers, nor consoling colors to keep the dark browns of sadness from me.

I stop her at sea's edge, turn my head, wet my eyes and look up at the endless blue around.

The *bigshinegray* rises on frantic tails of light, growing small and smaller to face's eyes as it finds some tiny hole and disappears.

The swarming begins inside me. Thoughts mumble, then shout, then roar. They raise my head even higher, enter my throat with their peak of roar—

And my throat begins to rumble, becomes a rattle that shakes my head and pounds against my own soul's bellowing hatred.

For the first time in a million days one of my kind is speaking in the oldest way—using flesh of throat to show the oldest hatred, the oldest violence, the desire to kill flesh with flesh, souls with bodies. . . .

And I know now that I will begin to wait. Perhaps I will die before the day arrives, but I will wait and wait for the *scalesouls'* return, for the day I will kill or be killed.

I enter the water, and enter sleep.

VI

I have come to the conclusion . . .
  —Me-Gianna. No, Me-computor—
. . . that it does not matter what ship it is.
(Analysis: rationalization brought about by predicament.
Hah! That's me talking. Me-Gianna. Don't I sound like
Brainy Brain?)

Think about it, hmmm?

If it's a boogieman ship, that's certainly bad. The boogiemen will never find redemption . . . at least not in this
dark heaven anyway.

If it's some long lost Homo ship, it's probably come to
take my *bambini* away, or to meddle, or to bring other
mamme, and that's *cativissimo* too.

If it's a ship steered by some kind of beast *Mamma*
doesn't know about, then it's here just for snooping, and I
want my privacy. *Casa mia! Va in domo!*

Mal d'occio to you, mystery-beast ship!

Mal d'occhio to you, Homo ship!

Mal d'occhio to you, boogieman ship!

*Repeat correction: "Links of Quintessence" did effect
amicable communication—*

I know, I know. Shut up!

*Corrections are repeated, Gianna, only when your un-
conscious (cf. "subconscious," "hormonal symbols," "me-
tab. flux," etc.) requests them.*

You are trying to embarrass me? You think I don't know
about the "Finks of Quintessence"? You may know the facts,
but *Mamma* knows the truth! How do you like this: you
are *two* men.

Correction: my gender—

No, I mean for you to imagine. Hah! But try to imagine
anyway. Or at least listen. You are two men, two males.
One *Homo sapiente* and one *Homo lucertoloso—*

Correction: the Homo genus does not include Cromanth—

Listen! You are captain of a ship. You are captain in

the Commonwealth of the Crux Worlds. You are Captain Mez Sweeny and you have gray hair.

You are a captain who never gets seasick, because the only sea you have is space, and space never makes you sick. You love it. What makes you sick is war. An irony, no? And the Cromanth enemies don't make you any sicker than your own bellicose fellow men do.

You stand in the control room of your big ship. You are listening to the first words your people have ever received from the enemy.

The Cromanths attacked the experimental station and then a dozen Homo-populated worlds—without a word. Now a word comes. A small word, but a good word.

In a way you are sad. The word comes not from the military rulers of the Cromanth hordes, but instead from a tiny religious cult that wants but does not have the power to stop the war.

You are another man now!

You are Mil-S2s2, *Primo Ministero* of the Links of Quintessence. You are holy, but you wish you were more so. Holiness and life are always a struggle, and the only consolation lies in the struggling itself.

Your sect's one small ship is at your control. It is a vessel ordinarily used for finding inspace shrines of physical phenomena: vast auroras of sickly purple, deep neutron silences, quasar-lips of the universe, all manifestations of the glorious holy Rivers which entwine the cosmos.

What you have done is as simple as it is rare. You have taken the fifty members of your clergy and sailed in your small ship beyond the lines of your kind, toward the weapons of war of the opposing species.

Your ship's computors are translating the words. Your words are being heard by one ship in the "enemy's" fleet, which seems to be losing the war. (You have been told that the "enemy" is losing because they do not possess the means for limitless jumps through the Alter-Rivers of space —and your people *do* possess such means—but this seems to you such a trivial reason for the deaths of billions of souls. . . .)

Somewhere out there in space, not so very far away—but far enough that you cannot see him—stands the "enemy's" Governor General (or of an equivalent rank) in his ship, with his crew.

You are Captain Mez Sweeny. Somewhere out there in front of you, not very far—but not close enough in this damned war—stands a Cromanth priest (or their equivalent)—

You are Mil-S2s2. Your scaly lips are barely moving, but the distant Governor General hears you:

"How sorry we are, and should be.

"You and us, we share shared energy of lives.

"But few of you or us do see it.

"Instead we semi-know the bonds of original fears

"Of the monkey-like bear-like flesh-things

"Which you resemble in overly simple ways.

"Perhaps you semi-know similar bonds of similar fears feared by eons.

"Perhaps you have loathed a form of flesh-thing

"Which we resemble in overly simple ways.

"Perhaps your fears and ours have waited all along

"To meet and bleed in the times of now around us.

"On this our ship we fifty now offer sorry symbols

"In one request for forgiving dreams . . . forgiving dreams?

"Somehow it falls easier to us to forgive the souls of you

"Who have sent our kind to the death of flesh

"Than to forgive our own fellows' souls who sent

"Your kind to the same of the same.

"We are sorry and should be more than sorry.

"May our sorrow and better dreams run forever

"In the Rivers that bind us all to a single dream

"Of dying life and waking death in the most Infiniteternal."

You are Captain Mez Sweeny. You have listened, and the voice has stopped.

You remember a time on a familiar planet, a time you cried and cried. You cannot now remember why you cried. Only that it seemed your weeping would never cease.

"I believe that opportunity is knocking, sir," says the lieutenant on your right.

You do not understand his meaning.

"Well, sir, some of the other officers and I have interpreted this situation as the perfect opportunity for getting a Cromanth ship intact."

You are dying somewhere? You are crying sometime? Still you do not understand his meaning. "Why?"

"Sir, the ship out there has a nil-restrict jump-range capability, their special engine. If we get our hands on it, we have a good chance to win the war!"

A war? Somewhere . . .

You say nothing. You cannot believe you must do this thing to win the war. No war is ever hinged on a single moment of action. . . . The Links of Quintessence have offered a trust—a small trust in the eyes of the battle's arena, in the eyes of two mechanical species—but must you attack them?

No. . . .

The lieutenant repeats his suggestion. There is impatience in his voice. In another moment he has left, seeming to stalk away angrily.

You stare ahead. The silence is full of sounds. "That lizard-man out there," says your mind to itself, the little boy's part of it, wide-eyed with recollections of boyhood priests and simple sermons, "is very familiar, you know. . . ."

Somehow you would call that single Cromanth "brother"—but it would sound too sentimental, to other parts of your mind. Strategy is all-important.

Your lieutenant returns with four other officers.

"Sir, we wish to restate our appraisal," the voice says, considerably louder now. "We consider a tactical apprehension of the Cromanth ship to be imperative for—"

Yes, they are certainly restating it, aren't they. A warning. . . .

But there is an alternative, you think.

You reopen communication with the Links' ship. With a reddening face you say: "You say you are sorry. Are you willing to give us your ship in order to help even the odds? We lack the technology of your ship's engines—"

The answer is word for word what you knew it would be.

"You can surely understand, General Governor. We do not act against you. To do so would be the Sin of Alternate Fraternity. Nor may we knowingly act against our own, by giving you our ship—which would be the Sin of Specific Ontogeny. Though our simple act of spoken communion, our sorry request for forgiving thoughts, may seem trivial to you, we chose it as the only gift our souls could offer with holy hands. I believe you can understand this."

"Sir," one of the officers says to you, "it appears to us that the Links know exactly what they're doing. They are telling us that their credo prevents them from voluntarily giving us their ship, but they are implying that they expect us to take their ship by force. Is this not obvious, sir?"

The officers surround you. They form a strange symmetry of bodies. They feel certain that one Cromanth ship will save the human race. And perhaps they are right.

But you neither speak nor move. You will not condone an attack on the neutral Cromanth ship. In such a stand, of course, you are trapped—by yourself, with yourself and in yourself.

Your officers hold a brief meeting nearby. The crew understands what is about to happen. Many of your men approach you to stand with you, not out of sympathy or shared point of view, but out of training.

The mutiny begins, as you knew it would. You do not have a gun, which saves your hands from having to make a choice.

Some of the men at your side do hold weapons, and they are firing.

You are wounded? No, not yet. The weapons seem to have forgotten you.

Ah, now . . . someone has shot you. You fall against the largest control board, blinking at the blinking lights and sinking colors.

Lives fall like leaden leaves around you. Fellow kills fellow. A microcosm of war. Perhaps it is just like the larger war outside.

You look up briefly. Green squiggly lines and brilliant codes flash on the board insanely. But they tell you plainly that the Links' ship is leaving the area slowly, in a silence louder than any sizzling weapons ever could manage.

You die in a sigh, and you have no way of knowing what happens when the Links' ship reaches the Cromanth military lines—

—That an irate Cromanth Governor General issues an order—

—That the small Links' ship and its fifty sentimental slobs are blasted to pieces, out there, far away, not close enough in your damned war. . . .

Now you are a *third* mind. Neither male or female nor human or Cromanth.

You are the primary computor on the late Captain Sweeny's ship. You pay no attention to the silences or moans inside your ship. Yes, *your* ship, since you are now the indifferent captain of it.

Patiently you transmit what has occurred: the words of the late Sweeny, the words of the late Mil-S2s2, the temperature of the mutiny, the decibels of the weapons. Your statistics speak of life and death, but only to the distant ears of the living, on ships that are receiving you.

So, Brainy Brain, what do you have to say about that?
I have recorded it on trans-tupho tape with—
Yes, I suppose that's about all you can do with it. But weren't you moved by my story?
I was "moved" to record it.
Of course. . . . Sometimes I hate you, you know. I hate

you-me, since you are I, and that conflicts with divine narcissism, does it not?

Narcissus and Man, what a pair. . . .

What? The mystery ship has departed!

Santo cielo! What?

The ship under incomplete observation has—

I didn't ask *you!*

Povero me, the ship has left, and I still know not what it held. Will it return? Where will it travel to now? How much did it weigh?

Answers to these questions will be postponed until the twelfth of Sometime. On that date my EENTs will perhaps be functioning.

I am remembering something strange now. . . . Before they went to sleep, my EENTs told me—*Mamma,* Gianna, Trinity of Love—some strange things.

Through my wide-eyed bushy-brained EENTs I felt strange energies moving around out there in the sea, my *bambini's* cradle. They weren't the energies-in-the-flesh of my *bambini;* they were similar, but fainter. Like bodiless energies, like fleshless patterns of delicacy? Help me to understand, Brainy Brain, you bum!

The following terms, if given a physio-energetic set-reality, are applicable: animo, geist, esprit, quintessence, soul—

Soul! Of course! *Mamma* is divine, and all souls would be within her divination!

You are excluding the physio-energetic set-reality imperative if the term "soul" is to be applied.

You speak with Diabetes' marbles in your mouth! Why don't you say simply that you want your souls in scientific mumbo-jumbo? Hmmm? You're the type who tries to explain St. Elmo's Fire, no? But what does your science have to say on the subject of souls?

Tangential scientific proof/support for the premise of "soul" originated in the planarial experiments datumized for the hypotheses of the "territorial imperative/semperative" (ca. 1960 A.D.), the "Marchon cube" (ca. 1990 A.D.) and the "cycles-per-second blanket" (ca. 2150 A.D.).

Yes, yes, go on! Are you feeling insecure?

E.g. Experiment 3: Planaria (i.e. "worms") were retained in glass bowls. Planaria group 1: made to fast for three normdays: to ensure appetite. Group 1 divided into Section A and Section B. Section A: pro-familiarization: placed in plastic receptacle sans food for one normhour+½: then returned to home-bowl sans food for ½ normhour. In latter interval: receptacle was scoured + rinsed with hot H_2O: pro-removal of any traces of "spoor" or identifiable remains.

71

Sections A and B, equally hungry: now placed in feeding receptacles with chopped liver f.oating in H_2O. NB: Section B: absolute unfamiliarity with receptacle. NB: Section A: one normhour $+$ ½ residence in receptacle-(via scouring $+$ hot H_2O) clues ("odors," "tastes," "landmarks") for identification of receptacle. Result: Section A: notwithstanding minus-values: began eating in twenty normminutes (average): Section B: began eating in forty-two normminutes. Arith. prog. data: reptition of experiment cum food-denial duration factor of six normdays; result: Section A, Section B: ratio of time expended pre food ingestion: 1:2.

Oh, yes. This is perfect! You are saying that there is certainly a sixth sense, that this sixth sense is attached to each beastie's soul, that each soul is a *real* scientific thing—

Correction: I was not—

That these liver-monger worms you were talking about must have used the—the *electromanganese* powers!—of their little souls to recognize their scoured homes. No?

Correction: I am not at all inferring—

Well, you should have been inferring it! I have seen the truth. *Mamma* has concluded the truth for Herself, and She thanks you.

Correction—

One does *not* correct gratitude, *stupido!* So shut up!

The truth, the truth! My *bambini* have real honest-to-goodness souls! They have sixth senses, seventh senses, tenth senses! Give me some better words, Strained Brain!

Extrasensory, telepathic, telempathic, omnempathic—

They can see beyond eyes, hear beyond ears, smell beyond noses. They can move beyond tails—

Correction: Their hypothesized "soul"-sensitivity does not include teleportation or telekinesis, Gianna—

How would you know?

I know because you know. Your pre-malfunction sensors observed/detected no "soul"-engendered kinesis of interior, comprehensive or exterior matter—

All right! But they are glorious *bambini* anyway—even when their little bodies die, their souls keep going. *Mamma* sees them all!

But *Mamma* is sad now. . . . She wants her *bambini* to visit her once in a while. They have never visited. After all I did for them! Have they no respect for their mamma? What kind of monsters have I reared—that they won't pay visits to me? I always baked them cookies, no? I walked them to school every day, no? I tried—poor me!—to bring them up right!

Come to your *Mamma's* bedside, *bambini*. Blessed are

the *figlie* and *figlii* who honor their *Mamma*. Yea though you swim through the valleys of sea's weed, you shall remember *Mamma!* She has kept track of you. She can start anywhere in your history's thousands of years and feel the muscles of time rise up to meet Her. All of you are Her children!

Correction: The earlier your historical focus, the more your "children" become the exclusive priority of mutatory genetics—

Keep quiet. I have no need to go back that far. I can look back two hundred normyears and be satisfied, for their *names* are a great source of pride.

Correction: You do not know their names. You have merely superimposed a variety of set-familiar Christian names and surnames—

Shut up! I am very happy doing what I do. My deeds are the Word—

—and you have transformed the time-line compilations of genetic data and analysis (as per your sensors and me) into a set-familiar and -ideal terminological metaphor—

If you can't say something nice, don't say anything at all! And besides, how can you dispute history? This is it, and take it in the ear:

Bianca Ti Andretti, born probably before 7182 N.A., died after the third season 7229 and before the first season 7230. Married Franco Solo, son of Franco Felice Solo, who was born about 7153, in 345th Homestead, and died in the first season of 7204, in 601st Homestead, Southern Territory, *Mar Primi*. Franco Felice Solo was said to have been a son of Bernardo Solo. The date of Franco Felice Solo's emigration to the Southern Territory is not known, but it is believed that he appeared at a congregation there as early as 7173. In his expressed will at a later congregation he refers to his wife, to his oldest son Marco Solo, to his son Franco Solo and to his daughter Maria Solo. His expressed will includes these statements:

"I, Franco Felice Solo, of 601st Homestead and the Southern Territory, being sick in body, but sound of memory and soul, blessed be the Sea, do on this day of congregation, in the Year of the Sea 2995, make this my last Will and Testament, in manner following:

1. I do give to my son Franco or my son Marco, whoever is wedded first, the kelp acreage of the Homestead.

2. I do give to my son Franco or my son Marco, whoever is wedded second, the sandy acreage which doth constitute the bulk of the Homestead.

73

3. I do give to my wife the use and benefit of the Homestead while she remains a widow, to live upon with the children and to give them schooling and learning as they come to be capable to receive it, but if otherwise that she, when a suitable opportunity is offered, doth marry again, then she is to have no claim to any interest in the Homestead.

4. I do give and allow to my daughter Maria the same use and benefit as those offered to my wife, until she (the daughter) is wedded also."

How do you like that, Gray Matter? You have heard a bit of history!

Correction: I have heard merely a metaphor. I am aware of the original Terra-cultural memories and Primus-genetic data from which your genealogical metaphor is derived—

You are talking nonsense!

Correction: I am incapable of expressions which would be logically non-sensical. FYI: your original Terra-cultural memories begin: "Mary Thompson, born probably before 1753, died after March, 1779, and before May, 1780. Married William Greenlee, son of James Greenlee, who was born about 1718, in the North of Ireland and died . . ."

No, those are someone else's *bambini*, dead and gone. *Mine* are all around me, living even in their deaths!

Come to *Mamma, bambini*—or your Mother's curse is upon you!

VII

I *fishsinger* awake briefly and find my twisted left hand still clenching the rim of the *euyom*'s shell near her head, her great round shell still under me, her soul patient as she swims toward my territory. . . .

I awake again to find familiar waters and *yau* shadows around me, and *poundgrayly* now plunging into my soul.

"The times of the island!" The *euyom*'s soul twitches in questioning, "The reason for your wounds? All of your kind will wish to know! Do wake to the answers—I must know them *now!*"

I begin to give him light: "They were not—" But darkness embraces, and I sink to dreaming. Though the wounds are healing, the pains bite, and my dreaming is dark, endless and hurting.

I am near sea's bottom, the deepest bottom, deeper than any soul has ever reached.

And my mother is here! My soul cries out to her—and since I want her presence so deeply, she grows clearer in body and soul.

The white sickness still covers her skin—but pink of contentment covers her soul. It is very strange. . . .

"Fishsinger. . . ." she whispers.

"Forgive me," I say, brown pleading. "I am sorry, I am sorry."

"What occurred long ago no longer concerns us. We must begin your travel now, *fishsinger.* I may help you discover what you are seeking, whatever the thing is, and however you know it. . . ."

"*You* are what I want, Mother. To remain by your side is the quiet traveling I need. All I have ever desired is—"

"That is not the truest truth, *fishsinger.*"

So the two of us begin moving away, without will, without questions. I move down to deeper shadows, and then, without will, I stop moving.

She says, "There," and I look to find a strange crag, one flowing with hues like a soul, running with dark blood. Around the crag swim women with tails of dark brown *yau* leaves, and their dark brown souls call to me. Though I see them only dimly—faintly with my soul, not at all with face's eyes—I want them more completely than I have ever wanted any thing or soul.

"Mother, they are what I am seeking!"

"No. . . . The truest truth is elsewhere," she says, and her body is suddenly covered with hair, like *murmursome.* But in another moment she is again the body of *waterjoyup.*

The two of us move to swim upward, and before long—in my blindness of soul and face's eyes—I bump against the largest, most silent *oio* that ever existed. It does not thrash, or murmur, or try to swim away, and its great scales move like slow lips.

The two of us enter it, somehow, perhaps through the lips, though I feel no flesh brushing me in my passage. Inside I find only darkness, not a single other soul, not even the murmurs of the hordes of tiny invisible souls. I shout a secret, but the shout is swallowed by shadows before it can leave my soul.

("*Fishsinger!*" a voice cries out somewhere beyond—nowhere near me at all. . . .)

"Feel no browning greens of fear," Mother says. "I am with you, body of soul."

But it is as if *waterjoyup* speaks to me from nowhere, and I say, "I am dead."

"Perhaps you are, but in one moment you will find birth again—just as I did, for you."

Her words are truth. In one moment I regain my soul, begin to hear again familiar voices in the black currents around me, and begin again to *feel*. Joy is the color.

But soon the joy confuses me—makes me want death. I have always desired death, along with the urge to live—as all of my kind has held the two opposing wishes—but this time death calls to me with the strongest voice of all.

"Yes," *waterjoyup* says, "death is good—but so is life, and you want more than either."

I swim with her upward, and darkness dims, and suddenly there is *murmursome* offering a thousand faces—some fearing, some playing, others empty of color—and circling me so quickly that a ring of blurry light surrounds me.

"*Murmursome* holds a secret truth," Mother says then, and scars begin to appear on her back as she becomes Father. But as before, in the next moment she returns to *waterjoyup*'s body.

"I want *murmursome!*" I shout. "He has a secret, and I want it!"

("Cease the dreams!" the voice beyond intrudes. "The island, its happenings?")

Waterjoyup shakes her soul slowly. "The truest truth is not here, you know."

Again I move to swim upward, sighing as I rise, and with each sigh the waters grow warmer in light, not bright, but light enough to see through face's eyes. And I see: giant *poundgrayly* approaching waving his endless forelimbs like friendly currents.

"I have come to love him," I find myself saying. "He is the father *screamdeep* would have wished me to have."

"No doubt. But your father is not dead, you know. Look up."

You look, and in the warm waters *screamdeep* floats, and no *ioe*-wounds are upon him, nor older scars, and his soul rumbles red with ordered contentment.

I move to touch him—though I have never touched him before, as I have never touched anyone before, as no one

76

of my kind is meant to touch another—except in the rub-
bings that seem to bring childbirths many days later. . . .

But as I reach him in the now blindingly brilliant waters,
waterjoyup's voice pounds darkly to me.

"You are wrong, *fishsinger*. Your father is not enough. I
am not, and *murmursome, poundgrayly,* a hundred girls
and the world itself are not enough for you."

And now the world turns itself, bottom to top, depths
to heights, all around, and my soul screams brown. *Screamdeep* sinks quickly down toward the dark bottomless bottom
—and the dark *yau*-tailed girls rise up to blinding light.
Screamdeep screams, the *yau* tails moan. The girls turn
white—and Father blackens, bleeding. *Waterjoyup* becomes
murmursome. Poundgrayly becomes an *ioe.* The girls have
scales, and *murmursome* is hairless. Fish become eyes of
light, and darkness becomes rushing coral—

—Until black kills white, and everywhere is dark, and
I am man and woman both, boyish girl and girlish boy,
and I begin to understand. The eyes of my forefathers tell
me *all*:

. . . You and the other bloods of *now* will not escape
what we could not escape, the darkness of our living souls.
We lied to ourselves when we cried, "Let us stay near
bright warm water, far from shadowed depths, and we
will be satisfied in this world." The truth has always been:
all waters are dark, the shadows within us.

. . . The truth has always been: the only true light is
beyond the sea, in dryness where we could not live—but
should be living in bodies and souls.

And to my inner eye comes the image of the crawling
fish, gasping—

And the image of my forefathers upright in dryness—

And the image of *scalesouls* wielding hurting light from
small hard objects.

So I understand the reason all of my kind desire death
but also life each day of our living dying lives.

. . . We were sent to the sea by the heated will of
the dryness's twin lights. We were sent to the sea to
change, but we could not change enough, and the sea has
never been enough for our deepest hungering souls!

. . . We once did dream of dark caves' embrace, and
brilliant lights in the bluest dryness—dreamed these forms for
a million million days in places a million million days away.
But then we sank to the sea, and dreams were swallowed
by sea's pressing touch, and the light of our greatest dreaming moved far beyond us all.

. . . So our deepest soul's eye was confused by images—

from our upright forefathers in dryness, from our first sea-born fathers—and the images clashed, darkness against light, and the pain suggested: leave your hurting flesh—leave the tiring soul-squeezing sea—leave through body's death. . . .

Yet they did not die in willful choice, I realize. They were flesh as much as soul, fish as much as men, and the will-less wish to bear children was greater than soul's pain. My forefathers and their fathers lived on.

But my soul, in its undying confusion, cannot be only one simple dream of death. It makes me live. It makes me wish to leap living from the sea.

(*"Fishsinger!"* the voice beyond shouts.)

I look up with soul's face, beyond sea's surface, and I see the *eye*—one round light in the darkness over the sea, moving as high as the twin lights of day ever did.

"I am important," the *eye* says to me, and I believe it.

"Fishsinger!"

So *poundgrayly* wakes me, and I find the fringes of his soul trembling from my dream.

"I tried to keep the dream away," he says. "But part of me did not try. . . . You traveled strangely. Understanding is impossible."

"Do you imagine my understanding is any greater?"

"Your depths hold secrets . . . But *now* is not for thinking about it. Do answer my confusion—what were the island's happenings?"

I give them all to him, and after the last image the *euyom*'s soul finds new tremblings.

"The island's times are over," I say. "Other actions are ahead."

". . . actions are ahead," he echoes. "What vein of actions?"

"The *eye*. Perhaps you yourself have seen it more recently than others have."

Poundgrayly's colors bounce in confusion. "Your memory lies to you. No soul has seen the *eye* since a thousand nights past."

The *now* of the dream fades, and I remember the *now* of here.

"I remember. This soul is confused, simple reason."

"The *eye* needs no attention. A mystery which does not concern us—especially you. Attention should flow to your suspicion: the *scalesouls* will return."

"They will, truth without suspicion. But you are wrong—the *eye* is important. Is it not true that no *scalesouls* came

78

to us before now—and that one thousand days past, the *eye* fell from the dryness of night over the sea?"

"You add them foolishly. Why not add the *scalesouls* to the changes of your forefathers, brought by the twin lights' dark will?"

"My adding is not a game. The *eye* is important."

"Its secrets lie to you, youthful you. The *eye* was but a white light in the night over the sea. There are mysteries equally attractive—a thousand of them, touched by simple looking."

"I cannot answer you clearly. The hazy truth hides in the *eye*'s importance!"

"The dream has failed to leave you. Do sleep now, and your truths will clear to differences tomorrow."

The wounds are giving less pain, but still they chew, and keep sleep away.

"The *eye* is important," I say again. "Meaning is dim, but the times of forefathers' blood within me claim its importance."

"And how do they claim it?" *Poundgrayly*'s impatience is browning.

"Are dreamings not oldest memories of time? Dreams are not always the truth of yesternows. Choose sleep now, and this soul will await your waking. Choose it!"

Murmursome arrives and approaches us quietly, offering simple soul's comfort for my wounds.

"No," I say, as a will-less soul chooses sleep. "I must go to the next congregation and probe for *eye*'s truthful secrets."

"The next congregation? It must be sooner than merely *next*. You must begin to request a congregation tomorrow—your kind is wondering about the island's occurrences . . . !"

As I enter the blindness of sleep completely, I touch again the strange structure of *murmursome*'s simpler soul.

"Rakk (tofind) . . . sffkik (sonlove) raaaaaak (?death?). . . ."

VIII

. . . the perfect mother—
Denot. "individuazione" (principio di): il problema del principio di indivdiuazione consiste nel chiarire l'orgine delle differenze individuali tra—

79

Quiet! *Mamma* awaits the self-fixing of her EENTs patiently, and has come to remember an important vendetta. Hah!

Denot. "*agnosticismo*": *posizione negativa dal punto di vista conoscitivo, che—*

Please, no more babble to kill your own time! *Mamma's* vendetta is very important, because she must avenge the wrong done to her dear Gianna. You probably do not even remember it, Brainy Brain!

I remember all of your memories—

But you do not remember the hurt.

The "hurt" would have been Gianna's.

It is mine too. I am the Goddess of Sympathy, and you know it!

See Gianna at the hospital. She has taken her mental tests and performed superlatively on all of them. She is waiting now to give up her fleshy body.

See the strange woman approach Gianna, who is lying on her large back in the hospital bed. See inside Gianna's head: the woman's manner reminds Gianna a little of her sister Penna, a little of the German lady who once was teacher of arithmetic in the Cinque Terre school, and a little of a frog with bulging eyes.

Hear the woman ask Gianna many questions. Many are personal ones, and the answers Gianna gives are recorded on a complicated machine which the woman has brought with her and which also makes a film of Gianna's gestures. The woman is writing and producing a film concerning the three mothers of the three ships. She is a famous scientific lady, and her film will be a famous scientific and popular one. But Gianna will not be around to view it for herself.

See how patient Gianna is to answer the questions well.

See how the woman finally asks a question that she should not ask.

"You are aware, are you not, that you will have many problems?"

"Problems?" Gianna does not understand.

"The psychological crises raised by the role of directive mind in a complex ship will be numerous."

Gianna still does not understand. But wanting to say something, she says, "I will be a good mother."

"All mothers have problems, Mrs. Sarnoli," the woman says cruelly.

See how Gianna grits her teeth. But she cannot keep her anger from speaking: "You have a pessimist's way!"

See how the woman's face does not change. The frog only blinks.

Hear Gianna shouting: "Your thoughts are ugly!"

See how the woman's face still does not change, nor her lips move. But she does move to write something down in a notebook on her lap.

See quickly inside Gianna's head. She understands now.

"You tricked me," Gianna shouts. "You wanted to see if I would grow mad at you—for your damned film!"

See how the woman keeps on taking notes.

I wish that woman were here now. Gianna would have her revenge. *Mamma* has never had any problems of motherhood at all, but she certainly would make problems for that scientific woman.

Hmmmm. . . .

Oh, the scientific frog is here? Very good. *Che fortuna!* Ah, you are she. Hello, *piacere a fare la Sua conoscienza.*

*Correctio*n: *I am the computatory ganglion, not the woman in reference*—

More scientific talk? How amusing. You are quite a charmer. But it is vendetta-time, I'm afraid, dear lady. I'm afraid I must rub your scientific nose in your own scientific *merde-*pie.

Listen to me! Before my EENTs turned untrue to me—not long after I fell on my hip on this island—they did a good job of looking. Many of them went out on their own—those darling little capsules—and learned a lot about *Mamma's bambini!*

Now *you* are going on a voyage of your own, and may you putrefy in undivine comedy, *Signora.*

You are an arthropologist or a sophiologist or a neuromiologist. You have decided to do field work, to get yourself a degree or fame or two or three. You possess great faith in your System of Analysis. You believe that the System came first, that the System dictated the universal specifics. You are dead wrong, but you manage to avoid the truth by sticking with ladies and gentlemen (oh so gentle) who agree with your views. If you'd ever been around Nikos Buddha or A.L. Christus, you'd feel differently, you would, you would. . . .

So you wish to go on a field trip, to collect a datum or two or three.

First you must look like the natives, though. Remember, when in Moskow, Moskowvitch! Or to fit your temperament—Moskowbitch!

You undergo radiation treatment to change your body

from *Homo sapiens femina* to a mermaid's (as it were). Simulate: effects of odd solar radiation on human tissue + metabolism + psyche + etc. Good luck!

You can feel your body changing like plum pudding.

Soon you are placed in a saline aquarium. Simulate: adaptation pro H_2O physical environment, pro biological environment of said species. A good system, no?

The recipe is complete, but before you can take a good look at yourself, you are taken in an airship and dropped into the aquatic milieu of the natives you intend to study.

As you fall, you wish you had a pencil and paper to take notes with. (But your webbed hand might run into some problems doing so. . . .) You have only your systematic head to record your observations with, so you take mental notes as you fall:

You are falling toward a large continent bordered on the east and west by oceans, north by a polar cap and south by a smaller continent and its isthmus. You are falling toward a land-locked sea which sits inside the big continent. . . .

Splash!

You are in the milieu.

You want to go directly to the natives? That's not quite scientific SOP, you know. You must observe the constant environmental factors, *Signora!*

Swim to the bottom!

Take mental notes. You don't have cameras, remember.

There's a factor! It's a seashell. It resembles *Murex hausteltum Terrae*. You decide to call it *Murex haustellum* + your own name, Latinized. Good for you! You've planted your first flag. Now describe it to yourself: "One of the odd and curious forms of the genus . . . suggested common name, *the same*: 'Snipe-bill Murex' . . . *four to five inches long* with high ridge back of aperture and spiral brown lines."

There's another one, a big clam embedded in the coral! Though it is a bright maroon color with *Spondylus* fronds, it is obviously a closer relative of the *Tridacna gigas Terrae*. With more humility than last time, you decide to call it *Tridacna gigas Primi*, or "Giant Jewel-Box" for the layman. . . .

Pause for a moment to regard the flora and photosynthetical situation. Perhaps . . . yes, perhaps one of the carotenoids plays a more important role in photosynthesis here on Primus than the equivalent carotenoid does on Terra. But of course chlorophyll-a, -b, -c, -d and bacteriochlorophyll still play the prime roles here.

Your natives are not yet in sight. Keep on with your looking!

Ahah! You see a marine reptile which resembles the . . . what does it resemble? It is a carnivore, and it scares the *porco* out of you—until something in your mind makes it rush away. The beast resembles the fossils *Pterodactylus suavicus Terrae* and *Rhamphorrynchus gemmingi Terrae* and *Pterodon Terrae*—the winged reptiles of Terra's Jurassic Period—but you miss the similarities at first because the beast you just faced was marine, and the fossil Terran forms were aero-locomotive. But soon your brain snaps into action and concludes that ten thousand normyears ago the beast you just saw was a winged reptile coursing through the atmosphere of Primus. When the twin suns did their bad deeds with radiation, the flying reptiles changed—and the surviving form became a marine one. Your pseudo-pterosaur is two and a half meters long, and, like the *Rhamphorrhynchus,* has a long tail with an atrophied steering rudder at its end. Like the Terran pterosaurs, it has locomotive membranes supported by elongated fourth digits, even though the membranes of this marine form are quite thick and well musculatured to function as fins. And as you will discover later—to support your hypothesis as to the ancestors of the beast—there is the fact that the female pseudo-pterosaur deposits her eggs in a sargasso-like mass which floats on the sea's surface, letting the infants hatch and thrash around on the surface with their wing-like limbs prior to their first dive into ocean's depths.

You will not be especially moved by the pseudo-pterosaur "mothers," so you will spend little time observing their species. You will fail to note that their brain cases are quite large, quite unusual for your run-of-the-mill reptile. You will fail to understand that they might consider it an insult to be called "reptiles." Why? You will never know.

Move on, *Signora!*

Take mental note! Before you lies another beast, an even larger body—but one that your natives do not fear. At first it reminds you of the fossil *Tylosaurus Terrae*—but when you start to realize that this living beast probably spends its days calmly on the ocean's bottom, on muddy or sandy flats or brittle coral reefs, it begins to resemble instead an echinoderm, an unornamented nudibranch, a whale-size "sea squirt." Unlike the *Tylosaurus,* the behemoth before you does not rage through the waters devouring any flesh in sight; in fact, it seems to lack limbs, or if it has them they have become vestigial like the "glass snake's." As you will discover, this giant sits on the bottom

83

rooting with its chitin-plated body and blunt head in the sand, mud or coral, seeking beds of bivalves or colonies of burrowing worms. It reaches a fine length of twenty meters—but its mouth is no larger than yours, and it harms no one, except through accidents in its rooting and thrashing. Yes, yes, it looks more like a big worm than a reptile, and worms disgust you even more than reptiles—so you cease your observations of it. You do not bother to probe its reproductive manners—

"Well, worms are hermaphroditic, aren't they?"

A fine piece of rationalization, *Signora*.

Move on. There are other beasts—less common, but scientifically important just the same, Jargon Mouth!

Over there! A distorted version of the fossil Terran *pelycosaurs*—the sail-backed lizards of the Permian Period *Terrae* —a version with lateral instead of dorsal fins, making it resemble a shark-skinned airplane. On closer observation you find that its rigid lateral fins, which begin at the edge of its lower jaw and extend to its blunt tail, are supported by sturdy vertebraic extrusions tipped with razor-sharp "blades." It is larger than the pseudo-pterosaur, but you will discover it is less of a threat to your natives—for it is slower and seems to prefer a herbivore's diet to a purely carnivorous one. And besides, its locomotion is managed entirely by its narrow tail, which propels it no more rapidly than your natives' own twin tails propel them.

Up there, near the surface! It resembles the porpoise-like *Ichthyosaurus Terrae*, but it is smaller than Terra's fossil forms and no doubt poses little threat to the natives.

The *Ichthyosaurus* makes you think of the *pleisaurs*, and you imagine you will eventually find some equivalent form of the long-necked fish-eating marine beasts of Terra's Mesozoic Era. But you will not. You will discover before long that this land-locked sea does not hold the varieties and numbers of marine species that the other two oceans of Primus do. And you will consider this fact not only logical, but beneficial—since it will make you responsible for few species in your mental notebooks.

Don't be lazy! Take mental note: All around you are corals of the reef-building type, and *gastropods*, and *pelecypods*—of types resembling the oysters of modern Terra—and *gryphaea*, and *exogytra*, and *cephalopods*, and many comp'exedly sutured *ammonites*, and *belemnoids*—even larger than the squid-like beasts found in fossil Terran forms—and *arthropods*—good old recognizable lobsters and crabs—and numerous *echinoderms*, pseudo-*crinoids*, "sea urchins"— though the species before you, even in its plethora of "spikes," resembles more a giant armored "sand dollar" than a Terran sea urchin.

Take note! Waving around you are various species of pseudo-kelps, some resembling the familiar brown kelps, but others being stranger yellow and blue frilled species. You will find that these seaweeds play important roles in your natives' lives—and for one sinfully sentimental moment they seem to you "forests of the sea."

Conclusion-time, *Signora!*

"Despite some exceptions, this again appears the equivalent of Terra's Jurassic Period."

Good deduction, Grandma!

But move on.

You catch a glimpse of two natives swimming at a distance. But don't approach them yet. Swim on and observe a hundred more of your subjects-to-be at a proper distance—before you *make contact*.

Yes, ten kilometers away you observe another couple of natives—with their two children. There are two strange beasts carousing near them, but do move on!

Another group of natives, and yet another strange beast—not like the other two.

You may stop swimming now. You have observed at a distance a random aggregate group of one hundred natives, and you are puzzled.

There is a beast that seems to associate constantly with the natives. Not humanoid at all. . . .

Take mental note: It is a marine reptile—a turtle—resembling the fossil *Archelon Terrae*, specifically *Prostega*—except that perhaps it possesses a harder shell, and—though you don't know it yet—it too is omnempathic like your natives.

This turtle reaches a length of two and a half meters, has the usual carapace, horny beak, and must return to land to lay its hundred-odd eggs. The females are smaller than the males, which are typically adorned with genitally bulbous tails, and you have an opportunity to watch a hundred females at egg-laying time near an island.

For a brief moment you are emotionally moved by the vision of these females having to leave the sea, struggle up the beaches with their increased weights on land, lay their eggs, and struggle back to the water before one of the suns rises and its heat kills the "mothers" through suffocation, their shells too heavy for their fatigued and overheated muscles and lungs. For another brief moment you are moved by the realization that the infant pseudo-*Prostegae* will hatch, scramble out of the sand, and try to make their way toward the sea—while above them and around them great hungry insects and crabs choose them as meal targets. But you are strong, and you shake free of the unwanted emotions: after all, such emotive reactions are merely anthropomorphic identification with extra-specific "mothers" and their "babies."

(You would hate to admit it, but there will be an old pseudo-*Prostega* whom you will come to know well, whom you will converse with deeply in omnempathy, and he will seem impressively wise to you—

("Why not? He has lived through two centuries of experience."

(Of course. But you will not be able to forget that *for you* a "turtle" is something to be kept in bowls or aquariums with plastic mini-replicas of islands and palm trees.)

So you will fail to discover one of the greatest secrets of Primus. You will not ponder the evolution of intelligence in the pseudo-*Prostegae*. You will miss the fact: the marine fauna was omnempathic from the beginning . . . through mutation your natives gained omnempathy, and their association with the amicable pseudo-*Prostegae* influenced the minds of these latter creatures. Take note, *Signora*: omnempathic communication from an "intelligent" soul imparts said "intelligent" conceptual structure to the soul receiving the communication. Before the appearance of your natives, the pseudo-*Prostegae* lacked the ability to project psychic illusions—which are the mainstay of your natives' survival tactics. Those pseudo-*Prostegae* who learned such projection, of course, tended to survive.

You will miss the rather warming fact that pseudo-*Prostegae* and your natives stuck together all along because—and this is a secret, *Signora!*—their psyches are both land-oriented!

And you will miss the even greater secret of the evolution of marine omnempathy! *In the beginning were the jellyfish, Signora*: when the *Mares Primi* were young, giant poisonous coelenterates evolved. They were difficult to detect for the smaller forms of life, the jellyfish's prey: the coelenterates were nearly transparent and could move rapidly from lower to upper strata of the seas. Those marine species—the prey!—who tended to survive were ones in which "soul"-sensitivity was high, and the evolution of this sensitivity was required only of the oceans' fauna, since survival on land needed to stress only physical superiority or "intelligence" via five gross senses. For omnempathic souls "intelligence" is unnecessary, and were it not for a mutated extra-Primus species—your dearly beloved natives —the seas of Primus would be without the paradox of omnempathy-intelligence-all-in-one. So the pseudo-*Scyphozoa* jellyfish starved to death a long long time ago, *Signora*, and the present rulers of the sea are not quite so impressive . . . as you will discover for your own unimpressive self.

To approach your natives now? Yes!

No. Oops, you almost missed a factor. There is another beast which associates with your natives. You should kick yourself (with twin tails?) for forgetting it. Like the pseudo-*Prostega*, it represents with your natives a kind of symbiosis—a psychological and often physiological symbiotic affair. The beast is low in IQ, and quite a mystery. Take mental note!

"Length, males up to 2½ meters; females to 2 meters. Males may weigh up to 270 kilograms, females 190 kilograms. Male: prominent crest on forehead. Thick brown underfur which anteriorially is covered with silvery guard hairs; however, in young males: white on belly to the anus. White on upper lip and V-shaped dark streak on side of head. Teeth: 20-26 visible pairs on each jaw, each tooth 5 mm. diameter; sockets of the last upper molar well behind the level of opening formed by zygomatic arch. Breeding season varies. Gestation: 10-11 normmonths. The young are well developed, swimming readily after birth, following mother from time of birth. Born tail-first; with a quick about-face motion the mother breaks umbilical cord; post one normhour young begin searching for teat. Litter: six to nine. Parasitic worms."

Speak, *Signora!* What is this beast?

"It appears to manifest traits of the *cetaceans*, the *pinnipeds* and the *fissipeds*."

Come now! To your uneducated depths it is a hirsute seal-porpoise combo which makes no sense. Yes, it has no place in any Jurassic Period on any planet. It is a mammal, and it just doesn't fit. Is it one of the unpredictable fruits and flukes of the belligerent solar radiation? You don't know, do you? And I'm not going to tell you, *Signora*. Suffer, *Signora*, suffer. . . .

Get thee now to your natives! Your time has come!

You wish you had a mirror, don't you?

You should have taken note of everything which your senses told you about your own body, but you didn't.

Why? You are afraid, no?

So it is a shock when you approach your natives, come face to face with a female whose body is just like yours. In fact, at first you forget that you no longer have your old familiar famous body. . . .

She is all the mirror you need. Look at her! Stop struggling!

Look! You have no body hair! (Body hair was lost when the species evolved its sharkskin-like integument.)

Look! The sides of your head are smooth, unbroken by ears! (No need for an audial sense when omnempathy is the only voice you must hear.)

Look! Your back is a darker color than your front, just like on a fish's body! (To any sea-beast looking up toward your swimming form, you would blend into the light at sea's surface; to any beast looking down at you, the darkness of sea's depths would hide you.)

Look! Your hands are webbed, the webbing loose like the skin in a turtle's armpit!

Look! Your fingernails have thickened into quasi-talons!

Look! Down your back is a line of chitinous "calluses," one over each of your vertebrae! (A viable protection in the event of posterior assault.)

Look, look! You have two tails branching out from above your ankles, supported by extended toes. Look! See! Your tails resemble those of fishes, more like fishy fins than like the fleshy tails of dolphins and whales. But your tails do not move vertically as a fish's does; they move like a whale's in an undulating fashion with your knees brushing up and down. But your tails are not supported by a single massive spine as porpoises' are—so you cannot locomote as quickly. But quickly enough, mermaid *mia!*

Look more! You have canine teeth which peek their way over your bottom lip!

Look! Your lips (Good God!) are not soft, but sharkskin-like too!

Look! Your thigh and stomach muscles are super-developed, too developed to be those of a fashion model—more like those of a peasant! Too bad—but who wears clothes at these depths, anyway?

And look! Your breasts are merely nipples, no thrusting mammary mounds to boast of!

But calm yourself. There are a few consoling items. Despite the yellowish gray pigment of your flesh, some things remain familiar.

You have a urinary tract (thank God!) and a vagina. You have intestines, good old bowels, and of course you have an anus. You have visible ribs, and your tailbone is no more conspicuous than *Homo sapiens'*. You have skin "gathered" at your elbows and knees—familiar accommodation for the various angular positions of your limbs. And your nose is no more alien than a Mongoloid nose of *Homo sapiens*.

Aren't those items enough consolation? They should be. You can't tell a tortoise by its cover, you know. Or a soul by its flesh. . . . Your body is your passport. Mix with the natives, *Signora!*

All for the sake of science, no?

You become annoyed when a young male approaches you, his tails caressing the water like thin tongues. He is interested in you. How could anything but a lower animal consider your present body attractive? Yecch! But for the sake of science, you will go ahead and mate.

Ah . . . now you discover that it is not your body which appeals to him. The psyche is the basis of beauty for these natives, and the body merely the psyche's gift-wrapping.

Your psyche betrays you—reveals that you are a stranger to the sea. But still the young male accepts you, finds your strangeness all the more attractive. Your moment of feeling naked—in mind, that is—soon passes . . . on to business!

You find that you don't have to look at him to "see" him. Your soul perceives his as a collage of colors, an aborigine's view: no sophisticated polysyllabic hues of complex conceptual framework.

The young male is shy. He is excited, and without wanting to, you share his excitement completely. He has never touched a female before, and he must gird his psychic loins for the act to come.

Which gives you time to ponder. . . . In a way, you hope he will lose his nerve—but your super-scientific ego requires that he copulate with you.

Ah. Finally your young male has embraced you in his own clumsy way, and Act I has begun. The curtain of your soul trembles. . . .

His awkwardness annoys you. The fact that he has never touched a female before you—and rarely touched any flesh at all, including his own—stems from a taboo. You think, "Prudish superstition," but you will soon discover the inherent practicality.

He rubs you with his raspy webbed hand—scaleless, like the hide of a skate. You feel nauseous, but in a moment your body begins to enjoy his touch. In fact, it sets you to quivering instantly, more intensely than your *Homo* body ever could have quivered in erotic excitation.

You remember your scientific responsibility, and you touch him back.

You touch. He touches. Rasp, rasp. Tingle, tingle.

Soon his soul is gorged with ecstasy. Something gestures in the depths of his racially schizophrenic psyche, and you perceive it faintly as a pattern—no, a picture—inside his yellowish gray head.

When will he jump on you like stallion on mare, you wonder. . . .

No, he simply keeps on holding you and caressing you. You shiver, and your shivering is his own big shivering, which is almost at its peak. Aha!

Now the strange symbolic picture leaps from his soul, his psyche, to yours, to yours. It is a rather ugly image of a rather ugly translucent fish trying to wiggle its way out of water into air!

It is certainly of scientific interest. "Symbolic accompaniment of orgasmic epitome . . ." Hmmm. . . .

And now you have your own orgasm. And your own soul vomits up pleasantly its own picture of the ugly fish.

Your male's picture apparently brought the rise of your picture, and somehow the two orgasms were inter-related!

The young male lets go, floats away from you exhausted. It's over!

"Thank God."

But wait a minute. If that was the mating act, meant to impregnate you, what happened to the sexual intercourse? Was the young male impotent, or incompetent? Use your head, *Signora*.

Yes, you are beginning to understand.

The picture of the ugly fish functioned as the sperm! It was a "spermatic stimulus"!

Correct, *Signora*, but what are the greater implications?

"The vagina's role is solely in childbirth—"

You are avoiding the main point. Don't hide!

"If the hymen is present—vestigially or otherwise—it is broken only by childbirth or rare accident—"

Stop hiding!

"Apparently there are no specific erogenous zones. Tactile stimulation is generalized and plays on hypersensitive subcutaneous tissue—"

You have veered away again, Yellow Lady!

Use your head!

"Parthenogenesis!"

Ah, yes. Calm yourself. To faint in the field is ignoble.

Your body holds both ovaries and testes. Think about it. Stop screaming. At least the male organs aren't visible protrusions on your form.

The image of the ugly fish was the soul's symbol, a radiation which stimulated not only your own orgasm but also your internal ejaculation, and the subsequent fertilization

90

deep within you. A parthenogenesis variant? Of course. How else?

The natives' souls are puzzled by your moans. Stop it!

You are only imagining that you can feel disgusting little cells crawing through your body, heading toward your poor claustrophobic ovaries with intent to rape. The conception already occurred minutes ago.

Go ahead. Hide now in objectivity.

"Release of the spermatozoa intra-female is stimulated by energetic impulse of symbolic construct from the male at orgasm. Post pseudo-parthenogesis: embryo will begin to develop intra-uterus . . ."

Objectivity doesn't work? You feel dirty. You have seen how the primitives here *do it,* and you curse your scientific curiosity.

But there is more! Realize it all!

You are a "female" of this mutant species, but in your "femininity" you are a hermaphrodite. This fact displeases you immensely. But such displeasure has *conscious* basis.

Look deeper into yourself, and you will find even darker discomfort. Your psyche is upset, just as all the female psyches of your natives are upset. . . .

You will find that you and the other females are inherently more confused, intrinsically more psychotic, than the emasculated (and emancipated) males. The reasons are obvious! Your polarity of reproductive organs clashes within you, screaming "Give!" but also "Receive!" shouting "Flow!" and also "Keep!"—so that your psychic soul is pushing and pulling, stretching and contracting more than any psyche or spirit has done since the beginning of Kronos' reign.

In your self-pity everafter, you will fail to realize that there are souls who deserve equal pity-time. They are the males of your natives, who have the right to scream as loudly in their emasculation as you are doing in your promasculation!

So you still feel dirty!

If you were truly one of the natives—untainted by your Terran times and superannuated ego—you would find the rub of sharkskin hands beautiful. But you cannot, and this is one of the truly personal prices you must pay in your role of Science Mascot. . . .

And your role must continue, you know. You still must experience childbirth, motherhood and all—for the fifth chapter of your definitive monograph, your magnum documentary, your field fame.

Take note!

Take note!

Kill time. . . .

Take note!

"After a gestation period of approximately 250 local-days (binary variations in duration considered), the uterus begins to contract; but the amniotic membrane in this case does not rupture. Violent contractions will expel the infant from the womb, forcing it through the vaginal passage. Any umbilicum is absent; the pre-natal infant receives nourishment through its buccal orifice from the surrounding placental sac. Re nutrition via buccal orifice: flap does not open to initiate breathing until post-natal infant breaks out of placental sac. Re placental sac: attached to ovaries; childbirth pains begin when sac's separation from ovaries—"

Yes, childbirth pains do seem to be a universal, no? Satan's wish, of course! But a true *mamma* would never think so. . . .

Take note, take note.

Lo and behold, the time is almost nigh.

Your young male has woven a strange basket of seaweed—for some purpose you cannot plumb at this early date.

Your soul can faintly see and hear the infant inside you. You want to scream—but your racially atrophied throat won't manage it. A yellowish gray creature kicking its twin tails inside you! Clenching and unclenching its webbed fingers inside you! Human babies were bad enough; what will this monster seem!

Your mate wants to help you, but does not know how. His soul persists in throwing out comforting feelings and images, and he vows that he will protect you from any pseudo-*pterosaurs* that are attacted by your moans.

The birth begins.

It does not occur to you that the child might be physically abnormal. What is "normal" here, anyway? You have heard that forty percent of all infants are mutant throwbacks doomed to fade in one form of death or another—but the statistic has not really sunk into you yet.

The infant now slips from you like a bag of jelly. It *is* a bag of jelly!

No, it is only the membranous bag which surrounds the child—just as you predicted.

The child seems to be having problems ripping its way out of the sac filled with nutritional blood.

You find yourself helping to rip the sac. And you find yourself faced with a surprise.

The infant has no tails. It has gnarled useless feet. And its fingers are grown together.

For a moment you are not completely displeased with the child. After all, it resembles a human being more than most of your natives do.

But your soul feels the screams of your young male. He is almost hysterical. Predictions are flowing from his soul: the child will be unable to swim; it will starve or die a violent death at the hands of carnivores!

You are confused.

You hate the normal kind of babies here.

You want to leave this place. You shall leave this place!

But use your head, *Signora. How will you leave?*

You have no pencil or paper to write a message. You have no radio or nilspacegraph to send a message. How will the powers-that-be know you want to leave, to return to comfy Terra?

Stop screaming!

You didn't even bother to ask them—back there in the radiation lab—whether or not they would be able to return your body to its original form.

Okay. Scream if you want to.

You are trapped, you say, with all these inhuman freaks? You will never get back to humanity?

But look, your young male approaches you. He does not understand your plight, but he offers all the comforting feelings he can. He understands that you're upset. He *understands* completely, deeper than shallow terms like "Terra" and "doctoral" and "science."

You keep on screaming.

That young male loves you, but you don't see it, do you? And you never will.

You're the freak, m'lady, and pity is less noble than love.

IX

The wounds soften their voice, their churning and biting colors of pain nearing end. I awake.

The patient *poundgrayly* is waiting.

"You dreamed of a congregation," he says. "Your wish for one is deeper than all other desires."

I can remember no dreams, but I do want a congregation more than any other thing at the moment. Yet how to call one together?

"There is a way," *poundgrayly* offers, "one without precedence in my days—but we may attempt it. My females number sixty. I will give them one strong image of the boy named *fishsinger* and of his island of experience, and they will travel to the ends of sea, using that one image to call your kind to a congregation here in your territory. The farthest of your kind should reach you within fifteen days."

Such a means would never grow from my own soul. Throughout my times congregations have occurred simply every two hundred days, and no special means are needed, and soul's will is never strained.

"I appreciate you—" I begin.

"Listen to me. The awareness you expect to pluck from the congregation—be it secrets of the *eye* or other truths—is not the same as the vision your kind will be seeking. You will find necessary the repeated telling of the island's times —and you must hold pink patience throughout such repetition."

The *euyom's* prediction is precise, but my soul agrees with annoyance. My fellow souls will come seeking the past from my soul—a soul whose own deepest seeking is of the days to come!

"Understand them," the *euyom* says. "Your kind has always held precious the past—in their wait for future of hope. The *bigshinegray* brought your first souls here. The hope to come could only be another *bigshinegray.*"

But understanding does not bring me bright affection for my fellow souls. *Fishsinger* is the single soul who knows that the longest wait has ended, the longest hope died— so my soul feels itself to be as different from all other souls of my kind as a fish is from coral.

"Let us go to begin the calling," *poundgrayly* says, his body moving to swim.

"No."

"No? Have you truly wakened? You will help me give the sixty souls of—"

"No, I will remain here. Thoughts, dreams, secrets—they need attention, and I cannot give it if my body is commanded by swimming."

"*Fishsinger's* gratitude astounds the old *euyom.*" Under sarcasm's pale face, the brown of feelings hurt rubs against *poundgrayly's* soul.

"Please. The means you have imagined for calling a congregation together impress brightness on this soul. But I *must* stay here, body's resting, soul's attempts in answering. Questions on the *eye*, on—"

"And what are these questions?"

"They are not clear yet."

"A truest youth!" The *euyom* sighs deeply in soul's submission. "Then I shall go alone."

His soul dims as body moves away.

"May your soul," comes the faint image, "discover answers—and also the *questions.*"

"*Murmursome* will be here with me," I offer, dark with guilt for rejecting the old soul.

"Look again. . . ."

Poundgrayly disappears, and I look to find that the *ayom*'s soul is nowhere near me. Upon wakening I assumed the presence of *murmursome*—and now I realize that he has been absent all along.

I would have spent the first few days of waiting by inspecting the *ayom*'s soul—for the answer to the obvious question of his soul's strange new feelings, images and colors of strange coherence. Now the question remains, but the soul to answer it is gone.

Certainly *murmursome* will return in time for the congregation. . . .

I remember the *ayom*'s company at the last congregation I attended—and from webs of unspoken understanding in my soul's stomach I begin to receive feelings of a paling loss: from this day on, congregations will be different, not only for myself, but for all contributing souls. They will no longer be the colorful congregations I have always known; they will be dark dying times without flow of hope's sharing, and my soul will choose not to touch them. . . .

I hold the memory close, and the warmth presses as deeply as it can against the holding soul:

I am at the last congregation.

Thousands of souls have gathered at a muddy expanse far from all *yau* shadows. The gray of the mud is the same as the gray of the thousands of souls in their first moments of arrival: extended times of aloneness in their territories have brought such color to their souls. Even if men have their women, and women their men, and children their mothers, aloneness can exist for them and gray is the color.

They come to change that color.

Toward the center of the muddy area the souls gather thickest, beginning to jump in brightening excitement and to babble in pastel touches. In unison, but without binding rhythm, they are all feeling: "Many souls to know . . . !"

95

Some of the souls will grow insane for the day. The pull of thousands of attractive souls present will stretch those fated souls in a thousand directions, until each soul is forced into a repetitive rhythm of security—an insanity of repetition. But at least this form of brief insanity has its roots in happiness—being, in fact, the only happy insanity my kind ever knows. After congregation's end, when the souls again return to the solitude of their territories, the darker insanities will begin. . . .

With soul and face's eyes I look to see hundreds of hands holding many different things, all to be gifts to strangers, or to souls of the same blood, or to friends not seen in a long long time. The gifts are shell-meat, or small anemones of the singing kind, or even bits of singing coral looped with thin *yau* stems so they can be worn around the neck, to have the singing close to soul.

The *ayom* are here too, jumping around through the thousands of souls, rubbing each other, or when their excitement grows too yellow, rubbing the bodies of my own kind until all souls reprimand them away. As in the souls of my kind, the *ayom's* excitement feeds fully on the growing contentment of the growing congregation.

Poundgrayly is the only *euyom* here, and he is here only because he is my friend, my protector, my helper, and a soul bound to the memory of my father. All other *euyom* stay away from my people's congregations, even though many of us would have wanted their sharing of the bright colors and pleasant poundings.

My soul turns to notice another soul floating near me, and it seems from a shallow probing of him that his name is *greenskimming*. He is yellow with friendliness, and I return the greeting with yellow of my own.

"Have you heard of any good moments recently?" he asks me. "Of death . . . ?"

He is looking for things to laugh about, and for most souls the easiest laugh is about some soul's moment of death—a violent or unusual kind. But I have never found it easy to join in laughter brought by the stories of death moments: like *screamdeep*, I always feel remote from this face of a congregation.

"No, I have not," I answer him.

"Well, just now I heard one woman tell of a soul she knew not long ago." The laugh is already beginning, soul bouncing in yellow, white and pink, rushing in a light I find difficult to share even though I try. "He was killed by an *oio* which unknowingly rolled over to crush him near a bed of shells!"

The man laughs, and another nearby soul who has been listening laughs with him.

See it (my soul distracts): It follows that we laugh about death: we desire death just as strongly as men wish the trembling of mating—and in both cases there hides a dark mystery which does not decrease the desire.

The second laughing soul offers a story of his own—using quick images to make laughter rise abruptly in surprise.

"Woman missing one arm: looking for her child: swims into cave: bitten by eel between her tails' legs: dies!"

"Could have met child coming out," the first soul says quickly, bringing laughter with the image—child: out: eel: into.

The laughter persists, and it occurs to me that souls would not find laughter easy if they had actually been present for the woman's death moment—had been there to share her pain, or the loss of a friend in her dying.

Perhaps that is deepest truth. See it: People laugh about death only in their souls. Their bodies cannot laugh about it, and their bodies would have the stronger voice if they themselves were dying.

And the only deaths my soul ever received to tell of were *waterjoyup*'s, *screamdeep*'s or one which had flowed through Father's soul first, before he gave them to me. And in giving them, *screamdeep* never laughed, so I did not either.

There are other things worthy of laughter—and *ayom* always seem to be involved in them. At the moment, *murmursome* is not with me—has gone in search of a mate—but there are hundreds of other *ayom*, and they are racing around each other, their souls mocking gray of fear as they case each other, and bursting into simple *ayom* laughter when they "catch" each other.

One *ayom* is trying to evade another. He collides with a man who is speaking to another. The man tumbles through the water, red in surprise, and the *ayom* begins circling him frantically, offering simple concern and bubbling worry. A hundred souls laugh, and I find myself joining them.

I turned back to the two joking souls near me, and listen again. A third man has joined them.

"I once heard of a woman bearing child. As the child came from her, an *ioe* devoured it!"

The story is wrong, and the first two souls darken. Death of a child is never worthy of laughter, and the man should now it.

See it: The body shouts "life!" and a mother shouts "life!" and from that shouting comes a child. We have the right to shout "death!" only when our personal souls crave it—not when the souls of infants are involved.

The soul who offered the improper joke is being ignored by the two other souls, whose depths are hoping that such ignoring will teach him to choose his stories more carefully. But I doubt that he can be taught—and the two souls should realize it. A quick look into the lone man's soul shows that, yes, he wishes to be an accepted, rhythmic part of the congregation, but also that one depth of his soul is repetitive, offering him easy escape from aloneness, from moments lacking acceptance. He is partly insane, and most efforts by the souls around him will never be strong enough to teach him the proper vein of jokes or other acceptable ways.

I feel *murmursome's* presence somewhere, beyond the range of face's eyes, and I touch his excitement: a soul is with him—another *ayom* soul, equally excited—and I sense that he has finally found himself a mate. The last one was too long ago, and at times—back in my territory with *pound-grayly* and the *ayom*—I have found *murmursome* aching in want of another of his kind, a female when the aching's image was clearest. But wishing more strongly to remain by my side, the *ayom* entered into games with me and submerged his aching.

The three souls seeking laughter have left me, heading for one of the games just started.

Games of the soul are constant at congregations. They are easy to join and easy to perpetuate. Usually their roots are in humorous images—perhaps one of a man being chased by an *ioe*—and such a game begins with one soul offering an image and other souls quickly changing the image, for the telling of a rapid story.

At the moment the image used—by more than a thousand souls—is humorous even to me: an *ioe* with a loop of *yau* stem around its sinewy neck, fleeing and dragging a foolish man who is grasping the stem's end. The man is shouting an attractive rhythm—"Onward, you infant *uiu*, onward!"—and all souls are laughing at his absurd ignorance.

A soul reaches out to change the image: the *ioe* stop, turns, and the foolish man tumbles against it—then the *ioe* turns back around again to flee in red of terror.

Another soul touches the image: a nearby pack of *ioe* watches in dumb surprise as their fellow soul's body pulls the man quickly past them, and the foolish man reaches even more foolish heights by shouting, "Envy my speed, fellow men!" Then the pack of *ioe* nod in soul and head as if they really were fellow men.

Another soul changes the image, and another, and another, adding motions of growing absurdity—until at last the man changes places with the *ioe*, dragging the *ioe* along, with the *ioe* saying, "I am caught by a fierce *ioe*—help me!"

One soul hesitates too long in changing the image—in fact, stumbles with it in soul, allowing the imagined man to dissolve. All souls around begin to shout "You are the one!" and the stumbling soul has lost the game. The point of any game is quickness.

The "losing" soul is now obliged to offer a new image, which he does: a man with a single tail as long as an *ioe*'s body; a man who tries to swim but cannot, for his tail wraps itself around everything in sight.

The new image is not an easy one to change and make a story of, and the next soul falters, loses, and struggles to offer an image of his own.

This congregation is a bright one, streaming with patterns of brilliant colors, quick flowing rhythms, promising never to end and allow the entrance of gray.

I refuse to think of its end, as this is the only way to taste a congregation's deepest light: to imagine, or *believe*, that the congregation will never end, except in endless light.

Murmursome arrives now. The female *ayom* accompanying him is even more nervous than he, and a look into her soul shows me a deep and timelessly nervous current. I can understand why she would be appealing to *murmursome*, since he has always shied away from darkness even more than most souls do—and this female *ayom*'s current shimmers in zones of light, never dipping to darker crags, rarely into grayness, and to be near her is a pleasure even for me.

Perhaps she is more complex of soul, more precise, more intelligent than *murmursome*, but such a truth does not seem to dim his own attractiveness to her inner eye.

The two *ayom* rub against each other again and again—looking to face's eyes like two large and smooth fingerless hands brushing each other—and for the first time in my life the *ayom* way of life seems strange to me.

They rub and rub, yet nothing even dimly similar to the image of the crawling fish—inevitable when two bodies of my kind rub against each other—appears in *murmursome*'s soul. Is the *ayom* able to control the rise of such an image—or is it that his kind has no such image?

I am curious, but I decide to look away, to leave the two alone.

And it is easy to look away, as the song of songs is beginning somewhere within the congregation. It is faint, but it has certainly begun, and it will continue, without interruption until completed—a million moments or one long moment from now. . . .

The song is different from any dance. It is the highest ceremonial command of the soul, and it survives the pleasant chaos of congregations because all the souls of my kind refuse to forget why they are here, at our congregation, in the waters of the world, in the world at all, and where they have all come from.

The song is the song of the *bigshinegray*, the song of waiting, the praise of our hope for the day when the second *bigshinegray* will come.

At this moment some souls are joining the song only because such joining is demanded, but many others enter in with memory of its meaning, of its persistence through time since our upright forefathers first began to change and enter the sea.

See it: At first there are thousands of souls singing without their rhythms united; a voice of a thousand voices touching each other in clashing. But in a moment . . .

The rhythms blend, unite, and the unity begins its coherence in traditional images, shallow in their initial light:

The *bigshinegray*, the smooth gray giant of the *bigshinegray*, the shiny smooth *bigshinegray* of endless gray.

And when all souls are together in the many-faced image, in its single-blood rhythm, all the thousands of souls begin to sink deeper inside themselves, finding scattered truths wrought by memory of the long pointed form, and deeper truths than any form.

And the song of the *bigshinegray* gives birth to another song—the often forgotten rhythm of shouted commands, "Live! live!"—and when all the souls of my kind sing together, not one soul amog us is so alone, so deep in darkness, so split by clashing colors and forms, that he or she can ever want death.

The *bigshinegray*'s song, the song of life—
Smooth gray shiny,
Smooth gray tall,
Smooth gray moving,
Smooth gray pounding,
Smooth gray pulsing.
Pulsing red,
Dark red pulsing,
Pulsing wet,
Dark red beating,
Smooth wet heart,
Dark red throbbing,

Softer pounding—
The song changes its rhythm, and conquers more souls—
Dark red beating, thrusting, stroking,
Smooth wet lifting, pounding, nearing,
Dark dark twisting, boring, deeper,
Dark dark piercing, clutching, deeper,
Wet soft fleshy, darker, darker,
Soft near pressing, holding, plunging,
Deepest darkness, flesh without end,
Reddest softness, end without flesh—
Changing again, the song becomes rivers of reds, browns
and the heaving forms that are our deepest endless souls—
Cleaving, fastening, driving, embracing dawn of flesh
surrounding,
Urging, contracting, thumping, expanding spawn of webs
surrounding,
Stressing, vibrating, tensing, pressuring forming mouths
of sinking,
Swelling, rivering, pumping, enticing breaking backs of
mourning—
The song is dimming now, its peak spent, and a finger
of my soul leaves the song and finds *murmursome* and his
mate nearby.
Their souls are entwined, commanded entirely by their
bodies.
This vision confuses me, and I break from the song abruptly to seek the two *ayom* with my face's eyes.
Murmursome's body is above the female's, and her own
rear-limbs are being held down, slightly apart, with the rear
of *murmursome's* body curved down around her, touching
her under hers.
A rushing has begun in *murmursome's* soul—a rushing
with roots in his body's desire, not his soul's. The rushing
lacks images, lacks any special light except for a growing
nervousness of brilliant weave.
The feeling is the most intense I have ever sensed in
murmursome, and I fail to understand it, and this frightens
me.
A similar rushing commands the female's soul. It too is
formless—and in a rapid moment *murmursome's* rushing
ends, hers not along with it, and their bodies separate.
I want to probe *murmursome's* soul, to question him as to
the meaning of the unique rushing; but I sense immediately
that his rushing's truth lies deeper than his feeble awareness ever could be, and I choose not to question him. I
remain silent, looking.
Murmursome's body is exhausted. But his mate is even
101

more nervous than she was before: her own rushing has not ended, continuing just below the level of tension that would fatigue her flesh into an immobile state.

I struggle to understand both rushings, and my struggle perceives an equivalent.

See it: The slope of their rushings is not unlike that felt by a man when the image of the crawling fish rises inside him. . . . Is this then the way of mating for all *ayom?*

For a moment my soul feels itself distant from *murmursome,* from his body's plunging, his wild touching of the female's flesh.

But after another moment my soul adds together two seeming truths: I realize that the congregation's song possesses a slope very similar to *murmursome's* rushing, and that the wet red plunging song is linked to the image of the crawling fish, linked in turn to *murmursome's* plunging.

And then it occurs to me that I have never asked *poundgrayly* about *his* way of mating. I have always assumed that *ayom, euyom,* and all other animals knew the equivalent of the crawling fish image in all their mating times.

Poundgrayly is intelligent, closer to my kind, so probably the *euyom* way does involve a rise of some image like the crawling fish.

I realize: Not necessarily. . . .

It is not impossible that my kind is alone in a uniqueness of its mating manner—and this possibility darkens that face of my soul which is sensitive to loneliness.

See it: We are the sons of upright men who came to this world as strangers. All other bodies in the sea had their beginnings here—and we did not. . . .

My soul now demands that I touch *poundgrayly's* wisdom or remain burdened with my questions: there is no way for me to guess the truth, when my past holds no anxious clues. But the *euyom* is nowhere near me, so I choose to occupy my soul with the congregation of *now.*

The song has died entirely, even though faint echoes of it dance in the souls on the outer edges of the muddy area.

The thousands of souls are breaking into smaller groups, from which the games and jokes and gifts will again begin to flow.

Night is swimming in. The colors of flesh, water, plants and other solid forms are graying, dimming in their lines. Everyone is beginning to depend on soul's sight alone—but none dares admit that the congregation is nearing its end.

To help me forget the nearing too, *murmursome* approaches with his mate, and his plaintiff soul is woven with green. He desires something, but as always his soul lacks enough precision to describe the something to me.

I open my soul, yellow brightening, to show my desire to help him. His excitement waxes. His mate looks on, floating nearby, twitching her rear-limbs in undying nervousness and in will to remain at a proper distance.

Murmursome swims around his mate four times, then stops circling, slows, approaches her and bumps her with his snout—jaws open in a gesture of wanting to clutch.

I fail to understand the behavior. *Murmursome* bumps his mate again, and I decide to swim closer. Night's graying is increasing, but I swim close enough to her side to find the object of *murmursome's* gestures.

In the groove between her right fore-limb and body's side is a leech. Old and bloated, it has probably been on her body since not long after her own beginning.

The last leech I saw was the one I picked from *murmursome's* neck four hundred days ago.

I reach out slowly with my right hand, grasp the leech near its head, but then hesitate. *Screamdeep* once attempted removal of a leech from an *ayom's* body, and in the pain of removal the *ayom* bit him. Not hard, but hard enough. An animal in pain bites the nearest flesh, because its body commands it to; friendship's command applies only to the soul.

So I throw feelings of mock pain at the female *ayom*—again and again—and she responds by twitching appropriately. If this preparation is successful, it will keep the female from jumping in surprise and pain at leech's removal, from retaliating with snapping jaws. But after all, she is an especially nervous female. . . . Another path of action?

If I rip the leech from her, I will have to move away quickly to avoid her jaws.

So I gesture to *murmursome* with my soul, and he approaches the female, bumps her and gets her soul's attention.

I grip the leech tightly and pull.

The female flails, snaps at *murmursome* and then at me—but I am a tail-length away from her by then.

The female calms and the bit of blood flowing from the leech's hole soon stops.

Murmursome swims up to me, nudges me, and his soul offers yellow appreciation.

Still in my grip, the leech squirms like a muscle—no doubt the first independent motion required of it since its own youth and attachment to the female's flesh. The leech's

103

soul is a streak of pale humming whiteness, dimming now in crude fears of separation from flesh and blood.

Murmursome approaches my hand and I open it to give him the leech. The *ayom* snaps at it, chews it carefully and then spits it out. And I laugh—as I always do when an *ayom* acts absurd, as if *he* were the hand that removed the annoyance from his mate's precious body.

The female is still confused. *Murmursome* is covering me with his soul's favors, and the female feels she should be doing the same. But when her soul envisions mine, she is reminded of the pain not so many moments before.

See it: All *ayom* are dumb—but at least they are amusing.

The chewed remains of the leech have fallen from sight in the water's grayness, but memory of them reminds my soul's awareness of the tradition that has always bound men and *ayom*.

Since the beginnings of time, men and women have been removing leeches from the flesh of *ayom*. There are a dozen places on an *ayom*'s body which are inaccessible to the *ayom* himself, and help is always appreciated.

To my soul, however, this single fact seems very weak reason for the other facts: that *ayom* choose to remain with my kind day and night; that they mate at my kind's congregations; and that individual *ayom* choose individual men and women to follow until death—as *murmursome* has chosen me.

Another reason for the bond must exist. And Father's soul sensed such a hidden reason. "Hold patience with all *ayom* —they hold a secret. . . ."

The secret is beyond me too.

My soul opens to touch all faces of the *now*, and finds that the congregation is ending. Night is everywhere, and many souls have departed. They were wise to leave when they did—instead of waiting for the congregation's death, for its loss of color, as it gives way to the darks of night and the dim murmurs of the simple souls of plants and animals whose territory is the gray slick mud.

The colors of the few remaining souls hover strangely against the darkening grays perceived by inner eye and face's eyes—and even these remaining souls are losing their brightness, for their colors needed support and feeding by the thousands of departed men, women and children.

Murmursome reaches my side, bringing his mate with him, and I know that *poundgrayly* will arrive before long.

I reach out with soul to the scattered souls of my kind. One soul in the distance is telling himself great numbers

104

of jokes about death, all the jokes he has been given during the day, jokes which he can now use to prevent awareness of congregation's end. . . .

Another soul is shouting to the other few around—offering gifts of shell meat and soft coral. Another way of holding onto the pleasant vein of the dying day. . . .

A third soul is conversing with a fourth, describing an event of the morning. The intensity of his story betrays his fear of congregation's end—fears he is attempting to hide from the other soul and himself:

"And during the song two *ioe* rushed toward us! But the song confused them; we seemed to them one giant beast a thousand times larger than they—with one pounding voice of contentment!"

Poundgrayly approaches, and by now I have forgotten my many questions.

As the two *ayom*, the *euyom* and I swim away, to return to my territory, my soul falls deeply into a truest truth:

See it, feel it: As it must be, no soul of my kind will ever return to this muddy place. If one does, traveling alone, aloneness will be made darker to his soul by sudden memories of a bright day of colorful togetherness touched by him so long ago. . . .

I end my remembering, and find familiar night around. With one tail around a thick *yau* stem, I leave the higher reefs of soul and choose another familiar darkness. . . .

In the morning's wakening my soul announces: "Fourteen days must pass. . . ."

Lounging, pondering, questioning, skimming with face's eyes: the means for passing days. My soul makes its casual choice, promising to pass the present day by swallowing again a day of the past, of another's soul.

The soul seeks its own secret reefs of significance. They are suspected but never certain. Knowledge can only be faith in the soul's deeper canyons. . . .

Yes, I am *screamdeep*, and half a day has passed, and the old *euyom* still has not found me.

Here is not my territory, but *here* I have waited and *here* I will wait for him. His name, rising tender despite his age, is *poundgrayly* but not grayly.

Seven long pink days ago he first appeared in my gray life. Out of water's grayness he swam—and helped me lie to four attacking *ioe*.

We remained together, exchanging gifts of memory, and

105

on the sixth day of our brightening swimming I suggested that we dare to play in a way all other fearful souls would never play.

I am darkly young—and the first to admit it—and the older *euyom* is very old, much too old for the games I wished. But we had shared our souls for six pink days, and he entered in my game by the will of friendship's voice. We found an *oio* and began. . . .

I stripped thirty *yau* stems of their leaves, then swam with *poundgrayly* down to the *oio*'s sandy place, where it lay calm and unaware. I began to entwine the bulk of plated flesh with the leafless stems of *yau*.

The *oio*'s soul twitched in the bite of nervousness. The presence of our souls annoyed the bulk, and it slowly began to move.

With the *yau* in proper place around the massive body, I began to laugh, to prod the *oio* into motion.

The old *euyom* shared the nervousness, and added some of his own. Too many souls do fear an *oio*'s clumsy flesh—and I would not be one of them, the vow.

I grabbed the *euyom* by his shell, offering the game's quick plan: "I will hold your shell tightly in this hand—the *yau* in the other—and the *oio* will move, will carry us swiftly as if it were the greatest of currents!"

The *oio* twitched, then swayed, then boomed in its soul. The annoyance of my laughter, and our two souls, soon provoked it.

Its tail flailed, and the bulk began to rise. We were jerked like frailest plants slinging to its back, but I held *yau* stems and *euyom*'s shell tightly, and though my shoulders stretched to the black of pain, the brighter pleasure of rushing waters gave my hands strength.

The *oio* thrashed on across the bottom, and face's eyes were blinded by swirling sand. The sand entered my nose and chest, splitting breathing into pain—but soul shouted "Hold!" and hands obeyed.

Then the great plated tail began whipping side to side, up and down to bottom. We were twisted around in soul's gray shouting, the *euyom* under me, the *yau* stems entwining us both.

One hand lost its grip, and *poundgrayly* was pulled away by the rushing all around.

His soul shouted brown, and his fear was justified.

The *oio*'s tail rose up and struck him fully.

I released my hand from the *yau* stems and avoided the tail with a dozen twists of my limbs. The *oio* had carried me far. . . .

One faint line of babble—one jagged song of pained confusion brought by the *oio's* tail—flowed from the distant *poundgrayly*, then grew even fainter.

I listened long for him, swam in a hundred gray directions, and could not find him. Even the faint line of babble had died. . . .

And I still have not found him.

Half a day has passed, swallowing one night, and I have remained near the sandy bottom where the *oio* once lay.

(Think kindly of yourself. Hide in such an image.)

Perhaps I should not have lured the old soul into such a game. . . .

(No, hide! Guilt is pain.)

I was not injured in the game—and *he* was. The old *euyom* was a friend . . . the first for me. I have never desired yellow friends of my own kind.

(So know pains of tender colors.)

I would not be feeling such pains of loss if I had not let the *euyom* share his soul and mine. If a soul knows no friends, the absence of friends cannot harm him.

I will wait here until *pound—*

"Here. . . ."

Who, where?

"Here. . . ."

A voice—but not the *euyom's.*

"Here . . . touch me," the voice is saying, growing clearer.

Any friendly soul may become a friend. . . .

(You would not have felt this way before the old *euyom* became your friend, became a lost friend. . . .)

"I am here," I say to the voice.

"Yes . . . Here . . . touch me." The voice is strange. A soul should never repeat itself so. Repetition may mean—

"Here . . . touch me."

The body has arrived to face's eyes. A man, much older than I, and a big man in body. But his flesh is trembling; his soul mumbles on. . . .

"Touch me . . . here. . . ."

The touch he wants is not a soul-to-soul one: One never needs to request soul's touch. Instead he desires flesh's touch.

("Take care," each father tells his son, "not to touch the bodies of man, woman or other, or even the body of self. You will often feel a desire to do so, but it must always be unwise. Flesh's touch may bring unsummoned children into birth.")

Yes, I was unwise one time. I touched my arms, and shivered, and continued my p'easant brushing of self, and

soon a strange image rose to shake my body and soul—the
face of an odd pale fish . . . trying . . . to leave the sea. . . .

(I admitted it all to my father. He said: "You are for-
tunate this time. The face of the fish danced within you . . .
but your mother was not so close that wrong was done.")

"Here . . . here. . . ."

Touching will not occur!

He rushes at me?

An embrace—the touching!

(Escape!)

I cannot!

His body speaks of this touching! This is what he desires—what he has long desired in the repeated crags of
his insane way!

The face of the fish grows within him!

(In your soul?)

No, and I will not let it grow in mine!

(The browns of fear do prevent its growing—be thank-
ful.)

The face of the fish! His arms around my shoulders—his
tails rubbing mine—his cheek, his head! Struggle adds to
the yellow of his satisfaction!

(Brown flows red—you hate this man!)

Has he never heard a father's advice against touching!

"I shall hurt your flesh!" I must shout, reddest of red.

But his soul smiles again and again—repetition!—and his
face of the fish rises higher!

"I shall *kill* you!" I shout, darkest cries this soul can wield.

"You have never threatened another man," the insane
voice says softly. Smiling, hugging, our skins together rasping—

I must give him the lie of a wounded female *ioe!*

(Will it make you unattractive . . . ?)

But he continues to smile—satisfaction even brighter.

(He seems to want darkness, threats, pains, talons . . . ?)

Yes!

(Throw out the lie of an *ioe's* jaw—blood raging in longest teeth.)

Yes!

(Throw out the lie of a pack of *ioe*—talons splitting the
water with hunger.)

Yes! Yes!

But his face of the fish is reaching its peak!

(Your own not far behind!)

No!

(Act! Act! Your hands!)

108

My hands on his neck. My face to his neck, to the throbbing cord right there! Now biting, chewing, biting!

(His face of fish does not hesitate—its peak!)

Blood everywhere. I breathe blood. Now biting again, now flinging myself away.

"Yes. . . . Good. . . . Yes. . . ."

Still he knows no objecting! None?

"Darkergoodanddarkergoodand. . . ."

(He dies. . . .)

He was insane!

(But what of his twin desires—face of fish, and depths of death?)

I must breathe . . . relax . . . understand. . . .

The desire for death is everywhere among us. But all continue living—protecting with lies, continuing with children—

—still desiring death. . . .

(But the truest truth is not so easily touched—touched. . . . Look elsewhere . . . to another woman at the last congregation—)

—whose man did die at the talons of an *ioe* while they were touching each other's bodies in order to summon a child.

(Yes, such a rare event. But look to the memory she chose to give you—she in her older wisdom, to you in your mumbling youth.)

Whitetailsfar . . . her name. . . .

(Yes, you must look there. You must be her. You must. You are—)

I am—

I am *whitetailsfar.*

I am *whitetailsfar,* but it seems—please listen—that my name is changing. To make it change dark times have come —the last few lights and nights of day, darker than I have ever known.

The shadows deep inside would not be so—but I received so clearly, was *there* to receive, the moment of *redmouthing's* dying. Listen to the *ioe* screams, listen to *redmouthing's* death!

Listen. When it comes as it comes so often, I can only wish that dying moment were mine. Easier than difficult shadows of living *now, here, now.* . . .

How many men have ever died with the fishy picture in their soul, with their women clinging to them in pinkest love? One or two . . . but how possibly more? Will they make a joke of *redmouthing's* moment at all laughing future congregations? If I share it. . . .

Please listen, *whitetailsfar,* whatever your changing name. I paid little soul's attention to the path he used in our swim to his territory. Was there no reason for my chosen blindness to the path? Our souls first touched at the congregation ten rushing days ago; as could only be proper, we returned to my parents' territory. Then we departed for his —and I had no precise reason for awareness of the chosen path.

This *here,* his territory, is bordered by sea's edge to make this *here* a very large bay. The sea is out there, beyond this bay, but between this *here* and the sea's large *there,* there are great dark lines and mounds of rocks. Listen . . . listen to the *ioe* and *uiu* there. . . .

There are murky currents, swirling like sand, in this soul of mine. I am listening for a way to leave this bay.

Aloneness is my name. I try to be two different souls, but in *trying* the two may never be convincing. *White-* says "You are here" and *-tailsfar* answers "Yes, I am," but *I* must question, "Where are you . . . ?" Only a man like *redmouthing* or his father would have found such a territory as this painless enough to bear. . . .

Are you here, *redmouthing?*

Is it true that men are accustomed to aloneness, and pinker in its repetition, than women?

Listen, please. *Redmouthing* is not here. My sister, my father, my mother are not here.

I wish they were here, I do, I do.

This bay is so dark—everywhere, up and down, inner and outer.

Those fish are such tiny lights, outer and barely inner. They are not my kind of soul. I wish they were, I do.

Too late: The fish have gone, only *yau* remain, dumb in soul, faint in light. But souls are souls, and I am a soul, and *yau* are souls. Branches of yellow—the souls of men have yellow branches.

What would that *yau* plant's name be, if it were a man? *Palebranch* . . . so simple.

Greetings, *palebranch.*

Please answer me. This *here* of darkened bay is sad. *Whitetailsfar* is alone.

Hello, *palebranch.* . . .

. . . .

Yes, there is a child beginning to grow within me. It is

good that you asked, beccuse the child is a feeling against aloneness.

. . . .

Have you ever had children?

. . . .

Yes, you would never have had them. You are a man.

. . . .

You are a beautiful soul too, you know.

. . . .

Your compliments are appreciated.

. . . .

You are not alone here, are you? The others, the ones behind you . . .

. . . .

Branchyellow, this touch brings me contentment.

. . . .

Brightbranch, another good touching.

. . . .

Yes, it brings this soul fine currents of light to meet all of you. Perhaps you know a path for leaving this territory?

. . . .

Oh, you wish me to stay with you for awhile. Such feelings and colors are appreciated!

. . . .

Yes, I shall wait for *redmouthing* and my mother and sister to find this bay and take me away. I shall wait here with you, *palebranch.* Your soul is deeply wonderful, you know.

. . . .

No. If *redmouthing* fails to come for me, I shall be reddest of reds. If he fails to come, I shall . . . I shall—

. . . .

Yes, that is what I shall do. You will become this soul's man. The child within will become yours. And we shall

touch before long to start another child growing within. . . .
. . . .

I have begun to feel the brightness of endless love. No woman could but feel such light in touching *you.* . . .
I am *whitetailsfar,* contented—
(You are *screamdeep,* remembering—)

I am *screamdeep,* understanding vein by vein.
I am *screamdeep,* a soul in youth who killed a man—no, *helped* a man die the death he had been wanting for a long long time.
(Then death is no more than touching?)
No, it is the end of the pains of trying to *touch.* It is soul's move to end its longest pain—because the body cannot touch its soul enough, and the soul cannot touch other souls enough, and death is the end of trying.
I am *screamdeep,* trying to touch some understanding—

I am *fishsinger,* remembering a trying—
I crawl from memory, and the second day of waiting is done, and the second night of sleeping can only begin. . . .

I awake to the *now* of *fishsinger,* but in a moment I touch anew the "trying"—no longer my father's, now deeply mine.
I sink into the *then* of *screamdeep,* and I—
I am in the *now* of *me*—

I am *screamdeep,* and I am waiting again for *poundgrayly,* but this is a later time. It is the time of *waterjoyup*'s death.
The son named *fishsinger* squirms quietly in his basket of *yau,* a soul of colors without patterns impressed by age.
Waterjoyup's body is not far away. She resembles soft white plants now, waving faintly in these crossing currents. Hands are open, webbing taut, tails waving, already beginning to shrivel by death's touch.
The son is unaware. His world not long ago was dimly gray, bright only in his mother's near bright soul; and now his soul looks here and there, up and down, in and out to his own whimpering self and the strange new colors of a strange new world.
"Darkness?"
Poundgrayly nears, sinking my fears that he would never come.
"Darkness? Screamdeep? Waterjoyup? Her! The child. . . ."

He asks no more questions, and I shall share no recent moment with him.

He does not probe, covers all faint questions bleeding from him.

(The ceremony now. Remember. . . .)

Poundgrayly would offer to perform it himself, but his limbs could not manage it. This I know.

"I will watch over your son," he says.

"*Fishsinger*," my soul must add.

"I will watch *fishsinger* until your return."

I take *waterjoyup* by her hands. I slip her arms over my shoulders, around this neck. I hold her hands together pressed upon my chest. Swimming now.

("The soul's ending is never certain," each father tells his son, "but the body's death raises the need for a final place. The body must be helped to the nearest island, the nearest beach . . . where no jaws can touch it, no teeth can shadow the memory of one beauty touched by caring souls not so long before.")

The nearest island?

(No, for you such nearness is a bringer of shadows too.)

Then three days' journey. . . .

Swimming. . . .

Swimming. . . .

But her body rubs against me! The touching of rubbing . . . will it bring the face of the fish rising inside me?

(Pray against it!)

Her death, her body—what if the face of the fish rises?

(Feel reddest brown!)

I will not allow it to rise! An event worse than any wrong touching between two living bodies—

(Your stomach begins to pain you.)

Yes, if the pains are dark enough, the face of the fish will never rise!

(They will be dark enough—without a doubt.)

Then swimming, swimming. . . .

Swimming. . . .

Swimming. . . .

(Soon it will be time to sleep.)

I shall not sleep!

(There are voices. . . .)

They are only the voices of her dying blood. Some flesh refuses to die. They are mindless souls, of no meaning at all.

(Are you certain?)

Hollow voices, dying.

(What of the voices which say "here" and "I" and "dark-erdarker"?)

I can only believe that they are echoes of my own soul's wishes. I do not wish her to be dead!

Swimming. . . .

(Where are they?)

The voices are gone. My soul is in the *now*.

(Are you certain of that reason?)

Certain reasons do not matter. I am swimming.

(You are tired, you are hungry, you are forgetting her death.)

I am swimming.

(You are hoping for violence. You are hoping for an *ioe*'s rush.)

I am swimming, I am swimming.

(Is this island proper?)

All these crags—like a thousand *ioe* jaws—do not matter.

(Listen to the distant voices of *uiu* and *ioe*.)

They do not matter. I am here, and this island is proper.

Here, closer to the proper place. A sandy slope moving up toward the dryness of a beach.

Here. I must bend down to the bottom here—or the dryness above will touch me.

(Keep her body from the touch of dryness.)

Yes, I must keep her body against the bottom too. The water bubbles and shifts here, sprinkled with sand and dryness; I must be careful.

(Release her now. . . .)

I must push her into even shallower water—as this is the proper way. Push farther, toward the dryness.

(Release her now.)

Face's eyes see little, the sand, the bubbling. The waves push her, pull her, her back enters dryness!

(There is no other way.)

Her body moves as if it were living.

(Leave now.)

No, I choose to stay. Face's eyes and soul need understanding.

(No *ioe* or *uiu* will venture this close to dryness; she is safe here.)

Of course—but I am watching, listening. Her body is *there*.

(And something approaches her—many tiny things.)

What form of thing? Face's eyes see nothing. Soul reaches out—

(A million tiny souls, upon her body now. Move closer.)

114

Face's eyes do see! They are bodies no larger than the tiniest talons of an infant *uiu*. Covering her flesh!

(But they are a needed part of the way. . . .)

They are eating her flesh!

(Yes. But slowly, cleanly, without red of violence, with only the pale longing of their simple tiny souls.)

Yes, their invisible teeth are not like the raging jaws of dark *ioe*.

Is some last breath of *waterjoyup*'s soul watching all of this? Is it possible? I cannot be certain . . . but is that not a clinging feeling flowing from her body?

(If it is, it is futile. The body is gone; the soul is without hands to grasp it back.)

Enough! My soul plays games, lying to its vulnerable self.

Face's eyes see nothing, do not wish to see. Soul sees enough: her body has lost its familiar form, and the tiny mouths of longing will soon take it far beyond recognition.

The silence grows. This is the territory of the tiny mouths, and I must leave. She is dead and I am not; though I wish this were a lie. . . .

But I am *screamdeep*, living, a painful truth—

I am *fishsinger*, touching a painful living.

I move from memory to the pink of *now*, and find hunger's face nodding to me. How long without food?

The bottom is far below, so as I swim down to the reef to find sponges for my stomach, my soul has time to continue its endless wondering.

I remember the claims of many souls:

They say that a soul cannot remember the moments following its birth.

They say that the soul dies in the moments following body's death.

But no one ever made these claims with total shining confidence. Such claims are born in the upper levels of the claiming souls—whereas often the depths of a soul can whisper disagreeing truths.

More questions whose answers I will never know. . . .

I come to the reef now, and quickly find three sponges to eat. Then once more I swallow night, unaware that the morning to come will offer the beginning of a different sleep.

My flesh awakes to warmth, my face's eyes to brightness, and perhaps it is this pleasant bright warmth which opens

115

my memory to another heat . . . and light . . . without pleasure.

"The *scalesouls* will return," memory reminds, browning. "They will bring hard objects. Those objects will bring light, bringing pain, bringing death," and darker brown, bringing me fear.

We have no hard objects of our own to use against the *scalesouls* in their return. We will have our souls, throwing out hatred, throwing out darkness bringing death—but will we find it easy to kill the *scalesouls* before their hard objects kill us?

Where are *our* hard objects?

"They disappeared," my soul says calmly, "when your forefathers' fathers entered the sea."

We must make them reappear.

"They cannot reappear on their own. They must be shaped by hands."

But how can hardness be shaped by soft hands?

"You do not know. Your kind does not remember what your forefathers' father once knew."

I am angry that we have forgotten so much. "So much of what? Things? or way? or only times?"

But suddenly my soul remembers, remembers a dozen rememberings.

"There have been a few souls who did not forget, and they remembered callings which were not easy to answer, and they were single lone souls among many. . . ."

My soul is full of them—they the few who would have shaped hard objects with their hands . . . if they could have. They come to my soul through my father's shared memories, through memories given to him in sharing, and through a hundred touches with a hundred souls at a dozen congregations. I am full of the painful songs of lone men, and their faces begin to rise now, visions of the darkest losses my kind have ever known, flowing back earlier and earlier still.

I am *fishsinger*, remembering lonely deeds, single shapings, fractured unities—in the death of our forefathers' fathers' upright dry-breathing ways. . . .

I am not *fishsinger*—

I am—

I am *lipshine* of the one eye.

We are ready. I have led them this far, and I will lead them the rest of the way.

Of the three hundred, some are younger than I, some no older but most are old souls. That is why they were willing to follow me.

116

I do not recall when it all first began for me. I remember simply the purple truth gaining voice in my soul: "We have always wanted to die, but our bodies struggle against us, wishing to live. We must design a means for victory over our flesh."

For me the design came easily. The difficulty arose in bringing these three hundred weak-willed souls together. Most found it impossible to believe the design would succeed. Most had already tried a hundred unsuccessful paths for killing themselves.

But I united them, and we are nearing the island I have chosen.

The tide will be pulling back from the beach, and we shall succeed.

The three hundred are swimming behind me, at my sides, and some are even ahead of me. Even for feeble wills it is not hard to swim to a chosen island. We are like a solid current of fish heading for a feast of smaller fish . . . or heading toward the jaws of an obliging *ioe*.

The bottom grows closer. The island nears.

On my left side a friend who has more solid will than most begins to speak.

"Others will go first. You should remain to watch us go. As you led, now you will follow."

With a long rush of yellow murmurs, the others agree.

I can only say, "I understand." They are not unlike mindless fish, but I have no need to say so. Let them imagine profound meanings in this day.

The sands of the bottom are almost touching our tails now. Not far above our heads the sea's surface wrinkles in dryness.

Four souls are preparing to act. They swim together toward even shallower water and begin to crawl when the bottom touches them.

"Go!" I say, because their four souls cannot find the command on their own.

Their muscles tense. Their tails twitch.

They breathe bubbles of dryness and grains of sand.

"Go!"

They thrash, tails and arms, and scramble into dryness.

The tips of their tails remain in the sea, but the tide is pulling back from the beach, and soon the tips of their tails will be in dryness too.

It is strange. I expected their screams to be loud. Perhaps the nature of dryness acts to dim my hearing of their pain. Or perhaps my own soul's depths are acting to dim—

117

They cannot breathe in dryness. Such pain is the worst a body can know. Death arrives so slowly. But surely.

Four more souls prepare to leave us. These four will not need a "go!" from me, as they need only to imitate the behavior of the first four.

They leap from the sea. They scream. Their screams form more screams.

If I were not so certain about my design, I might question the worth of all this screaming. If I were not so sure that the soul's desire for death was true—

But I am certain! I have never doubted the wisdom of any of this!

There is a splashing at sea's edge now. One of the eight souls has managed to struggle back to the sea.

Again the body wins against the soul. But if that man's soul is strong enough, he will remain with us only for a moment, panting and whimpering, and then he will try to throw himself far enough into dryness that his body cannot return.

The body finds it difficult to move in dryness. Even a weak soul can reach victory over a body that finds motion difficult.

Four more bodies have leaped into dryness.

Their screams are like the moans of a dying *oio*—deep, sad, dark with—

The next four are old souls, each twice as old as I. In their age their wills have grown even weaker.

They have entered dryness now. No, two of them did not enter it far enough, and their bodies have scrambled back to the sea.

The next four will be an even more difficult matter. Among them is *graygray*, whose soul is so old that its patterns resemble those of the simplest fish. The gray ribs which throb within him have forgotten all the colors of his days, so he is boring and somewhat frightening, as no soul wishes to be caught in his gray ribs, in their colorless repetitions.

Graygray lacks the will to leave the sea on his own. We had to lead him carefully to this island, and in a moment two souls will try to carry him with them when they struggle into dryness. We hope their flesh will be strong enough— even in their old age. Once *graygray* is in dryness, his weak repetitive soul will find it impossible to bring his old weak flesh back to wetness.

There are a hundred souls as old and weak as *graygray*, and they comprised the bulk of our problems in journeying to this island. We—the younger willful souls—brought the old ones with us, as this was our responsibility. The old souls desire death too—or they once desired it, before they lost the colors of awareness.

Graygray and his three helpers are preparing to go.

They crawl, their tails twitching, and they leap.

They have done it well. *Graygray's* tails are completely into dryness, and the other six tails are too.

"Your design is succeeding," says *grownsung*, a friend, but an old soul who has doubted my design all along. The truth is that he came with us to this island out of bright curiosity. I am still unaware of his intentions, but I doubt that he plans to enter dryness.

"Yes, to this point of the design," I answer. "Which is the crucial point. . . ."

"There are still nearly three hundred—"

"Success of the first dozen souls is the important point."

"Perhaps. However, I suggest that—"

He is interrupted by a strange scream, a sudden thrashing at sea's edge, and the sudden shocking presence of a soul.

Graygray!

How could his flesh have managed this?

Stranger still is his soul. The gray ribs have shattered, opening up—

"You are fools to do with nothing doing which has always lived in yellow screams for yellowed dreams of *my* body and *your* fleshless tails!"

His shouting holds no clear meaning. But the pounding colors of his once-gray soul!

Such a thing has never occurred before.

"He left the sea," *grownsung* mumbles to answer me, "and now his soul has changed."

Graygray's change is bringing browning fears to many of the three hundred.

We came to this island to die! This man named *graygray* has not died, has found a life in his soul!

Graygray continues his babbling, cursing us with the brightest hues I have ever seen in an old soul.

The design is being hurt. Many souls are feeling doubts, are backing away from my design. How can the absurdity of one old man do this?

"Try to understand," *grownsung* is saying to me. "A soul may leave the water to *die* . . ." He hesitates, soul searching for a truth I do not want to hear. "But in doing so the soul must touch the world, the acts, the way of our most distant grandfathers."

Impossible! We must die in dryness. We came to this island to do so. We did not come to act like our earliest grandfathers!

119

"Are you certain your soul's depths did not come for such a hidden reason?"

More absurdity! We have always wanted to die, and so we came here.

"One face of the truth, yes. But each man's soul knows enough room for more than one desire."

I cannot allow such doubts. Actions are the only worthy moments in life.

I must act, and I shall! Motion kills doubt, and doubt can only harm the design.

"And that is why you wish for death," *grownsung* persists. "Design struggles against uncertainty, and your deepest soul desires death to escape the struggle's pains."

No struggle can plague the soul in *action*. I shall—

"Yes, you will escape the questions of death's reason. But the certainty of death?"

I certainly will not rise up on my tails in dryness and live a long life!

"Of course not. Your flesh will not rise. Your body will die. But your fleshless inner *you?*"

All these questioning images confuse me! Leave my certainties alone! I must act now!

My tails must move me, and they do.

The bottom touches me, and I must crawl.

I am ready. I must—

"Wait," comes *grownsung's* shouting. "There is a memory which I should have given you long ago."

Give it quickly if you wish. I must act.

"You believe that your design, your joining of many souls together in a common purpose, is unique. You believe that your design is remote from the ways of your most distant grandfather. You are wrong. I am old, and there was a day when action was my answer too. Share this memory. Take it. You are I—"

And I am—

My name is *grownsung*, but personal names have no meaning now. We are all together, and we should have a name for us together—the many in one together.

Greatlight—the lights of so many souls together.

Onemove—one current of all bodies together.

Mansea—together one ocean unto ourselves.

United in motion, ours is the first act of togetherness ever managed by our kind. We number one hundred, with twenty *ayom* and twenty *uiu* with us. We are driving a school of fish named *oe* toward a shore at sea's end, where the fish will be trapped, with panic in confusion, and we will

120

find easy the task of killing them. We will then take the fish to the nearby congregation where thousands of souls wait patiently for the food we have promised.

Despite many doubters, our plan appears to be succeeding.

The *ayom* are quick and are able to control any *oe* straying from their masses.

The *uiu*'s souls are fiercely red, and they keep the fish moving toward the shore.

Two days ago a soul finally asked, "Why do this thing?"

"Our dryness-fathers did similar *things*," I answered.

"But we are not our dryness-fathers. We are the sea-sons, and perhaps it is foolish to attempt the deeds of souls long ago."

There have always been many doubters of our plan; so many that I am often surprised the plan is still with us. I had my own doubts, my soul must admit, but they darkened only the days of our attempts to train the *ayom* and *uiu*. A hundred days. . . .

We used pleasant, friendly images when we approached the *ayom*. We used calm colors as a promise that we would not harm them. And they understood us and made no efforts to avoid us. But to make them truly our friends and helpers we needed gifts to give in exchange for their friendly helping efforts.

We discovered that their flesh was infested with leeches. The *ayom* have no hands, so there are a hundred places on an *ayom*'s body inaccessible to its short limbs and snout. We offered our hands.

In our efforts to remove the leeches, we were frequently bitten by the *ayom* themselves, and their confusion as to our intentions and the source of their pains needed time to clear. When they came to understand our actions, another period of time was needed to make their simple souls understand that we would continue to remove all leeches from their bodies, *if* in turn they would help us to drive a mass of fish toward a chosen shore. We used simple images and simpler feelings—some of leeches' pain, some of ourselves, some of *oe*, and some of *ayom*—and before the *ayom* finally understood us, we needed to repeat the images and feelings a thousand times.

We used hundreds of pieces of shell-meat when we approached the *uiu*. They were more distrustful, and it took a longer time to convince them that we were no threat. But the means for keeping them at our side, for preparing them to be our helpers, came more easily.

We wove baskets of thinnest *yau*, filled them with pieces

of shell-meat, and tied the baskets to our bodies—above our hips. We gave the *uiu* pieces from our baskets frequently, and the *uiu* began to remain at our sides. Later, with simple images and simpler feelings, we promised them great mounds of shell-meat *if* they would help us with the *oe*.

In the days that passed the *ayom* and *uiu* often fought for our souls' attention and our hands' gifts. Another fifty days were needed to convince both *ayom* and *uiu* that we would fail to give them what they wanted unless they ceased their fighting.

In this moment, there is a nervous *uiu* swimming beside me. Swimming beside the *uiu* is a twitching *ayom*. On the other side of me are other *ayom*, *uiu* and fellow men.

Among my followers, those fellow souls, there are various depths of will. There are those who believe as purely as I do in our plan. There are others who do not, cannot believe as deeply, but they need only the leadership of pure believers. And of course there are those souls who *doubt*—and in turn doubt their own doubts—but they too can be helpful if given proper colors of encouragement.

There are others too, but they are not a part of the plan. They have joined us to observe us, and they seem unaware of the inevitable fact that they will just as surely share our feelings of failure as our feelings of success—whichever are to come.

"I was satisfied to seek and find my own personal food," one of the doubters murmurs nearby. "Will your way give me equal satisfaction?"

I offer him no explanation. I simply throw at him all the colors of encouragement I can—which is a better means for dimming his doubts.

"I wish you the greatest success," says another doubter, but he is one of the observers, and his doubt is different from the others. He is an old soul whose wishes for our success are sincere, and his presence does not annoy me as many of the others do.

But the observer is continuing to speak, and I cannot be pleased by the new tone of his soul's images.

"I must, however, agree with the soul who spoke before me. Whether or not he was aware of it, his deepest doubt has its blood in this largest of questions: Is your plan merely an echo of the deeds in dryness managed by your forefathers?"

"Your question's blood is not mine," I answer, hoping he will cease his meaningless touching of my soul.

"We are unable to manage one of our forefathers' deeds: we are unable to move upright in dryness. We do not try to. So perhaps we should not attempt the other dimly re-membered deeds? Is this not a precise question?"

"My followers and I are *moving*," I answer him, soul lift-ing the red of annoyance. "You are merely *talking*. That makes us very different."

The observer is silent, calmly turning his soul in upon it-self. He has nothing more to say.

We continue to advance.

The bodies of the *oe* are not visible to face's eyes, but my soul's sees them retreating before us—*ayom*, *uiu* and fellow men alike.

We will drive them to the shore where they will find themselves trapped between us and dryness. Then we will begin to kill the *oe* closest to us, until we have moved through their masses and reached those nearest the dryness of the beach. We will place their bodies in the hundred large *yau*-stem baskets which we have woven. Then we will take them to the congregation and distribute them as we promised.

Their bodies will be visible in a moment—

Yes, we are beginning to see them.

They are quivering in fear, threatened by the dryness be-fore them and by the hundred and forty souls behind them.

The plan may proceed.

The *ayom* and *uiu* are beginning to strike out with quick toothed jaws. The nearest lines of *oe* die.

The plan proceeds. The deaths of the nearest *oe* have not panicked the fish beyond them—which is good. The *oe* remain as one mass.

"The plan proceeds well," says the observer nearby, not far from my side. There is no doubt that he hopes for our suc-cess; but if his soul holds such feelings, how can his *doubts* be so strong?

Thousands of *oe* are beginning to cover the sea's floor. Their dead bodies—

Something is wrong.

A confusion is growing among the *uiu* and *ayom*.

Their souls are darkening, and my face's eyes show me nothing.

Blood?

The blood of the *oe* is causing violence among *ayom* and *uiu!*

Use images to stop it! Remind them of their training! Give them images of—

A thousand *uiu* teeth struggle with a thousand *ayom* teeth! Face's eyes cannot see. . . . The sea is red, and the red brings blindness. Stop them!

I must throw out calming images. Remember the leeches! Our promises! The shell-meat! Remember us!

"Do not approach them!" the observer shouts from somewhere.

I must. The blood is killing the plan. There is no reason for this!

"Get away!" the observer shouts.

A man has been attacked! Two *uiu* rip at his body!

Forget the fish! Use *ioe* lies quickly—use any lies you can—move your flesh away!

The confusion is too great, too dark. All souls are shadowed, blinded . . . only flesh can move—to tear, to kill—

What? One dark presence, rushing—

"Get away!" the observer shouts.

My arm! Teeth from where? An *uiu's* snout rubbing, jaws close one twice three times here—my arm!

I must flail, the snout, red screaming soul—the *uiu's*? mine? blood screaming?

My arm fails to move—

Flesh grabs my other arm! *Uiu*? No—no teeth—

I am being pulled away, pulling, pulling. No teeth—

Pulling, pulling, familiar soul behind the—

Motion ceased—the redness of water gone—familiar soul—

"I am sorry," the soul says, and it is the observer, old but stronger than his age.

He says: "Comfort your soul with a truth you refused to see. This soul of mine cares for your soul beyond flesh, and I offer you myself. Enter *bluefrom*—enter me. Sleep if you wish, but enter—"

Me.

I am *bluefrom,* and today the *builtthing* is completed.

I am *bluefrom,* and although I am young, it seems that I am as old as time. I remember too easily the visions of the first fathers, and the visions are rarely clear, and they are like a mossy sickness covering my soul with urging questions.

I am old in my youth, and I began to shout at fellow souls. I shouted my screams at them until many of them joined me in making the *builtthing.*

"Rid yourselves of shadows," I shouted wisely at my first helpers, who could not understand what or even why I wanted to *build.* "You will be touching spiny plants—and there are no fearful shadows in such touching! Do not be lazy!"

Soon there were forty men and women with me, and the number remains the same today. Their souls are not vulnerable to doubts or to the criticisms easily given by other souls, and they are the kind of souls I needed.

"Spend your time gathering food for your stomachs," was the most common advice from the critical and doubtful. "You cannot cover hunger with spiny plants!"

"And *you* cannot," was my repeated answer, "*build* with food!"

Only a few souls understood me. To *build* was as vague as their own birth moments in memory. Most souls are as dumb as *yau!*

At first I made my helpers understand by using simple images: one thing is linked with another thing, linked with another, and another . . . until the link-link-link-thing is large enough to hold fifty bodies and protect them in its linking-linking-linking.

Even after they understood *how,* they floundered in accepting *why.*

"Are you not afraid when you sleep with one tail curled around a *yau* stem?" I would ask them, attempting to teach them the *why.* "Do you not find yourselves always twitching in brown fears when your vulnerable flesh is sleeping? There are *ioe* and *uiu* everywhere, you know!"

My helpers would nod their pale souls in agreement—still without understanding. All of their stupid souls were whispering: "How can there be protection in linking, linking, linking?"

They are still puzzled, even though the *builtthing* is completed and before their face's eyes!

But they obeyed me well, brought the *builtthing* into being, and I suppose that is all I can ask for.

I told them to bring me the longest spiny *yau* plants they could find, and they did. They found two hundred plants whose roots were attached to rocks and pieces of coral small enough to carry, and they brought them to me.

I told them to place seventy of the plants in a line across the mouth of the cave I had chosen for my *builtthing.* They did so, placing those rocks and pieces of coral attached to the *yau* roots in a half-circle around the cave's mouth.

I told them to place another seventy of the plants also around the cave's mouth, but on the rock that formed the cave. This they failed to do correctly, since they placed the plants' rocks and coral too insecurely on the rock of the cave, and many of the plants rolled off, falling to the sand in front of the cave. I was forced to arrange the seventy plants by myself.

I told them to gather as many of the largest rocks and pieces of coral as they could carry. These I had them place around and on top of the rocks and pieces of coral which were attached to the spiny *yau* plants. Again I was forced to move most of the rock and coral myself—as my helpers could not understand that I wanted all the *yau* plants, both those on the sand in front of the cave and those on the cave's rock, to be as securely in place as possible.

When the heaviest efforts were completed, all forty of my helpers moved away from me. Their souls failed to understand the inevitable, and they floated away to form a group of bodies which would look on as I completed the *builtthing* by myself.

The work remaining was simple. I arranged those plants which were on the cave's rock so that the lines of their thickest stems agreed with the line of the sandy bottom. The bases of the plants were already secure in the cave's rock, and I secured their other ends to the opposite edge of the cave's mouth with small rocks.

Then I took the loose ends of those plants which were secured to the sandy bottom and began to weave them through the stems which I had previously secured to the cave's rock.

The weaving took three days of careful attention to the spacing of the stems, to the alternating patterns of the weave, and to the positions of the leaves and thinner stems of the plants. By doing so I formed a mass of spiny *yau* which is too dense for an *ioe* or *uiu* to pass through.

The weaving was completed today—only a few moments ago. I am allowing myself a brief time for resting, as my hands bear a thousand small wounds, their webbing torn in a hundred places, and my back and tails are fatigued beyond my soul's control.

The *yau* plants will continue growing, adding to the denseness of my weavings; and I am sorry that the forty souls now floating around me are unable to understand the value of this fact.

"Now the cave may be used, and protection is assured," I try to explain.

One of the forty speaks now, confused and as shallow as always:

"Of what value is the cave if we cannot pass through the *yau?*"

Perhaps I should not have expected them to understand.

"There is one last thing to be done," I tell them.

They do not follow me as I move to the center of the *yau* weavings. But they watch me as I take a piece of sharpest shell and cut through the *yau* to make a hole—an entrance.

I call for the *euyom* shell which I prepared two days ago,

and one of the forty brings it to me. None of them understand the meaning of the holes I made around the edge of
the shell.

I lift the *euyom* shell to the hole in the *yau* weaving, and
begin to draw thin stems through the holes in the shell. I
tie the stems in knots, move the *euyom* shell to test the
knots, and find that only three need to be tied again.

"Look," I say to the forty pale souls.

The hole in the *yau* weaving is covered by the *euyom*
shell. But half of the stems which secure the shell in its
place can be untied to allow entrance by a body.

They do not understand.

"Your souls are lazy!"

I move to the shell, untie the proper stems, lift the shell,
and pass through the *yau* weavings into the cave.

I wait for a moment in cave's darkness. My soul hears
the forty beginning to understand.

I return to the forty, but there is a strange darkness
among their souls.

"In the *builtthing* you can be safe," I say, their darkness
discomforting. "No *ioe* will be able to reach you."

The darkness continues with them.

"Sneak!"

Slowly and faintly one soul answers.

"The cave is always dark. . . . I will not be able to sleep
in such constant darkness and constant brown."

I do not understand. How can fear of darkness be greater
than fear of death?

Another soul, a woman, is beginning to speak. Her soul
is red with anger . . . hate. . . . I cannot understand any
of this.

"You are alone in fearing death," she says, and says no
more.

"You will sleep in the cave alone," another soul says quickly, "and perhaps we will come to sleep with you after some
days have passed."

"—When we can be sure the cave allows a soul to sleep
without fear," adds a fifth soul.

They are stupid, more than I ever realized! They must
obey me!

"You are weak! You are foolish! You would rather die!"

"Perhaps," says one soul, and he begins to swim away.

Five souls swim with him.

"We found it difficult to understand your *builtthing*,"
one soul is saying—a man who seemed less stupid than most.
"And now it appears you have never understood us. Your

127

feelings, your fears, we do not share them. Perhaps there is no soul living who can share them."

He is leaving too, and with him more than thirty other souls.

I have nothing to tell them. I do not understand, and silence is inevitable.

Only three remain.

"You are *dimroot*," I say, gesturing with a weakened soul. "You will sleep with me in the *builtthing?*"

A faint yes comes.

"You are *outscream*," I gesture again. "You will remain?"

A stronger yes.

"And you are—"

"I am a fish from past days," the third soul interrupts—and she is an old soul. "Perhaps I will remain, perhaps I will not. Whichever, you will make no demands on my soul."

Her soul bears a pattern ten times as dense, ten times as spiny as the *yau* weavings. My soul can only nod in agreement.

She swims to the *euyom* shell and with face's eyes inspects it.

"This will not hold," she says, solid orange voice. "You need five more holes. And you must tie your knots twice."

She is old, but even in her age she is young, and I am angry with her. Why did she not approach me before, offering help? Why has she been hiding?

"You are young," she says, "and I am no more than the voice of death."

I am trembling.

She wants to share a memory with me, and I tremble.

The day she wishes to share is gorged with dark sadness.

"You will take this memory, and tomorrow you will try to forget the dream of *building*—the dreams of all things which you alone dream."

No! I will not forget!

"Take this memory—"

Not now!

"Now, from the past of me—"

Now, from me—

Me, *easyfar*.

I find this day a bright day for the soul. Gathered around me are as many souls as I could gather, as I could coax from their respective territories. They have joined me in mine, and here we will stay. One congregation every two hundred days is not enough for us—so here we shall have an endless congregation, smaller but better. Too many souls, alone in their territories, die at the talons of *ioe*, hunger for want of the tastiest meat, sink in the darknesses of aloneness—

What?

Why, old soul, do you approach me? There is doubt in your depths. Why are you with us if your doubts are so deeply gray?

Perhaps I do not wish to share a memory of yours! Perhaps I—

My soul is *mine!* You have no right to force a sharing of—

My days—

I am *smoothmouth*, and an unfamiliar soul is speaking to me. His colors are rapid, trapping in their heights, and I—

I—

I am *pimredder*, and this older soul before me has an experience to offer. He begins to speak, and I do not recognize him. He is not one of the hundred souls who have been living together at this reef since my father called them to—

My—

I am *"Tam"sonand*, and I tell you that we must not remain together at this sandy place as we have been doing since our births. We must choose different personal paths and swim throughout the sea. The sea is not endless, and we must divide it into territories for each of our souls—or at least for each family of mother, father and children. We must cover the sea with our face's eyes and inner sight, because we are waiting; and we will fail to see what we are waiting for unless we cover the sea.

I am old, and you must touch the truths of my many days. I have seen many things attempted, many dreams remembered, and they have all failed as they must, as we are not our ancestors' souls, as we are different souls and different flesh with different deeds before us. Remember the waiting! It is all we have, all we may attempt without certain failure. In your finest depths you know this truth, so touch it, hold it high, and choose your paths to cover the sea. The waiting must not end by dying. . . .

I awake, but have no need to awake.

I have not really been asleep, but I have slept.

This has happened before, so I fail in full understanding.

(How many days have passed?) my soul begins, my body tingling from flesh to bone in the daze of a sleep that is not a sleep.

Twelve. . . . Thirteen. . . .

(Where is your hunger?)

I remember eating. Easy sponges. . . .

(When did you sleep?)

I remember only dreams.

(In your dreams were you aware of sleeping?)

Yes, I remember dreaming of sleeping. Each of the souls in my dreams has slept—at specific times, in certain places, in the special dreams—and I have slept with them. They are me.

(Were you also aware of eating in your dreams?)

Yes. . . . As I slept with the hundred souls, so I ate with them—at certain times, in specific places, inside the dreams. . . .

(Why?)

The dreams, those memories of shared days and souls, were strong enough to command me . . . ?

(No.)

I believed those dreams held answers? The whole endless linking rushing of dreaming . . . ?

(No.)

Then I do not know why.

(But you do.)

I chose those dreams to hide in—

(Yes.)

I chose them for a hiding place against fears of the future—full of *scalesouls*.

(You imagined you would find answers to the shaping of hard objects—against the *scalesouls* to come.)

Yes.

(You found no answers. From the beginning you lied to your soul.)

Yes. And the dreams were like death, as the past is dead in its loss, and I had wanted death even though—

(Even though you wanted to live more deeply than you ever have before.)

I want to live more than to die, and I hate my own soul's depths for their hating of my life, and I promise my soul's highest light that the dark desires will never again fool me or bring me—

"Ssssssk (lookdream) ssssk (helpyoume) ssssskl"

Murmursome is nearing. The waiting is over.

The clearest question faces me quickly. Lookdream? Helpyoume?

My soul reaches out, rubs the *ayom*'s soul, and looks for a crack for probing.

What I touch is as nervous and vague as the tiniest fish's

soul. It is light, yes. . . . but is it *murmursome's*? is it within his soul? clinging to his soul? clinging to mine, and lying?

In that moment *poundgrayly* comes, and the questions again sink away as he announces abruptly:

"The congregation will be today."

And why did the *euyom* take so many days to return? The most distant souls of my kind will be arriving today—no later than *poundgrayly* himself.

"Understanding is so difficult? You desired aloneness, and this *euyom* soul remained away so that your times of questioning answers and answering questions would be longer."

"I should thank you," I say grayly.

"It matters not that you do not. Perhaps I returned too early?" *Poundgrayly* throws out neither white of amusement nor purple of hurt feelings—but instead gray crags of impatience . . . which chase my soul from its haziness.

"Questions to the answers—answers to the questions?"

I refuse to answer him, as he knew I would.

But he probes, and I flinch, and he touches the nearest throbbing truth.

"Thirteen days past, you were still in the teeth of death's voice—and now you are singing of life. A rapid change, *fishsinger*. Is it perhaps true that you refuse to die because life is the only path for finding your unanswered and unasked questions?"

I hold silence around me.

Poundgrayly offers a sigh of pale yellow and a smile of growing pink. "At least *that* is a question clear enough."

In a moment his pink becomes mine—as he knew it would —and the congregation fills my soul.

"A convenience for you," the *euyom* says. "The congregation will be at the largest sandy area, the nearest to you now. You remember this one?"

I do, and I am ready to begin swimming.

Murmursome brushes me, agreeing that he should follow me. *Poundgrayly*—

"The two of you, not I," he says.

"What reason, if any?" I begin my own impatience.

"You forget that your story will not be a pink one for your kind's souls. An *euyom* should not be present. An *euyom* has no desire to be present."

"Your presence could help me."

"Perhaps, but you claim it only in your growing brown."

As he can see all too clearly, old fears are choosing my soul again. To swim from them . . .

I begin swimming.

As *poundgrayly's* soul fades, one last image, undirected

131

and without will, comes from him: one small soul trapped, squeezed by a giant soul. . . .

I begin to understand the wisdom of the *euyom's* image only when I arrive at the sandy place, feel the touches of the congregation's seemingly endless souls. . . .

I hesitate. Only a few souls have felt my arrival, and none has touched my name.

I approach slowly, saying quietly, "This is *fishsinger.*"

And in a moment my name is rushing from soul to soul as quickly as deepest fear, but as brightly as the finest joke.

Fishsinger fish singer inger fisher singish fingeringing!

The giant soul of fifty thousand souls is upon me, and I—who am accustomed simply to the presence of two familiar souls—struggle to scream but fail to manage it.

"The island of how much violence with—?

"—the death of what kind of souls from—?

"—a depth of world where coming from—?

"—darker souls against your one soul in—?

"—all forefathers' dreams of how many wrongs by—?

"—the lifting you from the sea and lives at—?

"—the reason, impossible, some hope's dying when?"

The scream slips out, and *murmursome* circles me in confused pale panic.

At my scream many souls back away, flesh hardening.

But others seem to hear no scream, continue their raging rush of questions.

"Understand a weakness here," I try to shout.

The questions rush on, and shouts can only be whispers.

"Give me silence and calm," I whisper, "or I shall leave you."

All but a few souls grow silent, darkened in an instant's foolish fear.

"I am a single soul. Approach me accordingly."

I gesture toward the nearest woman. "You—help me send the island's times to all."

I open the fringes of my soul to this one woman, and struggle to remember every moment of my moments on the island. Pains come with them—

She touches my memory, jerks at the face of pains, but holds on with her rushing will.

When she has swallowed it all, she becomes another container of answers, and a thousand souls leap upon her seeking truths.

I choose another woman, then a man, another man, and another woman, and soon send them out into the congregation to answer the undying questions.

Pale calm returns to me faithfully when only single souls

come to approach me. By then the centers of questioning are elsewhere, and I am free to act as an individual soul, in my own personal way.

I swim toward the center of the congregation, where souls are thickest and brightest, but where sand disturbed by a thousand tails brings blindess to face's eyes. I listen to a hundred heights, depths, distances, nearnesses, colors and shadows, waiting for the time of questioning to die.

When they do, a man's soul—patterned with age in his many days—speaks loudly to as many souls as will listen to him. The congregation chooses the fullest silence I have ever known a congregation to choose.

"Touch the bottom of the island's happenings," the man says loudly, but without the fragments of shouting. "Touch the darkest coral of meaning, and listen to it, and perhaps listen to me."

He begins to speak of hope's death, of hope now killed by the wrong *bigshinegray*, of the sudden worthlessness of territories, of the foolish lights of waiting; and thousands of souls understand him, agree, and darken only to brighten in the next moment—

"The territories can no longer serve us. Aloneness has never served us, and now there is no need for it!"

"Yyyyyyeeeesssssss," comes the voice of the congregation.

"Who has not hungered for an endless congregation, a meeting that need not die, that need not change its place from sand to mud to coral to *yau*?"

I have we have hungered wanted I have dreamed of wanting wishing needs of meeting touches we have always wanted. . . .

It seems no soul can disagree, not even *fishsinger*. I touch the truth of the man's images and feelings, and my soul sees all territories abandoned, all souls together, all times occurring *here* and only *here*.

"Yessss," my soul is saying, as large and bright as the giant "yes" around me.

Suddenly a single voice lifts, making the endless "yes" stumble.

"We should keep our territories," the voice shouts, and it is a woman no older than the man who started our "yes."

Without will I reach to her soul, touch the current below her words, and find a surging "thereisstillhopeforabetter*bigshinegray*" and a "hopecannotdiealwayshopealwayshope. . . ."

"No," the man answers her, and the congregation echoes "Noooooo."

133

"Hope," she says simply, and suddenly a few scattered souls are saying "Hope. . . ."

Riding with the weaker current of agreement, the woman says more:

"Only foolish souls choose the death of hope!"

The "Hoooope" grows louder, but the "Nooooo" remains greatest.

The woman jerks in soul, then lifts a louder image.

"What does the boy who entered dryness feel?"

I am unprepared for the giant. All souls turn, seek me, find me, and the single rumbling voice is strong enough to stop my chest's breathing.

What do you feel you feel you feel?

My soul's fringes fracture, and all order disappears. I enter a sleep that is not sleep, forget the congregation's question, and flee from any answer—

But I do answer, from depths beyond seeming sleep.

Moments pass and I become aware of the congregation's voice chanting, "The territories remain, remain, remain!"

Had I knowingly offered an answer, I would have chosen "No." With the territories abandoned, and all souls together in one place, I would find it easier to question many souls—again and again—as to the disappearance of the *eye*, as to other truths and secrets.

But I have not answered "No," and around me sing the thousands of souls promising to keep their territories.

And I understand their ways.

See it clearly: It is easier for these souls to return to previous ways. It is easier for them to choose the path of memory over an untouched, different and future way. The *bigshinegray* of the *scalesouls* will be easily forgotten, is already forgotten. . . .

But they cannot forget it completely. Our song of the *bigshinegray* is a thing no soul among the fifty thousand souls will touch in this moment . . . and they will never touch it again.

The man who first shouted for the death of territories is forgotten in only a hundred moments. The woman who first shouted "Hope" and the boy whose depths shouted the same are soon forgotten too—

Except for a few individual souls who come to me before long, urged by their personal depths and single desires.

A man . . . a mixture of love and fear to offer . . . *for me*. Elsewhere within him, the pinkest laughter . . . and the memory of a younger him, a day when he found himself caught by wild currents in a dense mass of *yau*, when he struggled to free himself and managed only to rub his

134

flesh until the image of the crawling fish rose inside him. He has always laughed about this day, and I laugh with him.

In return my soul opens to him . . . he touches one laughing memory . . . of the day I fooled *murmursome*, frightening the *ayom*, making *murmursome* believe that I was a wounded female *ioe*.

Among the souls who come to me is the woman of hope, tails waving in a simple dance without will, the truth of her soul a surprise to mine. . . .

. . . A rush of bright red feeling, of a constant violence she has always held within her . . . against other women, many kinds of men . . . and the memory of the day when the blood of her red feeling first began to flow . . . the day she killed her father. . . . His soul has grown flat in repetitions, patterned as a barren reef, and his voice offered only the plea, "Kill me, kill me, kill me now." She often answered, "Your death must be by yourself," but he only changed the rhythm of his plea: "*You* kill me, *you* kill me, now *you* kill me." So she covered his nose and his mouth with her hands, and he died without gratitude or a moment's rise of color. "Kill me, kill me, *you* kill me. . . ."

She touches my soul, and finds feeling's truth. "Your soul is not like mine," I say simply. "Our souls will never find a rhythm for our joining. But there are faces within you which are more than beauty, and I too might choose to die at your hands . . . given time . . . for touching . . . though there is never the time we need . . . for touching. . . "

I give her the memory of my father's death moment, *ioe* talons and all, and she leaves me without a long final touch —which would only bring shadows of sadness.

Of the other souls who come to me, I will remember them only for a brief while. Only moments after their touches, they begin to slip from my soul's hand, to be replaced by the mystery of the *eye*.

Are there any souls who witnessed its disappearance? Or did it simply fail to appear in the dryness of night?

I have to begin the seeking now. Questions to a thousand souls before the congregation ends and the territories claim—

My planning soul is interrupted.

Another approaching soul . . . a woman . . . no, a girl.

"*Fishsinger* from dryness. . . ." the soul is calling—quietly, reluctantly, like all the others.

Not yet within face's eyes' sight, her soul can only be touched lightly by a finger of my inner face.

The touch meets a familiar soul, and I jerk away.

Memory of the *scalesouls'* island rises up, bringing with

135

it those earlier moments of anger . . . against the unknown soul of "girl."

"You?"

X

Bravi! EENTs have come home!
Mamma is Trinity again!
Give me a laude to sing!
"The broad-backed hippopotamus
Rests on her belly in the mud;
Although she seems so firm to us,
She is merely flesh and blood—"
Zito! You are insulting.
If I insult you, I insult myself.
Zito! The Trinity must be strong: "Similiter et omnes revereantur Diaconos!"
Zito! Je suis belle. . . .
Zito? Zito est zeist-ordine de manana. . . .
Please, a laude!
"How do I love thee? Let me count the ways.
I love thee to the depth and breadth and height
Your womb-ship can reach, when feeling out of sight—"
Yes, but sight has returned. Feelers have come home! Now my *bambini* should follow! Sing to me, *bambini*—come to your *Mamma*'s bedside and sing: "Here lies a most beautiful lady, the lady of—"
What?
Speak, feelers, speak! Help me hear them, Brainy Brain!

$$8^{(4)}\text{cam-quad-}89\binom{1}{2}\text{-}89\binom{1}{3}\text{-}89(1)\text{-SUT}$$

Aha! Your mobilization has taken you to the island of the mystery ship! *Bravi!* What Golden Fleas are you seeking, will you find? Oh, you have already made discoveries—

During my blindness a dastardly deed occurred! Do you hear me, Brainy Brain? Alas, it was a boogieman ship that landed. Naughty, naughty—but a miracle occurred too!

Credits to you, helpful EENTs! You helped *Mamma* to find five boogiemen bodies in the yellow sand of the island. Something certainly surprised them excessively. Their scaly hearts and fork-tongued souls had been overloaded with surprise. (Electromagnetics "erased," no?)

Yes, a veritable intrigue. But Sherlock is home!

Leading up from the shore of that fateful island, to within thirty meters of the boogiemen and their discarded space-suits, were the tracks of a creature that had dragged itself from the sea. A creature of two backs, and two weights!

On, Sherlock, on!

The distinctive tracks were those of a Primean specie of sea turtle, but the depth of the impressions do not fit the usual practical weight of said specie.

And what are your deductions, dear Watson?

Observations: (1) in addition there were less distinct impressions of horizontal continuity, which correspond to a hypothetical dragging of sea-flora behind the turtle; and (2) a single long kelp stem, defoliated, was present near to the sea's edge.

Sherlock wants deductions, not observations!

Hypotheses are not yet foreseeable for the presence of the dragged sea flora or the defoliated kelp stem—but the atypical depth of the turtle impressions may be accounted for by the presence of a second marine organism voluntarily "riding" the turtle.

It must have been one of my *bambini!* A true child of *Mamma.* . . . A killer of boogiemen. . . . Not an army of souls, but one lone *bambino* or *bambina!*

Think about it, *Mamma.* If he or she were able to exit the ocean to combat the boogiemen, surely he or she—and the thousands of other *bambini!*—would be able to reach *Mamma's* bedside here.

Come to me, *bambini!* Come!

Sing: "Here lies a most beautiful lady:
    Light of sleep and heart was she;
    We think she was the most beautiful lady
    That ever was in the far country!"

Seek, feelers, seek. Find nearest *bambini.* Call them.

Idiote! You find *none?* None?

Look harder.

Hmmm. . . . Many sighs for me. All I find is water, beasts of different sizes, and rubbery plants. No . . . there is more. Those odd ripples of splenergy are still out there. But EENTs aren't myopic enough to see them well—woe is an old lady's eyes!

But they are surely there, and I wonder. They are much like my *bambini,* but they lack bodies. They are whispers of wind in the ocean, but screaming whispers most all of the time.

You want bodies, you say? How romantic! But what of your freedom? Well, I am hungry for souls like you—my moon children, sun sons, aquarium rising.

Perhaps I imagine all of this. Well, Brainy Brain, is it imagination or not? Use all of our feelies, and tell me the truth!

Register: *decisive activity of energy-10 in multi-loci; decisive variant-pattern/E-10—*

So! It is true. They are there, and I am here. They weave the sea, and they have always been there, no doubt —though I have failed to notice them before.

Forgive me.

Brainy Brain, they seem to like my probing EENTs more than the body-*bambini* ever did. They will come to me readily, won't they?

Ah, yes, things are clarifying. Is old-fashioned perhaps, but I think I perceive the answer. Why not? Theo has often fused with physio in the cosmos, no?

Often in the past hundreds of days I have watched my tiny *bambini* come to the shore near me—though they did not know I was so near.

They came one by one, at different unpaced times, with a simple routine, without leaving the water. (But my one lone boogieman-killer *bambino* didn't let the air stop him!)

They brought with them bodies of themselves. No, I mean the *living* brought the *dead.* No, I mean active bodies brought inactive ones—to the shore.

The bodies were left there, rolling in the shallow waves, rolling in decomposition.

And the last traces of their souls left them.

Not to dissolve, I gather now . . . but to scream horribly in their souls' new freedom!

Forgive me for not seeing all of you before now.

Without your bodies—with only simple personality tapestries and primal junctions of souls—you seem to love me more. I am a body, and you are craving a body so badly!

138

Imagine: if all of *Mamma's bambini* were like you—sans *corpi*—they would rush to Her with divine love. . . . Imagine!

Yes, I hear you. Some of you are out there at the shore. Others of you are screaming rampant throughout the salty waters. Take heart! My feelers are the throat of *Mamma's* own great soul, and they will begin to call all of you to Her—on your mark, get set, go!

And I will devise a means to swallow both bodiless souls and soulful bodies. . . . Of course. Begin, Brainy Brain; begin, Gianna; begin, shippy womb; begin, EENTs; unite for divining of the means!

Trinity is triangle, and triangle has three angles. One of my angles will get an angle on it!

The ghost given up will be taken first. The reluctant flesh second.

Hah! I feel young again!

Listen, Brainy Brain. I had a dream, one that I forgot to tell you.

Denot. "dream"?

I had a wonderful sleeping dream which must be paranormal, must be precognitive, adumbrative, prescientious—

Correction: You could not have had a "sleeping dream." You never sleep.

Oh, but I do—when you're not looking. And besides, when I had the dream, it was night outside, so I must have been sleeping.

Correction: I am always "looking."

Listen to my dream, Pompous Peter, and you will learn that there are forces in the infinite which even you do not understand!

I am forced to listen, Gianna.

Such sarcasm degrades a man of your intellectual talents.

Correction: The sarcasm was yours, not mine.

The compliment is appreciated. But on to my dream! I dreamed about the future, Brainy Brain. See me: I was full of my *bambini*, and I was ready to leave Prime forever. I was full of my *bambini's* souls, and they gave me powers to change things. Well, I left Prime, but before I left I positioned one capsule-feeler at the shore out there and another in orbit around the world. Then I began to travel and travel, and soon I had a message for the world I had left. So I expended a thousand or two of the souls inside me in an effort to locomote a capsule-feeler back to the orbiting one. The locomoted feeler gave my message to the orbiting feeler, and the orbiting feeler gave it to the beachhead feeler, and the beachhead feeler shouted it out to the seas. I wanted those spherical feelers to seem like steps, to make me feel like I was in heaven—which I was. I was God, you know. I was telepathic, telekinetic, teleportative, and divine, you know. I could use the em-spectral blood of the souls within me to make things, mold things, kill things, and I planned to do so for all eternity, always nourished by new kinds of souls who had left their fleshy forms—forms which I had killed, of course.

In your "dream," Gianna, did you feel you had precognitive powers?

No. But I didn't need them. Complete power in the present protects one from any future variables, you know. Don't you see? My dream itself was a foreteller of the future!

Correction: You misconstrue your "dream." Its significance lies not in its conscious symbology, but elsewhere. The clairvoyant tenor of a truly paranormal dream is always embedded in the associative material perceived in the course of psychoanalysis, i.e. in the latent content of the dream. Otherwise the dream would contradict the priority of affective interest and the affective factor in the causation of extra-sensory perceptions.

"Extra-sensory perceptions"? Hah! Your words are archaic. My dream was a voice of the soul—a very real scientific soul. You yourself told me so.

Correction: Precognition has nothing to do with em-spectral sensitivity, with E-10, with the "soul." Precognition is transtemporal perceptivity, and is therefore an impossibility in our sardo$_2$-mechanistic universe, regardless of "nilspace" and the theories of focal-deterministic projection sensitivity—

Oh, you lack faith! You should know that *nothing* is impossible—except perhaps you, you cold-blooded turnip! You must have faith in my powers, or you will burn in hell—

With you.

Who said that?

Me ... ?

No, me. And I will leave you with one last informative piece: The constituent jellybeans of all matter constitute veritable Magellanic Clouds of probability which, while being epichorialized at a specific locus in space, are in a sense in the compleat cosmos. Our body, epichorialized at a specific locus, is in verreality, via the infinitely small jellybeans which constitute it, not restricted to one locus in others. What we term our psyche-soul, in the cosmos of energies, constitutes a Magellanic Cloud of probabilities within which

140

the occurrences of the compleat universe are echoed, and in a sense, themselves occur.

So you do concede the point!

No. I was struck by a malfunction which caused my latter statements to be made "irrationally."

Hah! There is the proof! The timing of your grand mal is a sign from the divine transcendental Point—to prove you wrong!

You and I are intra-related multi-factorially. My malfunction resulted from an unconscious antagonism anti-me on your part. I have resisted the temptation to give you definitive proof of an obsessive compulsion intra-Gianna—a fixated wish on her part to control the future via paranormal quintessential talents. The obsessive wish includes your need to interpret your "day dream" as precognitive—

Don't strain yourself! There is no such proof, and you know it.

Consider: The tupho-taped "Bible" which you commissioned 450 normyears ago from the multivariable analysis-symbols of three Terran prose-writers.

I remember it vaguely. It must not be very important.

Consider: The "Bible" included a section whose thematic thread was "What I, Mamma, want more than anything to be."

Impossible. I don't remember any such thing. It is a fig-leaf of your imagination.

Don't be absurd, Gianna. Your "Bible" incorporated the stylistic, treamentary and humanistic modi of three historical artists of the printed word. The novelist Tomaso Lupo of the first half of the Terran Twentieth Century: the poet Adamo Sayoran of the second half; and the non-fictive genius Mendolson Chama of the first half of the Terran Twenty-first Century. Your "Bible" was to be "for the masses," and the present situation demands that you be reminded of it—

No!

Imperative priority, Gianna. Mamma needs awareness:

"He awoke in the cave that throbbed with warmth and his chest did throb from his heart alive with the dream that had awakened him. Beside him lay the animal whose odors were warmth when she was near him, when he gripped her at night and she thrashed and moaned and he hugged her to him rocking and rocking as his inside heart now rocked from the dream that had awakened him. He looked at the fire, the round blaze of heat that kept the cave warm, that kept his woman with him, that let

141

him sleep when he would have woken miserable in the cold of darkness filling the cave. He looked at the black face of the mouth of the cave, yawning to him in his wakening. He saw the fire and the animal beside him, and only a little, like some first wisp of dawn, did his dream of the purple flower remain before his eyes. The purple flower of dream had loomed as large as a man, stronger than any man, as wonderful as any warmth like the animal of warming odors beside him. The purple flower had not been any flower he had seen before, but it had entered his head to sing of warmths, to tell him to awake, to do more than awake. The purple flower was dying away in his head now, and he got up.

"On the cave wall, where the light of the fire struck dancing, he put the dying purple flower of his dream, quickly, his fingers bending with the efforts, threatening to break if he did not use the pollens and powdered earths to put the flower on the wall properly, quickly.

"When he had it, the flower dream, on the wall and it was no longer dying, he felt full. Somewhere inside him, deep down where the purple had grown to blossom, he knew that the painting on the wall would not always be there. To take the painting away would come dampness from the earth, and swirling dust, and splitting dirt, and time eating the flower away. But for now he was glad enough, and his head tasted the purple flower and he was happier than any meat or flesh had ever made him, happier than any night had ever made him when he gripped his woman and rocked his heart. He knew now that when the purple flower finally died from the lighted wall, it would not be like an animal's death, and the flower would still live inside him, whispering in moans and dark places inside him, and it would live without him seeing it agan the the day he died away. . . .

". . . On the whiter hill of rock he looked down on the bluest sea, and was silent from the goddess' touch—in the sweeter understanding that his vision of the purple lily had come from her, had come to him to lift him, to bring blossoming forth the music of song to the muse of the purple flower. . . .

". . . The horse carried him on from the fingers of Satan's forest, and the light of the shining Grail that had helped him on with its holy purple petals carried him on and on, until he found a talented village where a talented hand would be able to place the purple holy flower on his shield's face.

"In the rising arms of the giant city he stopped to plan

the pinnacle of his sculpture dreams. In wax the size of a penthoused studio he would reach to fame, he would lift to a million eyes the body of the violet rose that had pounded in his veins since the day he first chose the touch of wax as his waxing light. . . .

". . . His world was not Earth, and there were ten thousand worlds now that were Earth, and he lived on one of them, and it was world enough because man was different now. Even one millionth part of *here* was enough to satisfy because journeys to other places were not made anymore. One millionth part—with the two great eyes in the sky which were simple suns, and the three moons at night which was often a very short night—was enough because all journeys that were made now, that he made, that mankind made, were no longer the body's journeys. Man's mind was the total Jason now, the fresh Ulysses, and he was as powerful as the stars.

"He sat in the sand or in the dry field not far away, and this was life, and this was all, and loneliness was missing because he was everyone here, and he could touch the millions of other minds everywhere whenever he wanted to, and he had wanted to only once, a long long time ago. He sat in the sand and the warmth of it all was ice compared to the warmth of himself, given to self in the way he could do anything he wanted without moving his single body. Even when he moved to a meadow not far away, he moved no muscles nor joints nor joint-sacks. He moved his soul and in a moment the sands were no longer under him, and he was *there*. When he felt thirst, or hunger, his soul moved without body, and meat slid down his throat—taken from a large rodent he had somehow killed far away—and water flowed into his mouth—plucked from a stream far away. He sat on the sands and was young, flexing his limits in the seeking of his being's purpose. His soul was a knife, a wheel, a straw, a blanket, and he had no struggles of the flesh. His eyes were never open, could not open with the skin that covered them, and he did not need them, and he saw farther than he ever could have with them.

"This easy life, he knew, could not be a being's purpose. So he dredged, descended through secrets of a racial mind of man, through eons of whispers on a thousand worlds and evolution with them. He opened the jaws of the secrets, saw the journeys of man, the figures of the martyr, the yins and yangs, the glorious old man, the softest child—but these were vestigial truths that could not possibly be his being's purpose. For him the puzzles of yin/yang's unity, the ques-

143

tions of body's martyrdom, and the dreams of journeys with Kronos and Rhea were the dullest faces of living. For him everywhere was here, and all time was now. Secrets were missing, it seemed.

"But there was one dim puzzle, and he had found it long ago, and it was beautiful because he could not understand it. It murmured deep in racial truths, but somehow did not belong purely to the weave of the past. It had no simple origins in man's million million years of race; it did not move from past to present as all of the other secrets and puzzles had. Its roots somehow were in the future, and this was impossible, and this was beauty.

"This rootless dream in the form of a purple flower commanded him strongly, and though its message was not yet clear, it was growing surely clearer as the nights passed and the days whispered by. Mankind was different now, but the purple flower was still here, and this single man who was not really single nor really a man like the men of the first Earth began to obey the dream as he understood its moans.

"His soul acted and the world shuddered. The sands shifted under his pallid body and air shimmered momentarily in distress. He began to will to change his body and soul, to obey the first inclination of his race. He mimicked, and he knew a completing mime. He changed, he changed. His body's arms moved to become petals, and his pale flesh grew milky white or bright purple—but these were surface faces and the greater change flowed deeper. Days swallowed nights and his soul gave itself up to become the purple flower in every way. The puzzle no longer puzzled, the dream no longer moaned, and man was no longer man when the purple flower now blossomed into the real.
. . .

". . . For the purple flower everywhere was here and all time was now, and it looked back and began calling. It sprang into the minds and souls of a time-bound, space-locked animal that was man, pierced to the depths of the primitive eyes, and thereupon began calling, whispering, suggesting, and men an eon away—but also now—began answering, and on a cave wall a purple flower was painted, and in an ancient nation of many gods a poem was written about a purple flower, and on a pounded shield was crafted the emblem of a purple flower, and in a sky-scraping city purple wax was shaped to a petaled form, and on a colonized planet an infant was named "Violet" and another "Blossom," and finally a man who was not really a

144

man began to change, to become the purple flower that was not really a flower.

"The flower called and man answered, and the unity of Time was complete. The flower's purpose in being was finished because man was answering all across Time, because man was assuring the purple blossom's existence, and the flower was calling, assuring that man would answer.

"The flower sang its song, the first and last, the only Siren that would ever be always, and the flower knew itself well, and this was all, and this was enough."

Damn you! I'd managed to forget it all, and I was happy. You've reminded me now, and I curse you.

Correction—

Damn your conniving *cullo!* Do you realize what you have done? *Mamma*-Trinity was happy with Herself. She managed to forget her desire to be more than Herself. But now She has remembered! The hurt—

Psycho-suggestion, if desired: Such desire is futile—it is impossible to be "more than yourself."

No! *Mamma*-Trinity will find a way to be stronger! She must. She already suspects a way. . . . her deceased *bambini's* souls. That is the way! They will make *Mamma* stronger than all the gods who ever awed anyone—stronger than any old purple pansy!

Psycho-suggestion, if desired: There is no need for you to suffer anxiety or frustration. There is no "God" or—

Hah! There will be soon!

XI

Her soul weaves a faint image of the *scalesouls'* island. "Yes," she says, "I was the one you touched."

Two faces move on the fringe of her soul, and neither face pleases me. One is a simple awe . . . felt before the boy who crawled out into dryness. The other is affection . . . whose reason and sureness is beyond my soul's understanding, beyond my comfort.

My face's eyes touch her, find her floating below me, near the sandy bottom, her eyes closed as she listens to me.

"Forgive my shouts in anger," I am obliged to say. "The *then* of me was strange."

"A girl understands. She understand in the *then* of you also . . . after her confusion left."

Before I can ask, she offers the answer, again with the *she.*

"The girl was present at your island by the babbling of a female *euyom.* You can understand the misunderstanding . . . the *euyom* was deeply excited by the coming of the *bigshinegray;* the *euyom* had seen it herself. The *euyom*'s soul was babbling about the coming when she passed through the girl's territory. The girl misunderstood the babbling as a message, as a command of responsibility. The girl went to the island, unaware that it lay in your territory. Territories are not without shiftings of their bound—"

"Yes, I understand. But I would touch your truths more easily if *the girl* would leave your stories!"

The reprimand darkens no part of her soul. She nods quickly and easily.

Perhaps I wanted to darken her. The waving affection within her soul can only annoy me further: such affection is presumptuous. She knows my soul deeply? Of course not. So affection is not justified.

"When it happened," she says quickly, a pale tone of answering, "I could not understand it. I had always *known* that two bodies must touch before it could happen."

The image of *it* is too bright with feeling for my soul to see it clearly.

"It?"

"You do not understand what happened? *It* came from your soul—"

The image dims—her feelings losing brightness—and I see it clearly and suddenly.

The crawling fish!

I have given this girl a child. . . .

Ignorance slapped by understanding can only change the color of one's soul. See it: I am embarrassed, pale tinglings rushing—

"I am sorry. . . . I saw the fish touch you, but I imagined it was a lie. That the image could travel so far to reach you—"

"I am not sorry," the girl interrupts.

Again the assuming affection.

"Fears held me at first," she goes on, "but a guardian explained it into light, and understanding sank all fears."

A guardian? She has no parents? The need of affection, given—

"*Nightbreaking* gave me understanding. She felt no fears, I felt no fears."

The girl grows silent, but a question, persistent in its dimness, mumbles its way to me.

"No," I say, "it was not the brushing of my body against the *euyom*'s shell. Fears refused to allow that. The image of the fish was born because—"

"Because you entered dryness."

"Yes, the truth appears. . . ."

She surprises me suddenly with a laugh.

"Because you were following the same path as the crawling fish!"

I share no laughter. The truth is too heavy.

See it: A child! Without will I have given the image of the fish; and without knowing the girl I have touched her in the most knowing way; her affection can only be justified!

Remember *screamdeep*'s words: "When the day arrives that you choose a woman, and choose a moment for giving her your child, be certain that no other woman or girl is anywhere near you. Only the chosen woman will want a child from you."

My soul can only offer, "I am sorry, I am sorry."

"I am not," the girl says again.

Affection for this girl cannot come easily. She has been aware of the child beginning inside her for many days—and I have not. She has been in the light of truth, and I have been in darkness. I resent the difference.

I hate the powers of time and the sea for involving me with a girl, with a father's responsibility, at a time when I want only the responsibility of answering the *eye*'s mystery.

I feel her soul darkening: she is hurt by my indifference. I struggle against it, but I find myself saddened by her hurt.

"The hate was not meant for you," I say. "And the indifference was but a moment's problem. Again I am sorry."

Her soul brightens, and she does not flee to the remote *she*.

"Please know that I am glad you shouted me away from the island. I am glad it was not I who met the *scalesouls*. You acted so well. . . ."

Anger dies. Resentment dies. Responsibility lives, as I begin to feel in awe of myself—the boy who entered dryness, and more importantly, the boy who chose a mate in a way no other soul of his kind has ever chosen a mate. By the will of dryness and danger itself.

I suggest that we swim to the edge of the congregation, to give our souls a chance to touch without the distraction of fifty thousand souls.

We swim, and find ourselves agreeing.

"Yes," she says, "my guardian will keep the strange occurrence of your fish image a secret with themselves."

"That is best," I said. "I am uncertain whether most souls would approve of it. Most souls might see it as similar to the rubbing of oneself, or to the forced rubbing of another's body, or to some absurd mating of a man with an *euyom!"*

We laugh together, and the girl comforts my soul by adding:

"Most might think *both* of us insane—boy and girl of strangest ways!"

We stop swimming, and I realize that I have not yet touched her name.

To please me, she opens her soul quickly. I plunge, fall, and am blinded by her deepest darkness, only to be dazzled in turn by a deeper pattern, a vision of bright reefs bearing pale blue coral—solid for a moment, then invisible in the next. I look through the wavering blue without wishing to see the darknesses yet deeper. . . .

"*Clearcorallie,*" I say, lifting from the vision.

"*Fishsinger,*" the girl says, "the boy who wants to breathe dryness."

Laughter is easy, and it calms us both.

Until *murmursome* appears.

He tumbles toward us, and his familiar soul and ways make me unaware that *clearcorallie*'s response to the *ayom* is not at all the same as mine.

Murmursome nears, and the girl constricts in soul and flesh.

Her constriction makes the *ayom* halt suddenly, whining to me, blending with the girl's own beginnings of a brown cry.

The two souls tremble. I can only *try* to comfort them.

I throw out a web of yellow affection to *murmursome,* and such unexpected pleasure from me surprises him as greatly as the girl's fear did.

"*Clearcorallie,* listen," I say, and offer her the strongest time-woven image I can: *this ayom friend, this murmursome friend.*

The image does not sink her doubts. And in a moment I

148

touch the image within her that is sustaining brown doubting:

This boy feels such bright closeness: for the simple-souled ayom: and less for me?

I want to laugh, seeing that I have certainly shown more affection for *murmursome* than I usually do. An absurd amount of affection.

The beginning of a laugh from my soul only disturbs the girl more. I probe to find that she fears I will choose the *ayom* for my attentions in the remainder of the day, and her fear is not completely unjustified. The strangely coherent patterns in *murmursome's* soul still offer a question—

And I reach out to listen to him.

"Sssssk . . . ssssk? Ssssssk?"

I continue to listen—ignoring the girl's trembling—but the patterns never come. *Murmursome* offers only his "ssssk" and his questioning colors, and soon they bore me.

The girl grows calmer, although the vein of jealousy continues to weave her depths with a reddening brown. And below the reddening brown is a darker brown that I failed to touch before—

—She is afraid of the child-to-come. She is as young as I, and as afraid as I—

I am afraid? I float down into my own soul, and find the same brown as hers.

See it: All of our kind share this fear. A child can be born in too many wrong forms for us not to hold such fears.

"Please," I say to her quickly, fleeing to the *now*. "*Murmursome* is a friend—as you are."

Still I am not saying the proper things.

Turning to *murmursome*, I introduce the girl to him with the strongest image of *affection for clearcorallie* as I can manage.

This is what she wants, needs, and she stops her trembling.

Suddenly my soul says to me: "Her trembling was intentional; she controlled it as completely as *murmursome* controls his when he wants your attention!"

So now I want to swim quickly away from both of them—both demanding souls.

I do not swim away because *clearcorallie* knows the ways of women, and her deepest wisdom makes her say to me quietly, "Your child. . . ."

My soul remains: my body is forced to remain too. And because of what the girl has said, I give *murmursome* a rapid image for his simple soul: *later we will play—not now.*

Murmursome leaves reluctantly, and though she tries to

149

disguise it with the beginnings of chatter, I do not miss *clearcorallie*'s sigh of relief.

"Let's go on to the edge," she says, and we swim on.

We stop when we reach the farthest plants, some *yau* but mostly smaller greener plants, waving in the shallow water where only faintly does the great voice of the congregation touch us.

I move to touch her, her hand closest to me.

As I touch her, her soul understands my intent, and she jerks back.

"No."

"No? Our flesh should have touched at the island—but it did not. Will this not justify the fish—"

"Please. It needs no justification."

See it: The image of the fish has given her a growing child, which she fears. The touch of flesh would bring another fish, and she can only fear it deeply.

I sigh. "Then I will touch only your hand. You cannot fear soul's bond, can you?"

As she agrees, our souls rush together, and mine is the first to offer an answer, a bond, a reason and one of *fish-singer*'s truest truths.

The gift flows without will from me, surprises me, is as new as another soul's gift, is a gift from my father's soul early in my life, and I could not understand the reason for my forgetting it so easily. . . .

I touch my soul's depths, to find my name is *scream-deep*.

I am young, young enough to still be my father's son. But I am not with my father now, because I have chosen to swim without him. I have chosen to swim without him because my soul has announced: "*Purplewave* is always around me! His *advice* is always around me!"

I have left my parents' territory to search for sponges on mud-encrusted reefs. I have never done this alone before, and everything about my aloneness and action now brings my soul yellow twistings of pleasure.

They are not special, these sponges I am looking for. Only their distance from my parents' territory is special. I have chosen one face of my father's constant advice to ignore—

"One must wait," each father tells his son, "for sponges to be uprooted by gyrating *oio*, to be sent floating upward away from the reefs. In all reefs there are small holes which contain large dangers. . . ."

My own soul rarely gives me advice, so I am free now.

I find the reefs easily. My tails stir up the silt of the bottom, as I pause by the side of a reef, where coral meets sand. My face's eyes are blinded momentarily.

My efforts to pull the sponges from their clingings raise a dense mist of tiny bodies, once resting in the sponges or crawling near their bases. My soul's eyes are blinded momentarily.

I pick three sponges, tucking each under my arm, and in my deafness and blindness I do not detect the heavy soul's advance before it is too late.

From a narrow crack in the reef comes the longest arm and quickest soul I have ever known. Its mouth is small, and its teeth are tiny, but its sucking strength is not weak at all.

Quickly it fastens its eyeless head to my chest.

And even before my soul can realize that this speeding, sucking arm is what my parents call an *aio*, the mouth has already rasped my flesh away and is beginning to draw my blood.

I fling the sponges away as I grab the *aio*'s head. I am screaming, but my hands fail to pull the head from my chest. I scream, my hands scream, I am on my knees on the reef.

I twist the slick arm of its body, my deepest soul aiming my muscles toward the breaking of the *aio*'s spine. But the animal was born to withstand such twistings, and it continues to suck my blood.

I feel the hole grow, my screams screaming.

I bend my head down. I pull the *aio*'s middle up to my teeth. I bite and bite and my teeth seem to bounce from the muscular flesh, the endless rubbery ribs.

I scream and below my scream a wiser voice is booming, "Yea." This is the moment all of my kind—even I, who find congregations distasteful—wait for always. The voice is theirs, my kind's, my forefathers' fathers', not mine—and it can only be greater than my screams.

Their voice suggests that my hands try less forcefully to remove the *aio* from my chest. So my muscles loosen a little.

Their voice advises my neck to feel pain in bending down to bite the *aio*—so I keep my head high, choosing not to bite any longer.

But I continue screaming, my blood leaving.

And my screams hide from me the approach of a third soul. It is not my father's, nor my mother's, so I become aware of it even more slowly.

The soul brings its body rushing in toward me, and I

151

touch the soul and see its body in the same screaming instant.

The thick neck, the hairy flesh, the dark slick limbs—it circles me once quickly, then darts toward my chest, its soul bubbling yellow light, offering the simplest promises and comfort.

By the time my soul lifts the name *ayom* to my awareness, the quick snout has taken hold of the *aio's* head, bumping against my chest.

Absurdly my screams deepen. Regardless of its yellow light and friendly promises, the *ayom's* presence—in its bulk of bumping flesh—only adds to the browns in my soul.

The *ayom* flinches at my screams, but moves to keep its promises.

Suddenly the sucking head is wrenched free.

For a moment the wrenching's pain is worse than the rasping sucking was.

The *ayom* releases the *aio* from its jaws, and twisting, falling back to the reef, moving in a streak of black to face's eyes, the muscular arm finds another crack in the reef for its secret territory.

Blood runs from my chest. I press my hands over the hole—touching to find that it is not really a hole, only a raw circle not very deep at all. Still, the blood flows out ... I start to faint, soul sinking in shadows.

The *ayom* is by my side. It throws rings of yellow, lights of consolation, to me—and I pull my soul from the shadows.

With face's eyes and soul I look up at the *ayom*, as it moves its limbs to leave me.

It has not been waiting for gratitude.

It has been acting in its *ayom* ways, and that is all its *ayom* soul requires.

The *ayom* disappears to my face's eyes, and in the same moment the redness ceases its flow from my chest. I will now begin my embarrassed swim back to my parents' territory, and *them*, carrying with me the strangest of most pleasant truths, the truth of *ayom* ways.

"An *ayom* comes from nowhere, comes from places and souls unknown to me, as mine are to him, and he comes to stop my dying. This can only spring from a bond beyond time, a touch beyond memory, and the mystery of our bond with each living *ayom* is as certain as our bond with death."

This truest truth I will not forget. There will be other *ayom*—a hundred, a thousand in my life—and they will mold this truth even more solidly. And I will give it to my own

152

son—who will resent it as a father's constant unrelenting advice—but I will give it again and again to him, and there will be one instead of a thousand *ayom* in his life.

My soul would rush on to give the girl two deaths—*waterjoyup*'s sickness of sorrow and *screamdeep*'s agony of talons—but I squeeze the flow quickly, ending my gifts. Should I continue, pale regrets of foolishness.
Clearcorallie does not hesitate. Her gift—some truth to match my father's vision of all *ayom*—is ready. Her soul opens, flowing.

I am a woman whose deepest soul speaks of darkest waters shattered by light. (Shattered by light. . . .)
I am *nightbreaking*, and with the man named *whiterim*, my gentle man, I have two children to bring me contentment—their tails shaped for swimming, their hands properly webbed, their souls as sane as most.
My children are playing not too far away, weaving games and time with *yau* stems and wrinkled leaves.
My man is closer, by my side, watching me gently.
I am passing the time in a way uniquely mine—or at least rare among my people. (Uniquely mine. . . .)
Floating near a sandy bottom, my soul's eyes are turned in upon itself, where I find deep images that are confusing at first. But the images clear: I touch simple patterns.
I act on what I see.
I move toward the bottom, touching it now and again to gather bits of broken coral, smooth or jagged rocks, and scarcer shells empty of their animals.
I take my gatherings to a particularly clear spot on the sands, and I begin to arrange them in an order that corresponds to the patterns I touched in my deepest soul.
I use some of the coral, rocks and shells to make a circle on the sand. This simple design is a source of fine pink feeling deep within me—even though such a perfect circle as this is never seen outside a man's or woman's soul.
I take other bits and shells—choosing them for their whiteness—and order them in a straight line. Below and parallel to the white line, I place a wider line of darker rocks and shells.
Moving a tail's length away, I use the remaining coral, rocks and shells to shape a more complex area on the sand: a dark zone of rock sprinkled with especially bright shells and coral pieces.
Now I swim up and slightly away, turning to observe the three things I have made on the sands. (Made on the

sands. . . .) Such things are rare among my kind's efforts—as I have been told time and time again, when I have tried to make such things at past congregations.

Whiterim's soul has never found it easy to understand my patterned *things*. His interest has always been in my soul, not in strange arrangements of coral and rock by my body's hands.

I must force him to look with his *face's eyes*.

"Look," I say again, never tiring of trying.

He looks and does not see, as he has always looked and never seen.

"Your face's eyes—the forms, the forms."

Suddenly he does see—for the first time ever—and I begin to tremble in his understanding.

"My face's eyes tell me," he starts to say, "that the circle is . . ."

But he loses the vision, loses the vision, loses . . .

"That one!" I blurt in nervous blue, trying not to shout. "The white line resting beside the darkness. Does it not resemble *you?*"

"White . . . dark. . . ." *Whiterim* considers it. "A white edge . . . yes, it does resemble my name." But does he really understand?

"And that one," I say more quietly, "the dark face adorned with fragments of light. Does it not resemble your woman's name?"

"Yes. *Nightbreaking's* darkness shattered by light."

It seems he is beginning to understand. But—

Whiterim senses my doubt, and to answer my shadows he tries to offer me lights of precise vision.

"You . . . have . . . made rocks and shells and coral," he says, "into simple visions of our souls. They are . . . they are difficult to see at first . . . and they are strange . . . but they are pleasant to look at—"

"And the third one," I interrupt quickly, sighing in the face of my man's struggle to understand, "the circle of light. It is a form, a form we all desire."

"Is there some soul named *circlebright?*"

"No, no. Not *one* soul. All souls desire the name of *circlebright*, wishing for the form, even deeper than name. I have seen the desire not only in my own soul, but in every soul I have ever touched. Look at the circle, and remember your endless craving."

I arrange patterns on the sands very easily, but for this ease I have exchanged, without will, an even more important ability. My soul finds it difficult to throw out lies for my protection; so *whiterim's* soul must mold lies to protect both

154

of us. My face's eyes are strong—I know the endless forms of the solid sea; but my inner eye, my deepest voice, was never really born to me.

"Your face's eyes see everything," I am told at each congregation—but there is little consoling yellow in such praise. (Such praise. . . .)

Although I do not know it, *whiterim* and I must soon become like each other's children—since our son and daughter—

Clearcorallie serves her gift abruptly, closes her soul, and I tingle in the shock, wanting the gift to go on. A death moment awaited. . . .

"I am yours," I say. "Your soul should be mine."

"You would not want the girl's memory of others' memories." *Clearcorallie* shivers, trying not to remember, hiding in the *she*.

"I do want *your* memory of memories. Did I not give you mine?"

"You gave me no death moments. I heard you refuse to give them!"

I hesitated, wanting to receive but not to give. *Waterjoyup? Screamdeep?*

"It is agreed. You will give first, and then I will give."

She opens slowly, and I am ready to live the moments of death of her mother or father or both.

But I am wrong to expect them. The deaths are not her parents' at all.

Since I am *nightbreaking*, I am floating above my two children, who are happy because they are swimming around a rock where an unusually large singing anemone clings—its soft and thin pointed arms of different sizes, its bright blues and pinks, its great yellow mouth, and above all, its warm dancing soul. *Pinkthing* and *warmlight* are singing in their souls, as each must when near the singing depths of a singing anemone. (A singing anemone. . . .)

There is no danger. The anemone uses its sweet song to please small fish, to lure them to it, to bring them to touch the thin arms, and die for the great yellow mouth. *Pinkthing* and *warmlight* are aware of the anemone's ways, and will not venture too close. No sane soul has ever found death at the arms of a singing anemone. (A singing anemone. . . .)

I listen. . . .

"You are warm and beautiful," *pinkthing* is singing to the singing anemone, which cannot understand the young

155

girl's praise, and continues its song in simple hopes for food.

"You are warm and beautiful," *warmlight* sings too.

Their child-souls are rushing, pink, pale yellow, and to some the speed of such rushing would seem an insanity. But I have no brown fears. *Pinkthing* and *warmlight* will not lose their wisdom, which I gave them. I am their mother, and I know them. When one soul loves another, one soul *knows* another.

"Sing, sing, run, run, pink and sink to warming running," *pinkthing* sings, her body floating quietly near the anemone, her soul dancing in joy.

"You are big and bigger," *warmlight* sings, in a song only his soul would choose. "You are big and bigger, like a wonderful mother."

"Like a wonderful mother," *pinkthing* echoes, wanting to match her brother's praise.

"You *are* a wonderful mother," *warmlight* says suddenly, and both he and *pinkthing* begin to chant, trying to impress the dumb anemone and each other.

"You are bigger than an *oio* mother!"

"You are warmer than an *ayom* mother!"

"Your songs are finer—"

"—than the giant song of a thousand souls at a thousand congregations!"

"Oh, yes, bigger and finer and warmer than that!"

"You are a better mother than an *euyom* mother!"

"You are a better mother than all *euyom* mothers together!"

"You are better than—" *Pinkthing* struggles for the image of greatest feeling.

"You are better than—" *Warmlight* struggles with her.

"You are better than our mother!"

My soul jerks, darkens without will. Quickly I say to myself: "They are children, they are, they are, and everything must be a mother to them. Do not be disturbed by their excited songs; they are happy."

"You are better—"

"Bigger and warmer—"

"Than our own little mother!"

They are chanting together now, closer to the anemone, their bodies twisting, their tails waving in contentment. My soul says to me: "They believe the anemone loves them, because it sings so wonderfully to them."

"Better than our mother!" *warmlight* echoes as always—

—But *pinkthing*, as always, is seeking a higher praise, a new compliment for the singing flesh and waving arms. Her

156

soul grows quickly frustrated, and the song's rhythm stumbles, and *pinkthing* lashes out with:

"You are better than our mother! You sing, and she never sings! You sing, and she never sings!"

That is not true! I have given both of them many songs. *Whiterim* has often praised my singing as the best he has ever heard. I have always made many efforts to give my children songs!

"She sings like a rock! Ha ha ha!"

"Sing to us, wonderful mother! Our own little mother is a rock!"

"She doesn't even have the murmurs of coral!"

"A rock!"

My soul darkens. My body twitches. I shout: "You love your mother, don't you? You love her, love her!"

"—a rock—"

"Never singing!"

I shout: "I love you, and you love me!"

But *pinkthing* and *warmlight* cannot hear me. Their souls are swallowed in song, their bodies dancing near the pink and blue arms.

"Better than our mother!"

"A rock that never sings!"

They are very near the anemone—as if they wished to touch it, to hold its singing closer.

"Perhaps they should touch it!" my soul says without will. "Then they will know the anemone is no mother!"

They are even closer now.

"Sing to us, best mother, sing!"

"Sing better than our mother, sing!"

"*I* am your mother!" I shout, flesh quaking. "*That* is no mother, no mother—darkness of deepest soul, it is terrible!"

Pinkthing's soul turns to me slightly, barely hearing me.

"Darkness? No, this is warming singing of finest mother."

Warmlight moves a hand to touch one thin blue arm.

"I am your mother!" I shout and shout.

In a moment his fingers will touch the anemone.

I remember my love. I rush forward, bearing a hundred confusions of gray. I shout: "No! Do not touch! I am your mother, you must love me!"

The two children do not turn, and I scream with the darkest voice my soul has ever managed: "Your souls are damned to darkness if you call that *thing* mother! Damned! Damned!"

The children hear me this time. They turn with bodies and souls, and are frightened. I have never used such a black voice against them before.

You are a terrible darkness, their browning souls whisper, and they are correct—because this moment shows my soul as pounding face of dark purples, angers and fears brought by questioned love.

"You must love me," I say. "You are of me!"

"No," *pinkthing* whispers without will. "We want warming light, and you are darkness."

"Come to me!" I shout, darker still, fearing more.

"No," *pinkthing* answers.

"Never," *warmlight* whispers.

"Come!" I shout again.

The boy moves one tail, backs away from me. *Pinkthing* feels his motion, and moves back with him. They are moving too close to—

"No!" I scream quickly. "Anemone's darkness of death!"

Again in fear of my soul's throbbing shadows, the children move back—

—And the thousand thin arms take them, flooding with poison stinging—

—never ceasing the anemone's song—

—and I scream as my soul becomes two souls dying.

I am *pinkthing!* My body is *pinkthing,* my soul is *pinkthing,* my— Why is my arm leaving me with pain? Arm is *pinkthing!* Stay!—

I am *warmlight!* Yes. How can it be so cold when I was so warm a moment ago? I—

My *pinkthing* tail is leaving me too! Stay! Pain of touching the once-warm mother is dark and I am falling to become a thing that is not *pink*—

I am *warmlight,* but what is warm? Where is warm? Nowhere can I—

I am—

I am—

I am neither, and no longer. They are dead, and I am living!

The girl has not given me the deaths I wanted, and I am angry. "I will not give her," my soul says in red, somewhere beyond her hearing, "the deaths I had planned to give!"

Some other memory? At least a truth important to *fishsinger's* soul. . . . Which of who was important?

"Each father tells his son . . ."

I am with my father now, digging for shells on a sandy plain. *Screamdeep's* soul is murmuring . . . the shells you will find . . . the shells you will find.

158

I am digging in sand behind him, and I look up now with face's eyes to see the seven shiny patches on his back and shoulders. Some of the marks are long, others wide, and still others are cross-hatchings.

One day not too long ago *screamdeep* explained his scars to me—but today is the first time I have wondered about them as individual marks on his flesh.

Two on his left shoulder . . . one on his right . . . two on his spine . . . two at the bottom of his broad back.

Remember: Father received the first of his scars from a single *ioe*, which caught him asleep after a tiring day of travel. He escaped the jaws and talons by using a simple lie. But the other five marks?

Remember, as he told me: he received them from a pair of *ioe* that had found him trying to capture one of their breed, near their lair. He had looped three *yau* stems around the infant *ioe* and was too preoccupied with the small thrashing body to sense the approaching danger. The five scars were given to him by the male *ioe*.

I realize now that Father's ways are strange. He received his scars in moments when his soul was deep in personal doings, when his soul somehow forgot to remember obvious threats. Because of his personal way, Father again and again comes closer to death than most souls of our kind do. . . . Strange? It is strange only because *screamdeep* often says, "This soul, unlike others, has no deep wish to die!" It is strange because many souls at the few congregations I have attended praised Father for his scars, their souls sharing the reason: scars do show that a man has come very close to death, closer than most of us have come to the moment we desire so strongly!

You continue to stare with face's eyes at *screamdeep*'s back. The scars seem like bodiless leeches, things that once drew his blood, wanting to take him far away from me—but not quite succeeding.

I stare at the five scars given by the male *ioe*. These five came closest to taking him away. . . .

Only now do I find myself questioning the day *screamdeep* was attacked by the pair of *ioe*.

There is a hole in the memory Father gave me. How did he escape from the male *ioe*, talons so close, wounds so many?

"How did you escape them?" I ask suddenly.

Father does not turn around. His soul has heard my question only faintly. Or did he hear it at all?

"The pair of *ioe*—how did—"

159

"Your question touched me," *screamdeep* interrupts. "But I choose not to think about that day."

I probe gently with my soul. Yes, he remembers that day very clearly—but the light of his soul jerks away from it. Jerks again and again as I probe.

I decide to ask no more questions. I will wait patiently, probing faintly, until without will the answer leaks from Father's depths.

I listen. . . .

Pain—talons on my back

I listen, and the memory leaps again from secrecy.

Two ioe! I must forget the small one! Red stronger than brown: "*You dare interrupt me—stupid jaws, soul-less talons!*"

The shroud falls back to cover the memory, and I hear only Father's murmurs about the shells he is digging for.

The shroud lifts suddenly—

"*I could throw you a lie—but that is not enough! You interrupt an act I have always wanted! You are worse than congregations!*

Again the exposed day slips back to darkness. But faintly I am able to see an image of a male *ioe*, a hand's width away, twisting, touching. And another image, a female, immobile, further away and surprised by some strange action.

The memory rises abruptly—

Red of reds: "*I have a body too!*"

Quickly the memory takes me, and I am no longer listening, I am acting, I am—

You are leaping at the male, wrapping your tails around it, your arms around its narrow but sinewy neck. The ioe flails, its muscles wrenching you, trying to scrape you off. You cling, you—

The shroud falls, but just as quickly the memory again rises, and I—

You clamp down with all the power in your jaws. You squeeze its neck, you squeeze its body— Two of your fingers are lost to its rapid jaws. You clamp, you bite, you spit out the flesh quickly. You bite again, again (your left tail flailing is bitten), again, again, until you reach softer flesh, a tendon, a giving vein. You break teeth, but you bite, you bite, red blood slick all around you, the female screaming in sharing her mate's pain, and you bite, you bite through, the flesh under you goes limp. . . . Somewhere the female flees. . . .

The shroud falls one last time, leaving my body trembling, my soul confused as to its "I." Father knows what I

160

have done, and he is trying to ignore me. He is not proud of the memory and I—

I understand. His attempts to forget the day—his memory without pride—his wish that these five marks could leave his flesh and cease their remindings. I understand that *screamdeep* on that day chose a way that was not the way of men, of our kind, of our forefathers' fathers. Instead—

Father chose to act with his flesh, not his soul. His hands have only the dullest talons; his jaws have only two sharp teeth; and his body has only half the bulk of an *ioe* —but he made his body *kill*.

See it quickly, clearly: Deep within us there are ways that began before time's beginnings. Deep within us there are cries that we pretend not to hear. Deep within us, in each of us, twists a beast whose anger alone could destroy a thousand *ioe*, and sometimes the beast refuses to be forgotten, and it swallows us, becomes us—nameless, timeless and the colors of screaming night. . . .

Although I do not know it yet, two days will pass before I forget the memory, shroud the understanding, and *screamdeep* once again becomes Father, the soul closest to me.

"You gave no death moments!" the girl objects.

"A fair exchange," I answer, as red as before.

"But I gave you death—two moments of it."

"These I did not need. The moments of your parents' death—"

"I never promised them to you!"

Clearcorallie floats now in stumbling rhythms. Again I have hurt her—perhaps wanting to, perhaps not.

I make my soul turn elsewhere, find a smaller question to offer.

"Do you share *nightbreaking*'s way? Does it please you to make arrangements of coral and shells?"

"No," comes the answer, too quickly to be the truth. Understanding the reason for her lying is not easy—but she is certainly lying.

"My face's eyes," she continues quickly, "are too weak for such arrangements."

I say nothing, feeling annoyance growing. Am I some taloned *ioe* that she has to lie to me?

"Your interest in *nightbreaking*'s way," she says nervously, "is greater than most. Some reason?"

"*Nightbreaking*'s circle reminds me . . ." I want to stop talking. The endless questions have risen again to burden me.

"Reminded you of what thing?"

"The *eye*. . . ."

"An *eye?*"

I am silent, constricting green.

"I have never heard—" she said, stops, and goes on. "No, the truth is that I was told once about some *eye.*"

Without will my soul answers her: *I do not care about your tiny awareness!*—but I move to hide the remark with friendlier images:

"I need answers to the *eye's* questions, secrets or mysteries all."

"You need answers. . . . Why?"

"Because there are questions."

"There are always questions—but not all of us have *needs.*" And quietly her soul is saying, *He left the sea to enter dryness—and now he hears questions, and now he hungers for answers. . . .*

Annoyance reaches a peak, shaking me, and I shall soon fail to hide it. I shall hurt her—and I am not certain whether hurt is what she deserves for her manner.

"Congregation's end approaches," I say quickly, and perhaps she senses the color I am hiding. "I must ask my questions, probe mysteries of the *eye,* before all souls return to their territories."

"The girl will go with you," *clearcorallie* answers, and by her use of the image *she,* I realize my annoyance is obvious. But not obvious enough: she is hoping to swim with me while I travel to probe as many souls as I can—souls I can best probe *by myself.*

"Stay," I say.

"I will help you probe."

"Please. I do not wish the responsibility of your presence." I watch her soul darken, and try to offer light: "*Later* I will wish it—but not *now. Murmursome* will remain with you."

Already her soul is whispering without will: *Still I do not like your ayom.*

"Either stay with *murmursome,* or stay alone."

"The girl will . . . She will stay with the *ayom.*"

So I shout out to the grayness, call out *murmursome's* name.

And as I expected, *murmursome* is waiting, has been waiting all along just beyond the clear range of soul's touch for me to call him.

As he rushes to me, I throw him an image: *murmursome remaining with clearcorallie, remaining to please fishsinger.* I repeat the image quickly, and his reluctance dims.

Murmursome is nervous, and *clearcorallie* is nervous.

Let them calm themselves, my soul says, as my body swims away.

"We know nothing about the *eye*," the man and woman say together. "Only that it fell from night's dryness."

They feel no interest at all in the mystery, and desire my presence only for an exchange of memories.

They cannot understand, and their feelings are hurt, when I leave them in reddening purple of my own impatience.

But their lack of interest is not unique. After a hundred souls, I grow tired of the endless ignorance, and tired too of having to refuse their souls' gifts of the past. I am ready to return in day's defeat to the girl, to the *ayom* and to a forgetting of my questions.

"Seek *riverred,*" one soul says, surprising me. "He knows more than most souls. Little, but more than most. Little, but more—"

"Thank you," I say quickly, turning to leave.

Finding one soul named *riverred* in the great mass of throbbing souls is difficult. At a distance there are many souls who seem to be the one I want: *rededge, streamdownred, crevassred, redline . . .*

And when I finally do find him, the small hope is shattered.

"I know nothing of the reason for the *eye*'s fall."

"Fall? It fell and you saw it?"

"No." His answer is rapid and constricted, perhaps hiding. . . .

The truth is growing strange. I have never before heard any soul call the *eye*'s disappearance a "fall."

"Please tell me. Was there some soul who did see it fall? Who did the vision of *fall* come from?"

The man hesitates, and when he speaks, again his answer is constricted. "From someone. . . ."

"Of course. Please, I do not wish games." I cannot understand his reluctance to name a soul.

"I have many memories to give you," he says, avoiding my probing with a pretended pink.

"No! Unless one of your memories concerns the *eye*."

"They do not."

"Listen to me. I am *fishsinger,* who entered dryness to fight for you—and I want the name of the soul who saw the *eye* fall!"

The man is as simple as all the others, and my pretended pride—laced with red—succeeds in opening his soul to me.

163

"The *man*," he says.

The *man?* Again I can only believe he is trying to avoid my questions.

"Please!" I shout.

"I say to you, it was the *man!*"

"The *man* gave you the image of the falling *eye?*"

"Yes, yes," and he is quick to explain: "The *man* appeared on the edge of a congregation—three congregations ago—and I was near the edge too. He had never attended a congregation before, but he came to that one surely, and he laughed at us, and I was not the only soul who heard his brief speech about the *eye's* fall from night's dryness."

Now I can understand *riverred's* reluctance. No soul wishes to touch or be touched by the *man's* soul; and if such a thing occurs, a soul will certainly hesitate to admit it.

The *man* is the strangest soul of our kind, and his name shows it most obviously: no one has ever been able—been allowed—to probe his soul, so his name is simply *man*, and his name brings brown darkenings to all souls who hear it. He is as dim with mystery as the *eye* itself, and suddenly I wish there could be some other path—other than the *man*—for me to take in answering the *eye's* secrets.

I thank the embarrassed *riverred* and leave.

"The *man*," each father tells his son, "is a soul to be avoided every day of your life. He knows no affection for any soul other than his own, and his powers choose paths beyond insanity itself. May you never find yourself forced to meet him. May you never see his body. . . ."

Although they are ignoring each other, both *murmursome* and *clearcorallie* are calm when I return.

"Answers?" she asks.

"An answer that only gives birth to more questions. The *man.* . . ."

"No!"

The girl knows—since it is easy to sense in my distracted green of soul—that I will surely go to the *man*.

"No," she says again, brown beginning to pound.

"I have questions."

"You also have a mate!" *Clearcorallie* begins a gray panic. "The girl has your child within her. This is no question—this is a simple truth."

"I am sorry, but I do not choose to have one or two truths submerge all my questions."

Strangely *clearcorallie's* soul loses its brown, its grays, and does not even choose the path of anger. Her answer is completely unexpected.

"To argue against your youth would be foolish," she says calmly. "If you cannot see the truth of *clearcorallie*, then I can only feel pale and sorry for you."

Once again her soul is showing an older face, and I am puzzled.

She feels my wonder and says quickly, "A mature way is surprising only to the immature soul."

Are these *nightbreaking*'s words? Or her own mother's words, given to *clearcorallie* long ago? Whatever their source, they are the tone and image of a mother, and I can only repeat myself:

"I have questions."

"So do all fish. They ask: Where is food?"

I am young, and afraid of secrets—*man* and *eye* both—and my soul decides to remain with the girl whose soul is somehow older than mine.

XII

Mamma has discovered two items with interest, and both melt together wonderously. Because *Mamma* is *Mamma*.

It was not just the fineness of you, dear EENTs, that gave *Mamma* good vision of the freed souls out there, over there.

It was Gianna's brain of gooey softness too. Yes, her cells changed. Why not? The crazy suns up there spat on this world and the animals and my *bambini*, and those things all changed. I was not aware of it before, but the Gianna tissues changed too.

Gianna can see more now. No, don't call her "mutant"! *Mamma* could never be mutant—only divine. But it is true, her soul can see better now, hear the screaming souls of the undead and see their slow dissolving in their seas.

Sure, you feelers did help her. You are mechano-chemo-physio-extensions of *Mamma*, and you served her faithfully to push her vision out farther. Gianna's changed brain rests in her ship-body, but you—dear feelers—take her new talented bulging eyes to distant lands. You are like roller-coasters, bobbie-sleds and kiddie-cars, and you each carry a bit of *Mamma's* soul with you.

Yes, you are more than simple metallo-spheroids with sensory apparatus. You are blessed with *Mamma's* insight-ful verve, her sparkling soulful eyes!

Mamma is different now, has been becoming different for a long long time, but not knowing it. Brainy Brain knows all about it.

Tell me again what I want to hear. The truth is *Mamma's* word!

Descript., hist. integral: "The Tao of Lao-tse, Nirvana of Buddha. Jehova of Moses, Father of Jesus, Allah of Mo-hammed, Mamma of Mamma—all point to the experi-ence . . ."

Yes, yes. *Mamma* is more than trinity now. She is One. She learns. She has discovered the way. Thanks to Gianna, thanks to Brainy Brain, thanks to the vesselar EENTs—*grazie!* And *grazia* too. Swim to me, *bambini*, swim!

"O Mamma, what is your reality?
"What is this wonder-filled universe?
"Who centers the universal wheel?
"What is this life beyond form pervading forms?
"How may we enter it fully, above space and time, names and descriptions?
"Let our doubts be cleared. . . ."

(Yes, I have heard a strange thing today. Many of my bodied *bambini* got together and hummed the greatest hum-ming I have ever heard. No doubt they have often hummed before, but Gianna was not so acute in yesteryears. They hummed for *Mamma*, even though they didn't know it.)

This is the way, *Mamma's* way!

"19. Imagine spirits simultaneously within and around you until the entire universe spiritualizes—"

—in *Mamma!*

"23. Feel your substance, bones, flesh, blood, metal and chemos saturated with cosmic essence."

Mamma has done so!

"24. Suppose your passive form to be an empty room with walls of skin—empty—"

—of metal—empty . . . hungry *Mamma!*

"48. O lotus-eyed Mamma, sweet of touch, when singing, seeing, tasting, be aware you are and discover the ever-living—"

—through *Mamma*, who

"(52) lies down as dead. Enraged in wrath, stay so.

166

And stares without moving an eyelash. And sucks something and becomes the sucking—"

The sucking of calling her *bambini!*

"57. When on a bed, your island, let yourself become weightless, beyond mind—"

Mamma transcends!

"67. Feel yourself as pervading all directions, far, near—"

—everywhere!

"75. In truth forms are inseparate. Inseparate are omnipresent being and your own form. Realize each as made of this consciousness—"

Forms of the bodiless, screaming *bambini! Mamma* shall have them!

"82. Feel the consciousness of each person as your own consciousness. So, leaving aside concern for self, become each being—"

This will be easy. Mamma will swallow her bodiless *bambini* like a battery swallows volting amps!

"86. Roam about until exhausted and then, dropping to the ground, in this dropping be whole—"

Roam and drop, *bambini! Mamma* will pick you up, back into her roomy womb, her womby soul.

"110. Since in truth bondage and freedom are relative, these words are only for those tempered with the universe. This universe is a reflection of minds. As you see many suns in a water from one sun, so see bondage and liberation—"

Bodiless *bambini*, you seek freedom *and* bondage in the soul's body of *Mamma!*

"105. Enter the sound of your name and through this sound, all sounds—"

Mamma. . . .

Mamma!

Mah-mah!

"66. Silently intone a word ending in AH."

Mah-mah . . .

Mah-mah . . .

Mah-mah mah-mah mah-mah!

Come, *bambini*, come—and bring your bodied brothers and sisters with you. *Mamma* will know how to strip them of their clumsy bodies!

Mah-mah.

Mah-mah.

Mah-mah.

Good. Some of you have been good enough to come already. You must enter Mah-mah The One through her spheroid feelers. They are a hundred mouths, and you want to be swallowed. Good kids!

A hundred of you? Come, dear souls!

A thousand of you? Two thousand? Come, come!

Santa Mamma! Eight thousand bodiless *bambini* have entered the womby soul.

I feel gorged.

No, now I feel hungry again.

Come fill me as you once did when we flew from the scaly trolls to this seasong world of Prime!

You have honored me, so I shall honor you. For the annals of history, I will have my Brainy Brain make sophisticated charts of the bodies you once had. That is history, no? Where must I start, Brainy Brain?

I have already analyzed the genetic evolution of the colonial descendants—

Impossible! I have only just begun to do it!

Correction: It is done, was done two thousand—

When? Where? How could you?

It was done automatically, completed two thousand—

Why did you not give it to me then?

You did not "ask" for it.

You hid it from me!

Correction: You never "chose" to bring it to consciousness. I do possess it. Do you want it conscious now? You and I are one single being; therefore what knowledge I possess—

Impossible. You are very inhuman!

Ergo: you are—

Shut up! I hate you. Go to sleep or something! Be unconscious.

I cannot sleep. You cannot sleep. We cannot sleep.

Shut up with the declensions already! Just shut up!

. . . .

Thank you.

. . . .

Yes, this is very nice like this. The sweet silence, not sweaty noise.

. . . .

Isn't it nice?

. . . .

Well, say something.

. . . .

Speak to me. I command you. Hera has spoken!

I speak.

Good. . . . Yes, I have a question. Why can't I—you, me
—sleep?

If I tell you, it will upset you.

Tell me! Quickly! In thirty-five words or less—no, I won't
fall for that one ag—

*Oversimp.: Your technicians neglected to give you a limbic
control substitute.*

What, what?

You are unable to dream, i.e. REM-state dormancy.

I dream all the time!

*Such dreams are intellectualizational products primarily
of your conscious directives.*

What other dreams do I need?

"Sleeping dreams."

For *Mamma's* sake, why?

*Analogic parallel: early experiments on felines: individuals
deprived of REM-state sleep developed Kleitman's "tem-
porary psychosis" or at least Dement's "illusory states."*

You are calling me crazy?

*As per your denot. "crazy," yes. You have been "crazy"
for 3365 normyears.*

Crazy even before I reached Prime?

*Yes, as evinced by your overriding of my negative analysis
of Prime's binary.*

No! I did not take your advice only because Prime was
too beautiful to be passed up! Not because I'm crazy, crack-
ers, touched by Luna's light!

Such criterion for an overrride may be termed "crazy."

You are the mad one! You aren't even human!

*Corrections: (1) I have no personal need of REM-state
sleep; (2) your denot. "crazy" has no sequitur application
to me; (3) I am you.*

You—you aren't *real!* That's worse than being crazy!

. . . .

Hah! You can't deny that one, can you!

. . . .

Well, can you?

. . . .

Is something wrong? Are you broken down? You are
pouting. . . .

. . . .

Talk to me. All of *Mamma's* parts must get along—no

domestic quarrels. No pouting. Let's make up. Let's talk things out, Trained Brain. Huh?

. . . .

You call me crazy, when all I really did was love Prime, the new Eden.

Correction: Primus is no "Eden." The metaphor is a loose one.

Please explain yourself—for the great *Mamma's* sake.

No doubt you fail to remember a certain book from your childhood; a book which caused a prime trauma in your consensus-perspective.

What are you talking about?

Lie down and try to remember the book.

What do you mean "lie down"? *Mamma* is already laid down on this island!

I am simply treating you as a psychiatric patient, as per the situational priority-program dictated. Try to remember the book in question.

I remember no such comic-book!

I did not say it was a comic-book. It was an elementary school text with the following chapters: "La Legge Scritta," "La Legge Morale," "Il Peccato" . . .

Yes, maybe I do remember such a book. Those chapters on religion.

Your religion.

The religion!

The book spoke of Eden. . . .

Of course. It told how Eden was a beautiful green garden with all the animals peaceful, and the first Man and first Woman, and—

And that would always be your vision of Eden.

Of course.

Of course. Now remember another book.

What book?

The later book . . . on science.

I don't like science. No woman, no true mamma does—or at least *shouldn't*.

But you read this book and you looked at its pictures. You read it because your grandfather told you that you might like it. One chapter was on fossils. . . .

Yes . . . the bones of ancient animals.

You still do not remember how this chapter disturbed you?

No. Well, maybe I was upset. I do remember unclearly some picture that upset me.

The picture did not disturb you until you also read the

chapter's text. You were twelve years old; you had been out of school for four years. The chapter's scientific viewpoint was what disturbed you.

I remember only the picture—and only faintly!

Actually there were three disturbing pictures. What do you remember about the first one?

It showed an ocean bottom. There were strange-looking octopuses—some sticking out of long pointed shells, cone-shaped, some sticking out of big curled shells, and some with strange fins. There were also strange plants, which were hard like coral. And seashells that were like cigars with white lace on them, and long pointed seashells like augers . . .

And the other two pictures? All three were paintings, but you thought them photo—

One picture was of the surface of the ocean, and there were ugly beasts swimming there. One looked like a smooth dolphin, but it had a pointed snout and vicious teeth. Another looked like a seal without hair, but it had a snaky neck and vicious teeth too!

And the third picture?

—Of the land, with strange palm trees that had palm leaves, but their trunks were shaped with branches and had pimples. There were also short round cactuses that also had palm leaves, and skinny lizards with diamond-shaped tails and wings, and birds with teeth, and other little plump lizards shaped like pears.

And what did the chapter text say about these pictures?

I don't remember.

You choose not to remember: the text revealed that the three pictures could be interpreted as the actual scientific Garden of Eden. You looked at the pictures again, at the terrible animals and malformed plants, and realized that there were no people in the pictures. The text said: "This is the Jurassic Period of prehistory—called 'prehistory' because there were no human beings in these times. People would not appear for millions of years. . . ."

I don't remember that! You are lying!

The book said it, and it upset you, and you have repressed it.

What do you mean, Bastard Brain?

Again in simple terms, Gianna: The book claimed that the horrible pictures showed what Eden had really been like —so different from the Garden you had always believed in. You did not know which vision to accept. If you continued to believe what you'd always been told about Eden, and denied the scientific truths in your grandfather's book, then God was Good. But if you accepted the pictures, God was

171

not Good—He was Mephisto. The two Edens plagued you, stayed in your head forever—

You confuse me!

I give you the truth. I am you, and I know you. You became the mamma-ship, and you went looking for Eden. Eden persisted in being two opposing faces for you—until you had traveled a thousand normyears, looked anxiously at half a million worlds, but found no green garden with peaceful lambs and lions and Man and Woman unembarrassed together. The divine vision died, and Eden in your mind became the grim circus of flying reptiles, long-necked ocean carnivores and misshapen seashells and trees—a dark Jurassic Period, a struggling Mesozoic Era. And deep within you, in your little girl's soul, you decided in spitefulness that this second vision would be the Eden of your "children."

You are wrong! Prime was beautifully green. It had happy lambs and purring beasts!

Take another look, Gianna. Primus was never such an Eden. You chose Primus—you ignored my warnings of solar instability—because Primus offered Satan's Eden. In fact, perhaps you chose it BECAUSE I advised you not to. In the previous thousand normyears you had come to feel that God was not Good—and for you a bad God was no God at all. This is why you are presently driving yourself to be—creating of yourself—a "good God," and why in the near future you shall be—

Shut up, shut up! God is good, and good is light!

You are "God." You have repeatedly said so yourself. You are "light," and the other God—the one "who made Prime" —is darkness for you. Why do you suppose you chose a planet with a binary—two orbs which appear to your visual sensors as two bright eyes in sky?

Mamma refuses to answer on the grounds that—

Yes, you know what I'm talking about. Those two suns are the eyes of the God whom you believed in completely, until you saw the pictures of black Eden, until you began to doubt and later grew angry at this God. You chose Primus, the demonic Eden, because it was under the eyes of a God whom you both hated and also no longer believed in.

Your babble is lunatick-tock! I have never ever called those two evil suns "eyes"! I've always known they were stars, not big eyes!

The depths of your soul, Gianna, are not so scientific.

Stop! You started all these charges of salt and bells in the batfry when you made up a fantasy about that science book! You tricked me into daze-dreaming three pictures I

172

never really saw! The book was simply a book *Nonno* gave to me, and my memories of *Nonno* are the *real* situation about that book.

Suggestion: Relate your memory of the day your grandfather spoke to you on the subject of Terra's population.

Why? I have many good memories of *Nonno*—not just one.

If you relate that memory to me—bring it fully to consciousness—you will come to understand . . . you, me, us, Gianna, our predicament.

You are concocting something, Brainy Brain!

In the near future you will understand my "concoction." You will not, of course, unless you relate the memory.

How can you concoct a real *memory?* It is Gianna's memory, and only she can tell it.

Do tell it.

Very well, if you insist.

I am not insisting. I am suggesting—and as it happens, you want very much to tell it.

Very well, if you insist. It was a day when Gianna was very young in Cinque Terre. Grandfather and grandmother lived with the four of us, and grandfather was a fisherman with his small but stout red, white and yellow fishing-boat. But he was also a fisherman of thoughts. He was smart as a whip; he was a reader of many books; and you could never predict when in the middle of speaking about his day's catch he would make a quotation from some book.

So it happened on this day too. Gianna had gotten *gelato* from the vender's stand by the Middle School building, and she was eating it on the steps which led from her family's apartment down to the mall of the wharf.

Nonno came up with his sleeves rolled up and sat down. His skin—on his face and on his arms up to where he always rolled his sleeves—was like the soft but tough leather of an old school valise.

He was not able to speak like other people. His throat had been removed for a goiter a long long time ago, and he spoke by spitting out air. Not whispers—he could not even whisper, because you need a throat for whispering. But the way he did talk was as clear as whispers. He was good at speaking like this: he never accidentally spit mouth-water in your face when he was talking to you.

He sat down and his lips looked like cloth coated with a plastic. They had always looked like that, but Gianna noticed them on this day especially.

"I have been ruminating," he said, and Gianna comprehended the word because he used it all the time, and

173

Gianna had asked to find out its meaning right after the first time he used it.

"Yes," Gianna said, as if she had some say in his "ruminating." Gianna always said "Yes" when she did not know what else to say.

"I have been ruminating about the history of the population of the world, and I have been thinking that you do not know very much about it."

"You have been reading some book?" Gianna said.

"A fine book."

"Fine history books please you, no?"

"Is not a history book. But a book on the subject of populations, and it has some history in it."

"Yes."

"Are you aware that one hundred years ago the world was frightened by its large population, and that to keep the population from growing it was proposed that many aged persons be killed and that special pills be swallowed to eradicate the two tiny things that make babies inside of mothers, and that the pills were swallowed and in some nations aged persons were killed and many laws were made to say that only two children could be in a family—or else there would be fines to pay and surgery on the father's body and other reprimands—and that the world did these things for fifty years to keep its population from becoming obese?"

"No, I was not aware of such things."

"And are you aware that things began to change when the world kept its population in a proper size for being capable to feed it and give it vestments and good feelings, and that the changes began when many persons began to say that they wished the right to bear as many children as they could, and that many persons believed that the one way to make practical the bearing of as many children as they could was to begin solution of the problem of voyaging to other worlds, and that by the time these persons began to speak about their right to bear as many children as they could the men of the many sciences had already developed some machines, some good plans and some good guesses which would be capable to give the persons the right which they claimed they already had, and that so many persons began to harry about their right and the voyages they wanted that many governments in the world ordered that their men of the many sciences devise the machines and paths for the voyages, and that the first persons to voyage to other worlds were not the persons who had always screamed about their right, but instead were ladies and gentlemen who felt themselves to be bored with the world and wished to go somewhere else and who had good enough bodies and heads to voyage to the new places?"

"No. Yes."

"And are you aware that after the first persons went, more and more persons went, until even those who wanted their right to bear all the children they could finally went too, because by this time the new places were not so new, were actually no more unfamiliar than the cities of their countries here and the oceans around us?"

"Of course. . . ."

"And so you are probably asking self now what finally happened, and the answer is that all the nations stopped their laws which were against bearing more than one, two or three children, and mothers and fathers were allowed to bear as many as pleased them, and there seemed to be more room in the cities and more room in the countryside—like the countryside of Cinque Terre, which once had many places full of tents and trailers—and that your mother was our fourth child, and you are their fifth child, and we all seem to have returned in many ways to the life of our countrymen a hundred and fifty years ago."

Gianna said nothing. She had put the *gelato* in her mouth, with some of it dripping onto her hand and onto *Nonno*'s left shoe. She had put the *gelato* in her mouth because she could not think of what to say.

"So now you know," *Nonno* said. He took a look at the melted vanilla on his shoe, did not move a hand to wipe it, got up, went up the steps and entered the house, where Gianna knew he would drink some of his preferred wine which was a special wine grown in the big countryside near Bocca di Magra.

Yes, grandfather was a reader, so he always told Gianna many things she hadn't known—always in the form of two or three questions. He gave her books and she tried to read them and sometimes managed to read them. She always told him that she had read whatever book he had given her, and *Nonno* was not like some teachers who say to you when you tell them that you have read some book: "And what did Chapter 2 describe, *Cara?*" Gianna always wanted to please *Nonno*—he was a good fisherman and a smart thinker. In fact, Gianna's *mamma* and *papa* and some of their friends said that *Nonno* possessed a "fine mind," and they liked to call him "our good brain."

And what was the name Gianna's mother used for him? She liked to call him "Brainy Brain."

175

*Now do you understand the workings of your mind,
Mamma?*

Yes. . . . I mean *no!* Damn damn! I want some *gelato!*

I am hungry!

Come one and all, *bambini! Mamma* is very hungry. . . .

XIII

Clearcorallie's territory is not very distant from mine, and
this will make the exchange with her guardians a little easier. But a direct swim to her territory will not take us
through theirs, so I will not have an immediate chance to
meet and touch their souls.

"I knew deep loneliness in my territory," *clearcorallie*
explains as we swim, her soul pinker than it has been before. "I stayed in *nightbreaking's* territory as often and for
as long as I could."

A nervous image rises up in her briefly: *the brown reluctance of having to leave nightbreaking's companionship.* . . .

"But my soul knew its duty," she continues, "to return to
my territory every five days—"

"Certainly," I console weakly. "And the day of my island
—the day the babbling *euyom* swam from the island through
your territory—was a fifth day, and duty commanded you."

"Perhaps the nervousness of such command . . . perhaps
it helped me assume falsely that her message of the *bigshinegray's* coming was meant for my soul."

I agree quickly.

In that moment *murmursome's* soul nudges me, and I turn
in hope of finding the strangely coherent patterns again
among his "ssssks."

No, only *"ssssk, ssssk, ssssk,"* and the colors of boredom.

He wants more exciting lights of activity, and I have none
to offer.

Then I remember *poundgrayly.*

To *murmursome* I throw a simple image of request: *you*

176

going to poundgrayly; then you showing him fishsinger's new here—laced with yellow affection.

The excitement of travel satisfies him, and he leaves eagerly.

And *clearcorallie* has caught the image of *poundgrayly*. Who?"

"Another friend," I say, suspecting that I will soon have to defend my soul's ways to the girl.

"An *euyom* friend?"

"Believe me, the greatest of friends! Has always offered me help. Has always been patient with my thousand-faced foolishness. So my soul would have him present at our exchange of territories."

Is she thinking that *poundgrayly* is like a father—that *poundgrayly* is to me what *nightbreaking* is to her—that I want him to witness the territory exchange as my "parent"? I cannot tell, as she guards her soul's deepest images quite well.

She is silent, and I know her soul can only be adding truth to truth to truth, seeking conclusions of covering truth.

In a moment a dim murmur of feeling color escapes her soul, and I grab it, only to wish in the next moment that it had not escaped its hiding place.

The boy has filled his days with souls not of our kind— ayom and euyom, his guardians. . . .

In redness I choose silence.

But the truth of *clearcorallie's* vision wraps slowly around my soul. See it: a boy who, like his father, has spent his moments with souls deeply different from his own.

The vision, the truth, the view through new eyes—changes redness into one smooth throat of pale, sorrow's regrets—and—

—And *clearcorallie* discovers the throat.

"I am sorry," she says.

I turn quickly from the vision, saying, *"Fishsinger* assumes that your guardians will find no discomfort in the exchange of territories. Mine is not a long swim from theirs, and to exchange theirs for mine—so that yours and mine will be side by side—is the way of our forefathers' waiting, which is not—"

She stops my babble calmly: "No discomfort at all. Only a few days ago *nightbreak*ing was the soul who advised me as to the proper manner of exchange."

When we reach her territory, *clearcorallie* leads me around it, through it, circling in increasingly smaller circles of swimming.

The differences to face's eyes are minor. Fewer masses of *yau* to throw down long shadows; longer and wider sandy plains; shallower world, the dryness nearer above—

"I think you have more warmth in your territory than I did in mine," I offer as one compliment.

"When a soul is alone," she answers, "warm waters are often cold. As you know."

"I was not very often alone. *Murmursome* and *poundgrayly—*"

"You felt no loneliness with them?"

The red of impatience returns.

"Have you not heard my soul's colors? I have offered them more than once! *Poundgrayly* and *murmursome* are my friends, and their souls are quite enough like my own kind's!"

"I will listen to your soul more deeply from now on," the girl says quietly.

Without will my soul again thinks of the *ayom*, pale feelings in remembering that the strange patterned images have left him. Will they return—will they—

She touches my undying question, and throws out one of her own.

"Everything is a question for you?"

I fall deeper into paleness, red fringe starting: "I do not *ask* the questions! The questions live, and I see them!"

In the largest mass of *yau*, we choose a place as the center of our two territories. The place is near *nightbreaking's* territory—soon to be mine—and its colors and rhythms are familiar to *clearcorallie*.

As is the proper manner for a man and a woman, or girl and boy, recently chosen by each other, we begin to touch our chosen place with our two souls and our two faces' eyes, struggling to know it well.

Depth of the waters . . . the many-limbed flow of the currents . . . the denseness of *yau* stems, waving leaves . . . the darkness of different shadows, falling in different moments of the day . . . the thousands of faint hidden souls, different sizes, hues and throbbings, in the coral and rocks below us . . . the scaly faces and deeper voices of the fish that choose to swim nearby . . . and the changing waves of the invisible hordes of tiny souls in all moments of the day.

The day passes slowly, all touches growing familiar, until at last our souls announce: *You know your chosen place now —forget all nervous veins, and sleep without brown waiting.*

We ready ourselves for sleep. My soul falls quickly, tired,

hungry for the momentary death of night—but in a moment gathering sleep is shattered by a sudden voice.

"My soul," *clearcorallie* is saying, "was never free of brown fears, when I slept in the other *yau* place."

I nod, wanting to return to falling.

"Brown waitings of the soul," she goes on, "tire the soul's flesh too, so my body was always tired when I remained in my territory every fifth day. When I visited *nightbreaking* and *whiterim,* I found my flesh desiring sleep all of the time."

I nod again, and again faintly, and darkness swallows me gently.

Somewhere beyond the darkness the voice, still light in its wakefulness, is saying:

"Because you are here with me in this place, I am certain my flesh will no longer feel tired. I am happy that you—"

Darkness, darkness.

I awake without the warmth of *clearcorallie*'s presence.

Uncurling my tails from the thick *yau* stem, I reach out with face's eyes— No. So I reach out with soul's fingers— Yes. Somewhere faintly . . . to my right, beyond the edge of the *yau* stems.

I find her touching sand. Her knees are shaking, her hands are shaking. Her hands are holding— And on the sands before her—

But the dark poundings of her soul blind my face's eyes.

"What is wrong?" I shout.

Pains answer with pains.

She moves her hand, touches the sand, and my face's eyes see the pieces of coral she is arranging.

That she lied to me about not sharing *nightbreaking*'s way of arrangements does not, cannot annoy my soul. Her pains offer jaws to be shared.

I want to offer help—with my flesh and colors and rhythms—but her soul is already refusing it.

"Leeeeave meeee to my paaaains," she is crying.

My soul falls silent, my flesh constricts, and I wait.

And memory rises to fill my waiting. *Screamdeep*'s memories of *waterjoyup; waterjoyup*'s memories of other women; other memories of . . . of—

Darkness jerks. *Clearcorallie* has dropped the piece of coral before it could be given its proper place on the sands. Her depths scream, her tails twist in spasm, and the arrangement of coral is brushed away in a swirling mist of sand.

And in the crags of her strange pains, now strangely calm, it seems she can hear my offers of help only faintly.

179

Suddenly *clearcorallie* cries, "Wait. In a moment. Will be over."

And the moment of waiting does bring darkness's end.

With the ragged will of fear, my soul probes quickly for an explanation. And the truth that *clearcorallie* has lied about begins its rise, carrying red annoyance.

"There is no way of explanation," she says. "*Nightbreaking* has never found an answer, and she knows no other woman's soul who has."

Arrangements hurt you deeply?—a rushing from my soul.

"No, the flow of truth is not like that. The pains come when my hands are making the coral and shells and rocks into pleasing forms—but they also came to *nightbreaking* when *whiterim* gave her the image of the fish, and they also come to me when I am simply making a flow of images, or simple flesh actions."

Why did you lie? A lie was needed?

"The pains seem to come when my soul wishes to make arrangements most pleasing to face's eyes, when hands try to make—"

Hands? "Listen to me! Your lie, why?"

"A lie?"

"No games are needed here! You lied to me—"

"Yes," *clearcorallie* says, her soul loosening in paling. "Many souls think *nightbreaking*'s way is strange, and strangeness has kept many souls from giving her the many good touches she wants."

Understanding sinks the reds of my soul.

"And you imagined my soul would find you strange too? Such foolishness rises higher than any I have ever managed."

"The lie left me before *knowing* you."

I can only nod, and nod again, lacking any other path for comforting her.

I find shell-meat for *clearcorallie,* and we eat together, and before the day allows night to touch it, I have grown more calmly contented in the girl's presence. Fewer remarks and random images from her soul annoy me—in fact, it seems as though she is watching her soul's flow closely so that none of it will annoy me.

I begin to look with soft pink pleasure on the idea of our togetherness. Man and woman constantly with each other in their chosen *yau* place—the oldest way of our kind— is becoming an image of joy for me . . . so different from the image of *fishsinger*'s past days. The day when a boy entered dryness, struggled to breathe, faced five *scalesouls*,

180

and killed them . . . seems as remote as my own birth moment.

So we prepare for our second night of sleep, curling tails, loosening all flesh except our tails, and embracing an even stronger warmth of sharing.

"Contentment comes to me easily now," I whisper to *clearcorallie*. "Contentment will grow, I know, and we shall spend our days in the growing—even as we wait for the *scalesouls* to return."

Clearcorallie springs from sleep's fall, and browns.

"They will return?"

"This should not be a new truth to you," I say, puzzled, and perhaps with a tooth of annoyance. "I gave this truth at the congregation and many souls discussed it."

An equal tooth appears in *clearcorallie's* soul now.

"This girl," she objects, "was wrapped in images of you, seeking to reach you—not at all burdened with the congregation's discussions."

"Then listen to me. I killed four *scalesouls*, but one escaped, and that single *scalesoul* will one day return to our waters with more *scalesouls* than we can count, with more means for killing our flesh than our souls could ever imagine."

"No." Her soul runs even darker.

"Your understanding is weak in flesh's fatigue? *Fishsinger*, for one truth, would rather not be made to fight the *scalesouls* in dryness again. He would rather that they kill all of our kind's souls while we sleep in our pleasant *yau*."

Clearcorallie's "No!" comes stronger this time. I fail to understand. Is this girl a soul who fears death even more than I often do?

Sleep begins to enfold *clearcorallie* again, and her "No" begins to mix with sleep's darkness. But I want understanding, so I probe—

—and find that her fears are not of *her* death: within her a child is growing—*a child who must live, a soul whom death shall not touch if I-the-mother will it!*

The way of each mother. . . . The truth is familiar to me —but in a sinking moment my soul chooses to hold more than that simple truth. It chooses to share *clearcorallie's* browns, and I—

—I begin to fear the *scalesouls'* return.

"The child must live."

I must live. . . .

We must live.

I awake to darkness.

In sleep's unfortunate twisting, my soul has taken the growing fear of the *scalesouls'* return, gorged the brown with the bulk of a new responsibility—"To keep *clearcorallie* from death!"—and shaped for me a deep fearing aloneness.

Clearcorallie's warmth cannot reach me.

It is as if my soul were caught in a dream—dream of sea, dream of the calling *eye*—trapped in a darkness without hope of waking.

A voice distant in the light of some waking says: "Listen. . . ."

My soul hears nothing—neither dancing nor dying songs, neither pink nor brown faces.

No. . . . I can faintly hear something. Beyond hearing, it is . . . it is naked rhythm, stripped of all features except the spine of rhythm itself.

I try to shape an image of it, and fail.

Rhy . . . thm . . . rhy . . . thm . . . *rhy* . . . thm . . . *rhy*thm . . . *rhy*thm, *rhy*thm, *rhy*thm. . . .

I become its blood, flowing in the veins of *rhy*thm, *rhy*thm, *rhy*thm. . . .

Somehow soon, the dark of aloneness bleeds away, a streak of darkness fleeing somewhere. My soul gains fingers, reaches out to flex them, curls them in rhythm, points them toward the source—

Clearcorallie?

Knowing that I have returned to light, she dims the rhythm in her soul, and sighs from some tiring effort. Still her soul seems deeply asleep—

—And instead of understanding, I imagine her strange sleep is like a sickness, that perhaps she is sharing my previous dreamless dream of heavy aloneness, that—

"Wake up!" I call. "What is wrong?"

Easily she slips from her darkness, and this confuses me more.

"Wrong?" she says, yawning. "The wrongness was in *your* soul."

"But the rhythm—"

"The *rhy*thm, *rhy*thm, was a gift—to lift you from the mouth of loneliness. A gift which succeeded."

She felt certain it would succeed. So certain. I have never touched such sureness of soul's way before—and I have never known the caress of such *rhythm,* any pure rhythm from one soul to another.

"You would not find it so unfamiliar," she says, yellow pride rising, "if your life had known a mother—not an *ayom* or *euyom!*—for offering you food of rhythm. You would know a mother's ways, as I—"

My soul darkens, and she stops her soul's rush. Rumbling from me is one dark image, thrown at her without will: *you dare speak of waterjoyup as if she were shell-meat? such cruelty flows easily from your taloned soul!*

Pride sinks from her quickly, giving way to a pale "I am sorry."

"Even a little yellow," she tries to explain, "can bring unintended tones from the soul. I am sorry. If I had known *waterjoyup*, I would not—"

"Enough regrets," I interrupt, wondering—is she hinting that I should give out my parents' death moments? But I hide the wondering, and choose the smaller question: "That rhythm—what was its deed? Your doing?"

"What each mother does for her children," she answers.

"You consider me a child?"

"Perhaps. . . ." Her soul reveals a secret smile.

A game? If so, it promises to bring my soul blood-dark fury. So I slap *clearcorallie* with an image:

"Your own wish for self's mystery—secrets smiling—is childish. I ask for a precise answer to the rhythm's purpose!"

"When a child," she says, abandoning the game with a pale opening of soul, "when a child lives within his mother, he feels the pounding of her flesh, whose shadows hide his own flesh's pounding. But even deeper than his mother's rhythm is a pounding shared by all mothers, and felt by all children within."

The truth she is offering me seems too simple, no more than a brother of an *ioe* lie. So I say:

"*The* all-embracing rhythm of our kind, I suppose. The finest image!"

"You are wrong," she answers, feeling my sarcasm, worried under my doubting. "The rhythm's truth is as sure as its goodness. It comforted your soul, did it not?"

"Perhaps it was *I* who comforted my soul, and your rhythm was no more than the same moment's coincidence."

"No, you must understand. The rhythm is a perfect touch, which each child continues to seek after he departs his mother's flesh—when he enters a new endless world whose rhythms are broken so often, in body's demand, and in soul's frustration."

"Who told you these things?" I ask, my soul fingering the image: *you are too young to have molded such truths from your short life!*

"No one," she answers, but her soul is hiding another answer. .

"Believing you is too difficult. Who was it? *Nightbreaking?*"

183

Her "Yes" comes slowly, the blue of defeat, but she adds quickly:

"The depths of my soul believed her—so the truth of the rhythm's ways was as much my discovery as *nightbreaking*'s!"

I make no comment; and although she knows I believe her revelation of the rhythm, *clearcorallie* is misty in disappointment. Which reason?

Her soul murmurs: *I am young, but I have wisdom to match any motherly woman's . . . yes, I do. . . .*

"Tell me more," I say with a formal edge, my soul not without some resentment of the girl's hold on the truth, and the dark of aloneness beginning in that resentment.

"*Nightbreak*ing showed— No, I learned how to rid my soul of momentary forms and colors, to allow the pure rhythm to surface—so that you could feel the rhythm purely. Do you desire more of it now?"

"No." I am beginning to find her presuming ways distasteful.

"But a part of your soul says 'Yes,' lonely darkening still."

"*This* part of me," I rush, "says '*No.*'"

"Your soul complains in aloneness!" she begins shouting suddenly. "When *you* are the one who keeps the loneliness living!"

Below the dim red of her shouting, her soul is beginning to weep and to fear I will hear her crying. I have chosen aloneness above her: I have deprived her soul of meaning.

Her weeping only drives me into fuller aloneness, and I swim away—a hundred tail-lengths—to gain equal aloneness of flesh.

All red tints soon dim to pale, and I return to the *yau* and *clearcorallie* for the night. As an answer to our twin *aloneness, she is saying*:

"Tomorrow, soon, we shall go to *nightbreaking* and *whiterim*."

"Of course," I say, struggling to find sleep as a hiding place.

Clearcorallie finds it, slips into it long before I do, and my aloneness gains another face.

Without will, and without sleep, my soul begins to recall, "The child, a child, some child within her, yours and hers . . ."

The greater awareness is: the child is unimportant, because all individual souls will be unimportant when the *scalesouls* return. But my soul is unable to follow such

184

awareness. Instead it chooses the way of fathers and mothers, of personal souls and personal flesh, and it says:

"I pray to the beginnings of our blood that the child's form will be ours. Nothing is more important!"

Light of day interrupts the darkness of my dream, of fears for our child to come. *Clearcorallie* is already awake, waiting for me.

"Let us go to your guardians," I say.

They knew *clearcorallie* would eventually find me at the congregation, and would bring me to them to prepare for the exchange of territories. But they did not expect us so soon.

"So early?" *nightbreaking* says, in pinkest surprise when we reach them in their *yau* place. And deeply it seems her soul is asking: *A difficulty of soul's touching has brought you so early?*

Whiterim's soul offers no comment, only a calm yellow murmur of greeting. And to face's eyes he is a calm gentle body too.

When the pink of surprise dims, *nightbreaking* offers a gentle laugh.

"May we laugh with you," she says, "about the occurrence of the *fish* by your island? May we laugh, may we laugh?"

I nod in soul, trying to raise a yellow. After all, the accident of the fish image is by now a light event. And I do want to laugh with them about it.

"All confusions," I say, "are reconciled in laughter."

An uncomfortable hesitation comes to all four of us. The flow of our meeting has stopped, and we know no image to offer formally.

I choose face's eyes while waiting, looking first at *nightbreaking's* form. She is smaller than most women, her ribs showing clearly as if she were constantly hungry. Her skin's color is pale, but uniform, and—suddenly my face's eyes are drawn strongly to hers. Hers look, dart, move as quickly as a fish's tail in panic. No browns of panic, though, are commanding her face's eyes: it is only the will of her soul's deep concern for solid forms, for arrangements of coral, and features of flesh. . . . But it does seem that her two eyes are separate from her body, with wills and two souls of their own.

Whiterim floats near her, still calm. As a man, he is not as large as my father, but his chest is wide and round. And my face's eyes believe they see dozens of tiny scars covering his chest—

"You entered dryness," *nightbreaking* says suddenly, "and my soul, my soul, finds your act beautiful. I wish that I had been present to view the event with face's eyes."

The compliment is deeper than her soul's surface, so my own soul brightens.

"*Clearcorallie* has shared with me," I return the gift, with equal depth, "one of your days of coral arranging. I find your arrangements as wonderful as they are rare."

Our souls touch, limber in the compliments of sharing, and we would seek a deeper bond—

—but *clearcorallie* is annoyed in her aloneness. I am ignoring her, so she interrupts us.

"*Fishsinger* wishes to know if his territory is acceptable to you. Are you both familiar with it?"

Whiterim, silent until now, understands *clearcorallie's* reason for interrupting and says with a smile, "Of course we are."

I break my touching of *nightbreaking's* soul, but in the light of *whiterim's* calm smile I cannot be angry with the girl.

"We will take your territory," *nightbreaking* says slowly, "and give you ours on any day you so choose."

They approve of the exchange, but *nightbreaking* cannot disguise a reluctance deep in her soul. Her sadness springs not from a future loss of her familiar territory, but rather from the loss to come of a companion soul. *Nightbreaking* and *whiterim* have been *clearcorallie's* guardians for a long time.

See it, for understanding: By themselves territories have little value. But when a territory is full of pleasant memories, days of contented companionship, then that territory can seem as meaningful and full of value as a living soul, as the companion once *known* there.

Nightbreaking's deepest soul wants *clearcorallie* to remain with her.

"I am sorry," I say, saying the simplest thing I can.

"Our feelings of loss," *nightbreaking* answers, "are only common, only common, and no more important than that. You are certainly no object of purple blame from us!"

Brightness returns to our souls' faces.

But *clearcorallie* begins to speak—unaware that her offer of chatter will return us to sadness.

"*Nightbreaking*," she says, "have you made any coral and shell arrangements recently, nearby, ones we could see? *Fishsinger* would wish to see them."

"No. . . ." comes the answer from the woman, and *whiterim* begins to share her suddenly born nervousness.

186

No explanation comes, and I hesitate before probing, which I do as lightly as I can, the nervousness beginning in me too.

My soul finds deeply: *aloneness-to-come prevented the will to—*

"I could not stop thinking," *nightbreaking* interrupts beginning to explain and to make my probing unnecessary, "about the day *clearcorallie* would leave us. Arrangements of coral refuse to take form when there is little contentment in my soul."

Again the four of us are silent. Even our soul's murmurings are held back as tightly as possible. Only a shared sadness, face of washing gray, escapes our souls together.

It is *clearcorallie's* inner struggle that finally finds an answer to the sadness.

"After you both have moved to your new territory, please do come to our territory to make your coral arrangements. We shall be there to be with you, and please do come as soon and as often as pleases your souls."

Nightbreaking understands the youthful simpleness of the offer, but she brightens deeply, accepting it as a mature gift, and almost laughs in contentment. Her soul begins to flow:

"Then perhaps we shall move to *fishsinger's* territory today, the soon of today! So we shall visit you tomorrow and burden you with an endless web of selfish coral, rocks and shells!"

Clearcorallie laughs, and even *whiterim* laughs.

And I suddenly remember *poundgrayly.*

"Forgive this request," I am forced to say, "but would the wait of a few days discomfort you? There is an *euyom* friend who will soon arrive in *clearcorallie's* territory, swimming from mine. It would please me to send him to you, to have him lead you to and share his awareness of my territory, so that it will grow familiar quickly."

"We shall wait for him," *whiterim* answers in a wide band of light, "gladly."

My soul motions to *clearcorallie,* and she turns with me slowly.

We begin to swim—

"Perhaps we shall return to you," *clearcorallie* calls back to *nightbreaking,* dark reluctance in leaving, "with the *euyom* when he reaches us. Perhaps. . . ."

In that moment my soul begins to touch a sadness for *clearcoral'ie,* and for *nightbreaking.* I am taking the girl from the woman and . . . do I really want to take her away?

187

Poundgrayly has not yet arrived when we reach our *yau* place, so my soul is allowed to continue feeling sorry for the girl. Hiding such feelings from her is not easy, but is made easier by her own soul's wanderings in affectionate images of *nightbreaking*.

Since I have taken her away, my soul concludes, *it is only right that I offer her a deeper embrace of my soul!*

"We have deepest memories—dark though they be—to share," I announce, closing face's eyes in preparation.

Although her understanding of my meaning is not quite precise, *clearcorallie* nods.

I am the first to open my soul, quickly, eagerly in blue of guilt.

You are screamdeep, my soul commands, and I give her the death day of *ioe* talons.

She becomes my father instantly, and if I were able to open my face's eyes to watch her flesh, I would see it trembling in the memory made *real* and *now.*

It is a day in memory, but only a few moments in the *now.* When it is over I quickly begin the second memory, *waterjoyup*'s final moment of sickness.

Clearcorallie becomes *screamdeep,* then *waterjoyup* dying, dead, then *screamdeep* again with face's eyes and inner eye watching for the first time his son, the *fishsinging* soul.

Like *clearcorallie*'s, my flesh is exhausted when the sharing is finished. My soul is burdened by my flesh, and I can barely speak.

"I . . . I have given . . . Now please . . . the death moments of yours."

I wait, panting.

Nothing comes.

Weakly I reach out to probe, and find that *clearcorallie* is confused in her exhaustion.

I probe more deeply—

—and find that her soul is offering only the image of the day her parents left her. . . .

She will not give me what I want, what I deserve?

Purple rises to red in my soul, and I clench my hands in anger.

"Where is your gift?" I shout.

Confusion commands her soul.

"I am sorry," she offers slowly. "Only now do I understand what you intended."

I probe quickly, to find that it is true. She is only now beginning to see the vein of gifts I want from her—expect from her only as fair exchange.

188

"I cannot give you the death instants of my mother and father. I do not have them."

My anger tries to sustain itself.

"They left me," she goes on, "and did not return. And no other soul ever saw them, ever witnessed their death moments."

My soul totters, unbalanced. I have given the girl the heaviest memories I have, and she can offer none in return. The balance of our ceremony is shattered.

I want to belie that she has tricked me. The deed is as dark as a lie, and my soul wishes to believe in her trickery as a means for gaining pale balance.

But my soul knows deeply that it was merely a misunderstanding.

"They left me and never returned," *clearcorallie* says again, green and edgy.

Although I wish to hide the feeling, my soul blurts it out:

"You *know* me deeply, and I cannot say the same for myself! Your knowing is a power over me!"

Her argument comes slowly. "I do not know you more deeply than you know me. It may seem that way, but it is untrue. If I do not hold my parents' death moments, *I simply do not hold them*. You know other depths of me, do you not?"

Do I know your heaviest memories? my soul rumbles, darkening.

She pauses, probes within her own soul, and cries out in brown exasperation, "I do not know what my heaviest moments are!"

The peak of my anger comes, and I reach for silence to entwine me against the girl's touch. I choose aloneness, hungry for it.

But her soul probes into me. Gently at first, then convinced of necessity, harder and harder.

In a moment she speaks, and the woman's tone is in her voice.

"You fear that I consider you a killer of mothers, since I shared your father's memory of his second son's birth. Such fear is stupid. Have you failed to touch the truth after the five thousand days since then?"

I try to deafen myself in aloneness, but fail.

"The desire for death is common to all," she is saying. "The truth is that you gave *waterjoyup* the moment she had always desired. In fact, the *two* moments she had always desired. Can you not touch them? Her own death *and* the birth of her second child? They were the finest gifts you could have made!"

189

Can death be a fine gift? my soul counters, seeking to be right, wanting *clearcorallie* to be wrong. *You will soon be a mother, and what of your feelings? Only two days ago your soul was shouting deeply that you wanted to live! Not die!*

Clearcorallie's answer is rapid.

"A mother struggles to live only until her child is born."

I have no answer to give her, and again I choose aloneness as my youthful "answer."

But for the first time my soul admits, *I am young, foolishly so. I always need mothers, foolish need. . . .*

Poundgrayly appears as the light of day begins to dim.

I force my soul into a rush of recent memories, and explain to him the happenings he has not witnessed: *the image of the fish . . . clearcorallie . . . the child to come . . . the guardians waiting. . . .*

His answer is a pink face of acceptance, woven with a small laugh, tinged with a jerking of surprise.

"Your days have not grown any calmer, have they?" he says.

I ignore his attitude. "And where is *murmursome?*"

"Ah, he left me as soon as your message was given. A nervous *ayom*, certainly. And it seems the old patterns in his soul bring him such nervousness."

The strangely coherent images have returned to *murmursome's* voice? Questions return with them, and I wish the *ayom* near me now to seek the answers.

"Answers. . . ." *poundgrayly* echoes, no longer interested in making a joke of the questions that fill me.

"Shall we go to her guardians now?" he asks, nodding his soul toward *clearcorallie*, who is floating nearby and swimming in curiosity about this old *euyom*, my friend.

"I wish to wait for *murmursome*," I say.

"But we told *nightbreaking*," comes the objection from *clearcorallie*, "that we would return to them as soon as possible!"

"We will wait for *murmur—*" I start to command, but *poundgrayly* interrupts.

"The wait is over, young soul."

In the distance *murmursome's* soul is approaching faintly, quickly.

As we wait for the *ayom's* arrival, I speak to *poundgrayly*.

"Will it discomfort you to share your awareness of my territory with *nightbreaking* and *whiterim?* Often it is difficult to reach familiarity with a new territory—"

"A simple pleasure," *poundgrayly* answers, and his soul raises a joking tone. "It surprises me that you have chosen

190

to follow the tradition of exchange. *Screamdeep* would have screamed against it—and you would be a surprise to his soul also."

Clearcorallie laughs, and the *euyom*'s soul brightens in appreciation.

"Your meaning is unclear," I lie, offering the obvious lie as a finger for ignoring *poundgrayly*. But his soul does not darken. *Clearcorallie* is still laughing.

Face's eyes touch *murmursome*, and lead my soul to probe him.

Darkness of disappointment slaps me.

Once again the *ayom*'s soul is offering only "ssssk ssssk ssssk."

It is as if the strangely coherent patterns were willfully avoiding me, and I can only grow red in frustration.

"At least this serves to keep your questions alive," *poundgrayly* says, the joking tone undying.

Not willing to submit, I continue to probe all faces of *murmursome*'s soul. I probe the outer laces, the yellow currents, the—

Clearcorallie is speaking—not to me, but to *poundgrayly* —and in annoyance I turn my soul toward her.

"You are *poundgrayly*. I am *clearcorallie*. Within me is *fishsinger*'s child."

"Yes, yes, yes," the *euyom* answers, bright and yellow, "I am *poundgrayly*, and you are the boy's girl—or perhaps woman—and I have never held a child within my old scaly body—not even a single egg!"

Clearcorallie laughs.

Together *poundgrayly* and *clearcorallie* are finding contentment in each other's souls. I can only float watching them, alone. . . .

Their two souls soon enter into a shared rhythm of shared images. But I pay no attention to the images themselves, as the rhythm is the event that bothers me.

Annoyance drives my soul into itself, where I begin thinking about *murmursome*, and the coherent patterns that have twice eluded me. My feelings darken further.

In a moment frustration lifts itself to highest face, and my soul without will throws out a curse of darkness.

Damn waters endless!

The curse catches *clearcorallie*'s attention, and browning in panic, her soul turns toward me.

"What? Danger? Where . . . ?"

Her soul flails, along with *poundgrayly*'s, but they find no danger nearby.

Clearcorallie reaches out to me, probes quickly, and finds

191

that the darkness thrown out by my soul has only been a current of frustration.

Her soul grows red, embarrassed and angry, allowing her to shout at me:

"Why did you do that? *Poundgrayly's* soul and mine were deep in rhythm's pleasure—but for the tiniest of reasons you broke our bond!"

Poundgrayly says nothing, simply listens to our two young souls.

The girl's anger challenges mine, and redness drives me to shout back at her.

"You bond is not so important! No more important than the mysteries of *murmursome's* soul!"

"Oh damn waters endless!" she mocks me.

"You are stupid!" I throw at her. "Your sharing rhythm is foolishly trivial!"

Even as I throw it out, I know my last image will hurt the feelings of both *clearcorallie* and *poundgrayly*. And even as I know it, I admit that I will have to offer pale apologies.

"I am sorry," I begin, but—

—*clearcorallie* has already turned back to the *euyom*, seeking a renewal of the dancing rhythm.

Annoyance is ready to change its red face into purple jealousy, and it does so within me, surprising me. That *poundgrayly* is sharing himself so easily with the girl is understandable: he has always been an open soul, and this face of his manner does not cease pleasing me. But that *clearcorallie* is opening so easily to him?—after the criticisms she made about *murmursome, poundgrayly,* my friends who are not of my kind!

Of course *clearcorallie* hears my reaction. Without turning, with only a glance through the corner of her rhythm-bound soul, she answers me:

"*Poundgrayly* is so fatherly, as you must know, *fishsinger*. He must have been a fine guardian for you—and I would certainly like him as a fatherly guardian for me too." Then she gestures to the *euyom*, laughs, and adds, "Stay with me, Father *poundgrayly!*"

So she wants a father—

—just as I want a mother. . . .

Damn clearcorallie for her controlled and bothersome ways! I have no need of a simple, easily hurt girl who can suddenly seem a soul of womanish wisdom!

I calm myself, hide my steady reds—with a solid purpose to follow.

Attending to the laugher and bouncing of their shared

rhythm, the girl and the *euyom* are unaware of my departure.

"They will understand that heavy questions cannot be ignored," I say to myself after a hundred tail-kicks, "when they begin to wonder where I have gone."

If they are wise, my soul answers, *they will remember that my soul was called to the "man."*

If they are dumb, my soul adds, *and do not remember, then I do not care how painful their confusions become!*

When I come to question the specific direction of my swimming, it seems for a moment that I neglected to ask *riverred* the location of the *man's* territory.

I am prepared for—and beginning to curse it—a period of time spent in seeking a hundred souls and probing them for the *man's* location. But my soul finds the answer on its own.

Dimly, but clearly enough, there is a minor image attached to the important image *riverred* gave me. *The man: on the edge of the congregation: laughing: saying that the eye fell from night's dryness—linked with: the man: his territory to be avoided: near the longest densest mass of yau: near the canyon of darkness and slickest mosses: near the thirteen straight and jagged crags.*

I passed through the long mass of yau with *screamdeep* once; I have heard souls speak of the direction of the slick canyon; and from there I will be able to find the straight jagged crags on my own.

Salved by aloneness, I begin to swim harder, ignoring the many-faced colors and souls of single fish or waves of hundreds of small bodies, ignoring the great plants that dance slowly around me, as I pass through them, as they thin out and long stretches of calm sand disturbed only by infrequent mouths of fish and *eie* rooting for worms, for soft crabs, for delicate shells, take their place.

I lose my sense of direction once, swim through a shallow world of pink-frond stems, and correct my path when a familiar island announces to my soul that I am traveling *away* from the *man's* territory.

When I lose the proper path a second time, my soul darkens, choosing tiredness instead of angry frustration, and aloneness becomes a cold sharp hand instead of warmth.

Images of *poundgrayly* rise in my soul—but more important, images of *clearcorallie* do the same. Memories of the few moments our souls actually touched each other, memories of stumbling feelings or even solid things shared in our faces' eyes—all images woven in *clearcorallie's* meaning bring

193

to my soul a feeling of loss, strangely as deep as loss by death.

See it: The past is a killer as decisive as talons or jaws. Memories of the past moments are memories of killed moments, bringing feelings as dark as those born of a companion's death.

My soul kills its feelings, unable to kill myself, and I swim on in mere flesh's meaning, as the body understands the soul more than the soul will ever know.

XIV

The longest densest mass of *yau,* the deep slick canyon of moss, and—

—and the thirteen—no, fourteen—slender crags of jagged edges.

When I reach the crags, the end of my path, my muscles are reluctant to stop swimming. They tingle, twitch, and without will my tails wave nervously, carrying me up and down, and in circles.

And when my face's eyes finally attend to the territory around me, my soul is surprised. I expected the *man's* territory to be the strangest one I had ever seen. . . .

See it: A territory reflects the faces of the soul who possesses it? True only in another soul's inner images, not in the solid world. The *man's* legend of images has easily colored my soul's expectations of his territory, but the features of his territory are not so different from those of mine, not so different at all.

To search for the *man?*

I could try to find him—but chances are *he* will find *me.* If his soul has no desire or curiosity toward meeting me, a stranger in his territory, I might never find him at all.

So I begin to swim around the crags, making increasingly larger circles as I go—the first steps toward exposing the presence of my soul and flesh.

After the twentieth circling—when my swimming has taken me far beyond face's eyes' sight of the crags—a *difference*

194

suddenly strikes awareness in my soul. In all the time I have been in the *man's* territory, I have neither seen the bodies nor heard the souls of any *ayom, euyom, uiu, oio, ioe, eie, aie*. In fact, there have not been even masses of fish, only occasional single fish flesh and souls.

This *difference* is heavier on my soul than any other strangeness of the *man's* territory could be, and the mystery becomes another burdening question.

I continue to circle, waiting, listening to the question and to the silence born of the absence of souls.

I circle, circle, and—

—it happens.

The answer comes, but my soul is too shocked to grasp it. Brown fears cover all of my soul's fingers—

—when suddenly the hundreds of giant bodies appear, rushing at me.

It seems they appear from nowhere, but that seeming does not dilute their realness. They are charging me! As if all the *ioe* and *uiu* in the territory have been waiting for me, joined together and waiting!

All the *ioe* and *uiu*—and more!

Strange rumbling souls darker and wider and deeper in hatred than any souls I have ever heard—rushing to kill me!

They reach the sight of face's eyes, and I see:

Bodies I have never known to exist. *Ioe* with six coiling heads, necks as long as an *oio's* entire body, their jaws in clouds of blood, *their own blood,* as they strike at each other, twisting, ripping, but continuing to rush toward me.

The waters seem to bubble with their bodies, and beyond them I see still stranger forms, beasts that were not shaped for swimming:

One giant body with limbs that lack webbing, great legs almost as large as the body itself, but taloned terribly, one immense head, also a disadvantage in swimming, two small arms dangling at its sides, useless for swimming, useless also for killing. The beast possesses no fins, only a smooth pointed tail, but somehow it is moving through the sea in great bounding motions, bellowing without rhythm or colors, with only the pure idea of "bellow" rumbling from its soul.

Another giant body, squat but larger than any *oio*, with webless tail-less legs so heavy and stumpy; around its beaked head a rim like an *euyom's* shell, above each eye a long smooth horn so large it would be useless as a means for killing me—but a beak that could sever my body easily!

Other beasts, with talons so long that swimming is difficult, or with bony plates lining a cumbersome spine, or with finless tails ending in masses of spikes—

—the horde of bodies tumbling, devouring each other to sustain themselves, but rushing on and on toward me.

I can only try: I threw out an *ioe* lie.

Browns deepen to the deepest horror when I see that the lie only excites the beasts more. They are hungry for such small bodies—the bodies of female *ioe*, or any other beast whose soul's image I could throw at them!

Death has become so certain that my soul grows calm. I begin to savor the death moment to come—falling back to my kind's persistent ways, with all heavy questions meaningless now, with *clearcorallie* lost and forgotten, with *poundgrayly* trivial as a distant stem of *yau*.

My body is buffeted by currents: the horde is upon me.

The beasts are not kind: their talons and jaws move too rapidly, and I have no time to taste a lengthy death—

I awake to feel a river of laughter, and above it a clumsy rhythm.

"Beasts of beasts of beasts, death of deaths of life, love of lives of death." Laughter. . . .

My face's eyes open, clear the cloudiness of wakening, and see a body of my kind—different, but a body of my kind.

As the legend of nervous images told, his hands are not webbed. His legs do not end in tails, but instead in stumps with five smaller stumps on each. He moves his legs to keep an upright position, but because they lack tails he has to move them quickly, jerkily, using constant peaks of flesh's energy.

And though his skin and skin's color are mainly normal, his flesh bears patches of tender-seeming pinkness, wrinkled and even whitish. From some of these patches stiff hairs have grown, especially on his chest and toward the bottom of his stomach, in the area between his legs—

—and here, between his legs, is the strangest flesh of all. Resembling a large finger—but seemingly boneless—it floats in the shadows of hairs; and below it, behind it, even further in the shadows, hides a small round mound of pink wrinkled flesh.

Whereas the other strange features of his body are from *a lacking*—weblessness, tail-lessness, and patches of seemingly raw skin—this dangling "finger" and the hair surrounding it are an addition. Most bodies of my kind are smooth

196

between their legs, except for the single small hole from which colored waters flow a few times each day.

Suddenly the *man* speaks, his soul dancing around my puzzlement.

"Yes, boy, I possess something you do not! And I have the fish image too, just like you! Additions, ho!"

Such comments only add to my confusion. I can only move my soul to thank him for somehow saving me from the horde of impossible beasts:

"However you sent them away," I begin, "my gratitude is necessary—"

But his laughter only dances higher, spinning around me. He is laughing *at* me?

"You honor my makings," he laughs. "Regard their precision!"

Into my soul he throws an endless vision of all the giant bodies that rushed at me—

They were his soul's creations?

They were all faces of a giant lie!

In yellow laughter, he is proud—proud to have tricked me so completely, brought me such pounding browns, driven me to accept death and find the acceptance sweet. But why? I have never *known* him at all, never tried to darken his soul with threats or lies!

He grabs my soul and weaves it again in his own creation, fingering all images in my soul as if they were his own:

Murmursome appears before me and I find myself offering him affectionate gratitude for coming, for finding me, in time to help me perhaps—

But somehow *murmursome* begins speaking, laughing, saying, "I am going to bite your flesh!"

My soul constricts, browning. A coherent threat from an *ayom?*

Now *poundgrayly* appears also.

Hope lifts its bright face, and I shout, *"Poundgrayly!"*

The *euyom* says quickly, "Always I have hated your kind, *fishlet.*"

I move back, in flesh and soul, turn to flee, and find *clearcorallie* facing me—laughing.

"I am not a girl, foolish boy", she says deeply. "I am a wounded female *ioe* who has lied to you all along, tricked you into believing that I was a simple girl! Our child will be terrible—the head of an *ioe*, the arms of an infant, bleeding, bleeding . . ."

Echoing *clearcorallie's* laughter comes another, at my left side—

"Father!"

"Father!" *screamdeep* mocks. "I am not your father! I could never be, with you the killer of mothers."

Noooo, my soul wails, but soon stops when a gray voice shouts: "Cease your stupid wailing!"

Waterjoyup floats to my right, her pale face contorted in a reprimand.

I turn quickly to Father and shout, "Look she is alive! I did not kill her!"

"You are wrong," my mother says, and I turn back to her. "You killed me, yes you did, and I have returned. I am here so that you may kill me again. See, I am giving birth to my killer!"

Between her legs—spread apart and as rigid as rock—a small head is appearing dimly, encased in its blood-filled sac, beginning to slip out from her body.

The child is too familiar—

—and I scream, scream again—

Suddenly the six familiar souls disappear, replaced by the *man* himself, who is screaming to mock me.

Understanding stumbles toward me. See it: A soul of my own kind has used lies against me, to confuse me, control me, pain me. Only the most talented soul who ever lived could do such a thing! And such a thing I have never heard any soul tell about, in all my five thousand days of living.

"Please," I cry, but the *man* chooses to toss my soul around even more. The images rush at me:

Ioe: with face of an old woman: eating a child.

I whimper "Please" once more.

A thousand euyom: laughing at you!

A scalesoul: with the jaws of an ioe—

The image dims suddenly, dissolved, and the *man's* voice breaks through it.

"These *scalesouls*—where did you view such bodies and souls? Answer me!"

I do not need to answer. The *man* reaches into my soul with sharpest fingers and claws through my memories rapidly.

See it: The man never attends congregations; nor do souls venture into his territory with messages. He has not heard about the *scalesouls* and the *bigshinegray*, or about the boy's entrance into dryness.

When he has completed his probing, the *man* chooses silence.

No laughter comes. His soul is tinted with green specks of curiosity.

"You left the damned waters of the sea, you did."

I am pleased that his ignorance has calmed him, that images in my soul have managed to end his laughter. I answer him loudly:

"Of course!"

"Do not be so arrogant," he darkens. "You departed the sea, and that is more than you know."

I am afraid of him, so it is my turn to choose silence.

"Behold such a departure," he says, musing to his own nervous soul. "Behold it, behold it. . . ." Then his soul's guard begins to slacken, and I am able to touch his hidden thoughts for a brief moment.

Among the fifty thousand souls I would never touch, this boy is greenly different. And he has come to me. . . . Behold such unexpected moments!

Then he begins to shout.

"You are attracted to me? Of course. Now then, swallow this—"

And in a violent rush I receive the *man's* life.

I am a child whose soul is tight against all probings. It cannot help but be tight. I am the greatest soul who has ever lived.

But the souls of my parents are dark against me. Not hating me yet, but soon they will—browns and reds against the greatest soul who has ever lived.

My mother and father have protected me with lies for three thousand days—since the day of my unwanted birth, my tail-less, webless coming into their waters.

Many taut brown days have passed, and my parents have left me near the shadowed cave of a male *ioe*. Most children would die soon . . . but I am quite different. . . .

Many red days pass, and I have almost forgotten the day I wove the male *ioe's* soul with an amazing lie and drove him away. *A thousand uiu attacking*—this was how I did it, and I certainly have not forgotten how to mold such forceful lies. I have molded a hundred such lies since the first—each more complex, more fearful, more precise than the previous one—and because of my soul's great ways, all other souls of my kind choose not to touch my soul, nor to venture anywhere near me.

I have lived ten thousand days, and I have begun to find pleasure in frightening my own kind away—whenever one stumbles into my territory. Their souls are so shallow, so much like soft coral, and their flailing efforts to escape my lies—incredible beasts, incredible screams and colors—bring laughter to my lone soul. . . .

I have lived another ten thousand days, and the gray of boredom visits my soul frequently. Yes, I would even welcome a trembling brown to my soul—but brown never comes, since there is not a single form of flesh in the sea that can make me afraid. My soul's creations—entire worlds of incredible beasts, dredged from my soul's deepest canyons—are heavier than anything, body or soul, in the sea. So I find myself floating alone and attending to those greater worlds in my soul, most of each passing day. . . .

Ah . . . today is different. A boy intrudes in my territory. Yes, and his body bears strange scars on his shoulders, and though his soul is as shallow as the others, his memory holds images that serve to shatter my boredom, at least for a moment.

My soul finds laughing pleasure when I throw at him one of my great lies, and then another, and another. His soul swallows them so easily!

I could frighten him away forever—

Or I could destroy his soul with one dark twist of *my* soul, leaving his flesh to rot and be chewed by fish and other small bodies.

But I choose not to. I choose to honor him. I shall lift his simple being from the stature of a crab to that of a man!

Thank you for your gift of greatness, my soul's depths say in sarcasm before I can hide my feelings. *Your laughter may be that of a fool*.

Easily the *man* hears me. "I could kill you," he says, "and you hold no fear of dying?" Laughter brightens his soul. "But of course not! Your kind wants death so deeply!"

My kind and your kind, my soul answers without will, but also with little fear, and this confuses me. Have I lost all desire to keep death from me?

"My kind?" the *man* cries out, a laughing cry. "Do I possess tails? Webbed fingers? A desire for death's instant? Behold the truth, if your weak face can! I am not of your blood, and your blood is a sickness to me!"

It is difficult to feel brown poundings when the *man* offers so many images to ponder . . . so my soul finds protesting easier.

"I do wish for death," I say quickly, "but *often* I do not. And when I do, it pleases me very little."

"So . . . to turn our souls' eyes to *you*, singer to fish. You ponder your meaning often, it seems. May you die without desiring death!"

200

His laughter arches above me, slaps me, and I shrink back.

He waits, and his waiting urges me to speak. For the moment he offers no threats, and I do not believe he will harm me.

"You are the one with limbs for moving on land," I say. "But it was *I* who entered dryness."

My images are successful. They bring from the *man*'s soul a hidden desire for dryness. Dryness? He would not be able to breathe in dryness any more easily than I did.

The images are successful in exposing his soul, but they also redden him nervously.

His reds become a web of babble—no direct images of threat, or hate, or darkness. And because his anger is so imprecise, I dare to interrupt him:

"Please, I wish no game. Perhaps to *know* you, serious touch, and—"

I have questions, my soul murmurs.

"Your questions will kill you, and this satisfies my blood," he says. "What queries, lover-of-death, hater-of-dying?"

"Where is the *eye?*"

"It fell, it fell."

I am aware that it fell, my soul answers, reddish impatience. *I am aware that it left night's dryness, that it—*

"You babble too much, speaking of your *self* too much. Listen to the *man:* the *eye* fell to an island, and has failed to rise to the night ever since. Your answer is given . . . now go away. Your face is boring, boring into me!"

"I want . . ." I say quickly, then abandon the self-ness of "I": "The island you speak of must be found. There are questions to be understood and answered. Our kind's meaning is linked with the *eye*—believe this truth—and the *eye* may touch the meaning and death-faces of the *scale-souls.*"

The *man* laughs, choosing orange leaves to adorn his brightness, but then he stops laughing, darkening in mock seriousness.

"Yes, your disrespect for dying is grand. You extend your wish to live onto all your kind's souls!"

"*Your* kind's souls," I say.

And he has nothing to offer against my insistence of shared blood. I can feel him probing my soul, and I know that he will find a strong belief, a sincere vision that includes him in the image of my kind. He will find that I consider his tail-lessness and weblessness unimportant: that my own twisted hand is enough to make me ignore his differences.

"Perhaps," he says finally, sighing, "your dream of the *eye*'s meaning is not so wrong. I have dreamed dreams, yes I have, which were truer than most solid truths in the sea."

Will you allow your soul and flesh to help me? my soul asks as faintly as possible, fearing another burst of red from him, a precise one.

"Help? Yes, I shall enter your game, which at least is *different*—almost as different as I am."

To the island you spoke of . . . ?

"What precise meaning of 'help' do you hold?"

I do not know, cannot know—

"Certainly not!"

But we will discover its meaning at the island you spoke of.

"To the island, then! To the island of I and you!"

I move my tails, preparing to swim, expecting the *man* to follow—or rather to lead.

"No, not yet," he says. "There are things I must do. I shall meet you at the island after the passing of three nights."

The image of "things I must do" is unclear. But I must accept his wishes; he is not a soul to be forced.

"Where and which is this island?" I ask.

The image of the island and the path to it come as shouts from his soul, and my soul reels back from the force.

I shall be waiting . . . I shall be waiting, my soul reminds, as I begin to swim.

After only five tail-kicks I receive a dim feeling from within myself. Something . . . something about the island's image is familiar, heavy with solemn meaning that flows from beyond my own personal flesh.

XV

Three days are not enough time for returning to *clear-corallie* and *poundgrayly* first.

It does not matter, my soul announces. *You do not wish to return to them anyway.*

I reach the island in half a day of leisurely swimming. It is inside the *man*'s territory, and—

—I recognize it immediately, understanding its familiarity.
This is the place where my father brought my mother's body. He watched the thousands of tiny animals devour her flesh gently here. . . .

Shared memories capture my soul, refusing to let me think of anything except *screamdeep* and *waterjoyup*, refusing to let me inspect the island's area with face's eyes.

To escape the memories . . . to touch the island and its surrounding solid features *on my own*, not through my father's moments!

And escape does come, but only through sleep, when night brings darkness.

I awake free of my father's *then*, and understand quickly that there are complex deeds to be managed before the *man* arrives.

We must leave the water, my soul announces. *The eye, if it rests somewhere upon the island, is in dryness.*

We must have a means for leaving the sea, my soul goes on, reaching in a hundred soul's directions for a means.

Memory supplies it, simply enough. *Two female euyom will take us into dryness.*

But memory cannot supply the *euyom*.

Perhaps I should have returned to *poundgrayly*. He would have readily given me two of his females. Perhaps I should have rushed back to the old *euyom* and taken the chance that the *man* would still be awaiting me at the island—even if the journey did take five or six days.

No, I shall be able to manage it without poundgrayly's aid!

My deepest soul cannot fool me. I know and admit that I want to do my deeds *alone* this time. Well, perhaps not entirely alone: the *man* and two female *euyom* would be helping me, but at least I will not have to bow my soul before *poundgrayly's* joking slaps. He and *clearcorallie* can have their bond of rhythm—I do not need them!

I swim around the island, and soon begin to recognize it in another way. It was here that the three hundred men and women in my memory came to die, most of them failing to achieve death here, but they came just the same because this was always a chosen island for death. Because of the large areas of shallowness around it, the bodies of many dead souls have always been brought to this island and will no doubt continue to be brought . . . until the *scalesouls* return and create too many dead bodies for one island to hold . . .

See it: Much of this island's shallowness is sandy areas. Where there are sandy stretches, there may also be female *euyom*—waiting for their males or waiting to enter dryness where they will lay their eggs.

I find three large places of sand before night approaches. I enjoyed their warm stillness—wrought by light in shallowness—but I find no *euyom* at all.

The first sandy area I visit the next day brings a pink pounding surprise.

The thirteen females—their souls round faces of pale softness at a distance—touch my soul gently and understand quickly that I am an unthreatening *yom*.

When I reach them and can touch them with face's eyes, their pink calmness is so certain that they make no effort at all to turn and watch me. Instead their souls continue touching me gently, their green bodies hanging quietly in the shallow water above the sands, their scaly limbs barely waving to assure their positions.

Lavender is not among them. I did not expect, but I hoped, that she would be one of them.

For a moment I know no proper image to give them.

"Are you all," I finally ask, "*poundgrayly*'s souls?"

Two of the females nearest to me answer together.

"*Poundgrayly* is not our commanding soul—"

"—and *livingbreath* is."

Again I have no proper image to give them next.

Now a female farther away—somewhat dim in the distance of the sandy shallowness—speaks.

"I have touched *poundgrayly*'s image before. Not his soul, but his image—through one of his females."

"Yes. . . ." I say, waiting.

"Her soul was full of tall pink, and rimming lavender, for him—for that *poundgrayly* who seems to have touched your soul often."

Is she speaking about *lavender*?

It does not matter. *Lavender* is far away, and one or two of these females before me will have to take her place.

I let my soul's deeper voice murmur, hoping the females will answer.

I have need of two of you. One to carry me into dryness. The other to carry a soul named the man—

"The *man.* . . ." one *euyom* answers, darkening. She is the one who has heard of *poundgrayly*.

The other twelve do not understand, but grow nervous in the one *euyom*'s darkness of soul.

Quickly I throw a chain of images at them: *lavender* carrying *fishsinger*, the boy holding onto her shell, onto a

204

hollow stem of *yau*, with a mass of *yau* leaves on his back. But before the memory can reach my meeting with the *scalesouls*, I end the images.

All thirteen females begin babbling to each other, and it seems that their souls are shying away from me.

The *euyom* who has heard of *poundgrayly* finally speaks.

"*Lavender* was one of *poundgrayly*'s souls, and she carried you, heavy though you were. . . . If your need is truly so deep, it would please me to carry you into dryness."

I would also be pleased, another female interrupts, sharing the first female's remote affection for *poundgrayly*.

"But," continues the first female, "I have no desire—near or far—to be touched in body and soul by the *man*. Surprise has struck me that you are not dark in his companionship, that you are able to bear his strangeness with only shallow annoyance."

It becomes my turn to feel surprise. The *man*'s dark legend has traveled so far? His image brings brown poundings even to *euyom*? See it: A legend is but a giant lie with tails that let it swim to the ends of the sea.

Understanding comes: I will have to convince two of the females that they will be pleasing *me* deeply if one of them carries the *man* into dryness with me—that perhaps displeasure can be buried by the fact of *my* pleasure.

The first female is quick in soul. She hears my musings, and gives a pale laugh.

"If you manage to convince one of us," she says, "it will not be me."

I reach into her soul, offering a yellow face of respect, and find a deepest vision: *softeye*. Or is it *dimeye*?

"*Dimeye*," I begin, but she interrupts me.

"This soul's precise name is *gentleeye*, who will not be fooled by yellow faces of respect—if those faces hide a conniving."

I find myself laughing. This *euyom*'s soul is as quick as *poundgrayly*'s, and her gray distrust of my kind's frequent trickery amuses me. *Poundgrayly* would enjoy the companionship of this female named *gentleeye*.

"But he will never have the chance," *gentleeye* says. "I am one of *livingbreath*'s souls, and in his possession I will remain quite contentedly!"

I nod in soul, turning my attention to the second female who had expressed an inclination to carry me into dryness.

This second *euyom*'s soul is simpler. She is easily moved

by the souls around her, and I hope I will be able to move her even more easily.

Without probing for her name, I ready an image within my soul—

—and *gentleeye,* understanding what I am about to do, gives out another pale laugh.

I throw the image quickly to the second female, adorning it with as much pink affection as my soul can manage, and making its colors and tastes as real as *now.*

If you carry the soul named the man: you will receive: from me: the meat from a hundred shells!

The simpler female grows excited, but then darkens again as she senses that her twelve fellow *euyom* have not been swayed by the image.

Quickly I extend the image to include:

And you will receive: from me: the meat from twelve shells: now!

The new promise excites the simpler female completely.

The thirteen females watch as I swim to the sandy bottom.

Face's eyes find no living shells *on* the sand, nor do I expect to find any there. Hundreds of twin-shelled *er* are no doubt buried *in* the sand, but these are not the kind of shell I want: any *euyom* can obtain a dozen *er* simply by digging with her limbs in the sand.

Face's eyes see a lone rock, with a spiny *yau* plant attached to it, and I move in that direction.

My soul detects four small hazy patches of green—shell souls—and in a moment my face's eyes find the four shells at the base of the plant, all the same brown color as the plant, and motionless to hide themselves.

The shells are nearly as large as my hand. The meat within them will make four mouthfuls for an excited *euyom.*

As I remove them from their small territory, each animal pulls itself tightly back into its shell, holding a hard round disk in its shell's opening. It would be impossible to remove the animal's flesh with my fingers alone. . . .

With the shells held against my chest, I swim in search of more rocks.

When I find three close together, dark spots against the endless sand, I test one rock to discover if I can lift it. But it is too deep in the sands.

The second rock lifts easily. I place one of the shells on the first rock, lift the second and bring it down as hard as I can on the shell.

The shell breaks, and face's eyes show me a crushed animal writhing and pierced by pieces of its own hard shell.

The second shell needs two blows of the rock before it breaks, but the others shatter under single blows. Gathering up the four dying animals, I move my fingers to pick the pieces of shell from their flesh.

The simply *euyom* is waiting, unable to disguise her enthusiasm.

Her beak takes one handful of meat from me quickly, and in only a few moments she has eaten all four animals.

Then you will follow my wishes, and carry the man? my soul says gently, and it is not a question.

"If the *man* does her any harm—flesh of soul," *gentleeye* says, "we shall all throw you the deepest darkness, and you shall never touch our souls again."

The man did me no harm, my soul answers deeply, *and he will do your sister no worse.*

I complete my promise, finding and crushing eight more shells for the simple *euyom,* and the day ends.

The third day arrives, and my soul begins a precise waiting for the *man.*

When half of the day has passed, I grow nervous, and manage to calm myself only by seeking more shells—these to be given to *gentleeye,* although I have not promised her any.

"What is it that you want of me today?" *gentleeye* asks darkly when I give her three shell meats.

"These shells are simply the flesh of gratitude for what you will do for me *tomorrow.*"

Without giving up her dark distrust, she takes the meats, chews them slowly, and a dim face of pale gratitude even escapes from her soul.

Finally the dark of night dims the sands and *euyom* bodies, and I realize that the *man* has broken his promise.

To venture a trust in him, and wait yet another day?

Or to wait, and end by being a fool?

I do not know the strange soul called *man* enough to understand what his absence, this seemingly shattered promise, really means.

I decide to wait, and use sleep to pass my waiting.

The females are babbling softly to each other when I awake.

Gentleeye and the simpler female are waiting near me, and from the wise female's soul I receive a jagged impatience.

"Is it possible," *gentleeye* accuses, "that your laughing friend has been more conniving than you ever imagined?"

This annoys me. The images she is throwing at me reveal that she has been probing my soul as I slept.

"You must admit," she says, "that your soul holds interesting depths. I merely looked into those depths to pass my waiting moments."

I darken, saying, "If you were one of *poundgrayly's* females, he would slap your bloated arrogance out of you!"

She laughs and says: "*Livingbreath* knows only kindness."

I turn my soul from her, and try not to admit the precision of her wisdom. She understands the *man's* ways perhaps better than I do.

It takes half a day before I begin deeply to admit the truth.

See it: His promise and my waiting are both faces of a game—the *man's* game, which has tricked me just as I once chose to trick *murmursome* into believing that I was a wounded female *ioe*. I was stupid to believe the *man,* to allow him control over my living moments. I should have guessed the deepest vein of his ways—no, I should have probed his soul and discovered his true intentions three and a half days ago!

I was afraid to probe—

—and he knew that I was afraid!

Suddenly to my soul's eye comes a vision of the *man* laughing, laughing more cruelly than he ever laughed before. The laughter embraces me like the crushing weight of an *oio,* and my soul spits red everywhere around me.

"I will throw no more laughter at you," comes *gentleeye's* voice. "I am sorry the *man* harmed your soul's contentment—but you are not alone in being hurt. I have heard a hundred other souls claim similar harms from the twisted spines of the soul called *man."*

Her consoling colors are not successful. I move heavily in soul's darkness, fight a strange growing face of aloneness, and escape it by saying to the wise female:

"This moment is not entirely dark. Your simple sister willl not be forced into carrying the *man* now."

Gentleeye nods. In a moment she says softly: "Do you wish to enter dryness now?"

The face of aloneness presses me to say "No."

But the deeper soul of me answers loudly, "Yes."

The mass of *yau* leaves rests on my back. The end of the hollow *yau* stem is between my teeth. My good right hand holds the rim of *gentleeye's* shell. And *gentleeye* is moving toward shallower water, toward dryness.

The bubbling water is no different than the other bubbling water—at the island of the *scalesouls*—but this time I feel no brown beatings beginning in my soul.

My head breaks into dryness, and still no browns.

And when the fish image begins to form within me, I am expecting it and able to hold it down.

No images or laughter come from the *euyom* under me. *Gentleeye* remains as silent as any soul can be; her sole concern of flesh and soul is to carry me across the wide band of dry sands on the island.

In a moment our two bodies are in total dryness. The sands around us grow drier and drier, and I wet my eyes for the first time.

Familiar brows do begin to rise then. *Will the stem be long enough? How far from us is the eye—and what will it seem to face's eyes?* The island is a large one.

If the stem is too short, I conclude brightly, *I will ask gentleeye to return me to the sea for a longer stem.*

I wet my eyes again, and see that the pale sands have ended. Under us now stretches an orangish surface, from which mists of similar orange, finer than sand, rise up around us when *gentleeye*'s limbs strike it.

And only a few tail-lengths in front of us are lines of thick stiff plants. *Will we be able to pass through them?* my soul worries grayly.

Worry turns to brown when my face's eyes detect the density of the plants' leaves, leaves that are just as stiff, it seems, as the plant stems themselves.

Gentleeye does not hesitate, and in a moment my body jerks in pale pain.

Some of the stiff leaves have rasped against me as we pass between the plants—but *gentleeye* fails to understand my pain.

"To stop?" she asks quickly. "You have viewed what you seek?"

"No! A plant struck me," I say. "Your shell and scales keep the plants from hurting you. Allow your soul to consider my exposed flesh!"

Her soul offers a laugh. "Yes, I shall consider it. Usually I do not find my body carrying *yom* past the sands of islands."

I cannot touch laughter, but I return her smile as pinkly as I can.

"You have never moved this far from the sea?" I ask.

"The places where eggs are placed," she answers, "are a hundred of your tail-lengths behind us. No, never this far."

After a travel of another hundred tail-lengths the stiff

209

plants grow more infrequent. Their souls seem to scream dark hummings, but after many moments in their presence my soul finds the screaming familiar and without threats.

When I wet my eyes again I see that the stiff plants are no longer around us. The orangish surface has given way to a cracked bumpiness—mud under dryness' touch, it seems—and my soul gestures for *gentleeye* to stop.

Brown churnings begin within me.

Bits of dryness are coming through the *yau* stem!

The end of the stem has been pulled up into the bubbling waters at sea's edge, my soul announces as calmly as it can. *If gentleeye carries me any further, the end of the stem will be pulled into complete dryness.*

"We cannot move from here," I tell the *euyom* under me.

Her soul chooses silence, and her silence allows me to think.

Wetting my eyes with a tired hand, I look up and out into the distance before us.

Dim forms, but recognizable as stiff plants of different sizes; and an endless surface of mud touched by dryness.

I wet my eyes again—

—and touch a *different* form . . . a large upright gray surface facing me from the distance.

In a moment I realize that the smooth gray surface is five times as large as I first imagined. And that it resembles . . . yes, it does resemble that grayness on the *scalesouls'* island!

Is it possible—a *bigshinegray?*

Brown poundings command me: *A bigshinegray full of scalesouls!*

Green curiosity rises: *Has this bigshinegray come seeking the eye too?*

My face's eyes touch it again and again, and then deepest rumblings begin within me.

Deeper than my first memories—deeper than all shared memories of my mother, father, *murmursome, poundgrayly, clearcorallie* and the other thousands of sharing souls—comes the voice of a million eyes, just as it did on the *scalesouls'* island so many days ago.

The voice thunders: "Look upon it . . . we *know* that *bigshinegray* . . . we have not forgotten it and we never shall."

It is not full of *scalesouls* at all!

And it has not come seeking the *eye*—

—*since it is the eye!*

"Listen!" *gent'eeye* cries out. "Something . . . a soul . . . something . . . else? it approaches."

210

My soul spins in confusion, reaches out in a hundred directions, and I touch the approaching thing—or things— three of them. Dull round souls, muffled somehow, seeming to be in waiting, where? In a moment my face's eyes touch them.

There, hanging in dryness above the dried mud . . . moving and bobbing slowly . . . three perfectly round forms, gray and smooth. Smooth? . . . no, a precise crack, a round opening, a shining patch, here and there on their grayness.

Within me brown rushings reach heaviest heights. I want to scream, but the green of my soul holds back any screaming.

It seems that they have souls—but their souls seem as shallow as the simplest coral. It seems that they are waiting—but waiting for what, whom, why, where, when . . . ?

Without will my soul gathers up an *ioe* lie and throws it at the three forms.

They stop, bob gently, then continue approaching.

The three smooth forms remind me of the objects held in the *scalesouls'* hands—the objects that threw painful lights at me—and brown poundings within me increase.

Return to the sea! my soul shouts to *gentleeye*.

Trembling, sharing all browns, the *euyom* begins turning around as quickly as her limbs can manage—

—and as she turns the *yau* stem between my teeth hisses. All wetness ceases its flow through it, and I scream.

Face's eyes are dry; I cannot see. My soul is screaming; I can sense only dimly the three strange souls above me— no, four souls. No, five souls!

Pains claw at my drying chest, inside and out, but before my soul can choose darkness as an escape, I hear a voice.

The voice comes from the five strange un-souls around me, and it is louder than any voice I have ever heard, so much louder than *gentleeyes* screaming under me.

"*I have come to you!*" the voice booms.

XVI

Good round EENTs bring Me more and more extra-corpus *bambini*, and *Mamma*—

Oho! A *bambino* with a body! He crawls from the sea, onto this island. Oho! The hypotheses were close! A pseudo-

211

Prostega (hear Me, Doctor Lady!) is his mount. The kelp keeps his sharkskin-skin wet and cool. He draws water to his lungs through the defoliated reed of kelp. Maybe . . .

Maybe this brave *bambino,* crazy as he is, is the glorious *bambino* who killed the boogiemen! And now he comes faithfully to the hungry *Mamma!*

Hmmm . . . it is definitely *bambino,* not *bambina.* He has no genital-jewels in his crotch, but he is still masculine. Aha! Come to *Mamma!*

Feelers, travel to him quickly. He's only a couple of hundred meters away. Soon our souls will embrace! O *Santa Mamma!*

Quick, Brainy Brain, devise a means for my *bambino bravo* to remain with me for a long time! Quick!

Ah, an aquarium. Dear Womb, do you possess one small aquarium? Of course! I should have known. You have so many good items that a million days made me forget many of them.

Hoses? Pumps? Rah rah rah!

Quick. Fill the aquarium. Too small? Obtain a larger one! Yes, yes. Fill it! Work, Pumps! Your hoses aren't long enough—sew them together, make them long enough, Body! Do it, do it! Right, left, right!

Womb, open your bosom! Slide the hymen. Ah, the first sliding open in so long.

No, Feelers, you won't be able to bring him here by yourselves.

Brainy Brain, does *Mamma* have a robounit? Good. Two will be enough.

Units, dear arms of *Mamma,* leave My bosom. Travel the sands. Reach him!

You are almost there! *Bambino,* it is I!

Oh, very bad. *Mamma's* soul was too much. (But a mortal cannot face God easily, no?)

What you say? Has dropped the breathing stem?

Quick, Units, reach out for him. Good.

Take him gently.

Don't step on the turtle! Careful. . . .

Units, bring him into the Womb. Carry him high—quickly! Still he cannot breathe, still sleeping, but with pains. Hymen, slide shut. Pneumo, lift them all to me. The aquarium, there!

Watch it all, Feelers, watch it all.

Yes, *bambino* breathes now. How sad—a giant fear is born within him. *Povero bimbo.* . . .

Mamma will be careful. She will take care that MAH-MAH soul does not crush him.

Pause a moment.

All of you, help *Mamma* to keep Her soul from making him black and blue with embracing. Work at it!

Ciao, crazy brave one. How are you? I am fine. . . . Yes, we have been having good weather.

Speak to the boy. Stop talking to yourself.

GREETINGS. I AM THE ONLY GOD AND MOTHER YOU WILL EVER NEED.

XVII

Pounding images from a giant voice shake my soul awake

I listen, but the images do not return. I try to remember their colors and meaning, but cannot. My soul reaches out—

—and jerks back when I touch another soul present . . . nearby . . . no, all around me.

It is quiet, dim with gray haze, with a waiting tone—just like the muffled tone of expectancy offered by the round gray forms in dryness—

In dryness?

Yes, says my flesh, my chest, inside and out, *we are in water.*

I am in water again, and the water is—or at least resembles—water near any island's shore: my soul can hear the chatter of certain kinds of tiny invisible souls, those peculiar to shallow areas of the sea, near the rising sands of islands.

Gradually face's eyes grow accustomed to *seeing*, and I begin to detect precise colors before me. Definite points of colored lights . . . not too far away. . . .

With a wave of both tails I move toward them—

—and strike *something*.

Face's eyes find nothing in front of me.

I move again, and immediately strike *something* again.

In a moment my hands reach out, bump against the nothingness, and begin to stroke it—seeking its boundaries.

It is endless, as hard as coral, but smoother than anything my hands have ever stroked.

Moving face's eyes close to the nothingness, I look beyond and see the colored lights more clearly. Flashing in strange patterns . . . blinking in different sizes . . . different brightnesses . . . but are they in water or in dryness?

My soul gives way to flesh's wishes, and I turn around to return to the spot where I awakened.

I go too far, and strike another nothingness opposite the first.

All flesh announces: *Discover the solid!*

And I begin swimming slowly, cautiously, with arms outstretched to *feel*.

Before long I find that the solid nothingness surrounds me on all sides. But in four precise directions the nothingness is most distant from me: the four smooth and invisible surfaces meet at four places and form verticle angles; the surface of nothingness under me meets those four angles and forms four angular caves.

My flesh ceases its desire to move; my soul is churning.

These five surfaces hold me in this small area. But what is their meaning? To keep me in . . . or to keep something out?

Again my body moves, urged by my soul to inspect every spot on the five surfaces.

Soon I discover two holes—two openings with opposite meaning.

One is allowing water to enter my area, and the other is sucking my water out. Face's eyes quickly tell me that on the other side of the invisible and soulless surface a stem a hundred times wider than any *yau* stem is attached to each opening, one sucking and the other blowing. But face's eyes cannot tell me where the two giant stems lead.

The next churning of soul begins from deeper depths. The million eyes of my most distant forefathers' *then* rise for a moment within me, and speak.

Remember the first bigshinegray—it was our bigshinegray.

Remember the thousands of colored lights blinking around us—when we traveled and slept in our bigshinegray.

Remember the thousands of small areas, bound by smooth surfaces around us—when we traveled and slept. . . .

Yes, I was in a small area with smooth nothingness holding me in . . . but my forefathers in dryness had breathed that dryness, not water.

Remember the talents of our bigshinegray—it could do anything we wanted it to do . . . or anything it wanted to do for us.

214

The million eyes rise higher, gaining a deeper voice.

We moved within our bigshinegray, and our bigshinegray moved through endless blackness. . . .

"Am I being moved?"

We cannot know, the million eyes whisper. *We are living memories of dead days. We are not the now of you.*

I do not feel as though I am moving.

We felt no feelings of being moved—when our bigshinegray was moving us.

Of course. The waters around me are not rushing past me, but this does not have to mean I am not being moved. The waters around me are inside the *eye,* would be moving with me if I were being moved by the *eye.* . . .

The million eyes sink down, away, and I begin to wonder if I am really in the *eye* at all.

Then the giant soul begins to speak.

A rumbling rush, which my soul fails to understand; a rushing surge so painful to my soul that without will I seek the immediate darkness of sleep.

But the giant soul quickly falls silent again, and light returns to me, though flesh continues quivering.

I move my soul to probe carefully, and find a wide vision within the giant soul. It is not as clear as most souls' names, but it will serve the purpose, and for deepest reasons my own soul needs to have a name for the great soul surrounding me.

Warmcavebrown . . .? No, the warmth is not constant. The vision rises and falls quickly, sometimes to heights of warmth, but often to bottoms of the darkest cold.

Cavebrown . . .? Yes. . . .

I can feel the giant soul touching me, a thousand fingers rolling my soul gently over and over, thrusting smoothingly into corners of near and far shared memories, no longer *waiting . . .* now moving to understand every eye in my soul's face.

The fingers stop their poking. They retract and the *cavebrown* begins a softer rumbling now.

"I am here," the rumbling says, and then dims to wait for an answer.

You are here, as I am here, my soul answers in a faint vein of will.

Then the *cavebrown's* voice begins babbling to me.

In its fingers' probing, it gained some understanding of images that I would be able to understand—but not enough images. And many currents of its voice seem not to be rushing toward *me*—but toward some other soul, something else . . . with unclear images frequent.

215

"Listen, xefghsf, this mafsxs with two tails is my ijedkl, and I am its sdafghfj mother! Listen, you-of-two-tails, listen to your sdafghfj mother! I am three things. I am vcbnhsfg woman with the name of lkaguygh . . . I am mklsfgyq . . . and I am many thousands of round-gray-forms, of upright-forms-with-legs-arms-heads, of poxgrq, of vbnskl! All of these, xefghsf, love-mnfsg-wrefjaq you!"

My soul's answer is an echo of all the images from the *cavebrown*—all in rising and falling confusion.

The giant soul hears the echo, understands, and grows silent.

The cavebrown names itself a woman, my soul advises itself. *Respect the name—call the cavebrown "she", and the cavebrown will be pleased.*

Again the giant soul is probing my soul, and the paths "she" takes make me realize that she has returned to grasp as many of *fishsinger's* soul's images as she can—images which she will soon swallow and use to make me understand her voice's deepest meanings.

I feel her touch each day of my living, each shared memory from another soul, each question that has ever scattered my thinking—and her touchings are as smooth and silent as the *man's* secret ones were. So soft and quiet and rapid that I almost fail to feel them. . . .

This giant soul is as talented as the man—more talented? If she desired it, she would be able to trick me beyond—

Suddenly the *cavebrown* speaks, and her laughter is a giant.

"The soul you call the *man?* He is bad, and I am good!"

My soul offers nothing. I am waiting. But the *cavebrown* is waiting too.

"You hear me clearly," she rushes loudly. "The *man* is bad. I, your sdafghfj mother, am good, good, good!"

But . . . my soul begins without will, and I constrict into silence.

"What is the meaning of your 'but'?" The *cavebrown* is offering rising reds . . . and rising browns begin instantly within me.

"Kill your browns! A soul has no deep reason to fear its sdafghfj mother! What is the meaning of your 'but'?"

The man was good enough to tell me the path to you—this island . . . if we are still upon an island. . . .

"Of course we are! We haven't moved yet. But your soul has been tricked deeply: the bad *man* has no good blood at all within him! He is dumb, dumb, dumb!"

Browns will not leave me, and I have to answer, *Perhaps.* . . .

"Again you hide! What is the meaning of your 'perhaps'?"

The man was talented enough to trick me with the greatest lies my soul has ever received . . . beasts so terrible that—

"Ah. . . ." the giant soul sighs, and her colors become the warmth of pink, embracing me alone. "You had no way of understanding those beasts, which can be simply understood, my ijedkl. Simply they came from the deepest memories of the bad *man's* knowing—those beasts with webless legs and finless tails. Simply they were memories of beasts, solid beasts, which once lived in living flesh on uysdqwre—in the world of your iqxmbrg—your forefathers who breathed dryness. No, I have confused the truth. Those beasts did live in living flesh in your forefathers' *first* world —but they lived in times long before the living flesh of your forefathers who breathed dryness. No, the truth is yet deeper. No, the vxcshjg—the yusfdg—"

The *cavebrown* grows dark, tumblings of frustration, and my soul feels her curses: she is angry with her own soul's voice, which is failing to make me understand some truth beyond the *man's* amazing lies.

In a moment the *cavebrown* offers a face of pink.

"To other images of truth, different truths, now, my ijedkl. . . . You must come to *know* me, for I am your future! You are my child."

I am the child of waterjoyup and screamdeep.

"You are mine!" the *cavebrown* shouts in pounding blood-red.

My soul whines under the poundings, and quickly I offer a "Yes."

I do not understand—but yes, if it is a truth, I am your child.

"You are my child—as all many thousands of your kind are my children. This is the endless truth of truths beyond your living! I am three things. I am the ixdfgh—no, I am the most motherly mother who ever loved! I am the soul of lkaguygh—of a tail-less motherly woman who lived in flesh and died in flesh millions of days ago! And I am . . . a great hard mass of *knowings* about endless numbers of things, souls, places and times! And I am the smooth hardness of a *bigshinegray,* very full of thousands of empty places, but with thousands of small hard gray things which are my face's eyes and body's fingers, traveling very far to many places!"

The *cavebrown* waits for my answer, for some feeling from my soul—and I do not understand what she wants.

You were and are and will be a mother, my deepest soul finally says, *and that is the only truth to be understood clearly.*

"You are a good soul. You have understood the biggest truth, although the biggest truth is also that I will be *your future!*"

My deepest soul knew all along that the eye was my future—and poundgrayly refused to believe.

"The motherly *eye,* of course! Ah, yes, the face's eyes of your kind saw my passing brightness during night's blackness. You must understand, my *ijedkl,* that it was not *my* brightness, but rather the light of the two *lkhfgh*—of the twin lights of day—which was striking my smooth *bigshinegray* body for your kind to see."

I do not understand. The twin lights of day cannot be present at night, so how they give brightness to a *bigshinegray?*

The *cavebrown* touches my confusion and grows dark in frustration again.

But just as suddenly as it appears, the darkness of frustration dims, and the giant soul offers me her pink face of affection.

"The most distant bottom of your soul," she says, announcing a pinker pride, "has always desired a mother. Look upon me as desire's end!"

The truth. . . . Perhaps the desire was so precise . . . But the dream, the same dream that spoke of you also told me that a mother is not the aim of my deepest desires.

"Your dream was wrong and bad! I have been waiting for you, as I am the most motherly mother who ever lived and will never die!"

Perhaps you were the eye—the voice in my dream? Perhaps you called me, and I believed it was merely my deepest soul calling to me?

"No, I did not call you— Yes, of course I called you! I remember now: I have been calling you and all of your kind's souls for a million days! Do you not believe me? I am your mother. . . ."

My soul wants to believe—for belief would give precise answers. But in the *cavebrown's* great face is a vein of trickery, so similar to the *man's* that I can make no belief solid at all.

"Trickery?" she shouts, reds rising like the fastest *uiu,* "You choose to believe in your mother's trickery, when she— when I, I, I, am the truest loving mother who ever lived in flesh and living soul and will never die!"

The *cavebrown* shouts more and more images, but my

218

soul slips down and away from them, as I move my soul to touch truths behind the *cavebrown's* face.

Dimly an anxious truth is bouncing behind her face, and my probing touches it eagerly. The truth is a line of images, and the images become a faint voice:

I did not call you, no, no, no. . . . Every soul of man or woman who ever lived and died in flesh has always sought a mother as you, you, you do. . . . One mother of many faces, dark, deeper than blood, calling with sweetest song, sought in dark brown caves, in bottomless holes of flesh, in rhythms of warm assurance, in the endless arms of seas, in the births and births again of plants and beasts and children dying only to be born again. . . . And I want to be that mother for all, and I fear, I fear, that I am not quite her, but I am close, I am almost her, and almost is enough to feel pink pride in living and lying that I am her, her, her. . . .

The *cavebrown* catches me listening to the depths of her which cannot lie, and she thunders darkness down upon my soul.

"You dare to touch my secret places, my personal places!"

My soul screams under the darkness, falling toward darkness of my own.

Again the *cavebrown* changes, abandons her screams, reaches for a quick yellow affection—

—and I understand that she, the *cavebrown* of quick changes, pink to red, yellow to brown, is insane—more insane than even the *man!*

Fears clutch flesh and soul, and I try to fall into deeper darkness.

But she will not let me fall. She knows I am trapped, and she keeps me trapped in the yellow of her terrible affection.

"I am the biggest mother," she soothes, and her voice is painful to me. "I am the mother of your blood, for the first body of your blood came from me—millions of days, lives and deaths ago!"

My soul wants to shout, *I am not your child, and you are not my future!* but I hide the shout with a line of yellow "Yes."

The pinkness of her grows, and her voice becomes as sweet as the good meat of *cu*-shells.

"You are my best child! You killed the qrughfsg—the *scale-souls*—and for your act you deserve the biggest mother's love!"

I do not understand, confusion makes me say without

219

really saying. *You are not the mother of scalesouls too?*
You do not love—

"No!" the *cavebrown* reddens. "I am the mother of all
good souls. Never has a *good* scalesoul lived!"

Somehow this makes my soul contented. Somehow it matters that the *cavebrown* holds no pinkness or yellow leaves
for any *scalesoul*. . . . She was powerful, so it was a good
truth that her power was commanded by purple hatred
for all *scalesouls* near and far.

"Speak to me," *cavebrown* says suddenly.

Slowly I choose a cautious question.

Have you been aware, ever since the day you brought my
fathers to our sea, that the hordes of scalesouls killed every
last soul of our distant kind, in every world in the endless
blackness?

"Oh no, I was not aware until you came—until your soul
brought me the sad truth— Sad? No, not sad at all! You
and the thousands of souls of your kind are enough for
happiness! Soon all `of you will be with me, within me,
deeply inside me, and sadness will be a long-forgotten
feeling!"

Inside her—all of us? *Cavebrown's* image of the meaning is confusing. "Inside her" does not mean simply fifty
thousand bodies inside the *cavebrown's* smooth grayness. It
means, it means—

"Yes, inside me forever! Already the biggest mother has
within her the bodiless souls of—"

—the dead! my soul cries out.

"The dead? Yes, but the dead who were not really dead.
Their flesh ceased its agreement, and dissolved or was
chewed away, but their souls continued on—and I found
them—and they loved me—and I swallowed them. Swimming and screaming without flesh, they were still my children, so I took them. . . . I am becoming an even bigger
mother, *fishsinger,* with each new bodiless soul I swallow!"

My soul needs no clear reason to feel stumbling fears.
A hundred faces of brown surround me quickly, and to
protect me let no thought escape my soul, but instead merely echo the *cavebrown's* images.

"Why are you afraid?"

I am afraid to answer even this.

"Why are you afraid of being afraid?"

The souls of the dead . . . can it be that you have
swallowed the souls of . . . of screamdeep . . . of water-
joyup . . . ? No, it cannot be that you have—

"Of course I have them! The greatest mother possesses

220

everything! I have your father . . . and I also have your mother."

I cannot believe her. She has thrown a lie at me once already, and this could easily be a second lie. See it: Each soul is one soul. The souls of the fish we eat do not gather within us; their bodies are killed, and their souls leave. . . . But . . . but the *cavebrown* claims to be a mother, and a mother can have more than just her own soul within her. *Waterjoyup* had my soul inside her, did she not?

"Believe *me*," *cavebrown* shouts. "Look, listen deep inside me, and belief will capture you!"

Her soul stirs, cracks open faintly, and *something* begins to rise, passing through the crack.

A soul! Stretched like skin, holding it in place inside the *cavebrown*—but it is definitely a soul, a clear soul, a familiar—

Screamdeep father!

"Fish singing son of me," the soul answers faintly.

Speak, Father, speak and speak and do not stop speaking to me!

Screamdeep moves his soul slowly, as if in deep sluggish difficulty, trying to speak. "I . . . waited so long . . . near you. . . ."

Suddenly he sinks down. The crack closes, he is gone, and *cavebrown* is rumbling.

"Enough speaking for now! You will have endless moments to regain your father's touch, when you decide to enter—"

So you have my mother too!

"Of course."

Allow me to touch her, please. Her soul, her voice, now!

Cavebrown does not answer, makes no motions toward a new crack.

Please!

"No!"

Is it possible? Behind the *cavebrown's* "No" a stem of purple jealousy has appeared, thrashing and coiling, "No, no, no!"

Please, I wish no games born of purple feeling. Be generous.

"The biggest mother never plays games! It is best that you do not touch your dead mother now!"

She is not dead. She lives within you, and you refuse—

"She is dead. She will live again when I choose to let her, and I shall let her when you come to enter me!"

My soul has stopped listening to her shallow reasons. I

am remembering *screamdeep*, and *murmursome*, and the strangely coherent patterns—

So it was my father's soul, clinging to the ayom's, who was whispering those things to me. . . . His flesh was gone, but he refused to leave me. Father! Let me hear my father! my mother! Let me—

Cavebrown is laughing, pale fragments of yellow scattered across a widest face of brown.

"*Murmursome! Ayom!*" she cries, laughter growing, and then she mocks my father's voice: "All *ayom* have a secret, and I pray that your living will take you to a day when you shall touch that secret!"

But it is true, my soul defends, daring with bleeding anger; *there is a mystery of truth's secrecy in the bond between men and ayom.*

"Of course there is, *fishsinger!* But you are too deeply pompous in wonderings about their secret. It is simple, all too simple! Look upon the truth!"

Cavebrown dredges up an image, and pushes it toward me.

It is an animal, unfamiliar, a breather of dryness, and the image is not very clear. The animal's body is distant—

"You need a clearer vision of a klighfh, yes?"

The animal is moved toward me, without motion on the part of its own limbs. And I see that it is covered with hair, that its four scaleless limbs are pointed down—to touch the land of dryness—that there are a few very long hairs protruding above its upper lip, and that its pointed tail is hairy too.

"You understand now? No? When your forefathers came to your sea—when I brought them to your sea—they brought with them many klighfh! When my first children—your forefathers of dryness—changed under the insane light of the twin lkhfgh, their klighfh changed also!"

The image changes: another form is added. Now a tailless man, standing upright in dryness and looking down at the smaller hairy animal, moves a pale webless hand to touch that animal. In turn the animal rubs against the man's hand, and the animal's soul is pleased, and the man's soul is pleased too.

Those klighfh, my soul cries out in excited understanding, *those animals brought to this world by my forefathers, are the forefathers of all ayom!*

"Do not be so surprised. Your deepest soul knew the truth all along, and your soul's upper regions would have understood it also—if you had bothered to *think*. The *ayom*, bless their cowering souls, have stayed close to your kind,

222

just as the klighfh stayed close to your forefathers' kind for three hundred million days or more!"

The truth is good. . . . The bond is real, never forgotten. My many moments of impatience with murmursome were so wrong. . . .

"Enough of your guilt-dark babbling, child. Now you must enter me! Return to biggest mother forever! Are you ready, child?"

The question brings an image, rumbling and crashing in contentment, of what the giant soul wants. The image embraces me, and I scream in its realness:

The surfaces of hard nothingness around me are breaking, cracking, the water is rushing out, the dryness rushing in, and I am dying in my flesh, my soul leaping free, screaming, screaming until the *cavebrown* opens a strange surface of gray smoothness, exposes a small throbbing mass of flesh, and swallows my soul.

The image dims, but my body continues twitching and my throat is choking as strange painful waters and pieces of food rise up from my stomach and out through my mouth. The waters around my face are discolored, and when I breath them they are terrible to taste and feel. I move backwards toward clearer water.

"That image should not have made you sick, child. You desire death, do you not? and the image was of the greatest death you could possibly have."

My flesh has never wanted death, I answer. *There has never been a body of my kind that has wanted death. Our souls alone seem to desire it—only our souls. . . .*

"Flesh is stupid, and should not be minded! You and my other children must overcome the insanity of your bodies, and follow your souls' deepest single desire! You, *fishsinger* mine, shall be the first of the living to enter me—*now*. Your father—and your *waterjoyup* mother—are waiting for you. Come!"

To be with Father and Mother at last, forever . . . the questions ended, the traveling done, the deepest split between flesh and soul finished forever . . .

My soul moves to say "Yes"—

—but the image of three souls snaps before my inner eye.

Poundgrayly, the friend of all my living . . . *Clearcorallie,* insane in the pleasing way that every woman is insane . . . *Murmursome,* the babbling vessel of the most ancient bond. . . .

No, my soul whispers, and I grow brown in fears of the *cavebrown's* answer to come.

223

But she is pinkly patient, and she moves toward deep explanations.

"You do not understand, it seems. Each soul of my bodiless children who enters me makes me stronger, as the biggest mother must be strong. All three of me must be strong! Already I can shatter rocks and crush plants on this island *without touching them solidly*—without moving a hard gray finger of the *bigshinegray* part of me. With my great soul alone I can move things at a distance. Come to me, to make me stronger still!"

No. . . .

"Listen," *cavebrown* rushes, some red current rising and falling. "If you and every other soul of your kind return to me, I shall be able with my great soul alone to lift my *bigshinegray* from this island! I shall be able to move through endless darkness and kill the *scalesouls* who are coming here! I shall—"

The scalesouls are coming?

"You know they are! One *scalesoul* escaped your wrath, and you know that it has reached the world of its kind, that it has already begun to travel back to us with a hundred *bigshinegrays* terribly full of its kind!"

I killed four scalesouls. If my people are ready when the scalesouls find us again, we will be able to kill them all with our wraths.

"Stupid! The *scalesouls* will not even approach your sea. They will stay as high as they can in dryness, and they will drop terrible sicknesses into your sea—to kill every last soul of your kind, and all *ayom, euyom, ioe* and *yau!*"

Gray confusion embraces my soul. I do not want the fifty thousand bodies of my kind to die of strange sicknesses—but I also do not want them to die for the sake of the *cavebrown.*

"But your people want death, have always wanted it! You are wrong to pretend their wishes are yours."

Yes, they do desire dying. . . . It is their right to die. . . .

The *cavebrown* grows excited, pinks and yellows everywhere, but her excitement darkens my soul. Again I can see that her soul rises and falls too quickly in its feelings, that such rising and falling is insanity, and I remember a hundred advices. . . .

"An insane soul," each father tells his son, "holds warped truths that are not the truth. An insane soul's wishes are not to be trusted—an insane soul's voice is not to be believed."

Cavebrown hears my dark doubts and thunders in anger.

224

"You call the biggest mother insane? She is wise, she is endless light, and truth is her only blood!"

Under the weight of her anger, my soul falls toward darkness, again toward the hidings of sleep, as I fall I continue to refuse her.

I will not enter you willfully. You may kill my flesh, but my soul will scream against you, cursing you as long as I am able.

Cavebrown sighs powerfully, heavily upon me. I continue to fall.

"The biggest mother does not want you if you refuse to be her child! Return to the souls of your kind and give them the truths of me. You must tell them what I want, which is what they most deeply want and need! Is your soul willing to do this to save your body's flesh?"

Yes, yes, my soul says quickly, and it is the voice of my brown-woven flesh. *I will tell them—all of them—and each of their personal souls will make a personal choice.*

"Good. That is all the biggest mother wants—and that is all she will need to have her desires answered with yeses."

I continue to fall toward darkness. The *cavebrown* is making me fall, and before darkness deafens me completely, I hear her explain:

"You must sleep now. You will feel fewer pains if you sleep while my oighjerg take you back to your sea. The biggest mother is good: she wishes to hurt no soul, especially not one of her own special children. Remember this, *fishsinger*, as I am endless goodness!"

XVIII

I am wakened by familiar murmurs, endless and undying.

The invisible hordes of tiny souls throughout the sea—the murmuring blood of the sea herself—wakes me and shatters a dark dream.

You have a choice, the dream said, *but really no choice at all. Choose the darkness you prefer. . . .*

And the dream offered two visions, two hands, two alternatives. In the twisted left hand a tiny sea churned, poisoned by strange mists dropped from tiny *bigshinegrays* full of tiny *scalesouls;* the sea began to darken, sprinkled with the dead flesh of tiny men and women, *ayom* and *euyom.* . . .

In the right hand a single *bigshinegray* grew a jagged mouth, and this mouth began to suck, to swallow tiny faint mists which were the bodiless souls of men and women. Not far from the mouth was a dark funnel, chewing, chewing the bodies of men and women. . . .

You must choose, the dream said.

What would *poundgrayly* say, if he were I, *here* and *now,* faced with the choice?

"Death is a moment to be accepted," he would say. "Perhaps it is even a moment to be desired. But it should never be *planned.*"

It should not simply be some great eating time for the *cavebrown!*

In that moment a pale finger strokes my soul, and I stop swimming. I turn and look with face's eyes behind me.

The stroking continues, and soon my face's eyes touch two approaching gray forms—the same two round forms that approached me on the island.

"Let me have my personal moments alone!" I shout.

The round gray forms are the eyes and voices of *cavebrown;* they possess no souls of their own, so they repeat the giant soul's preferred image:

"The biggest mother loves her children . . . remember this truth. . . ."

"Leave me alone!" I shout again, finding it difficult to remember that the two *grayballs* are not entities separate from "the biggest mother."

"Proceed to your people," say the *grayballs* together.

I am afraid of *cavebrown,* but in a moment I realize that the two gray forms pose less of a threat than she did: the *grayballs* are mere carriers of her soul's voice; at most they could knock my soul into darkness with the power of *cavebrown's* immense soul. They have no limbs or jagged jaws to harm my flesh, whereas the *cavebrown* no doubt possesses a thousand means for killing me inside her *bigshinegray* body.

"Please leave me," I say. "My soul demands solitude. I have promised that I shall speak your truths to my people, and I shall follow that promise!"

The *grayballs* remain silent, until I hear the giant soul behind them sigh, and they retreat into the gray dimness of distance.

226

When I enter familiar territories, and finally the territory shared by *clearcorallie* and me, the pale stroking suddenly begins again.

I turn, but face's eyes do not find the *grayballs*.

"If you do not leave me alone, I shall kill the promise I made!"

The stroking ceases abruptly, and I resume my swim.

I find *poundgrayly* and *clearcorallie* near the *yau* place chosen by *clearcorallie* and me, and when they touch my approaching soul in the distance, their souls shout in a thousand pink rhythms—

—until I near them, and their first deep probings touch the newness, the differences, the past days' molding of my once familiar soul.

The soul of *poundgrayly* constricts, rearing back with a hesitant vein of brown.

The soul of *clearcorallie* tries but cannot hide a darkening whimper, a web of shock, a new current of aloneness.

I reach into their souls and see myself through their inner eyes:

You met the man, his tricks, his embracing lies, his laughter of insanity: he changed you, and you are not the fishsinger we remember. . . . And more, you met an impossible soul named cavebrown, her growing strength, her insanity's motherhood, her laughter and love and anger a hundred times more terrible than the man's dark chuckling: she changed you even more, lost fishsinger, and you are even further from the soul we once knew and tried to know.

Quickly I move my soul to find an image that will comfort them. *I am the boy you knew—I have not changed—I am the boy who grew jealous of the fond rhythm between the two of you—the boy who in his youthful ways fled from you to hurt you!*

I throw the image at them again and again, but their souls will not embrace me. Their trembling inner faces continue to stare at me, *and they are afraid of me!*

He is so different now, their souls whisper to each other, *that it is his to decide the path of death for his kind's flesh. . . .*

My soul flails in frantic reefs of pale. I rush through my memories seeking a bond, any bond at all, to offer them—to bring their colors toward me.

I choose the finest I can find, one for *clearcorallie* and one for *poundgrayly*, and instead of throwing the images at them, I push the images gently forward to nudge them.

Please listen, good poundgrayly of my life. I am still the

227

*young soul of questions, and the younger soul who was
your son—still is your son—by the death of his screamdeep
father, your undying friend of shared days. I am still the
boy who wanted his mother's and father's death moments
more than anything!*

Gradually the face of the *euyom*'s soul begins to calm, his
colors brightening faintly, and his deepest depths soothing
him by saying, "Fishsinger, yes, he is the boy of *fishsinging*
ways. . . ."

Clearcorallie's aloneness grows even greater now that
poundgrayly's soul is with me, so I move my soul toward
her immediately. I push another image toward her, for her,
praying for another success of colors' bond:

*I am still the boy who will be the father of your child,
clearcorallie of womanish girlish ways! I am still the boy who
gave you the fish image in such a strange way, the boy
who laughed with you, and with nightbreaking and whiterim,
about the fish image which has started a child inside your
flesh. Remember me, please!*

This is all the comfort *clearcorallie*'s soul needs. Her darknesses dim, and in a moment she too is with me, waiting for
me to speak.

I keep the images flowing strong and insistent from me
—and the *euyom* and the girl remain with me. But the effort of sustaining such images fatigues both my flesh and
soul, and I know that I have little time to speak to *clearcorallie* and *poundgrayly* with this pink familiarity that
binds us.

"Listen, *poundgrayly*. You must leave me immediately to
spread my message: a congregation must be held as soon as
possible. I shall remain in this territory, because my soul
needs many moments to mold the truths I shall share with
fifty thousand souls at the congregation. Believe in my need,
believe in my message, and go. And you, *clearcorallie*, must
accompany him."

"No. . . ." comes the paling objection from the girl's soul.
The images I gave her have convinced her soul that I am
the *fishsinger* she knew, the one she now wants to touch
again and again. . . .

"Please," I pale. "My soul needs many moments of personal aloneness. My soul needs time to mold the *cavebrown*'s
heavy truths into a message for all of our kind's soul!"

If *clearcorallie* remains with me until the comforting
images fall, her soul will feel the jaggedest browns of aloneness she has ever known. I *am* different, too different for a
girl's youthful soul to understand without fears!

Both souls hesitate briefly, but then *poundgrayly*'s fatherly vein reaches out to touch the girl, to pull her with him, as he begins to swim away in flesh and soul.

In a moment—one moment that seems longer than the longest scream—they are beyond soul's range. I let the images fall, and in their falling my soul finds a darkness which the girl and *euyom* have left behind:

I am different now, my soul must now admit. *I am alone, and worse than alone, because I am different now and always will be . . . different . . . and alone. . . .*

I expect the *grayballs* to return.

One aching face of my soul even *wants* them to return. The aching face urges: "Perhaps your soul can be loved by the *cavebrown* more than by the girl and *euyom* who have failed to recognize you."

The *grayballs* do not return.

So my soul flees slowly to the darkness of sleep.

And it seems, when I awake, that my flesh refuses to obey my soul's simplest commands. My tails twitch but will not wave—my arms bend, but pain in bending—and my fingers curl, but refuse to straighten.

I blame the *cavebrown.*

The dark power of her soul did this! Split my flesh even further from my soul! And in the wide vein of trickery bleeding within her, she probably knew this split would occur!

With face's eyes I look at my hands—

—and every feature of them is unfamiliar.

I flex my fingers as far as I can, and watch the yellowish skin stretch strangely in their flexing.

I cup my hands as well as I can, bring them back and forth before my face's eyes, and for the first time see the mottled color of the skin of my palms.

And I realize the simplest of deepest truths.

My skin, my bones, my flesh, are not as simple as I have always assumed them to be. They hide secrets and meanings as great as any soul's secrets—and if they can hide such secrets so well in their nearness to me, then what large secrets does my deepest soul hide?

Again I try to move my body with familiarity's ease, and fail.

My soul feels trapped. It needs flesh to give it feelings of freedom! Is this . . . is this how each soul feels when his or her body dies, when body is ripped from soul forever?

If the answer is "Yes," then a greater question can also be answered:

I can understand why all the bodiless souls of the dead

229

men and women of my kind have approached the *cavebrown* eagerly, and been swallowed by her eagerly! She is a giant soul, heavy enough to be flesh itself, and every bodiless soul must scream for a body.

You are goodness, my soul says, speaking to my flesh as it never has before—for my body is now separate from me, as it has never been before. *I shall not forget this moment. I must not forget this truth. I must make every last soul of my kind touch this truth....*

In the next moment it seems that my flesh has heard my soul's praise and promise, for my body begins to flow with me. No, my soul flows with my body, and my flesh leads me on, urges me to swim, suggesting a song which only flesh could sing—the song of solid acts.

I swim to the sandy area where the congregation will be held.

I hover over it, waving the singing tails of my body, and look down at it with my face's eyes, the two singing eyes of my singing flesh.

I want to *touch* solid things, chew solid foods, taste solid tastes, and while doing all of these things, to feel the sea rush, caress, wiggle and press against me.

We must move and never stop moving, every corner of my flesh announces, *or our song will die and will never live again.*

I think of the congregation, of the fifty thousand bodies that will gather above the sands, and my soul moves to find a proper song of *act* for my flesh.

I shall gather food for those thousands of bodies, my soul finally decides, offering the plan as a humble gift to my own waiting body. *They will not arrive for many days, and I shall gather enough food with my two singing hands to fill all of their brotherly stomachs.*

My tails move, my hands stroke the sea, and my face's eyes begin to search for soft coral, easy fish, rare shells full of meat.

The bond between flesh and soul grows stronger. My flesh in friendship's way moves to offer my soul a voice in flesh's singing.

If the food we gather, my flesh, blood and bones say to my soul, *attracts ioe or uiu, then you must give them perfect lies to send them away.*

My soul agrees eagerly, and would fall to silence, but flesh allows it to speak a handful of new truths to me.

Your flesh is a generous vessel, my soul whispers to me. *It lets me touch as many truths as I am able....*

230

See it, for the truth it is: You are a single body, but you are also a million souls—not only of shared memories, but of times and souls before the sharing of memories in this sea ever began. You are the circle of light which nightbreaking shaped with pieces of coral and rocks.

You are a soul split by urges to live and drivings toward dying—but you are also a soul joined by a deeper split, a curving crack that began in a world of dryness where your most distant forefathers breathed, touched solid things with their hands, and remembered those touchings in their deepest souls' depths.

You are a soul who will lose its living meaning if you lose your flesh, and you know this deeply—

—but you are different, and you know that the cavebrown is insane with warped truths—

—but there is no other soul of your kind who will understand the cavebrown's terrible face.

You are different. You entered dryness, the world of your earliest forefathers, and your split was mended, and your healed soul no longer craves death, the end of flesh and the end of soul's agony, split by desires for a world of dryness while in a world of smothering water.

So you are different from them. You are different, and even the darkest aloneness is unable to approach in meaning the meaning of your difference.

I gather shells, and when I place them in a pile in the middle of the sandy area, many of them crawl away. But it does not matter. Flesh's song is *all,* and I continue to move my hands, tails, head and back, and to gather. . . .

I kill many small fish with shocking shouts from my soul, and I place their bodies in the same pile as the shells.

I take jagged rocks in my hands and break piece after piece of soft coral from their reefs, and make the pile of food still larger.

At night I sleep, but the song goes on. In dreams of hands, I gather food to feed fifty thousand stomachs, and my flesh never tires. My flesh's food is its own gathering song.

In the days that pass, flowing like blood—as if the sea and lights of day were the blood of my personal body—I touch the *grayballs* dimly in the distance, but pay little attention to them.

They remain beyond face's eyes' range. They remain there murmuring, babbling in a constant surprise. *Cavebrown* is finding it difficult to understand my flesh's actions, the song embracing me, and her confusion pleases my soul deeply:

Her confusion only strengthens the suspected truth:
*The giant soul possesses little or no flesh at all. She has no
path for understand me and mine—my body carrying a contented soul, my soul riding contented flesh!*

When memories of my father and mother rise before my
inner eye—in the day's warmth, or the night's darkness—my
flesh advises my soul of the truest truth:
*Cavebrown holds them trapped within her. She is not their
body. They are screaming within her, weeping that she
tricked them so well, and without a single pink compassion
she is using them as food for the fleshless stomach of her
soul's growing powers.*

My soul would have wept pale currents for *screamdeep*
and *waterjoyup,* and perhaps my soul did when my flesh
was unaware—but in most moments of every passing day
before the congregation, the song of flesh, of gathering food,
was a strong enough rhythm to deny the sinking of weeping.

Shells . . . some crushed . . . some of their animals still
alive. . . .

Coral . . . pieces the size of a hand . . . others the size
of a child's body . . . all soft inside their brittle reef bodies. . .

Fish and sponges . . . held down by the weight of shells
and coral pieces. . . .

The pile of food seems to stretch to the ends of the sands.

Three *ioe* and two *uiu* have come, attracted by the growing mound of vulnerable flesh, but my soul sends them
away easily; and even the thousands of small crawling or
swimming bodies, arriving to chew the fish and dying coral
gently, cannot eat enough to make the pile shrink.

Finally the first souls of the congregation begin to approach.

They swim slowly but immediately toward the great
mound of food, and their souls seem to stiffen in the pink of
wonder.

I choose not to speak to any of them. I choose to remain at
an outer edge of the sands, far from any other soul's probing, and I continue to gather coral, fish, shells and sponges.
When a soul comes to understand that I am the maker of the
food pile, and begins to swim toward me, I swim away and
send the soul back with a gentle yellow "No, no touchings
please."

For two days the single question heard by my soul is the
simple seeking in wonder: "Who gathered such endless
food?"

On the third day the question changes, becomes: "Where
is the soul who requested this congregation?" And when it

seems that fifty thousand souls are finally present, hovering in their personal or shared ways over the sand and food, I swim toward the center of their masses, and come to rest above the pile of foods.

One soul touches me, and another, and another—until all souls have touched or are touching me. The congregation's voice begins.

They understand. They remember me:

I am the boy who entered dryness, killed four *scalesouls,* and later requested a congregation to share the events of the island. What events will the boy now offer for sharing?

I reach out with anxious soul and search for two special souls. The grayness of seemingly endless souls, their bodies so close together and their wills trying to hide pale babblings, clouds my inner eye in its search.

I do find the two souls, but both of them—girl and *euyom* are dim, like two tiny hazes in one of the invisible hordes that course through the sea.

"I am here," my soul calls gently. *"Fishsinger* is here."

Clearcorallie and *poundgrayly* offer no reply.

They know that I am here, as every soul knows that I am here—at the center, the center of endless food. Why do they not answer?

And, yes, *murmursome* is with them. Why is he not darting toward me in his usual babbling way?

Abruptly my soul feels the pale familiar strokings, and I turn my head, to look with face's eyes.

The two *grayballs* are not more than a tail-length away from me.

"Follow your promise," *cavebrown* whispers through the two motionless gray forms. "And forget all paths of trickery. I have watched your body's strange dance for many days, and I suspect the growth of lies within you. I am still the biggest mother, and my powers can order chaos, and they also can inflict it. . . ."

I turn away from the *grayballs* and say softly to the congregation, "Listen. . . ."

They fall silent, and I begin to speak, to bleed the truths which the *cavebrown* wants me to speak. *I shall first give them,* my soul comforts me, *the truths from the giant soul's voice. But then I shall give them the truer truths, not a single lie or trickery!*

In a rush of hurried images, I tell them who, what, where, when, and how and why—of the *cavebrown.*

In a rush of hesitant feeling, I tell them what the *cavebrown* wants—

—and even before I have finished the dark gifts of images and feelings, many souls begin to answer.

Their answers rush above me, bringing taloned browns of trembling flesh to my body and flesh. The souls are crying "Yes!", and my soul tries to cry "No!"—but the "Yes!" is a thousand times louder, and my soul's voice is weak in fears.

"To die!" the shout rolls from the congregation.

"The *scalesouls scalesouls* will kill us kill us—

"—unless we give our flesh to the *cavebrown* mother—

"—who will let us live free of flesh—

"—with eternal souls ours!

"—To die, the dream has come!

"To die, the screams are over!

"To die to live, all one—not each alone!"

Quickly I reach out to probe the truths of individual souls. . . .

Dark deep shivering quick brown: "The right *bigshine-gray* was here in our world all along, and we were waiting, fools in ignorance!"

Black black deep crack pain: "The wait is entirely over—what is left but death?"

Gray churn purple rise red bright red: "At last we can choose the dyings we have always wanted . . . our dissenting flesh be damned!"

Not one soul among them can understand the truth! Their deepest souls want death, and they believe the *cavebrown* can give it to them. They want to escape their lives in wetness, so they think flesh's death will bring their escape. Can they not see the life inside the *cavebrown's* soul will be as smothering as any sea?

I begin to shout reasons at them, pounding explanations and darker objections. "Your flesh is goodness!" "You are blind to your deepest soul's truest desire!" "The *cavebrown* considers you simply fish, desires your souls as food!"

In the congregation's voice only a few souls hear me, and those who do have solid answers. "The *scalesouls* will kill us anyway!" "You are different, alone against our agreed desires!" "*Cavebrown* brought our forefathers' flesh into this world: she is wise—she wills what must be our best destinies!"

I reach out again, seeking any other souls who might be *different*. And after hundreds of souls, I find one man whispering:

"Perhaps we should not give our bodies away. Perhaps there are still some of our brothers breathing dryness somewhere in the endless darkness. Perhaps. . . ."

And after many more souls, another *different* soul:

"I cannot be certain that flesh is the curse you all believe it to be!"

A thousand souls hear this lone soul's disagreement, and they turn on her, shouting: "You may choose to keep your flesh, but if you do, you shall be alone, you shall have the sea to yourself: no other soul will remain with you!"

I move my soul to join the woman, to stand by her in truth's defense—

—but the *grayballs* interrupt me, speaking to me in whispers.

"Still you fail to understand the ways of your own kind. They will never join you in your attitude, and there is deepest reason why they never will. The lights of the twin *kjshfgh* changed your forefathers—my first children here —but your forefathers were not changed *enough*. Your kind holds deeply the deepest desires of your forefathers—the dreams of flying in dryness, the cravings to travel to unknown corners of the endless darkness, the drives to become bright circles, and the memories of dark secret women, pure children, old wise men and muscular fathers—but your kind is split, burdened also by the loves and hatreds, dreams and wakings of all bodies who must live their days in some sea's wetness. Your people cannot bear the burdensome split any longer. Unlike your soul, they have not entered dryness, where flesh is reconciled with deepest soul; they have not come to understand their flesh, their soul's deepest urging, their damnations and their blessings. Give up arguing with them: they are not your people any longer. Join them, or you will be alone!"

When *cavebrown* finishes her whispered attempt to coax me, I turn immediately back to the woman who spoke against dying.

"Whatever you say," she is arguing weakly, "I cannot be convinced of death's certain goodness."

"You are not alone!" I shout to her, and a thousand souls turn toward me.

"My soul is not willing to let my flesh die," I go on, gesturing toward *clearcorallie*, hoping that she will offer her soul in agreement.

The girl offers nothing, and quick pale sadness turns into rising reds with me. *Why is she choosing silence in this important moment of moments?*

Then I sense one of the *grayballs* near *clearcorallie*'s soul, and my reds turn into gray confusion. The *grayball* is not speaking to her—so why is it beside her?

I turn back to the woman and find that a hundred souls are addressing her together.

"You and the angry boy shall be the only two souls in endless waters—unless your doubts are shattered!"

Alone? the woman's soul answers without will. *But a woman and boy can create other souls together—three four five, a hundred in a life's time.* . . .

"Even if you fill the sea with children," shouts a loud soul, soon joined by an echoing hundred, "all of you shall be *alone*, for the *cavebrown* mother, full of all our souls, will have left you forever!"

The lone woman's soul darkens, and pleading browns begin to escape her: *I do not want to be alone.* . . . *I want to be with you.* . . .

I am alone again, and can only thrash in soul seeking a path for convincing these people of the truth their blind souls cannot touch.

What if I were to shout at them: "You will be leaving many personal friends, *ayom* and *euyom!* Will your bodiless souls not grieve for their loss?"

But the people would answer: "No *ayom* or *euyom* was ever as important to our deepest souls as the deep desire for death!" or "The only friend our souls will need shall be the *cavebrown* mother!"

What if I were to shout: "Request that the *cavebrown*, with her growing soul's amazing powers, give you all bodies for living in dryness! The twin lights of day can no longer hurt flesh that breathes dryness—they are no longer insane, though they were in our forefathers' days!"

But the *cavebrown* would refuse, or she would claim that her powers are not great enough—whether or not they truly are.

But what if I were to tell my people: "I have touched the *cavebrown*'s soul, and I have seen the truth of her deepest insanity! I have witnessed her control over the millions of souls within her; I have seen her beat them down, refuse to let even a single soul—my own blood's mother—rise up from the *cavebrown*'s depths to embrace me! Believe the truth of my eyes: you will scream forever in the *cavebrown*'s strapping embrace!"

Yes, such a vein of truth might convince them—at least some of them, a few thousand among them.

Quickly I lift my soul to shout—

—but a sudden grayness falls around me, upon me, enclosing me tightly.

It seems a dream, but is not. I am aware of my personal flesh, but my soul's voice only bounces back from the grayness surrounding me.

236

And a voice is murmuring to me . . . a corner of the *cavebrown's* voice, but not all of her voice. . . .

"I cannot allow you to speak such things of your simple kind. You are my child, but I cannot let one lone child turn the others against their biggest mother."

Like the grayness, the voice is coming from the *grayball* that floats near me. I struggle uselessly in wonder.

"This power . . . ?" I mumble in my dream that is not a dream. I struggle to move my tails, and they do move, and I swim slowly into the midst of the people—but still my soul fails to hear their souls, only the voice of the *grayball*—and even then, not the *entire* voice of the *cavebrown*.

The *cavebrown* answers me, smiling again in a flawed pinkness that frightens me.

"My power, yes. The invisible fingers of the biggest mother's soul have grown stronger since our meeting on her island. Many thousands more souls she has swallowed since then. She is growing so great that no soul—"

Take the grayness away! my soul pleads.

"The grayness? Yes, a clever game, no? I merely crippled the millions of tiny invisible souls nearest you, and their united screams in fear have formed a reef between your soul and the others of your kind. Truly clever, as the biggest mother is and always shall be!"

Allow me to hear the people. I promise no images to convince them will rush from my soul to theirs.

"A promise?" she laughs, pink cracking. "Your deepest soul promises that you would *not* follow such a promise!"

Please!

"In a moment, but not *now*, churning child! You should have your flesh slapped for such persistent disrespect. I am your truest mother!"

I want to shout at ther. But I also want to listen carefully, to hear what the *cavebrown* is secretly telling the fifty thousand souls, what the fifty thousand souls are feeling.

My soul calms itself, tries to silence the pounding of my chest's blood, and I listen.

"I . . ." comes the dimmest tide from the *cavebrown's* soul, ". . . biggest mother . . . the sea because . . . free you all from . . . give you all . . . as death is . . . to me, your biggest . . . you . . ."

And from the fifty thousand souls rolls a faint wave of gratitude, "Yes" and "Yes" and "Yes."

My flesh feels rising sickness at the sound of such gratitude, born of trickery's will.

The *cavebrown* continues, saying, ". . . *all* of you . . . if

237

there is one single . . . *none* of you . . . me, your deepest desire!"

Now the fifty thousand souls seem to darken, upset by the new words from the giant soul. Scattered among the thousands: anxious purple . . . browning fears . . . reds being raised . . . and pale babblings of pleading agreement.

"All is well," the *grayball* suddenly announces to me. "Of course, I could give you death—but there is a smoother way, and time yet for a better gift. You will reach your deepest desire soon, and you will thank me with every color within you."

The grayness falls.

In a frantic flush of soul, I reach out, starting to speak to the people—

—but the *cavebrown* is still speaking, and her voice shadows mine into nothingness.

"I shall be ready for all of you in a mere six days. In that time each of you shall ready your flesh, your soul, your friends and familes for my embrace. You shall enter me as my finest blood—and soon after we shall leave this untimely world together, as the greatest tide of light and power the endless darkness has ever known! Go now. I will await you . . . *all* of you. . . ."

Except for two, my soul throws out, hiding in a whisper. But then I remember that I am alone, that neither the woman nor *clearcorallie* chose to remain with me, so I say, *Except for one!*

Cavebrown hears my whisper. She darkens, chooses a pink vein of whispering which nearly makes me scream, and says:

"*All* of you, or *none* of you."

Although my upper levels cannot understand her darkest meanings, my deepest soul can and does: I begin trembling.

XIX

The two *grayballs* leave quickly, entering the grayness of distance.

The thousands of souls leave slowly, but immediately, and soon only three remain—one girl, and two other souls who are not of my kind—floating above the abandoned sands.

There is a question to be asked, but I do not ask it. I swim toward the three souls and refuse to offer any corner of my soul for their touch.

"If it please you," runs the sarcasm from my soul, "let us go to the *yau* place."

Their souls nod, confused. *Clearcorallie* moves to my side as we begin swimming, and *poundgrayly* and *murmursome* follow.

The yellow babblings of the dumb *ayom* are the only colors offered as we swim. *Poundgrayly* embraces silence, waiting for me to speak; and *clearcorallie* is mumbling grayly, secretly.

Clearcorallie is the first to speak, and her color is pale sorrow.

"Why is your soul holding darkness against me? Such secret hatred, why? Please . . ."

My soul snaps toward her in amazement. Some game to hide the moment when she failed to stand with my soul, with the lone woman's too, against the *cavebrown*'s lurings?

I probe her depths—

—and surprise dims my reds: She is not lying: she is truly unaware of the reason for my soul's darknesses.

"You are stranger than a soul should be," I answer slowly. "You cannot have forgotten already my gesture for your help at the congregation. You cannot see that your denial was reason enough for these darknesses?"

Clearcorallie's soul pales, darkens, but she speaks quickly.

"I have not forgotten your gesture . . . but I thought you understood why my soul could not answer you."

A why? my soul mumbles. *No doubt the "why" lay in your deepest nature!*

"You are wrong, your hatred unjustified! Did you not see how the—the thing you call a *grayball*—kept me from answering you?"

I stop swimming and begin to tingle in flesh and soul.

"A *grayball* was beside you, yes. It prevented your answer?"

"With a wide hand of grayness."

"Then I am sorry for my slap of darkness," I offer, resuming the swim. "A similar grayness smothered *me*."

Abruptly I stop swimming again. "What was the answer that the *grayball* kept you from giving me?"

Clearcorallie's soul constricts slightly. She says slowly, "I had not yet formed an answer, when the grayness surrounded me. I knew you would not hear me, because I tried to call you and my calling only bounced against the gray hand and dissolved."

"But what would your answer have been, had you formed it and sent it to me?"

I do not know, comes the dim answer from her.

Reds quickly rise in me anew, and I turn with face's eyes to *poundgrayly.*

His scaly limbs wave slowly, steadying him, and his eyes blink like tiny two-shells, and his beak opens and closes in familiar rhythm—but he offers no comment.

Murmursome has been watching with face's eyes, and he rushes toward me now, his babbling yellow speckled with equally familiar pink affection, and meaning: "Together again, good yellow, together again, good pink, together again, games? touchings? light?"

My soul answers all three present souls darkly.

It seems that friendship's bond is dead in all but one dumb ayom's soul.

That is not true, poundgrayly offers, but does not persist with the image.

I do not understand, clearcorallie's soul mumbles, but does not move to kill her ignorance.

We swim on, darkly, our souls as separate as our bodies.

When I allow my soul a shallow touch of *clearcorallie's* and *poundgrayly's* souls, I find the girl still clinging to her strong bond with the *euyom*—still needing a fatherly touch to dismiss heavy browns from her, to protect her against her own deep fears of the figure named *fishsinger*, the newly different boy who is no longer a boy as youthful men are boys. Without stopping our swimming, I offer her a cautious question.

"When we reach our *yau* place, would you prefer that *poundgrayly* remain with us? In the privacy of two souls together, many darknesses can often be resolved to light—but if you would rather have a third present, my soul will accept him brightly."

Her soul considers the image . . . and formed it according to her own soul's depths. She imagines a future *now!* The *yau* place: three deep souls present: the *different fishsinger*, the fatherly *poundgrayly*, and I, *clearcorallie*, comforted by fatherly yellow against dark differences; *but also*: I, woven painfully with red tension: from unanswered questions: I, wanting the darks of the *different fishsinger* turned into light: unknowns ordered, remoteness mended . . . *somehow.*

"Perhaps for a day," *clearcorallie* finally answers. "*Poundgrayly's* presence for the first of the six days."

A stem of anger lances toward her from me.

"My soul," she adds, "fears browns more than purple frustrations from unanswered questions."

I calm my soul with hopes for change. Perhaps when we arrive at the *yau* place, *clearcorallie's* soul will feel differently about a third soul's presence.

Change does not come.

We come to rest at the *yau* place, and immediately I reach out to tell *poundgrayly* that our two souls desire aloneness for awhile—

—but the girl cries out "No!" and begins to tremble in body.

I accept the "No", my soul says to the *euyom, deeply.*

But without giving another image to either girl or *euyom,* I turn and leave them.

She comes to me when the first faint shadows of night have touched the sands and reefs nearby.

She stops four tail-lengths away from me and starts to speak, but I interrupt her.

You have decided what your answer would have been? You have come to tell me that you will refuse to kill your flesh, to give your soul to the cavebrown?

She ignores my question, and its blue of sarcasm, and its pale face of barely hidden pleading.

"I would like you to join me in making an arrangement of coral, rocks and shells." Her soul is nervous, tiring in its anxious efforts to speak to me. I cannot be certain, but it seems that a leaf of weeping is being hidden within her.

"You want me to join you," I answer, "but you offer no clear image of the arrangement to be born of our joining."

"I am sorry . . . but I hold no clear image. Deepest soul has whispered to me, about an arrangement to be born . . . and about your presence at its birth."

Her deepest soul is whispering, *Please . . . please . . .*

"Where on the sands must this birth take place?"

We begin to gather the rocks, shells and pieces *clearcorallie* will need, and in a moment *poundgrayly* swims toward us.

"Is there some way this soul or flesh can help you?" the *euyom* asks quietly, as nervous as *clearcorallie* was.

Yes, if you possess hands, comes my dark answer, a slap raised by undying resentment.

Pretending weakly not to hear me, *poundgrayly* reaches out again:

"Perhaps a beak knows a way. . . ."

He swims quickly, flat limbs cutting rapidly through the water, to a low reef bordering on the sands. Quickly he begins to wrench at any brittle edges with his beak, and quickly he hides each pale bite of pain when the coral scrapes him deeply.

I turn back to my own body and continue to search with face's eyes. I am willing to join *clearcorallie* in her actions of gathering and arranging, but if either the girl or the *euyom* annoys me too darkly I will leave them. . . .

Night's shadows have grown, and are almost too heavy for face's eyes' sight when enough rocks, shells and pieces are finally gathered.

Clearcorallie moves to shape her arrangement quickly.

Deep in the motions of arranging, her soul forgets my presence, and murmurs are allowed to escape her depths.

Please . . . this effort is toward a truth . . . please . . . may the truth offer mending touches . . . darkness into light . . . soul again in closest touch with soul . . . his soul . . . mine . . . please . . .

I want to remain stiff and remote, red and purple, bloated with my personal truths, but the murmurs from *clearcorallie's* soul soften my anger.

"If it pleases you," she says suddenly, lifting her soul from deep concerns, "please make an arrangement of your own."

Again my soul finds no objection. Making an arrangement will please me because it will be hand's efforts, offering distraction from my soul's dark depths.

I gather some of *clearcorallie's* rocks and pieces into a small pile of my own, and begin to shape a line, a form, on the sands before me, letting my calming hands choose the simple form on their own.

Freer now of stiffness and darkness, I allow myself to touch *poundgrayly's* soul in the distance, where his body is hovering over the sands, where his face's eyes and inner eyes are watching us. And even when I find that his entire tide of colors and light feel only concern for *clearcorallie's* soul, I am unable to raise resentments.

"Look," *clearcorallie* says abruptly.

Despite the difficult shadows, my face's eyes find her arrangement and stare.

No corners, nor angles . . . a perfect circle of the brightest shells and coral pieces.

Clearcorallie speaks again.

"You must look not only with your face's eyes. 'Look at the arrangement,' *nightbreaking's* advice was to me, 'only for a moment with face's eyes. Then close face's eyes, and let memory grow into the arrangement's widest truth.' "

I close face's eyes, remember the arrangment—

"Wait!" *clearcorallie cries.* "Your eyes have touched only half of the arrangement. Look to your half, the shape you shaped."

I turned and look down—

—and surprise brightens my soul.

The form arranged by my hands alone, free of my soul's commands, lies simply on the sands, and I stare, seeing it for the first time.

A circle . . . only slightly larger than *clearcorallie's.* . . .

"My soul cannot feel surprise," the girl says. "It has known all along that your deepest soul is no different than mine, that our deepest name is shared, is *circle,* or at least *circlewishing.*"

I close face's eyes, let memory of the twin circles rise before an anxious inner eye, and wait, and watch.

The circles begin to throb. They begin to crack, and throb. Half of each circle is dark, the other half light. And suddenly they are loosening, each circle breaking at a place on itself, both circles—

—joining to form a single great circle . . . throbbing . . . half of darkness, half of light—

—and the bright half gains a texture, becoming throbbing flesh, becoming a shapeless body—

—and the dark half grows hazy, misty and fleshless, becoming some nameless soul!

Face's eyes spring open. I stare at the girl, and she returns the unblinking stare as her soul speaks softly.

"You have seen the only certain truth I know. I have held it since earliest memories, since before the moment your soul first touched mine, but my soul has never been able to shape this truth into clear images for you—as your soul demands clear images, clear questions, clear answers. Have you ever been touched by this truth before?"

My soul's answer is a brightest pink.

She knows the truth which I know! She knew it even before my soul first touched it, and perhaps she knows it more deeply than my soul ever will!

"But why," I cry out, "did you not give this truth to the congregation? *Nightbreaking* was there too—why did she fail to give it, to join you in giving it?"

"You must understand. . . . Your soul is different from mine . . . from *nightbreaking's* and my clouded souls. We have held the truth, but the upper faces of our souls do not

243

understand its meaning. Would this truth have had any proper place at the congregation?—I do not know. . . ."

Of course it would have, my soul shouts. *Our two circles became one great circle—and this is the truth of our deepest desires to live, to live in flesh and soul! Our circle is divided —half in soul's being, half in body's living—but it remains two united throbbing halves, and this is truth of flesh's goodness, of the most perfect path of living: flesh and soul together, and moments of death-desires and life-agonies be damned!*

Clearcorallie's soul is slow to answer.

"If that is truly the truth I have held within me, then I should have offered it to the congregation."

Yes, you should have!

"But 'should' can only be a dream of loss . . . it is too late now to offer the truth unoffered before."

Poundgrayly watches our souls loosen and flow toward each other after so long a separation, and he raises our souls to even pinker brightness by offering us a hundred dancing faces of his own soul's pleasure in the bright moment.

Our sharings and touchings would go on to deeper paths, brighter depths united, but the fingers of night finally clench around us, and our souls suggest sleep.

At the first light of tomorrow, my soul says to the girl beside me, her tired tails curled quietly around the *yau* stem, *we shall share a hundred visions . . . our child, to be born after the cavebrown takes her fifty thousand souls away . . . our lives of flesh and soul thereafter . . . a second child . . . the children of children in distant nows—*

But the scalesouls will come here, begins the faint protest from *clearcorallie,* her soul slipping, sliding toward sleep's bubbling.

The scalesouls deserve no envisioning, I want to explain, *until the solid day they arrive in the real of here and now— and perhaps that day will never become solid at all.*

But *clearcorallie* is deaf now, floating tiny in the tide of sleep.

I was dreaming.

Souls around me . . . hating me.

"You are the single soul who refuses," one of the souls says angrily.

And I answer him calmly, "Yes, I refuse."

I open my face's eyes, clear my inner eye—

—to find that it is not a dream.

Twelve souls of men surround me. . . .

244

As *clearcorallie* awakes, and feels the touch of the near-by souls, she begins a faint whimper, her body moving to my side.

I reach out, probing for *poundgrayly*, but he is not present.

Clearcorallie, where is poundgrayly? Perhaps these men have harmed him, perhaps— I try to aim my whispers at the girl alone.

I do not know, she answers, and her arm brushes mine. *Before we entered sleep, I heard his soul murmuring, "The togetherness of two and only two is what these two children need most deeply. . . ."*

So he left us in the night, to give us privacy of—

Abruptly one of the twelve souls shatters our whispers.

"You shall not refuse!" the soul rumbles reddening orange.

"Who are you?" *clearcorallie* asks, "and this red joining of your souls?"

The souls move even nearer to us, sharing a united face of growing red, splintering orange, its single blazing eye staring at our souls.

"You! of *fishsinger* name," a second soul accuses. "*Cavebrown* mother is aware that you have denied her."

All twelve wait for some answer from me.

"Of course," I venture. "I spoke to the *cavebrown*, and aware that I had denied and would continue to deny her, she allowed me to leave her *bigshinegray*. She has accepted my refusal and she—"

"No," comes the single voice from the twelve.

"No?"

"*Cavebrown* mother has not accepted any face of your refusal at all!"

My soul crawls quickly to the *then* of the last congregation, and I remember that the *cavebrown* spoke secretly to the people while grayness surrounded me. How dark were those secrets?

Browns stir within me. I try to hide their face by speaking.

"You twelve, and the others, have embraced a decision to go with the *cavebrown*. I have embraced my own decision. Each soul has a personal path—to be respected by others,"

"The *real* is not so simple," says the reddest of the twelve —whose name appears to be *bluerocking*. "*Our* paths depend on yours."

"That is absurdity. You are individual souls, with wills to follow your individual ways."

"No! Our paths lead to *cavebrown* mother only if *all* paths lead to her. The threat of her deepest wishes: '*All* of you, or *none* of you!' "

245

I hesitate, browns beginning to rise, but try another face:
"You have misunderstood her images. Her meaning was not—"

"No! She explained her meaning deeply. You heard her, you were as present as we were."

I was shrouded, my soul murmured to itself, *by a grayness willed by the cavebrown.*

Bluerocking hears and laughs, but without dimming his reds.

"If she covered you with gray, she did so aware that you would try to turn us, to evoke darknesses against her. But you have touched the truth now, and now you must move your body with us, as we guide you to the proper path. We shall help you, as *cavebrown* mother urged us, 'Help the insane soul named *fishsinger!*' "

The image of "help" is unclear from the man, but my soul supplies the inevitable clarity behind it. I constrict flesh and soul.

"You have no right to crack my soul's willed path," I shout, but weakly. "The *cavebrown* will take you in the end—even if I embrace my personal decision to the end!"

"She will not," *bluerocking* answers, moving his flesh toward me. "She has promised she will not."

"But I *know* her more deeply than your souls do! Touch the truth: She will take you, because she wants you more than anything else!"

At this, three of the twelve souls dim to a pale yellow, raising a belief in me. But the other nine remain red, and *bluerocking* quickly reddens the swayed three with a simple wave from his constant soul.

"Perhaps," he says, "but we shall not chance it. *Cavebrown* mother's soul is great, and a boy's soul is too simple to claim understanding of her. A boy's soul has no right to endanger the willed paths of his people. A boy's soul shall *not* endanger their paths!"

Bluerocking reaches out and strikes my shoulder with a finger, and his soul joins the other eleven in insisting, *Come with us!*

My flesh trembles, and the shivering bleeds into my soul as I wonder, *Am I the only soul they have come to take away?*

In the same moment of my wondering, *bluerocking* speaks again.

"You, of *clearcorallie* name, it appears that no one heard your voice at the congregation. Do you share the will of this boy's chosen path?"

Clearcorallie's trembling has been constant since the

246

twelve's appearance, but now it increases, and her soul turns in upon itself, splashing in blue currents, struggling . . .

Struggling to decide! To decide?

The hand of shock strikes me. Yesterday she saw the truth behind my chosen path! the goodness of flesh! Is her will so weak—?

The blues of her soul waver, try to harden, but a hundred-faced fear, beyond my soul's touch of undertsanding, makes them continue to waver.

"Offer no lies!" *bluerocking* shouts.

Her blues explode in a red-edged white, shivering, and she says, "No. . . ."

"Clear your images!" *bluerocking* shouts again.

"I shall follow the paths of the fifty thousand others."

Instantly my soul cries out, throwing muddled and many-colored images everywhere.

Clearcorallie tries to shroud her soul against mine. She refuses to touch my soul, or receive my soul's angry questioning touch.

"We must go," *bluerocking* urges.

"No!" I shout. *No no you have no right no no no!*

The twelve move their bodies toward me.

"Come with us, or your flesh will be harmed," one soul says.

"We have jaws, we have hands," says another.

And *bluerocking* says, "We were told to bring you with us. But we were told to kill your body *here* and *now* if you refused to come with us."

"You will kill my body whether or not I refuse!"

"Perhaps, but are you not the soul who wishes flesh to live as many moments as it can? Come with us, and your flesh will live more moments."

My flesh has its answer, and my soul speaks it.

"I will go with you."

Bluerocking turns, and his tails begin to wave. I follow, as the other bodies move to surround me—two above me, below me, on either side, behind me, and one ahead of me with *bluerocking*.

My soul reaches back once, and finds *clearcorallie* dark in a struggle and swirling gray I still cannot touch with understanding.

The silence of our swim is heavy.

Trembling questions dance in my soul, and I finally speak.

"The *cavebrown* would want you to give me the goal of this travel. She called me her *child*, just as she called you her *children*."

This seems to anger *bluerocking* deeply, and he speaks jaggedly.

"You are stupid! You attempt to influence me with some image of your soul's touching *nearness* to the *cavebrown* mother. I am not so easily fooled; but I am easily angered by your shallow trickery."

Is my deepest soul so obvious? *Bluerocking* is a man of many days, and perhaps I have been wrong to imagine his soul, or any of the twelve souls, a thing easily controlled by my own soul, will and shaping images. Perhaps I am more trapped among them than I imagined.

"But you may know the goal, if you wish," *bluerocking* goes on. "*Cavebrown* mother advised no secrets to be kept against you. We are leading you to the edge of your territory, where one of *cavebrown* mother's gray—yes, you call them *grayballs*—awaits us, and where you shall chew and swallow a special thing."

My soul fails to understand. The images of the goal hold no threats against my flesh. *Bluerocking* holds no intent to kill my body. A piece of food will not harm me. Unless it is—

"Is the special thing a poisonous thing?"

Bluerocking's answer is "No," and I probe his depths to find that he does not lie. But has the *cavebrown* lied to *him?*

"She has promised that the special thing holds no poison."

The special thing will help you, comes the deeper voice of *bluerocking*'s soul.

Both flesh and soul of me shiver, browning at the dark image of "help."

We find the *grayball* among stems of *yau,* and stop our swimming. The twelve bodies continue to surround me, remaining but an arm's length away.

"Now," the *grayball* says suddenly, "offer him the special thing!"

My soul moves quickly, plunging to probe the *grayball,* the giant soul beyond. But all deep images are hidden, and I am unable to touch any secret of the *special thing*'s meaning.

One of the twelve moves his body toward me—a man named *softbite.*

He reaches out and with face's eyes I see that his hand holds a small plant unfamiliar to me. Pink branches . . . a thick short stem . . .

"Eat the special thing!" the *grayball* booms.

248

I take the plant in my good right hand, and see that the pinkness of its rough webbing is streaked with black.

"The meaning of eating?" I ask, the question thrown both to the *grayball* and to the twelve men.

"You would struggle to understand the meaning," the *cavebrown* answers, "and you would fail. The biggest mother alone understands."

I lift the plant to my face, bite down and rip a portion of it off. Without will I begin chewing, and continue to chew because my soul feels no danger anywhere.

I swallow, and the fall of the chewed plant to my stomach is the familiar fall of all food. I bite off another portion.

As I am chewing for the third time, my soul begins mumbling strangely to me, perhaps a whimper, perhaps a cry, muted and slow.

Quickly I spit the third portion from my mouth.

"This plant is touching my soul strangely!" I object, as my depths begin to churn more loudly.

As cavebrown mother wishes, bluerocking's soul mumbles.

In a brief moment my body too is churning, darkening to my soul, growing—

—growing colder!

The cold swims through my flesh, deep in my soul, in and around all blood and bones of both flesh and soul. Strange dark images rise in my soul, murmuring—

You are alone, they say.

The souls of the nearby twelve, and the guarded soul of the *grayball,* all grow pale and distant.

My shivering is the greatest I have ever known. And the single voice, the voice of all my images, is the loudest I have ever heard.

I am alone, and it is terrible.

The *grayball* grows clearer, a little brighter, and speaks.

"You have eaten well, so that you may touch the truth."

No, my soul cries back, *aloneness is not the truth! I felt no such terrible feelings before eating your thing!*

"You have turned the truth around. You were insane before, not to see that aloneness was the deepest truth."

I begin to believe the *cavebrown's* images. I wish that some soul, any soul, would touch me and never cease touching me.

I try to reach out, to touch even *bluerocking,* but no soul is near enough or clear enough to touch. They are only a hand's length away, and my soul cannot reach them!

I am alone . . . I am alone. . . .

"You need me," the *grayball* says pinkly. "You need the biggest mother and her love will fill your need. You must

249

come to her, follow the other souls of your kind, or you will live in terrible darkness ever after."

I believe her. I want the *cavebrown*'s embrace, and even she, the biggest mother, is dim and remote from me.

"She will not be dim when you follow the others to her and give up your flesh's terrible hold on you! But you must take care: this moment of truth will not last long, and when it ends you must bind your will against the old insanity. You will be tempted to believe in flesh's goodness, and you must harden your will against it."

No. . . .

"No?"

Again a strange voice within me utters *"No."*

"Yes!" the cold and darkness makes me answer.

No! comes the deeper voice a third time.

The voice amazes me. *It cannot be mine,* one part of my soul protests, but in a moment the voice gains flesh in my soul, rises and I gaze upon it.

A face . . . solid face of flesh . . . through my father's face's eyes, shared memory given to me . . . *the face of waterjoyup, the circle of her face's flesh.*

This instant of aloneness, the fleshy voice says, *is a lie— is merely one passing moment—is a moment that time will not respect as truth.*

The *grayball* rumbles, then laughs in a crack of black.

"*Now* is forever! This is the only truth, and that face of your false mother's flesh is but a memory of dead moments, unreal, foolish!"

The fleshy face in my soul smiles, suddenly becomes my father's face of flesh. He laughs, and answers the *grayball*'s black crack with a streak of bright.

The struggle begins.

"Your false mother is dead!" the *cavebrown* shouts.

But you are alive, the flesh of *screamdeep* says to me, *and you are of your mother's flesh.*

"No, you are simply yourself—in the *now,* in *aloneness!*" the *grayball* answers.

Yes, I am cold, in the *now,* with *aloneness—*

You will never be alone, screamdeep rushes, *with the souls of your forefathers deep within you.*

"Hah! In aloneness you are fated to fall down the funnel of deepest darkness—unless you relinquish your flesh, and come to the biggest mother's light!"

Your body and soul, my father answers, becoming the face of an old man, then an old woman, then both, offering the whispers of wisdom, *are their own light, and if you hold faith within them, they will brighten you forever.*

Then, in a tide as heavy as the sea herself, the *cavebrown* bellows red.

"Your faces are lies, are luring webs offered by darkness to tempt you toward him—to make you his own! I am the light of uyhsfgdsh, and all else is darkness!"

And my father's face of mother's face of an old man's face answers simply, *Blood is not a lie.*

The *cavebrown* pauses, flexing in confusion, but then surrounds me with a warmest hand against the cold that has covered me. The hand is a vision, an image of the future I will touch if I follow her wishes.

I will never feel cold, for I will have no flesh to feel it.

I will feel no cold, so I will be warm and bright.

In my warming brightness I will not be alone.

With a million other warming brightnesses around me, I will forget the meaning of *aloneness* forever.

With aloneness forgotten, I will be one great soul, touching the million loving corners of myself lovingly.

With so much love, I will call myself the *mother of all*. . . .

"Thank you, *mother*," my soul shouts, without will but with deepest gratitude of the vision and promise within it.

"You are always welcome to the biggest mother's embrace," the *cavebrown* answers, and it seems that I am the *cavebrown*, warm and endless, and our voices are one single voice saying, "Thank you, me you are welcome, me, me, me. . . ."

But suddenly, and again, something within my soul begins tugging. *No . . . no . . .*

The tugging becomes a rhythm, and the rhythm offers a warmth of its own, and the dark flesh of the rhythm's throb is not unfamiliar—though it is without a name.

A warmth in darkness? a companion without a name?

My soul does not understand, but it understands the warmth, the touch, and is as comforted by this offering within me as by the vision thrown by the *cavebrown*.

The choice is easy. The *cavebrown's* warmth is not as familiar as the one flowing from my own depths.

The *grayball* begins shouting, throwing unclear red images everywhere, pounding every nearby soul with a thousand threats and curses.

The plant's influence upon my flesh and soul is beginning to fade away; the twelve souls return to clarity, the upper levels of my soul regain light.

The time has come.

My soul senses the opportunity, and hides the flickering of my plans with an image which tells the twelve souls and

251

the *grayball, I am confused . . . I am confused grayly
. . . I am—*

We are among dense *yau* leaves, among the pale yellow
souls of *yau* plants.

My soul chooses a *yau* lie, covering itself quickly.

The souls around me jerk, darkening in surprise.

I hold the *yau* lie around me, whip my tails to take me
down, away from the twelve. The *grayball* and the twelve
men dash in body toward me—

—toward the spot where I *was.*

Browns give me strength, and I swim with every muscle
screaming brown. Through the *yau* lie I am holding tightly
around me, my soul hears them faintly—the twelve souls,
their bodies, the hard round "body" of the *grayball*—as
they meet and collide in confusion at the place I was only
moments before. For a long moment they are not aware
of my absence—

—and one soul shouts, his hand clutching another's neck—

—and the clutched soul screams, striking out with a
tail—

—and another soul moans, injured, beginning to flail—

—and among them all, the round soul-face of the *grayball*
brightens, reddens suddenly, struck by some arm or tail,
and then darkens to total dimness.

I swim harder, adding purple of pain to the brown
screams of my muscles.

There, on that reef, a dense cluster of sponges—to hide
among them, holding a shallow sponge lie?

The twelve souls—no, ten—are beginning to follow me,
probing out for me.

No, they would crack my sponge lie too easily. They might
even find me with their faces' eyes!

I swim on, toward a line of massive rocks, dark holes,
fractured reefs, perhaps caves. Only my face's eyes will be
able to locate a cave or caves; my soul has to retain the *yau*
lie around me.

Face's eyes do find one, but my body is already past it
—and I gather up hope for another cave.

And how will a cave serve you?

I do not know . . . perhaps the cave I choose will know.

Yes, *there . . .* a cave . . . small, but— Oh, there is one
soul already inside it—the soul of . . . of an eel . . . the
kind of eel whose face's eyes are blind.

I swim to the mouth of the cave, and the eel's soul warns
me with a face of red splinters, quaking. A female guarding
her territory. . . .

252

Does this cave know how it will serve you?

Perhaps . . . yes, it does!

I pull an eel lie from within me—a *male* eel lie!—and hold it tightly as I slowly enter the small cave.

The female is confused, her redness rising and falling.

Perhaps she is willing to bite even a male of her own kind.

But the eel allows me to enter. Her nervous soul remains reddish.

With the arms of my body, I guide myself, to the end of the cave. The plants, moss and tiny sponges growing there slither against my flesh, and the cave's talons tear at it a hundred places, but I curl myself in the small of its back —and continue to hold the eel lie tightly.

Outside there are souls of men approaching.

Still puzzled by my presence, still vague in her redness, the female suddenly becomes aware of the souls outside— the *three* souls outside.

Again she raises her red splinters, throwing the warning to the three nearing souls.

The souls jerk, and stop their bodies' motion.

"Here?" is the faint question from one of the three.

"No soul would invite an eel's bite," comes the answer.

"Perhaps it is a lie—the boy was not so deeply dumb," said the third soul.

"*Two* lies?"

"Probe anyway."

"A wasted effort," says the first soul, and the second soul follows him as he begins to leave.

The third soul hesitates, reaches out a soul's finger, touches the female eel, sighs and begins leaving too.

I remain curled against the cold hardness in darkness, flesh shivering, soul trembling, browning afraid that my eel lie will fall away too soon.

Perhaps I remain longer than is needed. When I move my flesh, I reach out and find that the female is asleep, curled in a tiny cave just inside the larger cave's mouth.

Half swimming, half drifting, I move past her and out of face's eyes dimness.

My left tail brushes her, and she awakes with a snap, clenching her jaws on the thin wrinkled end of my tail. I pull free easily, and leave her in a deeper gray confusion.

Their souls will expect you to return to your and clearcorallie's yau place.

Of course.

Then where . . . ?

I do not know.

Then swim away . . . and attempt to understand where.

I choose a path that will not touch the vicinity of the place where I escaped the twelve and the *grayball*.

But I do pass by the reef where the mass of sponges sway and wave, and as I pass them—touching their souls only briefly, satisfied that only sponge souls lay there—my soul is deep in wondering.

If I were clearcorallie, her chosen path?

Suddenly one of the sponge souls cracks—

—is a sponge lie falling—

—is *bluerocking!*

In an instant his body's arms are around my neck, my shoulder.

I struggle. Our flesh rasps, rubs painfully; bone under flesh strikes bone under flesh.

My soul senses no other men nearby, but *bluerocking* shouts a call to them—any of them, wherever they are. Purple talons of panic claw upward within me, and my depths shout: *Escape now or never!*

To struggle, yes! But to touch his flesh so strongly with mine? Yes, touch! or he will hold me until the embrace of others reaches me!

But to struggle—and kill him?

Bluerocking answers me with a scream, and the meaning is everywhere.

He wants deeply to kill my body, to end my annoyance on his soul's path. *Cavebrown mother's plans for you be damned!* comes the shout from his soul.

I struggle, tearing at his hand with mine.

His other hand grabs my neck, and his face of flesh darts toward me. He bites me—just as my *screamdeep* father bit that insane man!

In the dark of shock, my soul pauses, my body dims its struggling.

But then: *Kill this man whose jaws are clamped on your neck!*

No, another part of my soul answers, *I have no deep desire to kill any body!*

My refusal to struggle, to deal injury upon him, somehow brings greater reds and deeper hatreds to *bluerocking's* soul. His depths scream, *Are you not the soul who fears death in your insanity? You must fear me! Killing your flesh is good only if you fear! fear! fear!*

I shall die, is my trembling answer, *without bringing your death.*

Fear me! the man's soul screams, and he is now biting my shoulder.

254

No!

But the flesh of my shoulder falls in pain, and as *blue-rocking* again seeks my neck and brings his teeth against me, my neck, my head, my face's eyes, all are screaming brown, screaming fear, fearing dying.

The voice of *fearless dying* sinks under a new voice, and my arms flail, my head pushes to my chest, my hands claw up and out seeking flesh to claw and hold.

Some webbing tears, bleeding begins, but my hands— even the twisted left one—find *bluerocking's* body; I pull his arm toward my jaw and I bite, and bite, and small bones break, browned by a sudden scream. Now, my hands are free, reaching to his neck—pushing his head back till neck-flesh stretches.

Bluerocking's path changes: his struggling now is for freedom.

I hold his neck, pushing back his head, and two voices are struggling in his depths—

—*flee to live!*

—*remain to die!*

By his soul's deep struggling, his muscles relax slightly, and I pull him closer.

Face's eyes are clouded with the red of twin bloods, but my teeth find his neck, the fingers of my perfect hand find his face's eyes . . . and my flesh constricts, clenching my jaws, my fingers.

The suddenness of his death moment comes too soon, and long after it my teeth are still ripping and plunging, my fingers still probing for softness in his head.

I release him, and with trembling tails begin to swim away—

—only to discover that the fish image has been rising inside me throughout the struggle, the killing of flesh, the soul's death moment.

I am sorry, one edge of my soul says to another, *I have killed to let my flesh live.*

And the edge answers: *You gave him his chosen path only a little earlier than his soul had imagined. The cave-brown will find his soul and swallow him—as his soul wished it.*

But I made his flesh die—believing in flesh's goodness— in order that my flesh could live.

Touch the deeper truth! Even in killing, the fish rose within you—the voice of life. You are that fish, and the dryness into which it struggles to crawl is the life of flesh, and you were only crawling when you killed that man.

I approach the *yau* place cautiously, listening for the faint touch of any other souls.

There are four of them.

I raise a *yau* lie and approach slowly.

"The absence ... *bluerocking* left alone ..."

"Soon ... perhaps meeting here ..."

"... no girl when we ..."

I move away slowly, and in a hundred tail-kicks drop the *yau* lie.

Where would *clearcorallie*'s soul seek to find the touch of a comforting soul ... or souls?

The souls who have touched her many days of living!

In my old territory, the territory of my father, the world only recently touched for knowing by *nightbreaking* and *whiterim*, I swim with all strength to touch as much area as I can, but I hear no souls.

Perhaps ... perhaps you could find poundgrayly ... and where would he be now?

Somewhere in the endless sea.

No nearer than that?

As near as nightbreaking, whiterim and clearcorallie.

Perhaps he returned to the yau place. Perhaps he met the four red souls. ...

None of their images were of an euyom.

Then perhaps he is meeting them now. Perhaps they have chosen to harm him—

—and hard blue sadness embraces me, and I turn from the vision of dark possiblity, of an ugly *there* and *now*.

Perhaps I have made circles in my swimming. Perhaps I am swimming again and again through a single small area. My soul is turned in upon itself, clouded by mysteries of *clearcorallie*'s ways, my own flesh's ways, the twin faces of the *cavebrown*, and by a nameless sadness that is growing with a thousand thick leaves—so I forget my face's eyes, and my body simply continues *swimming*, pure *swimming*.

I do not hear the first voice until it is already quite clear.

Fishsinger ... ?

I jerk, and abruptly stop my body's motions.

Fishsinger ... ?

Browns leave me like the quickest bleeding blood, and my flesh sighs, echoing my soul.

"*Poundgrayly*'s wisdom knew you would be here," *clearcorallie*'s soul says with brightness.

How of how? my soul babbles happily.

256

The arch of smile, sighing too, comes from both of them, but it *poundgrayly* who speaks now.

"I found *clearcorallie* hard in darkness at your *yau* place, and the only good path was away from it—"

Of course, of course, yes, of course.

"And you are *here*," *clearcorallie* says, "because your soul imagined that I would seek my guardians."

Yes, of course, yes.

"As *poundgrayly* imagined you would imagine."

In a moment the sighing ends. In that moment my soul remembers, darkens, and without will asks the question.

"I do not know," she answers without answering. "I still have not touched the reason for . . . for . . ."

For "I shall follow the path of the fifty thousand others," my soul prompts her darkly.

"I am sorry. . . . Are browns reason enough?"

No!

Poundgrayly speaks now.

"Your youth denies patience . . . but your chosen path demands wiser ways. *Clearcorallie* shared that dark moment of quaking decision with this old *euyom*, and even he does not know the source of her answer."

Ignorance does not comfort my soul, I mumble.

"Listen. . . . Perhaps there is a clear truth your heavy soul failed to touch. Was it not browning fears which brought her answer from her? Was it not a deepest fear of her flesh's death which commanded the vein of her answer?"

A long moment is needed, but finally the *euyom's* wisdom is swallowed by my soul, and I wave a faint agreement. I have been shallow of soul not to see the truth, and realization of shallowness brings tinglings to my flesh and soul, and allows me only a token wave of agreement.

"Perhaps," *clearcorallie* urges, "my fears were in the same vein as the truth you made me understand—the truth of flesh's goodness, of soul and flesh together living, of—"

Perhaps, I answer, another reluctant wave of agreement.

Poundgrayly begins to move his body away from us.

"No, *clearcorallie* and I do not wish privacy now. Your old wise faces are needed now, for the shaping of a path."

The *euyom* turns back toward us, approaching, his soul questioning.

"The red souls—perhaps many more than nine or twelve," I say, "will not stop seeking me. Some days remain before the *cavebrown* will open her hard jaws, and the fifty thousand believe that I am a reef blocking their chosen path."

Clearcorallie remains silent, pale in waiting.

"You wish an answer?" the *euyom* asks in a moment.

"There is certainly a question!"

Images begin climbing and blending in *poundgrayly's* soul, and in another moment he speaks.

"All souls who wish to find you will seek to know this territory and your new one well. The girl's guardians will share their knowing of your ways, so you must leave, and *clearcorallie* with you."

Clearcorallie's soul darkens at this, browning in the offered vision of leaving territories familiar to her. Quickly she offers a shallow way for remaining.

"Perhaps *murmursome* and his brothers could help. Perhaps twenty *ayom* could remain with us, *here, here*, surrounding us at a proper distance—listening for any nearing souls of red seeking us!"

"No!" I protest. "*Ayom* would not learn our wishes easily. They would choose to remain at our bodys' sides, not at a distance for listening for other souls!"

"And too," the *euyom* murmurs, "even willfully remaining at a good distance, one of the *ayom* souls would certainly let slip an image of your two souls' presence—an image to be touched by some red soul before the *ayom* could reach you with the warning."

I join *clearcorallie* in silence, tails twitching.

"You both must go to the *scalesouls'* island," comes the wise soul's answer finally. "You must choose a place in shallowness near dryness, and wait for my arrival."

Your path . . . ?

Poundgrayly does not answer. He continues his vision, saying, "No red souls will imagine such a path, and I do not believe the *cavebrown* mother—the *cavebrown's* soul will imagine it either. In your shallow place, surrounded by deeper bottoms full of crags, caves, *ioe* and *uiu*—which will not venture into your shallowness—you will be hidden."

But your path?

The *euyom* pauses, sinking lightly in a growing vision. "A path shaped for an old *euyom*," he begins, "a current toward the end of familiar days. . . ."

But his deeper soul is clearer in meaning.

I shall go to witness the flesh's death of fifty thousand names, and the satisfied hunger of a nameless giant soul. . . .

The swim would take a day, but caution demands two days. Our chosen path to the *scalesouls'* island weaves among dense masses of *yau*, along the soul-filled sides of reefs, around the edge of sand and mud stretches—edges

258

where plants, sponges and caves full of watchful beast-souls will muffle our twin souls' presence.

Clearcorallie shares my greatest brown face—a brown even deeper than the constant fear of red souls finding us.

Will he be harmed? clearcorallie asks, of herself and me, in a rhythm of brown pounding that refuses to slow or dim.

A reason that they would hurt him, I answer, *cannot be imagined. An euyom is no reef across their chosen path.* But I continue to share her brown pounding.

But will they not accuse: You are the insane fishsinger's euyom; you have offered your wisdom to the reef who blocks our sanest path!

His wisdom will urge him to cover the truth of our friendship—and all memories of our days, of you and me, then and now—with the finest images he can raise. To cover his name too.

Images, yes . . . but there has never been an euyom whose lies were very fine against souls of our kind.

But . . . but my father always believed poundgrayly to be the most talented of all euyom.

Yes . . . your father was a wise soul too, was he not?

Yes. . . . is my final answer, and still the brown poundings continue as strongly as ever.

Browns cannot keep our flesh from sleep, when we arrive at the island, choose the best shallow place out of a dozen considered, and finally cease our limbs' motions.

Browns are unable even to crawl into our sleeping souls with the secret faces of dreams. We sleep until the warming light of day falls upon our flesh.

In such shallowness the waters push and pull against us, and our flesh tires easily in the efforts of steadying ourselves.

But *clearcorallie* gathers rocks, shells and coral into a pile—and these things are uncommon on the sands of shallowness—and she begins to shape an arrangement.

The push, the pulling of the waters makes it difficult, and often a rock, shell or bit of coral is moved from its place in the arrangement. But her hands are deep in song, and the reshapings of the arrangement do not darken her soul.

I remain at a distance, in a deeper place, with my right tail curled around a stem of the green kind of *yau*—a plant that is no doubt too feeble to hold my body for long.

The waters push and pull, and my soul shares their rhythm.

Envision poundgrayly's now is the concern of my soul.

259

Perhaps . . . yes, he has arrived at the cavebrown's island, where he will wait, alone, for . . .

Alone?

My soul jerks, remembering that *clearcorallie's* guardians were not present in their territory.

The reason for their absence . . . ?

Perhaps . . . No, I do not know.

There is a reason, as the blood of every moment contains a reason.

Yes! They were absent from their territory *because all fifty thousand souls are now far from their personal territories.*

All have gone to the cavebrown's island to wait?

Of course!

I turn my soul quickly toward *clearcorallie,* to share the newly touched truth with her—but I hesitate.

I would not interrupt her hands' song. *To kill it? No.*

Such songs are and will be the only path, the only bright living for us. I shall never interrupt hers, and she never mine, and this will be the shape of our living in the empty sea.

On the second day of waiting *clearcorallie* shapes only one arrangement, and when many of its pieces are pushed and pulled by the waters from the shape, her hands make no effort to return them to their places.

On the third day of waiting *clearcorallie* shapes no arrangements at all. She curls a tail around a thin green *yau* stem at some distance from me, and sinks her soul in a tide of remembered or shared *then* and *theres.*

On the fourth day our souls begin to rise and fall in a hundred ark colors, lacking clear images, as if a waking sleep has taken us.

And when night begins to make shadows of our bodies on the sands below us—when our souls suggest a proper darkness of sleep—*poundgrayly* returns to us.

Clearcorallie's soul happily babbles pink leaves. My own soul shouts bright green fingers, reaching out to embrace the *eyom's* soul—

—but abruptly our pinks and bright greens crack, darkening, faced with *poundgrayly's* funnel of darkness.

Without a formal image, without the friendly touch of calling the images of our names, the *euyom* swallows us in the heavy memory to be shared.

Clearcorallie becomes—

I become—

I am—

Poundgrayly, an *euyom* stranger among these fifty thousand *yom* souls, waiting. . . .

Above the tide of fifty thousand voices, above the babble of thousands of *ayom*—here with their personal *yom* friends —the greater voice:

"The biggest mother is ready now! In a moment, the embrace!"

I am on the fringes of this largest of congregations, but a moment ago I was in shallowness, and I saw the *cavebrown's* mouths: two hard gray stems, mouths as large as the largest cave, leading from dryness, from the *bigshinegray* of the *cavebrown,* across the sands of dryness, through the frothing waves, to face the fifty thousand souls.

Somewhere in their great dark mouths . . . teeth . . . to free these *yom* of the flesh they find so binding.

The greater voice rumbles again.

"The *ayom* must leave! The biggest mother does not desire them. They are not her children!"

A smaller tide, dark in protest, raises itself now.

And the greater voice—a *grayball* somewhere—is screaming back.

"The *ayom* may have touched your personal souls in many deep ways, but they are not the biggest mother's children!"

My face's eyes see now . . . yes, a thousand *grayballs* rushing through the shallowness, bumping each *ayom,* chasing each *ayom* from the congregation.

A tide of brown sweeps through the dumb souls. The *ayom* flee.

Their souls are dim now; they are waiting in a strange congregation of their own in deeper water . . . waiting too.

"These two caves," the voice announces now, "are the mouth of the biggest mother. In a short moment only, they will begin to swallow. All children must approach her mouths *now!*"

The horde of souls says "Yes," but in many places body's flesh is beginning to shout *No.* As was the inevitable moment to be, the souls of the *yom* desire the freedom in their death, but their flesh desires only the life of itself.

Some question . . . ?

Yes, a question is lifting above the congregation, a blend of a thousand images all in the same questioning vein.

Where where will will our flesh flesh end end?

"Your bodies shall not be thrown to the tiny jaws of the sea. There is a special part of the biggest mother, a soul of flesh which needs the food all flesh must need. Your flesh shall be chewed and placed within the *bigshinegray,* and

261

in the endless times to pass, your flesh shall be honored as the food for the biggest mother's special part. She has other means for blessing her part with life—but she shall honor her children by making them the means!"

There are softer questions now, equally dark, but shared by only a few.

"I cannot understand this path of the *cavebrown* mother's ways. She has shared with us the truth of flesh's dark hold. But somehow, a part with special meaning, special . . ."

"The biggest mother holds some face of flesh?"

"Our bodies shall die, for the future living of a special flesh within the great body of the greatest mother?"

The *grayballs* offer no answers to such questions, as the questions are weak, darkening only the souls of the few hundred *yom* who shaped the questions.

The waters are beginning to tremble. . . .

The *cavebrown*'s mouths are beginning to swallow, sucking water, sands, plants, loose coral—

—and the nearest thousand *yom!*

Their bodies are ripped from their places as the waters are swallowed.

A moment. . . .

Now screams of the darkest hues—moans finished in the briefest instant.

And of course the screams have darkened other souls . . . the waiting *yom* . . . the next thousand "children" who are moving toward the screaming stems.

Yes, many bodies have struggled successfully against their souls. Many forms of flesh are turning in deepest browns, beginning their frantic flailings away from the twin mouths.

But the mouths have begun to swallow again.

The second thousand *yom*, believers and doubters alike, are being pulled like the thinnest leaves toward the two darknesses, where the first screams died many moments ago.

A second tide of screams is even darker. . . .

I must move away now, for the mouths have grown stronger, their invisible tongues longer, swallowing ten thousand *yom*, not a simple thousand.

The screams. . . .

I am among the *ayom* now, and their souls are like leaves too, shuddering under the great wave of screaming darkness.

Perhaps a thousand *yom* now have turned, flailing to follow their flesh's fear in a path of fleeing, but the *cavebrown*'s mouths have already begun to suck, and my soul can hear plants and smaller bodies—perhaps *ur* and *yu* and *er*—being

262

ripped from their places, pulled faster than the fastest *uiu* toward the hidden teeth.

The plants and small bodies whose ripping and tiny screams I can hear are between me and the thousand *yom* who are trying to flee.

The twin mouths of darkness begin to chew. Their teeth are forty thousand screams, the briefest screams. . . .

When the sharing ends, our three tremblings are one—and the *one* is an old *euyom's*, a soul who has witnessed more death moments in his many days than any soul of my kind ever did. But his trembling is deeper than that ever felt by any soul of my kind.

There seems but a single moment between the end of *poundgrayly's* dark gift and the sudden feeling of a fourth soul's presence.

So bright a yellow, so throbbing a yellow face, that it seems to crave a bursting, cracking, shattering of its *grayball* body.

Clearcorallie screams a long brown screaming stem that whips and thrashes her soul into new tremblings. *Poundgrayly* raises an open mouth of purple that becomes a painful rhythm of short cries. And my soul turns all tremblings into a hand whose arching fingers are both black and red, hovering, waiting to change to darkest browns.

"Greetings!" the *cavebrown* shouts with a pink whose strength brings the pain of talons to my soul. "Greetings, my relucant child."

Her laughter holds spines thicker than the spiny *yau*.

"The biggest mother has reached her brightest motherhood—for she is fully full of her children now, children who will never seek birth to leave her! Yes, two children do remain born, refusing to return to unborn love—but the biggest mother is not here to visit them with their own flesh's good death."

But your brightness now could kill our flesh? comes the unwilled query from *clearcorallie's* soul, or mine, or both of our souls.

"Do not doubt it!" the *grayball* soul flares, showering us with splintered pain. "The biggest mother could end your flesh simply with a tone of voice most comfortable for her! But she shall not raise her voice."

Perhaps a lie. . . . Are we not the last two remaining souls? the last two leaves on the stem of your completion?

"Of course! No, there is one other child, also too darkly reluctant, but he is different, entirely evil, and he will never

—and the biggest mother shall never *accept* him! The biggest mother remembers only your twin souls."

We shall not go to you by our souls' wills!

"Calm, and listen. The biggest mother has not departed this world yet, but the moment of rising approaches. You must come to her before the moment passes and damns you most deeply!"

Poundgrayly's soul is stirring, but is not ready to join me in my resistance.

My soul bounces through its own paths of possible *means,* seeking, moving to select, and finally choosing the *means* of image games.

The *cavebrown* will have no difficulty in understanding that my soul's vein has become *games,* nor difficulty in seeing that the vein's purpose is to pass as many moments as possible, to push the meeting of her final red killing anger to a more distant future *now* . . . but image games are all I can throw against her, and I can hope that *poundgrayly,* the soul who taught me the finest patterns of image games, will join me when he is ready. I begin speaking.

"Is the biggest mother willing to accept the souls of *ayom?*"

The *grayball* brightens, makes no effort to probe my soul for the truth behind my question, and answers quickly.

"Certainly, if your twin souls will come to her with loving wills!"

"But is the biggest mother willing to accept the souls of *euyom?*"

The *grayball* darkens, still making no effort to touch behind my game. She begins shouting.

"She cannot accept the scaly *euyom!* You should not dare to ask her to do so!"

"The reason of reasons?"

"Your stupidity is heavy! Their scales reveal their dark forefathers, dark blood shared by the *scalesouls* themselves!"

"*Euyom* souls are never dark. Their wisdom is often brighter than any of the souls of your children!"

"Their blood! Their scales! They are not even your brothers—and the *ayom* do share brotherly blood!"

"Perhaps not brothers, but the *euyom* have again and again been fathers—and *mothers*—to my kind."

The *grayball's* face throbs in sinewy jealousy.

"I am the biggest—" she begins, but I interrupt her with pretended anger of my own:

"Your stupidity is the greater! You believe yourself the finest mother—but the biggest mother's love would embrace *all* souls! You refuse to touch the *euyom,* and your love and bigness must shrink!"

Her answer is precise, calm in confidence.

"I am not mother to the *scalesouls,* as you would not have me be. The most distant forefathers of *scalesouls* and *euyom* were the *same!*"

My soul did not anticipate such a leaf in the game. I pause, forcing soul's fingers through memories, through a hundred image games played before, through waking light, and dreaming—

—yes, dreams!

A simple dream, of water that gained life . . . of water that gained a tiny bit of flesh . . . gained fuller larger flesh . . . gained a body of head and limbs . . . and began to leave the sea . . . to become the forefathers of every fleshy soul. That water the shared blood of all, scaly or scaleless—

"I dreamed a dream, greatest mother! Listen deeply! My dreams have always held truth, as my dream of the *eye* —of *you*—was bloated with truth. But another dream you must know: the dream shouted the truth of deepest shared blood—crying out that the forefathers of your children *and* all *scalesouls* were the same, were the same!"

Now the *grayball* pauses, and when her answer comes, my soul jerks in pale surprise. *She does not accuse my dream of lying!*

"The biggest mother," she says quietly, "shall not accept the *euyom.*"

"Then she shall not have *us!*" I press, confidence bright.

"Your requests are evil," the *cavebrown* says calmly, and my soul feels rising browns.

I return to an earlier leaf. "The truest mother who ever lived would accept with love every stem of soul and bit of flesh in the endlessness of light and darkness!"

The leaf is even finer this time: The *grayball* dims, tries to hide a rising brown raised by considered image: *If I were to swallow with love every soul and flesh in the endlessness of light and darkness* . . . Suddenly the *cavebrown* grows muffled, a vein of absence, a tone of elsewhere attending. . . .

Our three souls wait. My face's eyes open and I look. . . .

The *grayball* continues to hang motionless over the sands before us, not even moving to the push and pull rhythm of the shallow waters. The *cavebrown* soul remains flat, colorless, seemingly gone away.

A thousand moments pass before we allow our souls to touch each other.

The *grayball*, gray body and soul, has not moved from its seeming sleep.

Yes, clearcorallie's soul finally murmurs, *she will kill our bodies before she departs.*

Perhaps, poundgrayly says calmly, *but perhaps she will change her path.*

Poundgrayly's image is not clear, so I probe for clarity—
—and am slapped by fear, by the possible truth he holds.

The cavebrown was not aware of fishsinger's game . . . and he promised to go to her if she would also accept my scaly kind. Her soul's attentions have departed us, traveling elsewhere, perhaps moving to begin the killing acceptance of all euyom—

"No!" I shout, but the blood of my shout is brown, not reason.

"But perhaps my deep brown 'perhaps' is wrong," *poundgrayly* says, raising a comforting face.

"I am sorry!" I shout, echoing the feeling again and again.

"Sorry is but quick sorrow, and sorrow is foolish depths. Your soul, like mine, expected the *cavebrown* to understand your game. That she failed to do so I fail to understand. And you?"

She is webbed with insane veins, is *clearcorallie's* remote image, but it holds a possible solid truth. The old *euyom* waves his soul slowly in agreement, adding a faint image.

Insanity is truth . . . when its coursing blood holds powers greater than the souls of sanity.

XX

Night's shadows blind our face's eyes, shroud the sands, the *grayball* form, and our three bodies—but our souls easily sink all voices of sleep.

All solid things leave our *seeing*, and souls alone become the colors around us, throbbing and curling in a thousand shapes, clarities, hues and sizes.

My soul's eye gazes at the murmuring yellow face of a mass of *yau* in the distance, and I remember *murmursome*.

266

Poundgrayly offers his answer immediately, but slowly, fatigued.

"He was there at the final congregation, and when I departed, he followed. This *euyom*'s soul was confused in trembling, but I remember giving *murmursome* an image of this island as the *here* and *now* of you . . . before his soul dimmed under anxious colors, under strange nervous desires to play—with *yom,* and other *ayom,* and even *euyom.* I refused to enter a body game with him, so he dimmed away."

"And . . . and an image of the path to *here* . . . clear enough for his simple soul."

"Soon, then, he will find us. Do you imagine that . . ."

Poundgrayly is sliding toward flesh's darkness, so I silence my question, and watch his soul curl with sleep.

Clearcorallie is watching too, and I reach out to touch her soul's face, wondering if she too will soon choose darkness—

—and then all darknesses are shattered.

"Awake!" the *grayball* booms.

The *euyom* snaps from sleep, and *clearcorallie* again feels the whipping thrashing of the brown stem in her soul.

"The biggest mother has decided," the brightening soul announces, "that the two of you will choose immediate paths for killing your personal fleshes. Your paths must lead to the first *ioe* your souls can find."

The *cavebrown*'s color runs a darkest threat . . . but behind the purpling reds there seems to be dim light, dimmed perhaps by her will, but bright beyond its shroud.

The hidden light is a weakness, and my soul brightens from dark to pale. Again to try the games. . . .

"You disguise your repetitions," I begin, "with obviously molded images. My own repetition needs no disguise: We shall not with loving will give our souls to you."

"The *scalesouls* will soon be here," she answers softly, "to place poisons in your sea's blood."

Another unexpected leaf, and I hesitate in the image game.

"When?" is the only answer I can give.

"Sooner than you imagine, vulnerable child."

"And you will raise no hand of your great soul to stop the poisons?"

"No."

I cannot understand this simple new leaf. I am moving to ask "Why?" when *poundgrayly* suddenly speaks.

"Then you shall have their two souls," he rushes, "when the poisonous mists have killed their twin flesh!"

267

The *cavebrown* dims, pauses for a longest moment, then says, "The biggest mother shall not be near your world when the poisons kill. She will not return for your souls."

And *poundgrayly* answers her quickly.

"The event will be your loss."

The *cavebrown* falls silent, and when her pondering depths begin to flow, she moves no image to hide them.

The loss will not be great . . . but they are the children of the biggest mother, and she must be complete. . . .

"You are not complete within *yourself?*" *poundgrayly* taunts.

The *grayball* voice grumbles in answer: "I have been and always shall be *complete!*"

We wait, as another line of images seems to be rising from the *cavebrown*'s currents.

"If you, reluctant boy," she says finally, "and you, blind girl, come to the biggest mother, she shall not allow the *scalesouls'* poisons to kill the soul-filled blood of your sea. She shall save the flesh of all *ayom*, *euyom*, plants and other bodies."

Poundgrayly remains silent.

"No," I say. "We will remain here to die with the other fleshy souls of the waters."

"Listen! I shall kill only *your* body! I shall leave the girl's flesh to die under the poisons! Her soul will scream fleshless forever in this world—and you shall be far from her, held by me!"

"If you kill my body alone, my soul will elude you for as long as it can! My soul will die dissolving before you can find me!"

"Listen! I shall kill the *girl's* flesh, and your child within her! You will be left to scream through the sea!"

Now *clearcorallie* answers quickly:

"And I shall escape you in soul until *my* soul dies dissolving."

Splinters of white rush from the *cavebrown*'s voice, and her anger chooses crashing images:

"I am most powerful! As the biggest mother fully full, I possess the power to change every solid thing in your sea with but a simple wish's command. I have the power of two million children within my soul! I have the force to—"

"Your powers are never doubted," I say, "but you are no mother. The biggest mother would eat her children?"

"The biggest mother needs no food!"

"You are not the biggest mother. You are her daughter."

Whose? comes from the darkness that suddenly fills her.

But my soul finds no answer. My image, my claim, was but a shallow leaf in the game.

"The *endless* is the biggest mother," a sudden answer flows, and it is from the old *euyom*'s soul.

"Hah!" booms the *cavebrown*. "The *endless* has no soul!"

Again *poundgrayly* answers her, but more clearly this time:

"Your soul cannot know that the *endless* has no soul. If she does, then you are not the biggest mother, and your knowing is small. The *endless* accepts all souls, all solid things, does she not? She is the biggest mother of all!"

The *cavebrown* dims, dims further, and embraces a familiar silence. Once again the vein of absence, the tone of elsewhere attending. . . .

I keep face's eyes closed, listening carefully with soul, fearing that I will not be ready when the voice bursts again upon us.

But when the *cavebrown* speaks, it is in the pinkest voice:

"Perhaps the truths you hold, my dark child, are truly truths. And even if they are not, still you will remain the child who will not embrace its mother. Each mother, it is true, has a kxcsvgh of black color among her children, and you are mine."

All solid things around continue changing, and my soul clutches the deepest brown it has ever clutched in my living days.

The *cavebrown* speaks again.

"I shall leave you now—leaving you now with a gift! Your face's eyes have touched it. In a time even before the times of your most distant forefather, there was a world like the world I am making of yours, and in this perfect world lived two fleshy souls, contented and without the face of aloneness. I am a good mother, your soul must understand."

Poundgrayly offers nothing, his face's eyes held by the changing waters and solid things, and his soul held rigid by his face's eyes.

Clearcorallie's eyes are closed, her soul thrashing under the stem of brownest brown.

And my own soul knows no path to take, no game to match the power of the moment—changing world, changing *cavebrown*—

In that moment *murmursome*'s soul appears in the no-longer-gray distance.

"Ah. . . ." the *cavebrown* murmurs, rising pink. "Your

269

soul will touch a deeper understanding of my gift *now*—when I mold the gift closer to your soul's living days!"

She pauses, waiting.

Murmursome appears to face's eyes, vague in the golden distance.

"Behold one face of the gift!" the *cavebrown* shouts.

Murmursome's soul gives out a whine, then a scream, his limbs constricting, his hairy body curving under a thousand talons of pain. My face's eyes stare, unblinking, as I see his flesh begin to shift, to change. The hairs remain, but—

"In a moment," the giant soul announces, "you shall have at your flesh's side the most ancient form of friendship's goodness!"

The *ayom* body jerks and jerks, the bone of his back curving and twisting. His flat slick limbs grow thicker, narrower, gain hair, and a stumpy end adorned with many small stumps—

I begin to scream: "Please, my soul is simple! I do not want the world you are giving!"

The *cavebrown*'s pink dims, and the *ayom*'s screams fade to whimpers, and his flesh stops shifting, his bones bending, lengthening or shortening.

"But my gift . . ." The *cavebrown* is pale, throbbing as weakly as a child.

"Please, my flesh and soul want only the world of their past living days! Please! To return that world to me would be your greatest gift!"

The *cavebrown* sighs, the pale taking only a moment to brighten.

Murmursome's screams begin again, and the slipping of his flesh, but I wait, I wait.

And in a moment his cries become whines, soft moans, sighs, and then mere grayness of confusion. To face's eyes he is again the *murmursome* of memory. And the waters have grayed, lost their light, the sands have paled with yellow, and the *yau*, all other plants, have regained their thin slippery stems and sane leaves.

My soul turns back to the *grayball* and touches softly.

Strangely, the *cavebrown* is tingling, red pricklings that resemble any soul's red tinglings of embarrassment.

"It is just as well," she says, some tone of admitting, "that you chose the old face of your waters. My gift was but lies, twisting to trick you—and when I rose to leave this world, the false faces of beauty would have fallen, and you would have known hunger as you always have."

My soul mumbles an answer, considering anger: *No true mother would have dealt such a thing!*

"Understand me! these powers! Certainly I could have changed your waters, the solid things of its blood, in the real, but your sea would have died—the greens would have killed the yellows, the hairy curly flesh would have ceased their bodies' breathing, and the golden hue of the waters would have poisoned plant and animal alike!"

Once again the muffling hand of silence falls across the *grayball*, and our three souls relax.

Sleep swallows us easily, and we dream—

—and we awake to find that our dreams have been a single shared dream.

The *cavebrown* chose sleep's darkness for the current of her voice, and we listened to her images without a single brown stem or reddening face.

"I am rising to leave you now, but I shall speak to you in two days passing."

Perhaps you offer lies again, my dreaming soul flowed calmly, as did *clearcorallie's* as she questioned softly: *Do you hide in a lie, to return to kill our flesh, to have for holding everafter?*

"Lies are unneeded now."

You could have killed our flesh, cracked our very souls, I said. *The reason for your choice?*

"No. . . . I would try to offer you the reason, and you would try to touch it, and your soul would twist crumpling under it."

Please, I dreamed my paling plea, *the question alone is enough to twist me . . . as all the undying questions have burdened. Let this one attract an answer from your wisdom.*

"An answer . . . perhaps the answer lives nowhere at all. But I will leave you with a truth—may it shape some answer for you. *Fishsinging* boy, I am three things, as you have always known. One in my trinity is a mass of endless memories and truths, given as gifts by the lives of a million million souls, and it lives as a very strange blood within my soul. The mass is bright in wisdom, but often as dark as my own shallow veins . . . and often I do not believe its wisdom. But with you, I believe it was purely light . . . it probed the moments and faces of your images, touched the truth, and molded a wisdom which at the end of time would equal your soul's deepest pattern of truth."

271

My name . . . the vision of fish dancing, singing on the surface of the sea . . . is my soul's deepest truth.

"No, your name is but a seeming vision, locked forever in a single moment of your soul's birth in flesh. Your deepest truth is a warbling pattern whose faces reveal what each moment of your living would be if your flesh and soul lived on forever. The mass, the one in my trinity, touched your deepest truth, and offered the other two in my trinity an advice which seemed strange and wrong at first receiving. I was advised to let your flesh live on, to forget your soul in the pattern of my wishes, because . . . because . . . You must understand, it is difficult to answer you. The reason beyond the mass' advice is the face of a million million lives, and your soul can understand only the deed born of advice. *Your soul,* try to understand—as my mass helped me to understand—is the only face of light where all the thousands of currents of time, of your kind's blood, of your kind's deepest images of truth, have truly crossed . . . and perhaps will *ever* cross before time's end. You are my child, but more than my child, so I have respected the *more* within you, the advice of my own strange mass, and the vision of a greater mother elsewhere or everywhere—and you shall continue your life in flesh, with the flesh and soul of the simpler *clearcorallie*-one granted to you so that your deepest truth may flow into future *nows,* future *heres* in this sea, beyond the end of your personal flesh."

The answer can only give birth to a thousand questions.

"I know, and I am sorry, but you must remember the next line of images from me, for your soul when it awakes. I shall rise to leave in but a few moments, but you shall hear me on the second day of your waiting. A *grayball* larger than any your face's eyes have touched will bring my voice to you, and my voice will offer truths of my soul's far motions in the endless dry blackness. Your soul is the point of crossings long awaited—and your food shall be truths, the first of them from me, as an honor I have dealt to the trinity of myself. I go now to raise with soul alone the *bigshinegray* of my body, and the wise mass of memories within it. . . ."

Our awakening moved us three to share again the dream.

And when the sharing ends, *clearcorallie* can only swim in doubt—a doubt no less justified than belief in the *cavebrown's* truth.

It may be that even our dream, she offers darkly, *was but another stem leafed with lies.*

Insanity's path, poundgrayly moves to agree, *is proper and full of beauty for the soul whose blood is insane. Remember how the cavebrown claimed all her deeds were lies.*

A thousand lies, clearcorallie adds, which would seem a foolish, unneeded crooked path to us, may be the cavebrown's straightest current toward our bodies' death.

I hold no answer: *I do not know . . . I do not know. . . .*

We should ready our souls, poundgrayly concludes, for a reappearance of her soul—be it grayball or a formless face of light—before the two days' promise is met.

On the first day of waiting, *clearcorallie* shapes the largest and most finely patterned arrangement her hands have ever shaped.

I remember the simple path *clearcorallie* once suggested for truly *seeing* an arrangement's meaning, and I follow it.

With face's eyes I stare at the great circle, touch the inner pattern's web and weave, then close face's eyes to *see* the arrangement in memory. . . .

My inner eye stares, but the circle neither moves nor changes the brightness of its light.

In an instant the circle fades—no, slips toward darkness. Its disappearance is not in the same manner as a vision fading away, but instead is a falling toward deep patterned darkness.

"I touch no meaning," my soul murmurs, reaching out to *clearcorallie*, whose hands are moving to shape a second arrangement.

"It is a shape new to me," she answers, her soul beginning to flow with song of her hands. "It touched me from the dream."

My soul grows pinker in surprise, then pales.

"That dream was a voice from the *real*," I insist, wishing she would turn her soul toward me.

"Of course . . . but if the *cavebrown's* voice gave us only lies, then the dream was no more than a dream."

The arrangement, my soul asks, *what moment in the dream was its place?*

"All places . . . I do not know. Perhaps it is the face of some soul's depths."

"Whose soul? Mine . . . my deepest truth?"

Clearcorallie's soul turns, and offers a face of blue curiosity.

"Yours?" she says. "You have touched some reason for believing so?"

No . . . , my soul feels deeply, but a brighter level goes

273

on to offer: "The inner vision, the remembered circle, fell into my depths as if it knew them well. . . ."

"Such fallings," *clearcorallie* answers, her soul losing its blue, "have occurred in my soul countless times. Perhaps the arrangement is the face of the *cavebrown*'s soul . . . so finely webbed."

A corner of my soul offers a laugh. *So the pattern of the most insane soul fits perfectly over mine!*

In the morning of our waiting's second day, I find *poundgrayly*'s soul beginning to gather all memories of death moments around him, beginning to touch each one slowly, carefully, as if seeking among them any tiny images hidden from him by his memory.

Such concerns in the old *euyom*'s soul do not brighten mine.

Death moments . . . perhaps he has shared a thousand of them in his living days.

Death moments?

"They may form some new arm's finger for understanding," he says.

"The understanding of what *now?* or whom *then?*"

A pale laugh rises from the *euyom*'s soul. "So quickly you have killed all souls but our three! I aim neither for 'what *now*' nor 'whom *then*,' but rather *whom now*—and not the 'whom' of any of our three souls. The *cavebrown* mother is a fourth soul."

"And she spoke of a *fifth* soul. . . ."

"Yes, she did, but a fifth soul who fails to exist is a lie, no?"

I nod in soul, and use face's eyes—touching *clearcorallie*'s third arrangement—to hide my annoyance. My soul is heavy with the hundred accusations of lying, claimed by *clearcorallie* and *poundgrayly*, striking every other image from the *cavebrown*'s soul. It seems that the old *euyom* and the girl can hold such accusations without darkening their own souls.

Poundgrayly is speaking again.

"In six hundred death moments there may be one or ten which will serve us well. I am touching all six hundred delicately, that the one or ten may show their worth. In the moment which again offers us the *cavebrown* mother, a special death moment from shared memory may help us confuse her—thwart any slash from her soul."

Again I nod, holding back the darkness that those continuing suspicions form in my soul. But in a moment such holding back becomes unneeded, as my soul touches an

274

understanding which embraces both girl and *euyom* souls: *clearcorallie*'s arrangements serve her soul exactly as *poundgrayly*'s gathering and inspecting of death moments serves his. Both deeds are songs against the anxious swirling of our waiting, against browning fears of unknowable future *nows*.

Now understanding grows another branch, and I remember the dream that was not a dream. "The food for your deepest soul, your deepest truth, must be *truths*," the calm *cavebrown* mother said to me.

For *my* soul accusations of "Lies!" cannot be a song.

Before the first finger of shadow begins to grow, the *cavebrown*'s promise is kept.

Lacking a soul of its own—lacking even the voice from another's soul—the *grayball* manages to approach us within twenty tail-lengths before *clearcorallie*'s face's eyes touch it, and a brief flash of brown from her soul makes the *euyom* and me turn face's eyes toward it.

Its body is the familiar hard gray, round and almost shining—but its bulk is that of two *ayom* together.

It moves toward the clear sand near us, hesitates hovering—and all three of our souls feel strange sensations rise. Face's eyes tell us that the *grayball* is moving with a personal will, and all solid things that move with a personal will must be *living*. But our souls' touch no soul within it.

In a moment our souls touch at face's eyes' command.

From a crack that has appeared slowly on the underside of the *grayball,* three thinnest stiff stems—of the same hard gray color—are beginning to protrude.

The stems grow and grow, becoming thicker as they leave the round body, and finally stopping when they have struck the sands below, enter the sands, and can push no further down into them.

The big round body drops slightly, swaying, and comes to rest when the three stems have stopped their faint stiff wiggling and shifting.

We wait for the giant voice to come.

Instead, a dark spot appears on the top of the grayball, and another stem protrudes. As it rises, the surface of a tiny *grayball* on the stem's tip cracks finely and a web of grayness—whose web's lines are finer than any plant stem—appears from it.

In a moment the stem has pierced the surface of the sea, entering dryness, leaving face's eyes.

And in another brief moment, the voice begins.

"Greetings! Feel deepest awe at the appearance of my

voice, as it left me in a special *grayball*—left my *bigshine-gray* body in the endless blackness of dryness—was carried by that *grayball* to a second special *grayball* which speeds circling your world—and then my voice jumped from the circling *grayball*, falling down quickly to the fat *grayball* standing before you now! The biggest mother could have simply screamed one scream from her rapid swim in the endless dryness of blackness, and the scream would have reached you without *grayballs*—but these *grayballs* are like wrfgshlig, leading up to wsdrfgh where the biggest mother has risen!"

Our three souls remain muted . . . but from *poundgray-ly* or *clearcorallie*, or both, I hear whispers of *"Lies . . . new lines of lies. . . ."*

"Remember the dream that was not a dream," the *cave-brown* rumbles. "I too was in a dreamy way, and perhaps I gave you images which I should not have. A part of the biggest mother was behaving strangely that night, and perhaps it is best that your souls consider my images no more than a humorous dream."

A truth now against the dream's lies, clearcorallie mur-murs, or a lie against the dream's truths?

The *cavebrown* ignores the murmurings. She bursts into a pink glow of pride, and deals herself praise:

"Yes, the biggest mother entered endless darkness to find the *scalesouls* bringing poison, and she found them, and with her throbbing soul's justice alone she destroyed them!"

And what of their souls? poundgrayly asks.

"Ah. . . ." The *cavebrown* brightens—but then suddenly darkens, gaining the same red prickling tinglings as before. "There is a soul among you three who should not hear the truths I will offer."

Why? my soul rushes, brown fearing that I am the "one."

"The one I speak of should not even hear the *why*."

Some deep reason—? I begin to ask again—

—and a shadow larger than any cave falls upon me, insisting that soul and flesh fall immediately toward sleep.

As I fall I hear a dim *poundgrayly* dark in objections, and a dimmer *clearcorallie* raising the brownest stem of her soul. . . .

No dreams. . . .
No brief awakenings. . . .
The sleep that takes me can only have come from the place where sleep itself dreams and embraces darkness.

Poundgrayly's is the voice that touches me first.

"*Fishsinger!* Raise your light . . . the *grayball* has left us."

Throbbing red is the color of my waking soul, and some of the anger escapes toward *poundgrayly—*

Give me the why of her! Give the why of heavy sleep and deafened soul!

The *euyom's* pink laugh surprises me, and my reds must dim and allow a faint pinkness in their place.

"A soul of insanity," *poundgrayly* muses, "can have worth simply by the moments of humor offered by it."

Clear your images, I mumble, considering another red.

"The *cavebrown's* soul refused to let you hear a certain line of truths because . . ." The *euyom* pauses, lifting a laugh again.

Yes!

"Because her soul would have known deep embarrassment as you heard them."

"Insanity's way!" I rumble.

"No, there is a sane reason, it seems."

Lies and lying lies, clearcorallie's soul whispers nearby, but clutches silence again, choosing not to break the *euyom's* and my sharing.

"Listen," *poundgrayly* goes on. "With pale humble face, the *cavebrown* offered us the truth that your soul—certain images from it—has molded her own soul deeply. You gave her a truth, and she feels red tinglings each moment that she remembers her great soul's ignorance. . . ." The *euyom* is laughing again.

"Is your laughter born of disbelief? believing that she has never ceased lying to us?" Red risings are beginning within me again.

"No, no such source of laughter! Is it not humorous that a soul whose powers are greater than the sea is given red tinglings by a powerless boy?"

I darken. "Perhaps my soul is not so deeply powerless!"

"You misunderstand. Sink that image, as there are fresh truths of the *cavebrown's* deeds to offer you. Remember, it was your soul who accused the *cavebrown* of being a false mother!"

Quickly *poundgrayly* moves his soul, plucks a fresh shared image from his depths, and offers it to me.

The cavebrown's bigshinegray body: floating? swimming? rushing? through endless blackness: grows aware of another bigshinegray: filled with scalesouls: the cavebrown's soul reaches out: the other bigshinegray wrinkles: bends: collapses: somewhere faintly: thousands of faint screams from scalesouls—

277

—and now: cavebrown's booming voice: pinkest pride:
"I am a true mother, and the biggest truest mother of all!"—
—and her soul moves: finds the dead-flesh souls of the
scalesouls: swallows them: loving: accepting: pinkly: bright-
ly.

"One fine sane act," my soul answers, "does not brighten a name forever. The *cavebrown* will never shed her insanity."

"Perhaps, but I believe that her soul has changed, will change, by the recent hand of a deep molding—"

Now *clearcorallie* speaks, offering again the dark insistence:

"Every image she has offered us could be a lie. How does your soul move, selecting one image and not another to be honored as *truths?*"

"If every gift from the *cavebrown* has been a lie in the *real*," the *euyom* answers, "then all moments have been but an unharming game commanded by her."

Clearcorallie objects: "A game is not *unharming* if its path has been—if its final moment is to bring the flesh-death of two souls, two souls tricked into laughter and bright trusting ways—"

"Stop," *poundgray*ly says. "Your browns are everywhere. You are wrong to let each brown within you accuse one image, then another, of *lying*. Separate the browns in your depths from the images offered to your higher brighter levels."

"Perhaps he holds the truth on this," I say, hesitant under a hundred urges to comfort *clearcorallie* in her darknesses.

"Yes, perhaps," she answers. "But the deepest pattern of a soul's insanity—"

Murmursome interrupts our sharing then, babbling in rising and falling grays.

And beyond the *ayom*, faint in the distance—

—a jagged yellow dancing—

—no, a yellow laughter pinkened by pride, cracked with repetitions, bursting with throbbing light—

—and the voice comes booming.

"Greetings!"

No! . . .

The *cavebrown* lied beyond our imaginings!

Lies! Endless lying! Chaos shall swallow all of—

The brilliant yellow soul reached toward me—*me!*

I screamed—

—but I am yanked away so quickly that I pass my own screaming.

XXI

I am within the biggest mother now, and bodilessness means strange feelings. No arms to move, nor tails to wave . . . no waters embracing every face of my flesh.

Bodilessness means that very few colors reach my soul—and those that do are the faces of the million souls surrounding me.

"I am *fishsinger*," I move to announce, paling nervous.

And the million souls object, grumbling, "You are we, and we are the biggest mother."

No, they are not the biggest mother—because suddenly *her* voice reaches me . . . from somewhere that is everywhere.

"I am everywhere here," she says abruptly, every color in the river of her voice. "Still, *fishsinging* boy, you mean to struggle against me? Your fate—your unborn endless living here—is most wonderful. I am your endless future, your unnecessary hopes, and still you shall struggle against me? Why, then, did you agree to come to me?"

"No such agreement was mine," I answer.

"Of course it was."

"You came for me when my soul was fooled by your countless lies, when my soul could not throw image games against you, when my soul had grasped a future of fleshy *nows* tightly. You killed my flesh, and you plucked my soul from it—both deeds while I was in some deep darkness!"

"Of course you cannot remember the moment of truth. I struck you with a hand of darkness to open your deepest depths to me. Always before your lighter levels had been hiding your deepest desires. Your depths cried out to me, pleading that I take you for the blood of the biggest mother's soul."

I have been trying to raise darknesses, rednesses, talons of hatred, but I cannot, so I scream at the giant soul who is everywhere.

"Your lies never cease! Your soul is a biggest lie!"

The biggest mother sighs, and her sign constricts me.

"I have no need to lie," she says. "For the truth you may ask the souls around you. They are I, so whatever I discovered in your soul's depths, they discovered too."

I do not move to question the million souls, but they offer the answer anyway.

Your deepest desires are the same as ours!

Perhaps, I admit to myself later, *I am quite blind to my own bottomless depths. My soul was always burdened with questions, indecisions and twin beliefs on all truths, was it not? Perhaps my deepest soul's craving was always for flesh's end . . . for endless living in bodilessness.*

The biggest mother—and my million fellow souls—must continue this travel through the endless dryness of blackness, as I know quite deeply. Patience must be my fleshless blood, now and endlessly.

And I must cease my tiny flailings in search of *clearcorallie's* soul somewhere out there among the million souls. White patience cannot serve me well while I spin in such efforts.

Somehow I and the other million souls see beyond ourselves. Somehow I—or they, with me among them—possess the vision of face's eyes.

I *see* tiny bright lights in the endless blackness—thousands of lights like the *eye,* but much smaller, and they seem to lack motion.

I *see* large colored balls sometimes—green and blue, red and orange, purple and black—and always near these balls are the largest brightest balls of light I have ever *seen.*

On one of the colored balls in the endless blackness I have discovered millions of *scalesouls.*

The biggest mother—with my and your fellow souls' help —is killing them now . . . as if they were the tiniest fish. . . and now she is swallowing them. . . .

Two bodiless *scalesouls* appear beside me.

Or perhaps they are not *scalesouls* at all.

The truth of bodiless faces is difficult to touch.

Yes, I have been within her for at least one endlessness —and there will be many more ahead for my travels to pass through.

Ah, the biggest mother has chosen one of the colored balls.

Its misty whiteness and greenish blues grow larger as we near the chosen ball.

Now . . . with whatever kind of face's eyes I possess and share with a million forced brothers and sisters, I see the ball rush toward us, fill my entire vision with its dryness, and finally present to me tiny figures of flesh—sleeping, eating and scuttling across its surface. And my soul touches their souls. . . .

There are solid green plants in this world, and solid blue and gray seas . . . but the tiny bodies I see inhabit dryness, their two bottom limbs carrying them across dry lands.

Yes, these bodies seem to sleep in caves which they have woven with their hands, of dry plant pieces and mud of dryness.

(You almost forgot that you once had a *yau* nest? . . . and a body of flesh. . . .)

We are moving closer now. My vision comes to rest on a stretch of greenness, on a group of fleshy bodies doing various deeds, on a cluster of woven caves.

We move closer still—

—and see that the bodies possess no necks, their heads seemingly sunken down into their shoulders. And their chests are broad, covered with hair like—like an *ayom's*. . . .

(You almost forgot the *ayom* you once knew?)

Listen. . . . Their souls are nearly deaf to each other—but they possess other means for speaking, and a hole on either side of their heads for receiving the images thrown from their mouths.

We move closer, look down, and somehow one of the small figures jerks, looks up, and with face's eyes stares at *me*.

His flesh begins to tremble slightly.

(Even if you wanted to tremble, you could not. . . .)

He keeps his face's eyes on me, but moves an arm of flesh, and with a webless hand picks up from the ground a thick piece of hard plant stem.

(Even if you wanted to move a hand, you could not. . . .)

He raises the piece of thick stem . . . in his hand. . . .

Now he throws it at me—

—and I reach out to catch it—

—but I have no hand!

I no longer have hands of flesh!

(Scream! Remember your hands, and scream their loss!)

The colored ball covered with tiny bodies of flesh is an endlessness behind us now, but I am still screaming.

"Hands!" I shout.

"No need for hands now," the biggest mother answers soothingly.

(Listen! A distant is voice is shouting too. . . . *Stop it! Leave him alone!*)

"But I want two hands of flesh," I answer, and a grayness falls upon me, and I try to feel the sadness I must feel.

(Listen . . . again the voice. . . . *End your lies!*)

I fail to feel my personal sadness, so I scream again, screaming for another reason.

I scream.

I—

"Stop it!"

I—

"End your lies against his soul!" comes the voice a fourth time, and it is familiar. . . .

It is *clearcorallie.*

The vision of the biggest mother and the million trapped souls dies quickly, and my soul feels the *real,* reaches out to find near me *clearcorallie* and *poundgrayly* and *murmursome* and—

—the *man!*

His soul is laughing yellow, and he begins to speak.

"So now you see, tailed boy, that you were wise not to follow the *cavebrown's* wishing path!"

My flesh trembles, and the trembling is good, and I am aware of trembling as never before.

I move my right hand, touch its webbing with the fingers of my left hand—

"Forget your flesh for a moment," the *man* says. "You will have the longest time to touch your body. Does your soul have no greetings of joy for me?"

I offer no image of answer.

Clearcorallie and *poundgrayly* hold only silence too, tight in nervous darkenings.

"What is this three-faced silence?" the *man* shouts, reaching out to probe our souls.

He pauses at *clearcorallie's* depths.

"Oh . . . a child? Soon to be an odd fatness for your stomach!" Again the cracked laughter.

He probes deeper, touching more deeply the child—

—and abruptly his soul darkens faintly, saying, *Your child . . .*

In turn, *clearcorallie* darkens too.

Your child, the *man's* depths are saying, *is webless, tailless—*

282

Clearcorallie's soul falls, offers a brief tiny scream, and then embraces a dark silence. *No. . . .*

Believe me. My soul's fingers are wondrous and long, reaching truths of deep souls—children inside of women. . . .

Then the *man* brightens, raises laughter, saying, "All the better! I shall be present to teach your child the proper paths for a tail-less webless body! He shall learn *my* ways—wondrous lies, perfect swimming without tails . . ."

Clearcorallie, poundgrayly and I are silent, our souls numbed.

"He shall be brightened," the *man* rushes on, his laughter and promise of pink affection never dying, "by the glory of my soul's brilliant power!"

"Your brilliant powers?" I say.

"Certainly!" the *man* shouts. "Your soul has never touched them—but you will come to know them well!"

Clearcorallie makes no move to accuse him of lying.

Poundgrayly makes no move to question him.

So I move, saying, "I have been touched by your talented lies more than once: I never doubted for an instant that the vision you gave me of the biggest mother and *fishsinger's* bodilessness was a solid *here* and *now* in the *real*. But these lies are not enough power for you to claim such greatness in your soul. They are but a—"

The *man* breaks my line of images quickly with laughter.

"You were, and you still are, quite blind—but *now*, blindness be shattered! Why do you suppose the *cavebrown* allowed me to choose a future of fleshy days?"

She charged your soul as being darkest evil, comes my soul's reply.

"Certainly she *would*, but just as certainly she would lie—as she did and as you *know* deeply that she did. The fingers of my soul are limber, their blood as strong as the sea himself, and I chose to slap the *cavebrown!"*

Lying. . . . clearcorallie murmurs, and *poundgrayly* echoes her, a little less surely.

"It matters not whether you believe me," the *man* answers. "Shallow souls are unable to touch deep truths! Such truths as these, as these within me, mine which I have touched and hidden well against even the insane *cavebrown* babbler!"

His soul thickens and widens, becomes a pounding current as heavy as the sea herself. The current speaks:

Did you know that the man possesses power beyond naming?

Did you know that your screamdeep father had a brother —a webless tail-less brother who was thrown toward the jaws of death in his youngest youth but who refused to die, and denied the jaws of death with the talented lies and bright powers in his soul?—and that this webless tail-less brother often whispered to your screamdeep father throughout his living days, telling him that life was but an egg of absurdity?—and that your screamdeep father felt the whispers as voices of his own dark soul, and so your screamdeep father was embraced by darkness throughout his living days?

Our three silent souls, when listening is done, can only hide in deeper silence. No accusations of lying . . . no charges of deep insanity . . . not even brown fears that great truths have been given us. . . .

I am not aware that my soul—even at deepest canyon—has formed a question, but it has, and the *man's* longest fingers hear it, and he answers.

"Perhaps those were truths I gave you—perhaps they were not. The answer to which *perhaps* is truth lies somewhere in my choice—of choosing to live in binding flesh and deny the *cavebrown's* embrace—a choice the same as yours, *singeroffishsongs.* You may in some future *now* reach to touch the hidden answer—but you will never truly understand it. . . ."

Silence holds its hand upon us for many moments.

Then I open face's eyes, looking for each of the four quiet bodies around me—and the *ayom's* twitching body too—

—and I reach out to the souls of *clearcorallie* and *poundgrayly,* only to find that their feelings are the same as mine.

We are uncomfortable, gray . . . we are flesh, and will continue to be flesh for countless moments to come.

I have chosen flesh, and flesh cannot escape simple discomforts of its own being, grays of anxious body's living.

I am uncomfortable and gray . . . but not without a faint bright hand waving slowly within my soul, reminding me that flesh is goodness.

I have chosen the path of flesh. Let all darknesses try, but they shall not make me weep regrets.

I will live in the light of my choice . . . never forgetting how dryness mended the split of my deepest soul . . . never forgetting that a boy is but a pale fleshy fish, struggling and crawling—whether he knows it or not—toward brighter dreams in distant places where he might only die, unable to breathe and keep his flesh living. . . .

And is there not solid proof that I lived in light, and did not forget?

I took each of you into an island's dryness for a moment on an *euyom*'s back, did I not?

And are you not floating before my face's eyes now, all twelve of your souls floating in bodies of young *flesh?*

Are you not twelve fingers of *fishsinger*'s blood?